# The Lantern

*A NOVEL*

# Deborah Lawrenson

HARPER LUXE

*An Imprint of* HarperCollins*Publishers*

HarperCollins books may be purchased for educational, business, or sales promotional use. For information please write: Special Markets Department, HarperCollins Publishers, 10 East 53rd Street, New York, NY 10022.

FIRST HARPERLUXE EDITION

HarperLuxe™ is a trademark of HarperCollins Publishers

Library of Congress Cataloging-in-Publication Data is available upon request.

ISBN: 978-0-06-208872-7

11 12 13 14  ID/RRD  10 9 8 7 6 5 4 3 2 1

"I often stopped before that wild garden. It was in the most silent fold of the hills . . . All around the wild hair of the undergrowth was waving and there was the strong odor of the hostile earth, which had a life of its own, and was independent, like a beast with cruel teeth."

—JEAN GIONO

"Don't let us make imaginary evils, when you know we have so many real ones to encounter."

—OLIVER GOLDSMITH

# Prologue

Some scents sparkle and then quickly disappear, like the effervescence of citrus zest or a bright note of mint. Some are strange siren songs of rarer origin that call from violets hidden in woodland, or irises after spring rain. Some scents release a rush of half-forgotten memories. And then there are the scents that seem to express truths about people and places that you have never forgotten: the scents that make time stand still.

That is what Lavande de Nuit, Marthe's perfume, is to me. Beyond the aroma's first charge of heliotrope, as the almond and hawthorn notes rise, it carries sights and sounds, tastes and feelings that unfurl one from the other: the lavender fields, sugar-dusted biscuits, wildflowers in meadows, the wind's plainsong in the trees, the cloisters of silver-flickering olives, the garden still warm at midnight, and the sweet, musky smell of secrets.

That perfume is the essence of my life. When I smell it, I am ten years old again, lying in the grass at Les Genévriers, on one of those days of early summer when the first fat southerly winds warm the ground and the air begins to soften with promise. I am twenty, as I toss my long hair and walk on air toward my lover. I am thirty, forty, fifty. Sixty, and frightened . . .

How can I be frightened by a scent?

# Part I

Part 1

# 1

The rocks glow red above the sea, embers of the day's heat below our balcony at the Hôtel Marie.

Down here, on the southern rim of the country, out of the mistral's slipstream, the evening drops as viscous liquid: slow and heavy and silent. When we first arrived, the stifling sultriness made sleep impossible; night closed in like the lid of a tomb.

Now, in the few hours I do sleep, I dream of all we have left behind: the hamlet on the hill and the whispering trees. Then, with a start, I'm awake again, remembering.

Until it happens to you, you don't know how it will feel to stay with a man who has done a terrible thing. Not to know whether the worst has happened or is yet to come; wanting so badly to trust him now.

We **cannot** leave France, so, for want of anywhere better to go, we are still here. When we first settled in, it was the height of summer. In shimmering light, sleek white yachts etched diamond-patterned wakes on the inky blue playground and oiled bodies roasted on honey-gold sand. Jazz festivals wailed and syncopated along the coastline. For us, days passed numberless and unnamed.

As the seasonal sybarites have drifted away to the next event, to a more fashionable spot for September, or back to the daily work that made these sunny weeks possible, we have stayed on. At this once-proud Belle Époque villa built on a rocky outcrop around the headland from the bay of Cassis, we have found a short-term compromise. Mme. Jozan has stopped asking whether we intend to stay a week longer in her faded pension. The fact is, we are. No doubt she will tell us, in her pragmatic way, when our presence is no longer acceptable.

We eat dinner at a café on the beach. How much longer it will be open is anyone's guess. For the past few nights, we've been the only customers.

We hardly speak as we drink some wine and pick at olives. Dialogue is largely superfluous beyond courteous replies to the waiter.

Dom does try. "Did you walk today?"

"I always walk."

"Where did you go?"

"Up into the hills."

I walk in the mornings, though sometimes I don't return until mid-afternoon.

**We go** to bed early, and then on to places in our dreams: places that are not as they really are. This morning, in the shallows of semiconsciousness, I was in a domed greenhouse, a ghost of itself: glass clouded with age; other panes shattered, glinting and ready to fall; ironwork twisted and corrupt with rust. No such edifice exists at Les Genévriers, but that was where I was.

In my dream, glass creaked audibly above my head as I stood mending bent iron shelves, frustration mounting as I failed repeatedly to straighten the corroded metal. Through broken glass, the pleated hills were there, always in the background, just as in life.

By day, I try not to think of the house and the garden and the hillside we have left behind, which ensures, of course, that my brain must deal with the thoughts in underhanded ways. Trying is not necessarily succeeding, either. Some days I can think of nothing else but what we have lost. It might as well be in a different country, not a few hours' drive to the north of where we are now.

**Les Genévriers.** The name of the property is misleading, for there is only one low-spreading juniper, hardly noble enough to warrant such recognition. There is probably a story behind that, too. There are so many stories about the place.

Up in the village, a wooded ten-minute climb up the hill, the inhabitants all have tales about Les Genévriers: in the post office, the bar, the café, the community hall. The susurration in the trees on its land was their childhood music, a magical rustling that seemed to cool the hottest afternoon. The cellar had once been renowned for its *vin de noix*, a sweet walnut liqueur. Then it was shut up for years, slumbering like a fairy castle on the hillside, and prey to forbidden explorations while legal arguments raged over ownership in a notaries' office in Avignon. Local buyers shied away, while foreign bidders came, saw, and went.

It is more than a house; it is a three-story farmhouse with a small attached barn in an enclosed courtyard, a line of workers' cottages, a small stone guesthouse standing alone across the path, and various small outbuildings: it is officially designated as *un hameau*, a hamlet.

"It has a very special atmosphere," the agent said that morning in May when we saw it for the first time.

Rosemary hedges were pin-bright with pungent flowers. Beyond, a promenade of cypresses, prelude to a field of lavender. And, rising at the end of every view, the dominant theme: the creased blue hills of the Grand Luberon.

"There are springs on the land."

That made sense. Three great plane trees grew close to the gate of the main house, testament to unseen water; they would not have grown so tall, so strong, without it.

Dom caught my hand.

We were both imagining the same scenes, in which our dream life together would evolve on the gravel paths leading under shady oak, pine, and fig trees, between topiary and low stone walls marking the shady spots with views down the wide valley, or up to the hilltop village crowned with its medieval castle. Tables and chairs where we would read or sip a cold drink, or offer each other fragments of our former lives while sinking into a state of complete contentment.

"What do you think?" asked the agent.

Dom eyed me complicitly.

"I'm not sure," he lied.

# 2

Bénédicte drifts through the rooms of the lower floors, into the dust of venerable scents: flecks of the lavender held in the corners of drawers; flakes of the pinewood armoire; the soot of long-dead fires; and, from the present, the deep mossy aroma from cloud formations of damp above the rose-tiled floor; the sharp white smells of late-spring flowers outside.

These visitors are new. She is sure she has never seen them before, though she closes her eyes and tries to think calmly, to count her breaths, slowing her intake of air, scouring her memory to make sure. When she opens her eyes, they are still there.

The strangeness is that they stare straight into her face, just as they look around her so intently, into the corners of the rooms, up to the cracked ceilings, the fissures in the walls, yet they don't acknowledge her presence. All is silent, but for the tapping of the catalpa tree in the courtyard and the creak of a newly opened shutter that lets in a shifting band of brightness.

I will sit a while longer, Bénédicte thinks. Watch to see what they do next.

Breathe. Breathe deeply.

# 3

The property drew us in immediately. Not love at first sight, exactly, not as explosive as that: more a deep, promising undertow, as if it had been waiting for us, and we for it. It was familiar, in that it was the same sensation as when Dom and I first met: recklessness muted by instant empathy, surrounded by beauty.

Meeting Dom was the most incredible thing that had ever happened to me. A classic whirlwind romance. Deciding so quickly to throw my lot in with his was the most daring, rash, life-enhancing choice I had ever made. My friends and family wondered if I had lost my head, and of course I had. Head, heart, mind, and body. I wanted him and, miraculously, he wanted me.

**Dom and** I met in a maze.

It was on the shores of Lake Geneva. I'd seen a photograph of the château at Yvoire while flipping through a magazine in a coffee shop that Saturday morning. If the accompanying description was beguiling, the name of the maze in the garden was irresistible. It was called the Labyrinth of the Five Senses.

According to the waitress, it was only twenty minutes out of town, across the border in France. But it wasn't hard to take a taxi, or even a bus. I was doing nothing else that whole weekend, staying in one of Geneva's soulless city center hotels, sleep broken by the roar of traffic, bored already by the thought of more dull meetings on Monday morning.

So I went.

It was a picturesque little place. Golden spires thrust up from narrow alleys, catching the winter sun. The château, curiously small and homely, seemed to rise from the lake itself.

I wandered quite happily on my own, unconcerned by the maze but ever more certain with every sense that I had taken a wrong turn somewhere in life. My so-called career was in a dull phase, and, as such, a reflection of my own limitations; it was one of the reasons I accepted the job that had brought me briefly to Switzerland. As for any social life, it seemed as if high tide had receded, leaving only wrinkles and minor wreckage to show for the fun.

Then everything changed.

There, in a living cloister of hornbeam, the air richly perfumed by a line of daphne, there was Dom.

"I seem to be lost," he said.

He spoke in French, but leaving no doubt that he was British. The atrocious accent gave it away, of course, but it was a very British thing to say, under the circumstances.

"What about you?" he asked, and we both laughed, because the eponymous labyrinth was nothing more complicated than a few low hedges that linked the gardens.

His face was tanned, and there were strands of gold and red in his bear-brown hair. A good smile, his eyes hidden behind sunglasses. Tall, but not towering. I had noticed him earlier. He was on his own, too, set apart somehow from the other visitors in more than the sense of not being half of a couple or part of a family. Partly it was the intense self-assurance in the way he walked, loose and confident like an athlete. I saw him take in a particularly pretty view of plants and stone set against the water but somehow remain detached. He stood still, absorbed it, and moved off. While other tourists attacked with cameras, greedily capturing the scene, imprinting themselves on its beauty, he simply looked and went on.

We started talking, inconsequential nonsense about mazes, then, imperceptibly at first, moving in the same direction until we were walking the same path together. Through the Garden of Sound, where he talked, unexpectedly, about Debussy; through the Garden of Scent, where the cold air was spring-sharp with narcissi; on through the Gardens of Color and Touch, where we discussed synesthesia, and settled on Fridays being orange and shiny-smooth. In the Garden of Taste, we stopped.

"It's supposed to be full of edible plants," he said, reading from a leaflet.

We looked around. It was February, not a good month for garden crops.

"You could try that ornamental cabbage," I said.

"Tempting—but no, thank you."

So we kept walking, out of the château gardens to a dark, warm café where we drank coffee and ate cake. We had more coffee. And still we talked. It was so easy. It became a conversation that continued and sustained and bound us as hours became days became months.

That day at the lake, I could have taken a different turn on those labyrinthine paths and we would never have met. I might have taken a taxi instead of a bus, arrived an hour earlier and missed him. I might not have agreed to attend those extra meetings on Monday and spent the weekend alone in Geneva.

But you can't think like that. It is what it is. Either walk on, or accept.

**He had** been skiing with friends but decided to cut his losses a few days early. The winter had been unseasonably warm and sunny, and the snow had yielded early to mud-stained slush.

"Didn't you want to stay just for the company, enjoy the rest of your time off together?" I asked him over that first coffee. Now that he had taken off his sunglasses, I could see he was older than I'd thought, a fair bit older than me. A low lamp on the table lit his eyes, so I could see they were gray-green. Lovely eyes, full of intelligence. A bit of mischief, too.

"It's not really time off for me in the same way it is for them."

"How so?"

"I don't have a job like theirs. Not one I have to go back to, anyway. Sitting around drinking all day watching the snow melt doesn't give me quite the same release it does them."

"I see," I said, although I didn't.

He cut off the obvious question. "I'd rather listen to music. What about you—what do you like to do best of all?"

"I love to read."

"What kind of reading?"

Sometimes you can tell all you need to know about a person just in the way they ask the question: politely, or with genuine curiosity, denoting a fine understanding of all it might reveal—from a rich inner life to a point of compatibility between strangers. It was also a hard question to answer, its simplicity lethal as a narrow blade.

"Anything that makes me think, and dream a while, and make connections," I said at last, as the incoming rush of a hundred thoughts pooled into coherence. "Modern fiction, some classics, biographies, travel books, some poetry occasionally. Beautifully written cookbooks . . ."

I watched his face. "Don't ask me my favorite author," I said quickly, not wanting to be disappointed too soon. "I can't bear that question. I can never think how to answer it, which gives the impression that I hardly read at all, or that my tastes never change, or I never make new discoveries, when nothing could be further from the truth."

He smiled. "Understood. So long as you don't ask me for the title of the best book I've read recently."

There it was again, the ease between us.

"Never," I said. "I can hesitate over that one so long because I'm trying to find a match for whoever's asking, to think of something I'm sure they would think was perfect, that it leaves me tongue-tied . . ."

We both laughed, and I felt a tightness inside me loosen for the first time in a long time.

**"I'm American,"** I said, when he asked.

"You don't sound it. I couldn't place your accent, but I wouldn't have guessed American."

"I'm kind of a hybrid."

"Meaning?"

"My dad's a New Yorker. My mother says she's from Sussex, but her father was French. They met and then married in Paris. I went to school in France and England, college in the U.S., but I've lived in London for years."

"You live in London now, or here?"

"In London. I'm just working here for a few days."

"What do you do?" he asked.

"I'm a translator."

He didn't say, "Love of words again," or some other trite comment.

"What kind of translating?"

"A very ordinary kind. Commercial stuff mainly—advertising and promotional brochures, contracts."

It was hard to resist telling him how bored I was with the vapidity of it all; the false premises of product desirability; the ugliness of urban life; the hot rush of the subways; the jostle of the intent, white-faced crowds; the dirt; the sirens ripping through the nights. I almost did, then stopped myself, not wanting to sound negative or petulant, both of which I felt too often for comfort when I was overwhelmed by the city. I was only a few years out of college but already it felt as if I had taken a wrong turn and trapped myself.

Did he sense some of that in my tone? "And if you weren't translating?"

"If I didn't have to work, you mean?" I asked, reminding him there was still an explanation due.

"If you could do whatever you wanted every day."

"Apart from reading, obviously. I would love to translate books if I could get a commission. There are some fantastic French writers, like Pierre Magnan and Chloé Delaume, who aren't often translated into English. I'd love to have a try myself, and really do them justice in my own way."

"Making the books into your own, partly?"

"Well, you can't do that, because you must always be faithful to someone else—to the details and the spirit of their work. But you're right in a way; you can be subtly inventive and the joy of it would be to achieve that special balance."

"You're a faithful kind of person, then?"

"Always. It's important." Then, realizing what he meant and how naïve that sounded even though it was true, I laughed and said, "Are you, though? I suppose you're married?"

He shook his head very slowly, looking into my eyes. "No."

I failed to find an adequate response.

"It will come, what you really want to do," he said, breaking the sudden awkwardness. "You're still young."

"I can dream."

"Of course it can happen."

My face must have betrayed the skepticism I felt.

"Why not?" he asked. "It happened to me."

**Dominic is** a writer—of music. After college, he and a friend started a geo-technology business with one computer and a clever idea. Dom thought it might give him some kind of income while he worked on his music. He didn't do much music for the next twenty years but the business did better than anyone could have predicted. And, as they sold just before the downturn, he's considered doubly lucky—or astute, depending on your point of view. I could vaguely remember reading in the business section about his company, although it wasn't so high-profile that I could have put his name to it. In any case, he would far rather people knew his name for a piece of music than as someone who made a pile of money.

At Les Genévriers, he would disappear for hours into his music room. Notes floated out into the courtyard from the new piano he bought in Cavaillon, followed by expressive silences that suggested the transference of sound to paper, or computer screen, or the inner process of composing, or sometimes a siesta on the plump cushions of the sofa he installed there.

That first summer, like the deepening love and understanding between us, the property kept growing. Armed with a fistful of medieval keys, we discovered new rooms, hidden chambers revealed below and beside the rooms we thought we already knew.

The attached stone barn in the courtyard was the first surprise gift. When we finally managed to unlock it (a feat of strength the real estate agent had not managed), we found it was a large, light, and well-proportioned room with a tiled floor, plastered and whitewashed walls, and an enormous fireplace. Dom knew immediately what it was: his music room.

Underneath this room was a flaking, splinted wooden door accessed from the sloping garden. We broke the obsolete lock, expecting to find a tool store or some such. Inside was a paved antechamber to a warren of caverns and Romanesque vaults. In the row of cottages, crudely modernized, then abandoned, we found semi-underground chambers by opening a cupboard door.

And in these hidden places were the discarded objects we claimed as gifts from the house: a bad painting of a peace lily, a hoe, a vase, a set of ramekins pushed deep inside a kitchen cupboard, a pair of rubber boots, an iron birdcage, much rusted and with a broken catch.

Dom's laugh rang under the curved ceilings of the half-open cellars of the lower ground floor. Down there we found pillars and arches, and under these ribs of the main house, drifts of wine bottles, glass frosted opaque by long use. Up in the kitchen, where the units were ingeniously formed of cast-off wardrobe and cupboard doors, waited the spicy Vacqueyras wines celebrating both our territorial expansion and the happy expansion of ourselves.

Outside, our northern pores sucked in the warm blue sky, the astringent bracers of rosemary and thyme, the dust of ages, and we looked at each other and smiled. A home of our own—and what a place!

# 4

The visitors are still here.

Bénédicte waits for them to go, holding herself tightly in her chair, pushing down the terrors that will follow if they do not. Breathing deeply, she makes herself see—behind her tightly closed eyes—the precious valley with its long southern screen of mountain.

Beyond, in the rising hills to the east, the first shivers of the Alps heft the land further into the sky. There the fields are corded purple, forever that long-ago summer when she scythed and bent with the other girls, the women, and the elderly to pick lavender flowers for the perfume factory.

Higher still the land is stubbled with sheep. They say that each troop of sheep keeps the scents of its particular grazing land deep in its fleeces, so that its provenance can be established by what the nose detects in the matted, unwashed wool: thyme and dry rocks, acorn-mashed mud, slopes where the herb savory grows in abundance, the pollen of gentian fields, hollows where leaves rot with windblown spikes of lavender.

Breathing slowly.

Breathing in scents of the fields and sun-warmed stone.

Hearing only the sound of a lightly running stream made by the wind in the trees.

## 5

The approach to Les Genévriers is wide open. The Luberon hills are like a great wide curtain, falling in folds created by steep gorges like a stage backdrop behind our land; all paths south through the property seem to end in ridged blue hills that deepen with the passing of the day. By early evening, the folds are sharply delineated by black pleats, the crevasses that trap the dark.

This property is not enclosed. We fling open all the flaking wooden shutters, and all is light and air. The blue is all-encompassing: the sky, the hills, the distant towns that cling to other hills along the valley, laid out before us.

Living there, waking up to it each morning, I felt as if life—my real life, that is, the life I had always been hoping to have—had truly begun. In every way imaginable, I was happy, exhilarated even. And, at the core of it, I had found Dom, and he had found me. We were embarked on a new life together.

Does this sound reckless? All I know is that I never thought this would happen to me, but when it did, I seized my chance.

After the momentous meeting in Yvoire, he came back to Geneva with me, and we went out to dinner, walked for hours around the black, wind-ruffled lake lit on all sides with advertisements for the most expensive watches in the world. Indeed, it was one of those names that had provided the work that brought me to Switzerland.

He pulled me in toward him. Against the light, he was a black outline with no visible features. We kissed, and I knew at the first, feather-light touch of his mouth that this was special.

"Eve . . ." he whispered.

It's not my real name. It's what he called me for the first time that long, lamp-lit afternoon in the café by the lake. He likes to claim I was seriously suggesting he take a bite of the Château d'Yvoire's ornamental cabbage in the Garden of Taste. It's a gentle tease that stuck.

"You're not married?" I asked him again.

"I was," he said. "I'm not married anymore."

The same thing happened the next night, nothing more, and the day after that I returned to London, my translating job finished. Dom went to stay with friends in Paris before he turned up in London a week or so later. We went to the theater and to the Tate Modern. I tried to play it cool. So did he. But we both knew.

**So we** went away together, to Italy: a flight to Naples, then a hydrofoil across the bay to the island of Ischia. Four days, it was supposed to be. As a freelancer, I was able to juggle jobs. Arriving in Ischia's harbor out of season in a lemon-yellow spring was like stepping into the set of a fifties movie. The jumbles of tall stucco houses perched over the water, the buzz of Vespa motor scooters, the shouting, and the sulfurous baths. In a hotel that was once a palazzo, we shared a bed with ridiculous gold silk sheets and stayed for a week. Until I met Dom, I never knew what it was like, physically, to find the perfect fit, to be aroused by a glance or a single passing contact. It was a revelation.

So was he, that first night. He had a wonderful body, broad-shouldered with well-defined muscles; a physique that made sense of the athletic stride. I had not yet known a man who looked so strong yet was so skilled in gentleness.

"Not an athlete so much as a swimmer," he said, in response to my admiring question. "Long-distance swimming. When I was much younger, I swam competitively."

"And you still do it, obviously."

"Not seriously, anymore. I didn't swim for a long time, but I went back to it a few years ago. Being alone with my thoughts, plowing up and down my line in the pool, working out, body and mind. It helped a lot during a tough time."

"What kind of tough time?"

"Oh, you know. Life, sometimes."

"Tell me," I said gently, tracing his upper arm with a fingertip.

"I'd rather not talk," he said, pulling me over him with a smooth, sinuous movement.

I did try asking again, much later, but he made it clear I should drop the subject. And so, I let it go. Who hasn't had a tough time of some description? If I'm honest, at that stage in the affair, when I didn't know how serious we were, any hint of trouble was only important in that it played to my bookish fantasies that somehow I would be the one to rescue him, the romantic heroine who would restore what he had lost.

Reluctantly, we went back to the mainland, but didn't move from Naples until two days later. In Menton, just across the border with France, we checked into a hotel with full business facilities, and I managed to finish one piece of work I had promised, and sent word to other regular clients that I would be on extended leave until further notice.

We trailed blissfully and aimlessly along the French Riviera for a while, feeling decadent, of another age. Was this how it had been for all those rich artistic people: the Scott Fitzgeralds, the Bloomsbury group, the Picassos and Somerset Maughams? It was idyllic. We were idyllic. The whole scenario was exciting, and fun, and all-consuming, and stage-managed, of course, but it was also a manifestation of a profound understanding between us, which had taken both of us unawares.

I had never consciously looked for an older man, but know now that I shouldn't have left it to chance. Dom was fifteen years older than me, and everything I hadn't realized I'd wanted all along: confident and sophisticated but undercut with a vulnerable creative streak I understood all too well. We went back to London together and we stayed together.

**"I'm thinking** of moving," he said one Sunday afternoon as we ambled around Hyde Park and the Serpentine gallery in that semi-exiled way of self-obsessed lovers who had spent the whole morning in bed, and lunchtime, too.

"Are you?"

"I've had my eye on somewhere special. Somewhere I've always wanted to live, dig myself in, put down roots."

There it was again, that natural empathy we had. The idea of roots struck a chord with me. Deep down, throughout all the years I spent shuttling between divorced and still-warring parents and their separate continents, I yearned for somewhere I really knew as home.

"I've looked at other places," he went on. "But this is the one that stays in my mind that everything else has to match up to. But nothing does compare. Like it's cast a spell—I even dream about it!"

"So—it's what, a house—apartment?"

"It's an old farming hamlet. In Provence."

"You want to move to France?" I asked weakly. A sudden shaft of pain in my chest expressed the dread I didn't dare articulate. It was an effort to keep my voice even.

"It's the most beautiful spot. And I know the area well. My family used to rent a villa in the Luberon for summer holidays. We went back year after year while my sister and I were growing up. I think my parents would have liked to buy somewhere there themselves, but couldn't afford to, or thought it was impractical."

I knew by then that his father was a senior civil servant and his mother had stayed at home in the traditional way. His elder sister was a doctor, a general practitioner in Richmond. Dom talked vaguely about introducing me to his family, but it hadn't yet happened.

"Anyway, now there's no reason I can't buy a house there . . . as I say, it's an extraordinarily beautiful place, and well, this is something I've always wanted to do. I really want to do this." He was speaking too quickly. Then he stopped walking, right in front of a Rebecca Warren sculpture titled *Perturbation, My Sister*, and faced me, searching for some answer he needed from my eyes.

My heart pounded uncomfortably. I stared into the distance, sure he was about to tell me it was over between us, that this was the parting of the ways.

"Come with me—come and see what you think. If you think you could live there." His delivery was offhand.

Less than two weeks later, we were standing in the courtyard of Les Genévriers for the first time.

**That was** how it began. A whirlwind and a new start: one that had immediate appeal. Perhaps it wasn't as odd for me as it might have been for someone who had always lived within the same boundaries, in the same place, in the same country. Sure, I realized it was a risk, but I felt excited and optimistic rather than uncertain. It seemed like the outward expression of our joyous discovery of each other, our unexpected and intimate happiness.

I didn't ignore the practicalities. I decided not to sell my tiny flat in London but to rent it out furnished, which would cover the mortgage. I stored most of my assorted possessions at my mother's house. In the end, all I brought with me were enough books to fill two bookcases, a laptop, and a suitcase of clothes.

"I'll still work, contribute my share," I said. "I like to work."

"You can do what you want. Why not find that special book to translate?"

"You mean that?"

"You know I do."

There's always translation work around, and I did have every intention of finding out exactly what was available, but somehow I never got started. Dom. The landscape. The life of books and music. It was all enough. How lucky were we?

There are plenty of cynics who would say that it was too good to be true.

**What did** Dom see in me? I did wonder sometimes. Beyond the physical attraction, was it my lack of experience, the borrowed sophistication, the unblinking adoration in my eyes? Or just that I was happy to sit and read for days on end without asking anything more of him?

In the early days of a relationship, we all pretend to be something we are not. It might be as simple as pretending to be more outgoing than we really are, or more tolerant, or feigning cool when we feel anything but. There are infinitely subtle grades of pretense. Perhaps I was pretending to be more self-sufficient than I felt, making a conscious effort not to repeat past mistakes of neediness and possessiveness, though with my family background it was obvious why I would be.

A bad marriage and a worse divorce. It didn't do any of us any good. I still hate any kind of confrontation. As a child, I made myself believe the myths my parents spun; the collusion was necessary, especially for my brother and me. I can let myself see it now, but I won't mock self-delusion. In the pulling together to weave the fantasy, we were achieving the impossible dream: we were fastened securely together in the teeth of financial disasters, remorseless moves, separations, and fundamental incompatibility between husband and wife.

But now, being with Dom was like being shaken awake. Everything was clearer, sharper; my senses were more acute. From the moment we met it was as though I had found the home I had always dreamed of having. I wanted to put down roots, deep and lasting ones.

**That summer,** the house and its surroundings became ours. Or, rather, his house; our life there together, a time reduced in my memory to separate images and impressions: mirabelles—the tart orange plums like incandescent bulbs strung in forest-green leaves; a zinc-topped table under a vine canopy; the budding grapes; the basket on the table, a large bowl; tomatoes ribbed and plump as harem cushions; thick sheets and lace secondhand from the market, and expensive new bedcovers that look as old as the rest; lemon sun in the morning pouring through open windows; our scent in the linen sheets. Stars, the great sweep of the Milky Way making a dome overhead. I have never seen such bright stars, before or since.

After several abortive attempts to penetrate the arcane bureaucracy of France Telecom—including a trip to Cavaillon, where we waited hours in a store only to be told to come back with more documentation—we made a conscious decision to live as simply as possible. Not forever, but for now. With the prospect of major building work, Dom suggested, there was no point in spending weeks trying to install telephone and Internet lines only to have to jump through more hoops to replace them later. For a while, apart from a couple of cell phones that didn't always pick up the unreliable signal, we would absent ourselves from the modern world.

And so we did, just as we embraced decrepitude, from the house's small sighs as more plaster cracked and fell, to the dry bodies of dead insects and husks of scorpions. None of it mattered. It was a kind of release from the normal worries associated with owning a house. All would be fixed in the end; fixed but not spoiled.

Besides, the place contained a history. In the wooden lintel of the oldest part, what must originally have been a simple cottage, is carved the date 1624. A lopsided stone arch at the end of the main house, which would once have let carts into the courtyard, bears testament to its construction in 1887.

We filled the main house with relics and prizes from the local *brocantes*, the secondhand flea markets. However badly rusted, flaking, dented it was, we were charmed by each item. Castoffs, objects near the end of their life, their usefulness already given to other people in other settings, could play out their final years for us, until they crumbled finally into the dust that fell steadily from the ceilings and walls.

Baked red tiles on the ground floor—*tomettes*—stamped with incident, finger and animal prints, like fossils, told a possible tale of the playful farm dog who would not obey and came running across the earthy work while it was still wet. There were stains on some of the tiles in the kitchen that might have been there for generations. I rubbed and scrubbed and sanded, but the evidence of bygone carelessness—an eye taken off a great pan on the range, a bowl of boiling hot soup sent flying from the table—remained indelible.

After a while, I began to relax into it, to accept that the place would never be completely, surgically clean; that was impossible. Live with the dust. Live in the dust; call it a light dusting of magic.

I was talking about this to Fernand, one of the village elders who came down the track one day and introduced himself. He was friendly and helpful, and had soon organized a small team of gardeners for us, led by a hardworking but lugubrious individual called Claude.

Fernand nodded sagely. All these tiles were hand-made, he said, some were perhaps a hundred years old.

*"Chaque tuile a son secret . . . cherchez-le!"* he said. Each tile has its secret—look for it!

And that was exactly what it felt like we were doing, looking for delicious secrets. Discoveries: not only about the buildings, but about ourselves. I don't think I have ever felt closer to anyone. It scared me a bit, the depth of the intimacy, as if on one level it couldn't be sustained. Maybe that tells you all you need to know about the person I used to be before I met Dom.

As the great range of hills slumbered in evening shades of rust and indigo, we listened to soupy jazz on the CD player. We'd cook together, drinking rosé and talking in companionable murmurs.

Sometimes we'd light the sconce on the wall outside the kitchen. It is a sinister creation: a disembodied arm emerges from a wrought-iron picture frame, extending a candle. It was left by a previous occupant; we would almost certainly not have bought such a grotesque artifact; yet we left it hanging there, and often lit it.

Inside and out, pools of light burned from hurricane lamps, candelabras, chandeliers, tea lights, and the rusty lantern we found in the courtyard and used on the dining table on the terrace.

During the long, gilded evenings, we touched compulsively as we exchanged our stories, raking over their import gently and unhurriedly as the tide stroking a beach of pebbles.

"Happy?" asked Dom.

"Very happy."

The glow lit a green-gold lace of our fingerprints on the neck of the wine bottle. His warm, brown hands took mine. His eyes were soft and utterly serious. "This is exactly what I've always wanted," he said. "I've never been as happy as I am with you, here. Thank you for coming, thank you . . . for everything."

"It's me who should be telling you that," I said, leaning over to kiss him. "You're the one who's made all this happen. All this . . . it's just enchanted!"

He put a hand up to my face. "I adore you, you know that, don't you?"

I smiled even wider. "I love you too. More than I can say."

"It just feels right, doesn't it?"

I nodded, suddenly overcome by the magnitude of our good fortune.

The isolated flowering of lights in the valley beyond. Nights warm as black velvet. I loved those evenings. I had never felt so completely at ease, so close to another person, so happy, so lucky, so loved and loving.

Throughout all those evenings, he never said a word.

# 6

That summer there was much talk of La Crise, the world's financial crisis. It was brought up by everyone who came to the house, from the gardeners to the man who sold us the desk at the *brocante* market in L'Isle-sur-la-Sorgue, to the builders who came to estimate the cost of the renovations we needed, and naturally needed to judge whether we would be good for the considerable costs involved.

When the local newspapers weren't full of financial worries, layoffs at fruit-packing plants and the crystallized-fruit factories, and falling prices for the farmers, they were reporting a series of local girls who had gone missing.

We heard the talk and saw the headlines, but we managed not to register any of it. We took refuge in our foreign status, bound up in our own little world, where nothing could touch us.

Dom, dressed in worn T-shirts and filthy jeans, seemed in his element ripping into the overgrown parts of the garden. We both soaked up the sun, moving fallen stones, digging and pulling. I loved the way that sheer physicality meshed with our more aesthetic pursuits; it seemed a perfect balance. One afternoon, we saved Pomona, goddess of fruits and gardens. She was lying in the bottom of the abandoned, mossy swimming pool, legs broken in the green rainwater shallows.

Dom knew who she was, because he had already been introduced to one of her other likenesses at the salvage yard on the Avignon road. He was becoming a regular there, what with his search for a mantelpiece for the main living room and his grand designs for the garden.

Together we managed to haul out what remained of the statue (head and torso and one arm), cleaned her battered body (but not too much), and propped her up against a wall, where she slumped, exhausted, a study in survival against the odds.

"Do you think she might preside over us?" I asked. "When she recovers, obviously."

He laughed, still out of breath. "I'd hope so, after all that."

"We could find her a nice spot."

"A plinth!"

He found her one, too: a plain cube of sandstone. After a visit from a blacksmith, she was fixed in place and installed below the terrace, framed by another of the faux-Roman stone arches. She sat well there, holding her tray of petrified fruit and flowers, the coy tilt of her head drawing the eye down the grassy slope.

I liked the way the roughness of surfaces was a part of the setting, the wide, descending terraces held up by broken stone walls. Nothing was overdone—the reverse, in fact; it all looked as if it had been thrown together, weeds and dying plants all part of the whole.

Inspired by Pomona, Dom was back at the reclamation yard as soon as the bones of the garden were laid out. A Greek boy, pox-ridden with lichen, cast an anguished look back at the house from the parterre; what should perhaps have been a parting glance had it not been petrified into a stare. Fragments of old stone pillars and pediments were placed to amuse: a granite pineapple; a hand that seemed to beckon as it rested on the low wall leading to the pool, a leaking basin of green water.

**For about** five days that first August, the hills bruised purple under black clouds. The wind whipped up and temperatures plummeted.

The gardeners were downcast. "We never know what to do with ourselves when it rains in the summer," said Claude.

We reminded them that there had been no significant rainfall here for five years, and the water-storing *bassins* and underground reserves needed replenishment. Everyone had told us that. The architect had been particularly keen to explain how the drought had worsened the fracturing of interior walls.

The men shrugged. It was true, of course, but that didn't make the loss of sunshine any easier to bear.

Dom pointed down the valley. "That's full of cloud and mist on autumn mornings. It looks like snowfields."

He could have left it there and I would have assumed he was just speaking generally.

"And the garden is full of wildflowers again—the moisture must bring them out," he went on.

"How do you know?"

He barely missed a beat. "Rachel and I came up here."

It seemed an odd way to phrase it. As if he was using simplicity to cover a great deal more information.

"You brought her here, to this house?"

There was a pause, as if he had given himself away. As if he hadn't thought before speaking and wished he had. "Sh-she brought me, actually."

"Why didn't you say?"

"Does it matter?"

I knew about Rachel by then, of course I did. She was Dom's wife—his ex-wife, rather. She was one of the reasons we would definitely not be getting married any time soon, no matter how well our relationship worked out, and it was all fine, really. He had no desire to get married again, and I respected that. It was a golden time; what we had was so precious we were happy just to be.

**Looking back** though, there had been clues.

The day we saw Les Genévriers for the first time. I remember asking that day, sensing there was a clear difference emerging between me and his ex-wife: "Did Rachel not like Provence?"

And he laughed. "What makes you say that?"

"It just seemed—"

"She loved Provence," he said. "Never wanted to leave."

"Where does she live now?" I asked, aware suddenly that I knew very little about her present circumstances and had never thought to wonder.

But the real estate agent was approaching again, urging us toward another door he had managed to open with the great ball of rusty keys, and the question was lost through another sequence of stone-flagged rooms and their echoes.

And now that we were immersed in each other, in the landscape and the house, Rachel was the one subject we never discussed.

# 7

énédicte has never believed in ghosts.

Yet the house is full of spirits. Wherever she looks, in every corner is the outline, in her mind's eye, of a person who once occupied it, of an object that once stood there, right back to Grandfather Gaston, leaving his hunter's pouch at the door and threading small birds on skewers to cook over the fire, and Mémé Clémentine in her dusty black skirts, busy chopping vegetables or kneading dough at the kitchen table. Maman and Papa, Marthe and Pierre; the Poidevins, the Barberoux, and the Marchesi, the tenant families. Old Marcel, who lived out back by the sheepfold, who worked here man and boy, jack-of-all-trades. Bénédicte's great friend Arielle Poidevin, who was the same age.

Only Bénédicte remains.

She takes a deep breath, and then speaks clearly and slowly.

**The haunting** began . . . one afternoon in late summer.

It was one of those days so intensely alive and aromatic, you could hear as well as smell the fig tree in the courtyard. Wasps hummed in the leaves as the fruit ripened and split; globes of warm, dark purple were dropping, ripping open as they landed with sodden gasps.

I remember it all so vividly. The pulse that pumped out the sweet, heady scent was quickening as I bent down to pick the fallen figs, then pulled them apart to find insects already drunk on their scarlet hearts.

For nearly three weeks, the heat had not abated, dense heat that sends you to sleep between the hours of three and five in the afternoon. But it was coming to an end. I could feel it in the air, the sky was subtly changed, closer down to earth, the light was flattening. Soon it would become heavy and begin to press down. Then the first drops of rain would come, splashing the wounded fruit; then the first flash of lightning.

For now, though, the full trees swayed in the remaining sun, taking the wind. The light in the courtyard dipped and dappled across the ground, painting underwater scenes on the patchy grass and earth.

I remember going inside, my senses heightened.

Breaths of basil and mint and rosemary rose from the pots outside the kitchen door. The wandering cat that came by from time to time brushed by my legs, releasing hot, dry earth and animal rankness in musky gusts. The scents made me think of Marthe, of course.

The shutters in the kitchen were closed, but I do recall that the room seemed strangely light. The upholstery on my mother's old chair by the black iron stove was starkly defined so that the green-and-red pattern seemed to spring renewed from the shiny gray sheen of long use. I sat down in it and half-closed my eyes.

For a few moments, all was drowsy calm. Then a shadow fell, calling me back to consciousness.

A small figure had stolen in. It was my brother, Pierre. He was standing, waiting expectantly in front of the hearth, silent, as if his intention was perfectly clear. That was so typical that I simply took no notice. You had to play it like that with him, or you would give away more than you had intended, and he would get the better of you, as usual.

I raised myself reluctantly and went to the larder, taking out the basket of vegetables I had cut to cook that evening. It was never a good idea to give Pierre the impression you had time on your hands.

"You can help if you like," I said sleepily. "About time you did something to help me, for a change."

He didn't reply but followed me over to the work-table and stood by, leaning insolently against the wall, still in silence, eyes large and dark in a muddy face under matted hair, bony bare knees badged with their usual bruises and gashes from boys' adventures in the woods.

I put tomatoes on the chopping board, unable to shake off the afternoon torpor. The whir of cicadas outside intensified. A few minutes must have passed before a jolt returned me to reality.

There was no Pierre. How could there have been?

I blinked hard and turned around. The wall was blank. The kitchen was darkened by the shutters. In front of me, the tomatoes on the board were rough, red shapes in a mess of seeds. Slowly, shakily, I put down the knife. I was alone, as usual. A rumble of thunder raked the air overhead.

That was the day it began.

**It upset** me greatly. What was I to make of a vision of Pierre, more than fifty years after he had been that muddy ten-year-old boy? Pierre, after all these years.

There were three siblings in our generation of the family: a family that had lived at Les Genévriers for so many generations that no one knew how many. Marthe was the first, born in 1920; Pierre followed three years later; and I was the youngest, arriving on the last day of 1925.

For hours after Pierre's visitation, my heart beat too vigorously. I felt light-headed yet my limbs were like lead as I moved slowly through the rooms on my usual round, from the kitchen to the little sitting room where I now have my bed, through the hall to the bathroom. I was aware that I was holding my head rigidly, staring straight ahead, not wanting—not daring—to look into the periphery of my sight, into the corners of the rooms. When the light flickered, as it always did when the wind shook the leaf shade in the courtyard against the clear, bright sky, I jumped and had to clasp my chest and stop, the breath caught in my throat.

He was there, or so I imagined, in every sudden shadow and burst of sunlight through the glass above the big door into the courtyard. At any moment, the ever-shifting patterns of brightness and dark I had always known and loved, which gave this place such life, might bring him back into view, as he once was: Pierre in his child form, the boy with the wild, demonic streak. The capacity he had for coming out ahead no matter how unpropitious the circumstances. The glee with which he would torture stag beetles with lighted sticks, or hook ever-larger objects on to their pincerlike antlers to see how much they could pull. His pinches that left dark stains on my arm. What if . . .

No, I could not think it. I am the sensible one. I don't think that way. My imagination is poor, with none of the inventive associations of his, or Marthe's. I take after my grandmother, Mémé Clémentine: hardworking, frugal, and practical, with no time for silliness.

# 8

By August we were sleeping with all the windows thrown open. That was why, when I became aware of the scent, I assumed it had come from outside.

It was a voluptuous scent: vanilla with rose and the heart of ripe melons, held up by something sterner, a leather maybe, with a hint of wood smoke. The first time it stole into my consciousness, I was half-wakeful in the early hours, in the act of coming around from one dream before settling into another.

I allowed it to envelop me, this pleasant, slightly heady aroma. It was a lovely sensation, as if my reverie was so sensuous that it had a tangible perfume. Warm and content in the bed with Dom sleeping beside me, I was wrapped in this delicious concoction.

Then, as minutes passed, I became fully awake. These were real thoughts, and I was breathing real scent, and my mind was trying to make sense of it. Was it rising from the garden outside our open window? Had shower gel spilled in the bathroom? A bottle broken in a handbag? There was nothing I could recall that might explain it, yet the scent was all around us.

Dom slept on, handsome and half-smiling, oblivious.

It was a romantic fragrance, I'd say. Fruit and flowers and smoke, soft and warm, alluring. It was starting to cloy.

Gradually it faded, and I must have gone back to sleep. In the morning, I examined every possible source but nothing came close to replicating that fragrance.

I decided it must all have been a highly charged dream.

After an absence of about a week, it returned, and continued to do so, though with no discernible pattern to its reappearance, and with slight variations on the ingredients of the scent. At times it carried essence of vanilla, sometimes a robust note of chocolate and cherries. It might linger only for a few minutes, but strongly, or less distinctly for up to an hour. Some nights it was carried off by a whisper of wind in the courtyard trees, an ethereal, smoky lavender.

The first time it happened, thoughts of Rachel came stealing into my head. There was no logic to it, except that perhaps I had been associating the scent with another woman and to think of her was the obvious progression.

But after that, despite my best efforts to change the pattern, each time this strange, thought-provoking aroma stirred from its mysterious source, I found that the unknown Rachel was there, too. I didn't want her there, but she was locked somehow into the experience. A voice in my head kept up an insistent refrain, as if trying to remind me that I knew, that I had always known: Rachel was there with us, unacknowledged but still exerting her influence.

**I did** ask Dom about her, of course I did. At the beginning, it had seemed only natural to want to know about his life before he met me, and what had happened to end his marriage. He was reluctant to discuss it, and, as all the advice to those contemplating new relationships is not to make too much of the failures of the old, I assumed he was following that tack. As we grew closer, I tried again but the result was always the same. And I knew him well enough by then to understand that the self-contained man I had first seen in the maze had a chilling capacity for detachment if I pushed him too far. It was this intensity that had first drawn me in, of course. But in the months we had been together, I'd come to recognize that what seemed like an electric charge between us when his mood was sunny could switch without warning, leaving me adrift in a cold, black void.

"It ended badly," he said, the first night we spent together. "If it's all right with you I'd rather we didn't talk about it." Whenever I tried in a casual way to find out more, he would reach out and draw me to him, putting a stop to my questions with soft kisses.

But that morning, after the night when Rachel had first stolen into my consciousness, the enigmatic perfume still vivid in my memory, I asked him again.

"What did happen between you and Rachel?"

He moved to get out of bed, offering his smooth, sculpted back to me. I could see the muscles of his shoulders tense.

A few seconds passed.

"I can't talk about it. I know you want me to, but I can't. It's . . . very painful. I'm still . . . in fact, the one thing I'm going to ask you, very seriously, is that you respect that and don't keep asking about it. It has nothing to do with us, here and now, and if it's all right with you, that's . . . the way I'd like to keep it."

He finally turned to look me in the eye. "Promise me that?"

His face was strained. He seemed eaten up with sudden unhappiness and the vulnerability I sensed below his surface. A wave of guilt washed over me, and I nodded. Then I flung my arms around his rigid shoulders and held him to me, rocking gently.

**M. Durand,** farmer and head of one of the largest families in the village, appeared at our door with a yellow melon. The last of the summer, he said. His leathery face creased like an accordion when he smiled.

"Come to us for lunch on Sunday," he said. "Now the hunting season has begun, there is every excuse to sample the excellent casserole and pâté my wife makes."

We accepted with a great deal of pleasure and anticipation on both sides. This was the country life we had hoped to find, the adventure of new people and customs we were part of together.

Dom took advice at the local cave and chose some wines carefully. The Durand house was a twenty-minute walk down the track from Les Genévriers. Neither of us suggested driving the long way around on the roads.

That morning, the silence of the hillside had been splintered by bursts of gunshots. On our own land, clearly visible thanks to the rapidly thinning trees, we spotted an illegal hunting blind, spent cartridges scattered around the damp wood. Wood smoke was rising from the decomposition of the summer's delights. We tramped down through a grayness unthinkable back in July. Clouds hung like wisps of bonfire between the hills and the ground exuded damp, fresh, rotting smells.

And clumps of wildflowers, I noticed. Just as Dom predicted: comfrey and meadow clary, autumn squill, watercolor-blue chicory in scrubby clumps, and scabious.

The track of loose stones, earth, and fallen leaves wound down the hill past the ruined chapel and joined a wider farming path that had been paved with concrete. An unforeseen climb later, we arrived glowing and slightly out of breath at the traditional *mas* occupied by the Durand family for the past century, a longer, lower building than ours, redolent of the kind of sharp animal odors that had long since faded from Les Genévriers.

Inside, it was darker and warmer, too, thanks to plentiful wood paneling, a log fire, and a generous gathering of guests. Mme. Durand bustled out of the kitchen, a short, well-padded woman in a chef's apron.

"Welcome, welcome! Eat! What will you take as an apéro?"

Her plump face bobbed over a plate of diced salami and olives that she offered up to us immediately.

According to Dom, who first met M. Durand at the end of our track and cemented their acquaintance at the village bar the next night, Mme. Durand had been a teenage heroine of the Resistance during the Second World War, bicycling messages between underground cells in the surrounding hills. That put her well into her eighties, but she might have passed at first glance for a good twenty years younger.

Pinned down by sturdy oak furniture and our curious neighbors—almost every guest was a village inhabitant, it seemed—we sipped pastis cautiously if respectfully, and drank in their stories.

"There's an underground river, flowing right under the property," they told us, though the real estate agent hadn't.

"You should read the village newsletter," said a man who introduced himself as Patou, a big man with wild, dark hair and a beard. "There's an article about the great freeze of fifty years ago. The children from the outlying hamlets—including those from the five families at Les Genévriers—were unable to attend school for almost a month. A month! It's only a ten-minute climb up the hill. Only fifty years ago."

"Five families . . ." I said.

"At Les Genévriers? Sometimes more. It depended."

"On what?"

"Times of plenty. Times of need. War. Charity."

"There's treasure buried at Les Genévriers," added another bulky man who came to join us.

"And this is the man with the machinery to dig for it, too," said Patou.

The man mumbled his name but gave his profession clearly as *terrassier*, the village excavator and landscaper.

Dom smiled indulgently. "Seems odd that no one has found this treasure yet, after all these years and so many people living there."

"That's the legend." They drained their glasses in a fluid movement that elided drinking and shrugging.

"And watch out for the spirits!" said Patou.

There was laughter at that, as if everyone knew the stories and assumed that we had heard them, too.

"What spirits?" I asked brightly, but the moment had passed.

**Around a** great oak table, afternoon became evening as course after course appeared: pungent braised meats and herbs, exquisite vegetables with oil and garlic, and full-strength cheeses. Bottles of red wine appeared and were quickly emptied. Talk grew louder, of memorable games of boules, curling roots, many vintages, the drought, sun flares, the local soup-making competition, and hunting.

At one point, M. Durand filled my glass yet again, and leaned in conspiratorially. "Do you want to hear a Provençal story?"

I nodded eagerly, mouth full.

"In the next village there is a high escarpment. They say there is a great black boar there that portends disaster for those who are unlucky enough to see it. It appears to lone walkers, or farmers rounding up errant sheep. It is a terrible sight, for they know that soon they will be presented with a situation that can only end badly."

He paused, maintaining eye contact. Was there a twinkle there or was it the lamp that was now blazing?

"Does it really exist? people ask themselves. Those who believe say that there is proof. The escarpment is formed of a special kind of rock. It is hard as steel, but, inexplicably, up there set into these stones are the foot-prints of the beast."

Like the tiles on the ground floor of Les Genévriers.

"Could the footprints be the remains of fossils, perhaps?" I suggested.

"It's why we need to hunt," said M. Durand emphatically.

"So you think the story must be true?"

"We need to hunt," he repeated slowly.

I became aware that other conversations had stopped and that he had a wider audience as he added, turning to Dom now, "We have always hunted on this hillside, it's traditional. We will continue to hunt, no matter who nominally owns the land."

There was a pause, before Dom asked, "What do you go after?"

"Pheasant, partridge, rabbits and hares, a boar if we find one."

I missed the point, at the time. I asked Durand if there was a good collection of these stories I could buy, but he did not know. He supposed they must be written down somewhere, but he had only ever heard them spoken from memory.

"Shepherds' tales," he said dismissively.

We were about to leave, rummaging for our jackets in the hall, when the woman came up to us. She had been sitting farther down the table, and we'd not spoken.

"It is you, isn't it?"

She was in her mid-thirties perhaps. Her wide mouth was glossy with newly applied plum lipstick, which was a striking combination with her well-cut auburn hair. The kind of Frenchwoman who maintains a slim figure and immaculate grooming at all times as a demonstration of national pride. She was smiling and nodding, looking Dom directly in the eye.

Very charmingly and in much-improved French, he explained that she must be mistaken. He seemed genuinely puzzled, amused even. There was no reason for me to think he was holding anything back.

"But—a couple of years ago, no?"

He smiled but shook his head.

"The villa down the hill—the Mauger place . . ."

Sadly, he assured her, she was mistaken.

**Outside, clouds** were thickening, now rising, and creeping up between the trees like spirits. The sun hung low and pink-tinged above fields of muddy sheep, streaking the dead sky lupine, mauve, and apricot.

Dom strode ahead. As I hurried to keep up, I realized he was furious.

"We've been given fair warning," he said.

"What?"

"The hunters."

He explained angrily, as we walked, that we had been drawn in and firmly informed that we should not attempt to interfere in local life. Any complaints if the hunters appeared on our land would be futile.

**Dom was** still sleeping upstairs the next morning when I crept down for coffee and some pills for my headache. Wine-induced, most likely. My thoughts were racing, as they always do the morning after too much alcohol. Scenes from the previous day ran on a self-lacerating loop through my mind. Had I made a fool of myself? Were M. Durand's words really a threat? Had Dom understood correctly?

I stood at the kitchen window. A solitary magpie perched on the stone wall, then took off suddenly, a black-and-white dart. I was absurdly relieved to see another, a few moments later, coming in to land in the great ivy-clad oak farther down the garden.

Gradually, one incident jumped out from the previous day's tangle and became my focus. The woman with the plum lipstick. There was something that had gone over my head at the time. It bothered me now like an itch. Why hadn't the woman said anything until we were about to leave? Unless . . . It would make sense, I rationalized, if the woman was not wrong. If she had indeed met him before, a couple of years ago as she said, when perhaps he had been with another woman—Rachel—and she had been exercising some discretion, as the French always do in such matters.

Dom might simply have forgotten meeting her. Why, then, had he been so defensive?

**While Dom** stayed in bed for most of that morning, I took direction from that disembodied stone hand and dosed my hangover with fresh air, doing a job I'd been putting off. We had drained the old green swimming pool. Wet leaves had sunk like damp brown stars into the empty basin. I climbed down into the dirt. Fat scorpions lurked malevolently as I began to clear the stew of windblown twigs and sodden tangles of ivy, rotted petals, and grit. Underneath this soggy mess, as I suspected, there were ominous cracks in the concrete, which would explain why the water had seeped out over the course of the summer.

My head improved, but pain was replaced by uneasiness.

In the kitchen, I made myself a strong tea in the English way, letting it steep.

The sun had emerged, quick and sharp. It seared into the wall, on one small patch, lifting layer after layer of surface tints, from cream to burnt brown; so mottled, hacked, knocked, replaced, corroded that the effect was of a decrepit fresco. It would be a bit of a shame to paint over it now, I was thinking; it was part of the fabric of the building's history, like the various places in the house where the ghostly outlines remained of old doors now bricked up and plastered over. They were a fine counterpoint to the doors we found opened into new rooms that hadn't seemed to exist.

A shadow fell across the wall. I turned and saw a dark blur pass the glass in the door, announcing an arrival. I waited expectantly, but the seconds passed and no figure reappeared, no knock came.

Sipping my tea too soon, I felt it scald the roof of my mouth. I put down the mug, went over to the door, and pulled it open. No one was there.

I stepped outside. The little terrace was empty.

"Hello? Who's that?" I called down into the courtyard.

All was quiet. I retreated, puzzled.

Back inside the kitchen, a patch of weak sunlight flickered, making me jump. Perhaps all I had seen was the effect of sudden movement in the branches of the lilac at the entrance to the courtyard. Or a wisp of cloud, I told myself. But that did not alleviate the instinctive sense that someone was there outside, that I was being watched.

I listened closely, detecting a rattling sound that might have come from the alleyway. Perhaps one of the shutters had loosed its moorings. I went over to the window over the sink, and peered down. Nothing unusual that I could see.

I opened the back door and went out again. The courtyard was empty. Not a sound beyond the rustle of leaves. I was standing at the top of the stairs, about to turn and go in again, when a movement caught my eye farther down the garden, in the direction of the old pool. A scrap of gray-blue movement.

Wrapping my sweater tighter, I ran down the steps and out of the courtyard, keeping my eyes on the spot. When I reached the pool, nothing was there. The abandoned orchard beyond was empty, too.

I shivered again, this time with cold, and walked slowly around to the public path. The great hills were fringed by rain clouds. But there—

There was a movement and a darker, blue-gray shape.

I squinted. A figure? A woman in a long coat? I couldn't be sure. It seemed oddly insubstantial.

A blink and it was gone. I stood staring at the vanishing point on the path where it seemed to dive into the base of the hills, waiting for the apparition to reappear along the path and reveal itself.

It did not reappear.

**Everyone wants** answers and tidy conclusions, but in life they don't always materialize. You settle for the best outcome you can manage, and accept that you can't explain everything. The subconscious mind sometimes makes surreal connections, like the ones in dreams. Tricks of the light were all around. Look how the setting sun carved bloodred clefts in the hills that then turned to black rivulets.

I shrugged and tried to regain my rationality as I went back to the house. What had happened to make me so anxious all of a sudden?

Breathing deeply, feeling embarrassed by my over-reaction, I walked slowly around, checking for any signs of disturbance. Nothing was out of place.

On the kitchen table, my tea had gone cold.

# 9

After Pierre appeared, I found it hard to concentrate.

Each evening, when I sat with my book, the lamp grew dimmer as I struggled to find a comfortable position and to bring my vision into focus on the pages. In the glow that makes an island of the armchair and side table, the lines blurred and seemed to imitate waves. Individual words moved and stretched themselves, until they were impossibly gigantic, then suddenly snapped back to become impossibly small and slanted.

I would blink and close my eyes again, this time against the unbearable thought that I would lose one of my greatest pleasures. That I, too, would be afflicted like Marthe.

Surely that was a cruelty too far.

———

**I have** always been a reader. As a child, I loved books, though there weren't many at home. But as soon as I went to school and was given one to look at the lovely pictures, and turned the pages to find more of the same, I was happy. Such colors and strange and vivid images! I marveled at how they were all closed up, asleep with their secrets unseen until you reached up and took the book down from the shelf.

The teacher, Mlle. Bonis, noticed my reaction and, as soon as she thought I was ready, she gave me books that I could read on my own, books that made sense of the lessons the class was learning on the blackboard. My parents used to say they never knew where it had come from, but I seemed to be aware straightaway of the importance of books and words. The connection between the fantastical pictures illustrating the story and the images the words suggested in my head.

By the age of ten, I was reading Dumas, de Maupassant, and abridged versions of Victor Hugo's works. Very often, when my work on the farm was done, I would run up the path through the woods to sit reading on a hard chair in the village library in the corner of the *mairie*. I can still recall vividly the terrible shock I had while reading a passage by Giono, in which a man was killed by a storm. Lightning "planted a golden tree between his shoulders." The image has been imprinted in my mind ever since, both as a picture that is as beautiful as it is horrifying, and as a monument to the immense power of words.

I kept it quiet, but I wanted to be a teacher myself, just like Mlle. Bonis.

I feel him here all the time now. Pierre. He is at my back, in the vulnerable hollow at the base of my spine that acts as a warning sensor.

Why has he chosen to come back? After all these years, why now?

So typical of Pierre.

Always here, behind me, at my side: a presence beyond the familiars of the house, the well-known shapes and voices from the past that live benignly alongside me. Odd noises are disturbing now, and I am unsettled by voices when I know it is only the wind in the trees. My skin prickles as if a change has occurred but is not yet completely revealed.

Finally, four days after Pierre's first visitation, when he hadn't reappeared, I allowed my shoulders to drop. It was when I began to relax, of course, that he returned. This time he was standing by the hearth in the kitchen, quiet as you like.

I was making bread, which I don't do so often now, as the girl brings me bread from the bakery every two days. But I had a sudden craving for the bread that Mémé Clémentine and Maman used to make, when there was a brick bread oven at the end of the cottages. Into the mixing bowl they'd put a fistful of dough kept back from the previous batch; they called it the spirit of the bread, so there was continuity, a link down the years and generations, living and breathing in the yeasty pillows of the new loaves.

I was at the table, arms floured, kneading, and sad that there was no spirit of the bread to be placed inside, when Pierre strolled in again.

He didn't follow me this time, just stayed where he was, hands in pockets, guilty smile playing about his lips. A cut bottom lip, I noticed, as if he'd been in a scrap, which he often was. This was the Pierre who set snares in the woods and caught rabbits and larks with sticks and twine: the clever, grinning ten-year-old boy who provided the meat for Maman's herb-laced casseroles. The look on her face when he presented her with a fat animal or string of dead birds was beatific, like the face of the Virgin Mary at church, but she never knew that for every one he gave her, he had sold two to the restaurant at the foot of the hill and spent the money on cigarettes: real cigarettes, not the rubbish made of dried clematis rolled in leaves, which most of the village boys learned to puff on.

Head down, eyes almost closed, I scuttled past him down the few steps to the hall and into the sitting room, scrabbled in the drawer next to the bed, and drew out my rosary. Holy Mary, Mother of God. Bless us and keep us.

The third time he came, he was the first thing I saw when I opened my eyes in the morning. I was still bleary, emerging from sleep. But there he was, standing by the side of the bed, waiting for me to rouse myself.

I knew for certain then that Pierre, in the guise of the unsettling child he once was, had come back for good. He was staring at me mockingly, wordlessly, as if to make sure I had understood that there should be no mistake about it. His fingers were playing with the smooth twigs and the twine he used to make his most effective traps.

# 10

At that stage, it was only a wisp of suspicion, but it was the first time I had ever had reason to feel it about Dom. There had been bad times with other men, but never with Dom. He was different. I trusted him absolutely, in every way. Obviously, there was an element of disappointment in this small intrusion of reality. But at this stage, it would be more accurate to call it a dread of disappointment rather than the fact of it.

So, when I started asking questions, it was in the spirit of wanting to be proved wrong. I knew that in pressing him I risked one of his cold moods, but it wasn't fair of him to expect me never to be curious about his ex-wife. She was part of who he was, for better or worse.

"Are you still in touch with Rachel?"

It was a few mornings after the lunch at the Durands'. The hilltop lay on the cloud like a lushly vegetated island, long and low on a spumy sea. On the other side of the valley a village high on the Grand Luberon emerged in golden light from the same cloud waves, so that the great fortified walls appeared as seafront buildings.

The question clearly irritated him, as I had known it would. "In touch with Rachel? No."

I searched his face, the frown, the eyes, which avoided mine, staring past me at the floor, at the wall, and only then finding the great vista on the other side of the window.

I couldn't help but pursue it. "No, not really . . . or no, not at all?"

Again, a beat lost.

"No, I'm not in contact with her."

"But you know where she is?"

Just the tiniest fraction of a second. "Yes."

"What does she do?"

"What is this?"

"Just . . . curious."

"But why are you asking?" A flash of anger now, with a sarcastic bite. "Have you overheard me phoning her, found some texts between us, or—God!—perhaps you think I'm still in love with her!"

"Of course not."

There were so many other questions: How long were you together? How did you meet? What's she like? Is she anything like me? Why did you split up? Whose fault was it? What was so bad that it has hurt you so much?

But the look he gave me before he walked out of the room ensured they would remain unasked. Don't go there, it said. I asked you not to. You promised.

**Before the** incident with the woman at the Durand party, it never occurred to me that I might be jealous. I thought I knew as much as I needed to about Rachel, and accepted that she was a part of Dom's past, without wanting to know more.

But from that day on, it seemed Rachel was constantly there: hiding unacknowledged in the background of stories Dom told me; beside him in the pictures that reinforced his memories; informing his opinions; smiling inside his silences.

I brought her on myself, of course. I alone allowed her into my mind; I can't blame Dom for that. Dom did not talk about her. It was not as if I had moved into the house they shared. I was not living surrounded by her old belongings, or even their shared household items. Her hands had probably touched his books and pictures, but that was the extent of it. (Her hands on him, though; that was a different, altogether trickier, matter.)

But it was not as though I was condemned to sleep on sheets or walk on rugs that she had chosen, or wonder at her taste in wallpaper. There was no eating from her forks, taking food from her plates, sipping from her glasses and cups that would have underscored how far I had come in and taken her place.

Surely, though, it was only natural to want to know their story. It was precisely because he would not talk about Rachel that I found myself wondering more and more about her.

Who was it who said that what is hidden or cannot be said grows more powerful? "I told my wrath, my wrath did end . . . I told it not, my wrath did grow."

I remember now: Blake. "A Poison Tree."

# Part II

Part II

# 1

They say this region was once under the ocean, many millions of years ago, that the rocks were shaped by the tides, and the stones contain the outlines of forgotten sea creatures from the dawn of time. I would say there are days when all history stands still and all the spirits gather.

You can feel it when the air in the valley is so hot it ripples the horizon. The blue hills rise and fall in waves, a mirage of the sea, and the breezes rush and expire like rollers as they form and collapse on distant shores.

Bénédicte's voice breaks here. She takes some deep breaths. The audible suck of air into her lungs is imitated by the pull and hiss of the tape moving through the recording machine.

This is important. She must go on.

She must remember it all, not only the bad. She must not let herself be defined by the worst, not when there was so much that was good, and there is so much to teach.

**After Pierre** came back, I knew I had to find a way to ground myself in the present. Forget the past. What was real now was bad enough.

There was silence when I opened up the cottages, four in all, to assess the condition of the damp and the cracks. Spiders and scorpions rule the cool, musty emptiness, and dead insects crunch underfoot. The human inhabitants are long gone, to the towns, to the bad, to the sky. No guests come to stay. The bread oven is a locked storeroom, stacked with pieces of wood and iron that might once have come in useful.

Above the main house, the roof is falling in. The walls are weakening and the worst damage is in the stairwell, the walls that form the height of the house where the staircase winds up to the bedrooms. The staircase itself is breaking apart; the cracks in the banister wall and between steps are as wide as my thumb. Plaster dust has begun to seep out in thin streams like sand in an upended hourglass. One day, the whole staircase, the four half-flights up from the kitchen, is going to give way in a roaring tumble of bricks and plaster and tiles.

I have moved most of my possessions down to the ground floor. All that remains in the rooms above are wood-wormed cupboards and iron bedsteads that are impossible to move, since the screws that hold the struts and sides together have rusted so badly they will not turn. The beds that once held the family are fused black skeletons, too large to fit through the doorways. Abandoned, and trapped.

What a big, rambunctious family it was, not only the five of us but all the others who lived here with us. I miss them. I miss them all so badly sometimes, even Pierre.

The house is already full of ghosts, friendly ghosts. Wherever I look, in every corner is the outline, in my mind's eye, of a person who once occupied it, of an object that once stood there, right back to Grandfather Gaston and Mémé Clémentine. Papa so strong and silent and hardworking, not a particularly tall man, but, like many of the subsistence farmers here, wiry and tenacious. Our gentle *maman* with her soft, wide face and the smile that lit up our enclosed little world on the hillside. The tenant families. Old Marcel in the sheepfold. My friend Arielle. And here am I, the only one left, the one who was so clear about where her duty lay and what tradition demanded.

Outside, the figs fall, the wasps drone at the sugar bursting on the ground and on the branch, the scents of summer are overblown in the heat.

**When I** was a child, we were lucky in so many ways. It's only now I realize how poor we were and always had been. Such was the pride of the Lincels. Set apart on our land with our buildings and tenants, the family seemed like ruling nobility, to us at least.

In summer, the hillside was a kind of paradise.

By mid-June, great, white candelabras of blossom opened on the catalpa tree, and waved acid-green leaves like flays against the clean, new blue sky to mark the return of the long, hot months. Mulberries dropped from a soaring tree by the sheepfold into an obscene river of plenty. Arielle and I would cram the fruit into our mouths, letting the watery sweetness burst on our lips and tongues and stain our faces and hands purple. The plum trees and olives on the terraces below the main house were loud with birdsong, drowning out the first feeble cheeps from the cicadas.

In the mornings, we woke early to a warm shock of the brightness that suddenly filled the room as the shutters were thrown open, and the deep blue of the morning outside. Hearts singing with the knowledge that there were no school lessons to detain us, we tumbled downstairs to grab whatever was on the breakfast table.

A splash of coffee in boiled milk, a hunk of bread dipped into it, and we were out at our chores while the air was still cool. Later, as the hillside heated up and duties were done, we were off and away, out across the tough, hardy grass that soon scorched to hay, into the infinite sunshine. The hills were so blue it seemed they had soaked up the sky. Eagles and hawks hovered, riding the thermals, puppets suspended on invisible wires. The thyme and rosemary and lavender patches released their musky incense. Tender puffs of wind were silken on the skin: a gorgeous *vent roux* from the southeast.

As children, we spent whole days in the woods above and below the house, collecting treasures, climbing trees, watching the insects: complicated towns of ants, scarab beetles, copper-green rose beetles, and the hummingbird-like hawk moths.

Marthe and I once sat for an hour, observing a huge hornet dragging a cicada up the stony wall of the courtyard barn. Twice it almost reached the top but then fell at the last obstacle with a scratchy flop at Marthe's feet.

We shared a capacity to stay very still and just look, and touch, and smell. Toward the end of summer, we would lie facedown in the courtyard. After the brief, hard rainstorms of late August, the earth was caramel-sweet and spicy, and the warm, smitten flesh of fruit gave off a smoke of incense. I may be imagining this, of course. Perhaps memory has rendered these interludes larger-than-life, but it's true we did spend hours simply looking and inhaling, feeling life slowly, in close-up, burrowing into our surroundings, eating vanilla pastries with dirt on our fingers.

Marthe loved to talk about the scents and smells of the farm. My sixth sense was never as acute as hers (as I said earlier, my imagination has always been poor, which leads me to worry that the present situation is indeed precisely as I fear) but I could almost always smell what she smelled. Perhaps there was a family nose we both inherited that enabled us to read aromas, some small quirk of nasal membrane or nerve setting that provided an extra sensitivity. Old Marcel up by the sheepfold always claimed he had no sense of smell at all. Well, that went without saying; there's no way anyone else would have chosen to live in that fetid, dungy quarter.

Marthe wasn't blind then, or if she was, she never said.

Of course, there were many other hours (more hours than any child these days will ever know) spent working: gathering fruit and picking vegetables; washing and scrubbing; digging and clearing irrigation channels; sewing and mending for us girls as soon as we could hold a needle, and knitting in winter; running errands and taking messages between our farm and the others and the village at the top of the hill. That was thirsty work, in this country of drought. In the summer, we rushed back to Les Genévriers for great, gasping drafts of the pure, cold spring water.

It was precious stuff. Some years, in other hills to the south, the wells would run dry by May and the locations of springs had to be kept secret. At times like that, so it was said, the men used wine for shaving, though none of our menfolk would ever admit to such a thing, even if it was the rankest brew.

In any case, we were lucky. There was always water at Les Genévriers: there was even said to be an underground river beneath the house, though this was never proved.

What we had for certain, linked to our abundant water, was progress. The pride of the hamlet was a large brass tap in the lower kitchen-cum-laundry. My mother and the other women of Les Genévriers no longer had to traipse up to the village with their bundles to sit at the communal washing place, that mysterious, echoing stone room open to the street where mothers and grandmothers gathered to gossip around the long, pitted trough.

It helped, of course, that the house was situated on a hillside, so the pipe from the spring could be laid downhill, ending in that magnificent tap. When it first went in, groups of neighbors gathered around it for weeks after, marveling at the engineering and ingenuity. When we were children, our showers were a hose attached to that tap and hung out of the kitchen window over the alleyway between the big house and the row of workers' cottages. The wastewater ran down the hill and fed one of the vegetable patches. For other, more personal ablutions, there was a toilet built in a kind of sentry box attached to the side of the barn.

There was something else that was special about Les Genévriers. As our father had told us, "There's treasure here." Right from the time when he first started telling us stories: "A legend says so, there is hidden treasure." It was a subject he particularly enjoyed, and the ensuing conversation would be a variation of the following:

"What kind of treasure?" we all wanted to know.

"No one can say for certain. Most people say it's a cache of gold coins. But it might be jewelry, or Roman swords and cups. The Romans were here, you know."

"So why haven't we been looking for it?" asked Pierre, skeptical from a young age.

"Why do you assume we haven't?" countered our father.

"What if someone has been and stolen it?" asked Marthe. That was always her concern, and probably well-founded.

"It might have been, but surely we would have noticed the hole where it was dug up."

"So it's buried!"

"That's most likely. It must be in the ground, or beneath the stones of the house."

But why? But how? But when? And so we would go on, round and round in circles of perplexity as the light faded. The oil lamps would be lit. Inside or out, the method of generating light was the same. In Marseille and other great cities, they had *le gaz*, but we children had never seen it. We relied on the lamps, which drew flying insects and moths to butt hopelessly against the glass, and candles set in jam jars, in which they finally succeeded in killing themselves.

Papa sucking on his pipe, nodding as he apparently gave serious consideration to all our theories. None of us really believed it, but it was fun to dream.

If there was ever any trouble caused by our free-ranging activities, and in those we were no different from any of the other children in the surrounding countryside, it was inevitably caused by Pierre. He was the one who fell off walls, was injured by loose rocks, and tumbled off a bicycle he stole not knowing its brakes were shot. His thin legs were always notched with cuts, scrapes, and bruises.

Once, he broke his wrist at the abandoned chapel when a cord of ivy failed to hold his weight. Another time, he was bitten by a fox and his hand swelled right up. Next, he went missing for a day and a night until someone heard his cries from a well, the rotten rope he had lowered himself with had frayed and pulled apart, leaving him unable to climb the slippery, moss-covered sides.

"The boy is a liability, a danger to himself," Papa would say. But he was never as angry as I thought he would be. Nor did anyone seem to consider he might be a danger to others, although, as it turned out, they should have.

In between his climbing games and insect-torturing interests (my brother had recently acquired an apprentice in the form of a *prégadiou*, a praying mantis, which had a formidable record as a vicious slayer of butterflies, including the elegant swallowtails that wheeled around the garden; he and the mantis were learning a lot from each other), Pierre had a scam running.

It involved old bits of machinery, screws and bolts, broken pots, odd plates and cups, a framed picture from a raid on the attic. The objects were nothing important in and of themselves; no one ever noticed. Things were always appearing and disappearing; it was a facet of having so many people threading their way through the house, needing things and taking them, forgetting to put them back in the right place.

But these weren't simply disappearing in the usual way. Pierre was taking the objects and going into town to sell them on market days, when he was supposed to be at school. I don't think he even bothered to lie about his absence to the schoolmaster, M. Fabre. He told him he was going to market, just like that, and naturally it was assumed that he was working the family stall. This was the country, after all, and it was understood at that time that there were certain students who would not be in the classroom on a market day.

He took these items down to a junk stall, and was allowed to keep the price they fetched in return for a morning working the crowds for the stallholder. And Pierre kept a little bit more than that, as it happened, for the *brocanteur* was an inveterate tippler and spent most of the morning in the Lou Pastou bar, and wouldn't have noticed if Pierre had stolen twice as much as he did.

My brother, at that time, was such a charming, cheeky little monkey, with a certain gift for closing sales, that the man must have reckoned that kept him ahead of the game whatever was going on underneath the counter.

# 2

The summer was dying.

Blackberries crisped on dying brambles and fungus jutted like trays from the trunk of the big garden oak, hard to the touch and caked with dead ants. The trees farther down our hillside were in sharp relief: first the cleared terraces and then the black trees reaching down to the sea that was not a sea.

I showed Dom my dismal discovery in the old swimming pool: a gaping tear at the deep end where the western wall seemed to have broken away.

"Looks almost like the ground's shifted," he said. "More damage there, too." He pointed into the corners. "Same story with the house."

Dom was sanguine, as always. We'd get some advice; we'd get it fixed. It was all part of life here. We'd known what we were taking on.

So we paced the garden. If we had a new pool, should it be ten or twelve meters long? How far from the semicircular walled structure that we could keep as a natural focal point? How wide should it be, and how deep?

I wonder now what would have happened if we had never decided to replace the pool at all. With hindsight, would we have gone ahead if we had known all we would uncover, and what effect it would have?

**We made** an appointment and drove down to the industrial zone at Apt to talk to the owner of a company that built swimming pools. M. Jallon had been highly recommended, and we liked him from the start. Avuncular and practical, he assured us that anything was possible. Like almost everyone we met in Provence, he seemed to combine professionalism with a laid-back manner so effortlessly that by the end of the meeting we were firm friends, partners in a glorious endeavor that would enhance not only our personal surroundings but the landscape and history of the entire region.

The first step would be for him to come and look at the old pool to see if it could be salvaged. We might then decide that we wanted a more efficient, modern version, but the correct course would have been followed. He knew the property, of course—as did everyone, apparently—and was particularly concerned that, given the openness of our land, we might want to consider a high-tech, reassuringly expensive, retractable cover for the pool.

We should also be aware that a lining of ice green–gray was in vogue for new swimming pools: it tinted water the color of glacier melt, inducing the brain to lower the body's temperature just by seeing it, he said. M. Jallon was a wonderful salesman.

On the way home, I turned to Dom and tried to sound as light and teasing as possible. "I hope this isn't all because you need to get your laps in."

He gave a short laugh, letting me know he'd gotten the point. "This is the last situation I would ever want to escape," he said.

**Now that** high tourist season was over, the streets were quiet. We discovered anew the enchanted villages of the great valley: Bonnieux, topped with a church, not a castle, opposite the bleak ruined fortress of Lacoste; Ménerbes, shiplike on its low outcrop at the foot of the range; Roussillon, perched on the edge of surging cliffs of red ochre amid green pines; Gordes, majestic in its autumn emptiness, incomparable views framed to artistic perfection by its own limestone ridges planted with candles of cypress.

Hand-in-hand, up the winding cobbles we climbed. I claimed kisses in the shadows of stone buildings and against the rough stucco of golden-baked walls. The steely purity of the midday sun, shutters closing. Lunch with wine. Always talking and talking.

Only one subject we did not talk about.

So, in the absence of being able to ask Dom or, rather, not wanting to provoke one of his black moods when everything was so lovely, I had two leads: the name of the house that the woman at the party seemed to associate with him, and the Durands, who might be able to put me in touch with the woman herself.

Yet even then, part of me was wondering what exactly I was concerned about. It was such a tiny, unimportant incident, after all. I tried to push the information to the back of my mind, but I couldn't help myself. I was curious.

I asked Marie-Claude at the post office about the Mauger house.

**One morning,** when Dom was visiting another swimming pool company to get a second quote—he wanted to prove, I think, that he had not entirely lost his business sense to the Provençal spell—I followed her directions and headed down the hill.

It was a pleasant walk in bright sunshine down to the ruined chapel. My footsteps crunched loudly on the gravelly, stony path. The warmer air released a scent of pine; it could have been summer but for the silence of the cicadas.

The autumn huntsmen were out, though. A red plastic sign was tied to an oak branch: ATTENTION: BATTUE DE GRANDE GIBIER EN COURS. I assumed the "big game" it referred to were wild boar, but possibly it meant deer, too. The guns released occasional splatters of sound farther down into the valley. I remembered what Fernand had told me at the start of the season: "If you must walk, you wear a bright coat and go before lunchtime or even at noon, while the men and dogs are eating and drinking in their ramshackle blinds. After lunch, you don't venture out. Not far north of here, a hunter has already killed a Sunday cyclist."

*La Provence*, the local newspaper, reported that the tragic event had been caused by *une balle perdue*. The words for "stray bullet" sound almost playful to an English speaker's ear: just a lost ball.

It didn't take long to get to the ruined chapel. It's hardly more than two parallel walls covered in ivy, stems as thick and twisted as trees. Oaks grow in the nave, which is open to the skies. A first glimpse of a red roof made me quicken my pace.

The house was clad in tangerine stucco, too new and too bright to be a long-term fixture in village history. My heart was thumping uncomfortably (I couldn't understand why) as I approached the steel gates at its entrance. It was a low, modern building, fairly charmless, surrounded by a neat garden with a pool. All this was visible through the wire-mesh fence that topped a stone wall.

There was no car in the driveway. The sage-green shutters appeared to be tightly closed. The place had the air of a holiday villa, closed now for the winter.

Clearly, there was no one around to ask. I hadn't passed a soul on the track down. The only confirmation that I was not alone on the hillside was the intermittent sound of hunters' salvoes.

A postal delivery box on the gate pillar offered the sole indication that I had come to the right place. On a label the size of a Band-Aid was the name MAUGER in capitals, written by hand in black felt pen.

I hesitated.

Standing by the wall, unsure how to proceed, I stared into the property as if trying to see some trace of Dom, impossible though I knew that was.

Was this really a place that he and Rachel once rented for vacation? It seemed so unlikely, such an odd choice for a man who loved the time-honored quirks of Les

Genévriers, its atmosphere and views. This house occupied a dull position on a lower slope of the hill, with
no views. The village on its proud rock was hidden by
a bank of ill-placed trees. The place was uninspiring,
the kind of villa he routinely dismissed. Why on earth
would he have come here?

If he had come here, I reminded myself.

Trailing along the garden walls, rooted in shallow
crevices, ivy-leaved toadflax was beginning to run
rampant. On the other side of the fence, the land was
cut back primly, a dull, flat area of grass with few trees.
It told me nothing.

I retraced my steps up the hill, feeling sheepish. Of
course, Dom was right. The woman at the lunch had
made a mistake.

**3**

I sleep downstairs under a vaulted ceiling, hoping the arch will bear the weight of the creaking house and protect me. In what is now my bedroom, a traditional three-person country bench stands by the window, piles of junk on its rush seats. My few clothes are folded carefully in Maman's lovely walnut chest of drawers.

Maman always seemed to love Pierre the most.

Pierre, who laughed at others' concerns, and whose insolent grin grew more and more a permanent feature of his handsome face as he reached manhood, though Lord knows it was better to be his sister than one of his women.

"He's a boy," she'd say, and the pride in her voice made it painfully clear that the fact would forever obscure his shortcomings. I didn't understand then about mothers and sons; or about only sons and the continuation of the name, of the line, of the work on the land. At the time, I could only wonder, in abject frustration, how it was that she had not noticed his casual cruelties, his lies, and his acts of contempt.

It was all such a long time ago, yet in so many ways the circle is closing. I feel closer to the past now than I did twenty years ago. Bats have recolonized the lower rooms. My clothes are torn and patched, and I care as little as I did when I was a girl who ran all day in the hills. The generator has broken down, so I live by candlelight and oil lamps. Life is reverting to the ways I knew as a child.

**My ambition** may have been to become a teacher, just like Mlle. Bonis, but my first taste of a career was altogether less glorious. I unwittingly became a criminal.

Pierre came to find me, where I was reading in the shade of a plum tree, and ordered me to take something into the woods for him.

"Put it in the blind, under the dog rose."

I knew the place he meant. I had paid for that knowledge, several months earlier, when I stumbled upon him by accident, crouching down and smoking.

He tried to put out the cigarette and hide the evidence in the hollow under the bush, but it was too late.

"You're too young to smoke," I told him. "You're only twelve."

He said nothing, but dug his long thumbnails into the flesh of my bare leg with the kind of gleeful ferocity he usually reserved for killing and skinning small animals.

"You don't ever tell," he hissed. A warm, acrid trail of smoke escaped from the side of his mouth, the nails embedded sharper. "If you don't want this every day."

I struggled but it was no use. "Are those Papa's? Have you stolen Papa's?"

He laughed. "Why would I need to do that? I have my own money."

The need to boast overrode his discretion, as usual. He never realized that was his true weakness.

Somehow, it turned into a situation where he won, and I lost. I did his bidding from that day on, never quite understanding how it had come to that.

**But that** time, when he asked me to go to the dog rose hiding place in the woods above the sheepfold, I planted my feet and crossed my arms. "No," I said.

"No?"

"No."

He walked around me, as if observing me closely for the first time. He was carrying a long twig he had stripped of bark, and switched it through the air as if he were practicing a rapier thrust.

"I think you will," said Pierre. "Because I've asked you nicely."

I knew that meant he would not ask so nicely the next time, so I seized the initiative. "I will—if you promise to leave the swallowtails alone!"

"The swallowtails!" He said it as a teacher would, like M. Fabre, who liked to make an example of pupils who gave stupid answers. "And would you care to explain what you mean by that?"

"You know very well what I mean. Leave them alone—it's cruel."

He continued walking around in a most disconcerting way, now rubbing his chin like M. Fabre, who, it was said, was a relative of a famous learned man and liked to live up to it.

I was wishing I hadn't started this, when Pierre gave one of his nasty laughs. At least it started as a stage version of a nasty laugh, but quickly became genuine. Like the pleasure he took in pulling the wings, those beautiful wings like arched gothic church windows, off the butterflies.

"Your face!" he said, when he eventually stopped.

I said nothing.

"All right, all right. If the swallowtails mean that much to you . . . You do this for me, and I'll leave off the butterflies—though if you think that will see off the real predators you're living in dreamland."

He told me what to do and, feeling quite pleased with myself, I set out on his errand, imagining I was learning at last how to get something back in return from him. At the time, I had no idea what he was up to, of course, nor of the significance of the heavy object in the sacking that I carried. Following instructions, I placed it carefully in the root-veined hole underneath the dog rose and covered it with the biggest stone I could move.

# 4

Days of crystal brightness opened with cold that cut the morning air and stung our cheeks.

We huddled close as the temperature dropped. Inside: reading, cooking, eating; the scent of herbs steeping and piano notes rising from the music room. Outside: purposeful pacing around the garden, happily engrossed in discussing stone surrounds, screening, and pump systems.

Dom decided the new swimming pool would be sited nearer the odd semicircular structure built of stone, which sprouted rosemary bushes, a dead cherry tree, and other spiky clumps of scrubs I didn't recognize. That way the old pool would be demolished and the hole it left would form part of the new, larger one.

"Excellent decision," said M. Jallon, at his well-ordered office at the pool construction company. "If you like, I can arrange for you to see a pool we built at a property quite near to you—it's the kind of design that would work well at your place, but also might give you some more ideas, and show you our work."

We accepted without question.

**Dom was** right. There were days in October when it was like being imprisoned in a cloud. In the library we made upstairs I read the Brontës.

As we stayed on, glorying in not having to pack up and leave for a city winter of work, the fig trees yellowed. I had never seen the seasons turn in a southern country before. I only ever thought of these places close to the Mediterranean in their summer form, hot and bright and lush. Now, before my eyes, purple spears of buddleia transformed into rotten corn kernels. Walnuts dropped.

It was wetter and darker than we had anticipated, but we counted ourselves privileged to be there to witness it, adding another layer to our understanding of the land. I had all the time in the world to read, and was keeping a notebook of colloquial phrases that might, just might, come to fruition if I ever found the right book to try translating. In a burst of insane optimism,

I wrote to an esteemed publishing house in Paris, and a smaller one in Marseille, putting my name forward, but I suspected I would be better off finding an appealing book myself and simply playing around with words to see what came of it.

I had every chance to do so. Dom was often at his piano and filled page after page with notes on staves. One early evening, he took me down to the music room, sat me on the sofa, and played an evocative romantic piece I had never heard before.

"It's lovely—just gorgeous," I said as the last chord died and he looked up expectantly, perhaps even a little shyly. "One of yours?"

"For you," he said. " 'Song for Eve.' "

**I spent** hours wandering around the buildings, trying to decide how best to use the rooms. We scarcely went up to the top floor of the main house, but at the end of the winding stairs were two interconnecting bedrooms under the eaves to one side, and to the other, a bare attic room with warped wooden floorboards. A hayloft, perhaps. The only item of furniture in the room was a lopsided cupboard. It creaked as I opened it, but it was empty.

Where the roof leaked, the floor was stained. In places, the boards were so riddled with holes they were like planks of Emmental cheese. Mice? I wondered. Without thinking, I pulled up a board to see if I could. It gave easily, revealing a small, dark emptiness that released a moldy dampness. I left it out and pulled at some others.

One of the cavities right over by the wall was different. It was packed with straw, and under that I felt a smooth surface. I drew it out and saw it was a book. I sat back on my heels, marveling. It was a volume of Provençal tales, written for a child, with a pretty dust jacket, much damaged by age and moisture. I opened the title page. Thick, black print, dated 1935. The badly spotted pages crackled as I turned them. A silverfish darted into the tight cleft of the binding. What was the book doing under the floorboards? Was it hidden, and if so, why? I felt inside the cubbyhole again, but it was empty.

Once again, the house had given, but with these gifts came mysteries. With each one, the echoes of the past resonated ever stronger. The longer we stayed, the less it seemed to belong to us.

I showed the book to Dom, wondering aloud about the children who must have lived in the house. "Why would one of them hide this? Was it to keep it safe? Perhaps one of the others wanted it for themselves . . . and they wouldn't have had many books like this, would they—too expensive . . ."

Dom smiled and raised his eyebrows. "You do know, you have the most extraordinarily overactive imagination," he said. But his tone was affectionate.

**The October** mist was thick as fog as we bumped down the track from Les Genévriers, negotiating new ruts and potholes gouged by the rain. During heavy cloudbursts, there was a stream running between the main house and the row of tenants' cottages.

We turned up to the village, and then took the road into damp whiteness toward Viens. The plateau flattened on either side of the empty road—fields and trees, the occasional house. In the passenger seat, I consulted the map spread across my knees. Tucked into tightly packed contour lines not far away, I noticed for the first time the words L'Homme Mort, the dead man. What was that, I wondered: a hamlet, a memorial at the site of a tragic accident, perhaps?

The whiteness in the air had begun to glow pale amethyst as we progressed, and as the cloud lightened, the sun finally broke through. The Luberon range was an irregular black smudge above the line of cloud. Only a few kilometers away from where we had started, and it might have been another country.

"This isn't far from the place where the mysterious black boar is supposed to roam the high escarpment," I said.

"What?"

"M. Durand told me. There's a great black boar up here somewhere, which foretells disaster for those who are unlucky enough to see it, or so they say. Now and then it materializes to shepherds and walkers."

Dom said nothing, so I lowered my voice and leaned closer. "It is a dreadful sight to behold . . . for it means soon they will be faced with their . . . doom . . ."

His mouth twitched.

"They say that . . . set into these rocky ledges . . . are the hoofprints of the beast . . ."

We both laughed.

It was a modern house, built in the style of a Provençal *mas*. Substantial, attractive, but strangely lacking in atmosphere. The pool was neat and clean, with an impressive electronic cover. The bearded man in a hunting jacket, who gave us a tour, was not the owner but the caretaker of the property. The owners were Belgian.

In the garden, a shaggy maturity ruled. Bushes were studded with vermilion beads, berries beginning to glow against the season's premature browning.

A winter chill pinched the air as Dom asked about electronic pool covers and infinity effects. I wandered off when it became clear Dom had no need of me as a translator. What he could not say in French, he made up for in sketches. It was interesting to see how other people had ordered their surroundings, even if they weren't to my taste.

On the way home, clouds were finally rising from our hillside, curling up between the damp trees.

**A few** days later, Dom returned with another purchase. It was a shifty-looking monk in highly polished wood, half life-size. Dom installed him just inside the door of what passed as the hall of the main house, which had a medieval atmosphere that probably had as much to do with the pervasive damp as our spiritual sensibilities. I could see why Dom thought the monk was an appropriate addition.

"Another sinister figure," I only half-joked.

I hadn't told Dom about the incident on the path. I didn't want him questioning my rationality. Privately though, I'd been thinking a lot about the objects we'd chosen to surround ourselves with: the chipped plates and bowls; the secondhand mirrors and scratched paintings; the crazed broken statues. The way they spoke of a history that didn't belong to us, even in their inanimate state, the way they blurred the distinction between the living and the dead.

Absently, I stroked the fine rosewood of the monk's arm, trying to find something to like about the piece.

"Might be nice to see some living people up here," I murmured.

Then I glanced up and saw the anguish on Dom's face.

"What do you mean by that?" he asked. His voice sounded different, as if he was struggling to keep it under control.

"Nothing! It was just a— We don't just want to surround ourselves with dead old statues, that's all . . . What's wrong?"

There was no answer. He had walked away.

It was all too plausible to think about ghosts, or spirits at least. It hadn't occurred to me before that I was uncomfortable. But I must have been, subconsciously. How else was it that I had been spooked by some shifting play of light and shadow on the wall, and made it into a frightening presence in the garden? My overly active imagination, Dom would say.

All those people who had once lived here—naturally, there would remain vestiges of their stories, joys, and sorrows as well as the dull drudgery of daily life. This was a land of plenty, but it had been created by hard toil. Think of the shepherds and the tales they told as they wandered, how many hundreds of miles each year was that to keep the flocks fed and healthy?

The next time he came, I asked Claude the gardener, "What is L'Homme Mort, the place marked on the map over there?" I pointed vaguely north across the edge of our land.

"It's a hamlet—like here."

"What's there? A farm?"

"Yes, I believe so. It's still a farm."

It was up to me to volunteer why exactly I wanted to know. He scratched the side of his face and waited.

"It's just the name. I wondered why it was called that." I made a face I hoped he understood: simple, light curiosity, but an interest, too, in the history held in these hills.

"I don't know," said Claude. "I'm not from around here. I'm from Apt."

I smiled, then realized he was serious.

"Have you heard?" he went on. "They've found the body of one of the missing girls."

"Which one?"

"Amandine. The one from near Roussillon. A man with his truffle hound, out over by Oppedette, came across her remains in the forest."

"Dreadful . . ."

"It's bad news and good news," mused Claude. "The worst for her family, and the families of the others breathe again. They still have hope."

"I guess, but still . . . it must be awful."

"The man who's doing this . . ."

"I know . . ."

But I didn't know. Like everyone else, I wanted these events not to be happening, for our fantasy of a new life to last a while longer.

"Everyone's talking about it. The truffle hound was the brother of one of the dogs bred here by the Millescamps at Les Peirelles."

# 5

When the wild cherries had dried on the trees, too small to pick, too hard for the birds, but chewy and delicious and left as treats for us children, we knew it must be close to the fourteenth of July. The date was marked every year in Apt with a party in the big south square and a fairground and fireworks at ten o'clock.

Apart from the village *fête votive*, also an annual event, this was the highlight of the summer. School long-forgotten and too far in the future even to think about, we celebrated Bastille Day and freedom with a few traditions of our own.

Having spent the afternoon baking, Maman, in her best dress, hair gleaming, would climb daintily (helped by our proud father, suited in brown serge) into the front seat of the *charrette*, the little cart. The baskets would be handed up.

Then the rest of us piled into the *charrette*, and our neighbors in theirs. The horses had a last drink at the trough and were hitched, and off we went. It was quite a party. We could have walked, or even taken the bus down from the village, which stopped where our track joined the road, but it wouldn't have been the traditional event without the family crammed into the old cart, eating sugar-dusted doughnuts Maman had made that afternoon and singing as we bowled down the hill, swapping jokes and invitations to race with the other carts, the blue of the sky deepening as the orange glow trickled like honey over the mountain ridge, the rippling hills growing taller and more mysterious over us as we descended.

**In town,** the streets were warm as day with all the crowds and fires and lamps. Legions of glasses and bottles stood to attention on tables in the square, restaurants were full, and a band was playing at full strength.

"Midnight, in the usual place," said Papa sternly, and we were off to enjoy ourselves in all the unaccustomed light and noise.

Marthe, Arielle, and I linked arms and paraded around, stopping to see what the boys were up to at the fairground. For them, that meant the shooting gallery and the desirable prizes to be won by hitting the tin targets.

For Maman and Papa, and the other adults, the dancing was the great attraction. For hours, they showed off their steps, waltzing and fox-trotting, twirling and bending. I was awestruck to see them perform a passable tango, and wondered where on earth they had learned it.

The band was indefatigable, the accordionist mastering the complex rhythms and changes of direction with aplomb and liberal swigs of wine.

**The fireworks** had exploded, leaving smoky trails across the night and a drifting scent of burned excitement. Marthe, Arielle, and I were already at the stage of utmost tiredness, which must never be admitted for fear of not being allowed to stay up late for special events.

We were sitting on a low wall, watching the parade of dancers coming off the dirt floor, the men drinking in the bars, the lights strung up between the plane trees, the musicians beating and blowing and pulling, when Pierre emerged from the inner town.

He passed under the clock tower gateway, rubbing his face with his sleeve. There was an awkwardness to his walk and the slope of his shoulders. Up went his sleeve again. Expression set in anger or disgust, he was about to turn away when three of his friends came running up, shouting to get his attention. One put a hand up to his head and was shaken off.

I strained to see what was happening in the half-shadow of the archway. Now there seemed to be some kind of argument going on. Pierre's mouth was moving quickly, hands were being raised. It was intriguing. Perhaps there would be a fight. It was about time my brother was on the receiving end of some pain, and it would have been quite satisfying to witness the event.

At the very moment, Marthe pulled at my arm and asked me to take her to the stalls where the doughnuts were frying. In the time it took to take in her request and stand up, Pierre and his friends had been swallowed up by the darkness.

**At midnight,** we assembled on the corner of the square, as arranged. We girls were the first, followed by Maman and the ladies of the party. The men fetched the horses and carts. Papa had taken out his fob watch and was about to comment, when Pierre and the boys came running up.

Pierre claimed that the crusty red mess on his face was the result of a nosebleed, and thanks to the silence from his friends, my parents had no reason not to believe him.

The next morning, Arielle told me, in whispers in the woods above the sheepfold, that her brother had told her what had really gone on. Pierre had been beaten up for stealing by the stallholder he worked for in the market.

The other boys had wanted to go and find the man and his gang, and give them a kicking in return, but Pierre had ordered them to leave it. It was as good an admission of guilt as any.

I don't know how much of this, if any, our parents were told. Not much, I suspect, but I may have been wrong. Luckily, Pierre's nose was not broken, or surely our father would have extracted the truth from the boys, and seen the man from the stall subjected to some rough justice.

Whatever theories I had, I decided to hold on to them in the event that they might prove a useful lever against my brother's excesses.

**For our** return, the lanterns were lit on the cart and, tired, mouths sticky-parched with sugar, the stars so hard and clear above that you could make out the gleaming path of the Milky Way, we allowed ourselves to be jolted back up the hill.

Later, unable to sleep for the excitement, I got out of bed and went over to the open window. Below, in the courtyard, was an oil lamp burning on the ground beneath the olive, and around it, silently, majestically, Maman and Papa were dancing, alone. Her head was on his shoulder, her eyes were closed, and her lovely smile stretched right across her face. Papa was singing, at least I think I heard him, under his breath, so that only she knew what song it was.

# 6

I t is only six kilometers down the hill to Apt, but, to me, the journey signified much more. Until then, sliding into the car, I hadn't fully realized how little time I'd spent on my own away from the house. Our world of two had been so enjoyable, so comforting in a way I'd never really experienced before, that I had been perfectly content to drift in the flow.

The road down is bumpy as well as sinuous. It makes for an uncertain ride, even before the locals in their extravagantly dented vehicles swoop around the blind bends and out of hidden turnings at top speed in the middle of the road, oblivious to the possibility of encountering anyone else. In town, the Calavon River was high, running through the valley here in its casing of concrete. During the summer, it had been a sad dribble of water along the bottom of the basin, so unthreatening that lush outcrops of grasses and scrubs had grown up on the stones of the riverbed. Warning notices to exercise caution when using the car parks contained within the embankments still seemed unnecessarily alarmist. I took one of the many empty spaces and then walked over the bridge into the main part of the little town.

The last time I was there, it had been market day. It's one of the most famous in the region; they say that there has been an unbroken line of markets every Saturday morning in Apt for eight hundred years. The narrow medieval streets were crammed with stalls and people, shouting, discussing where to buy the best vegetables, the most succulent game; Dom made for his favorite cheese stall and started bantering with the owner; smells rose of roasting chickens and chestnuts and freshly made pizza; three squares—north, south, and west—offered meat, fish, fruit, carved wood, spices, kitchenware, linens, racks of Indian-made clothes and leather goods from North Africa, bead jewelry, the scented olive oil soaps from Marseille, and all varieties of products made from lavender.

Now the narrow paved road through the center was almost empty. My footsteps echoed loudly, and the same goods had been moved behind shop windows.

The warmth and scent of food were gone. A winter smell rode the light wind: the wood smoke of mountain villages. It was possible to look up without fear of obstructing the flow of the crowd. In the bookshop opposite the Hôtel de Ville, I found what I'd been looking for: books about the area, the way life used to be when it was a lost and remote area of France.

Then I bought a newspaper and read it as I sipped a cup of coffee in a café on the square, with only one other customer.

The missing girl's body had been removed from the wooded ravine below Oppedette; a photograph of police tape that marked a forlorn muddy site. Other stories crowded the page; pictures documented the aftermath of a bad car smash, fatalities involved. More businesses were in trouble. The only good news was to be found in the small announcements of personal success, the civil marriages, and sports prizes.

As I drove back, there was a traffic jam, not unusual on the main road through town toward Manosque and Sisteron. Stationary behind a line of cars and vans, I looked around with interest rather than annoyance. That was the best of this life: there was no rush, no work stress, no beating against the clock; it wouldn't have mattered to me if we were stuck here for hours.

Opposite was an Internet café I hadn't noticed before. A couple of men in North African clothing were standing outside talking. Then another came out to join them and the wind caught the tails of their long, white shirts. Useful to know, I thought. It had never seemed odd until now that on our hillside we were all but cut off from the twenty-first century, living with no television, no fixed telephone line or broadband access. Then the car in front began to move and I pulled away.

**7**

October winds post crisp deliveries of dry leaves, torn petals, pine needles, and grit-rolled insects under sun-shrunken doors.

For generations, we women swept them up with the brush and pan, on our knees. Twice a day, when the mistral raged.

There are one hundred and eighty different winds that blow across Provence, all with their different and special names: the mistral, of course, from the north-west; the tramontane from the north; the south wind; and all the minute grades in between. They say there are more than six hundred different variations of the names of the winds.

Here in the Luberon, where around thirty of them are regular visitors, a softer wind from north-northwest is called a *biset,* a little kiss, but the might of a cold north wind is *l'air noir,* or *bise noire,* black air, black kiss. It is violent and chill, like a storm in the depths of a winter's night without a moon.

A northeasterly is *l'orsure,* or *le vent de l'ours,* the wind of the bear—which, they say, is the wind of melancholy poets, artists, and dreamers. The north-northwesterlies are the *vents de farine,* the winds that grind the millers' flour. The kindly *vent roux,* the russet winds, are east-southeasterly, close in spirit to the North African sirocco, bringing warm, dry breezes ridden by pollinating insects and rusty Arabian dust.

**During autumn** and winter, when the worst winds howled, the summer lived on in the red and orange and green of the fruit and vegetables pressed into glass jars and sealed. As the temperature dropped, olive oil went cloudy in the bottle.

Once, when I was still too young to dispute the facts, Pierre warned me that the eerie white shapes held in the oil were imprisoned spirits.

"Like ghosts?" I asked.

"Bad ghosts."

"Will they escape?"

"They might," said Pierre.

"If they do, what will we do? Will they catch us if we run?"

"We will be pinned to the ground, unable to move, while they do terrible things."

"Like what?"

While I stared in wide-eyed horror, he went over to the glass jar with a devilish look on his face, which made his chin look more pointed than ever. He made to drop the jar on the floor.

"Don't! Don't!" I begged him.

He gave one more unsettling laugh, but then slowly replaced the jar on the shelf. He would have gone through with his threat, I was sure, but for the rattle at the back door that announced our father's return from the fields.

Change is not always visible, as the turn of the seasons is, or the natural process of aging. We are so many different people in one lifetime. But even now I think Marthe can sense my thoughts, would feel the rough textures of my indecision under her fingers, and taste my failings as easily as she could smell the changing seasons.

As for Pierre: what disturbance occurred inside his head, under his skin, so early in his life? I never understood him.

Why had he come back now? To laugh at me and mock my efforts? Why couldn't it have been gentle Maman, or Marthe, or, best of all, Mémé Clémentine? A grandmother would have been in the natural order. I might have welcomed her return, given a choice of phantoms. Hers would have been a watchful presence by the hearth, by the entrance to the wine cave maybe, or in the quiet spot in the orchard or the kitchen garden.

I still grow my own food. I eat vegetables mainly, and fast-growing chickpeas, that peasant standby. I keep as fit as possible, though my joints are not as flexible as they once were. When I wring out the washing, and try to pinch the pegs to hang it out, my fingers take longer than they should to grip. I've noticed that after a few hours in the vegetable patch, soil gets stuck in the deep grooves of my hands. Such a lot of scrubbing it takes to get out, and when that's done, the things are red and bent like claws. It creeps up gradually, old age, all the more insulting when you were convinced it was a state that would never happen to you.

How much more I understand now, though! I still use the same utensils and pots that Maman used, and clean the copper with lemon juice, just as she did, the acid biting into the cuts in my fingers, just as it must have into hers, though she never complained. It's important to keep up tradition.

"Go to town for work?" she'd cry. "But there's always so much to be done here!" A countrywoman to the bone, she found the very notion of leaving the hamlet, let alone the village commune, for work unbelievable. It was enough to make it necessary for her to sit down (a rare event) with a restorative cup of lavender tisane. I don't think I ever told her how much I would have loved to train as a nurse or a teacher.

Do I look like a mad old woman now? I suspect I do. Maman's little mirror is long gone. What would be the point of looking in a mirror, anyway? The only visitors are the birds and the wild animals, and the children who dare each other to play mean tricks and risk catching sight of the madwoman who lives here alone.

Better to be invisible.

# 8

The river Sorgue flows green and glassy through Fontaine-de-Vaucluse. The green is extraordinary, a malachite composition of underwater meadows of emerald weeds, reflection of the deep greens on the steep valley above, and the ice-blue purity of the mysterious spring that boils up from a pool beneath the cliffs, a pool so deep they say it has never been accurately measured.

The village is a dead end, a beautiful place at the end of the line held captive on three sides by fractured precipices that rise steeply into the sky to the great Vaucluse plateau. The remains of a castle cling to the sheerest escarpment, so few of the stones surviving in place that it's awe-inspiring it was ever inhabited.

This is where the Italian poet Petrarch wrote love sonnets to his Laura, though the undoubted romance of this association is undercut by the leaden references in every touristic souvenir. In the center of the village is a granite column, which was raised in 1804, according to the inscription, to mark the fifth centenary of Petrarch's birth. It stands on what has become a roundabout.

As Dom and I studied the menu at our table in the restaurant closest to the bridge, where the iridescent water seems to still itself to fall over a weir, a wedding party emerged from what must have been a registration session at the *mairie*: a laughing couple in their twenties; he dark and handsome, she a pretty blonde.

"You're quiet."

He reached across the table and rubbed my fingers.

"Am I?"

"World of your own."

That was true enough. But it's strange, isn't it, how once you've started to notice something, you can't escape it. Seeing the wedding party was like a trail opening up. I could not resist the temptation to follow it, compelled to know what lay at the end, even though I was well aware that I would almost certainly not like what I found.

I had tried to put the wild-goose chase to the Mauger house out of my mind. Any stray thoughts of Rachel, too, and her former status as his wife. It had nothing to do with me, or this new life of ours. Marriage between us had never been mentioned. I had accepted, though the subject had never been aired, that I would not be Dom's wife when we decided to live together in France. As I had never particularly wanted to be married for the sake of being married, that was fine by me. I had certainly never been the kind of girl who dreamed about her wedding day and its swirls of white gossamer, traditional vows, and tiered white cake.

But my curiosity was whetted. What was she like, what was so special about her that made him want marriage? Was it a large and triumphant family wedding, or an intimate city hall affair?

It was at that point that it began to dawn on me how little I knew about Dom. There was no one I could ask, no points of reference. I had met very few of his friends and none of his family. That was not quite as odd as it might have been, given that he had met my mother only briefly (an early-evening drink in Brighton) and only a couple of my friends (a farewell dinner in a London restaurant). It hadn't seemed to matter that we existed in an intimate, private universe of our own devising. For one reason or another, it felt like what we both wanted and needed. Other people were just background noise.

Of course, even as I write this, I know now how strange that sounds. But it is the truth, and that is what I'm trying to inch toward here, trying to order in my own mind what really happened, as opposed to what I imagined or inferred. At the time, it was all part of the romance of our situation.

So I bit my tongue and said nothing.

**After lunch,** we walked.

The river, crashing white over mossy boulders, took on the opalescent green-blue of a mallard's head in the stiller reaches. Above, the rock of the cliffs was stacked in diagonal ribs, emphasized by the occasional tipsy line of small trees and scrub that followed the angles.

Past the sunken arcade that joined the working paper mill, where I couldn't resist buying a notebook of stiff, thick handmade pages and a packet of plain cards, and past the heavy wooden presses powered by the waterwheel. There were few other people on the dust and gravel path to the spring. Past the line of souvenir stalls, mostly open, several selling tablecloths of iris-blue and purple, mustard-yellow, in the traditional patterns of black olives and silver leaves, flowers and sprays and diamonds.

"There's an old Provençal story—'The Shepherd of Fontaine,'" I said.

I'd been engrossed the previous evening reading the stained and crinkled book of Provençal tales I'd found in the hayloft; strange and compelling tales, full of fairy-tale characters: the shepherd of Fontaine; the magician's daughter at Castellane; Picabrier and the perfect garden; the ruins of Grimaud. And always there, as shadows over the land, the troubadours and the threat of the Saracens.

These stories were all rooted in place. The gray limestone crags of the Alpilles, the bare stone range to the south of Avignon. The hot plains and scrubby hills south toward Marseille. The empty uplands of the Lure to the east.

Dom smiled.

So, as we walked, comfortably arm in arm, I told him the story of Paradou, the shepherd of Fontaine-de-Vaucluse.

"Paradou was a wild outcast, living with his sheep as if they were his family. He slept in the fields with them, and had little contact with any other humans. He did not wash. He barely spoke, and could not read or write. But there was one old woman who was kind to him, a wealthy widow who lived in a grand farmhouse in Fontaine. Instead of kicks and shouts warning him to keep away, she gave him food.

"One winter's day, when Paradou had brought his flock down from the cold high ground on the plateau, one of his sheep climbed up the steep rocks above the spring. Paradou watched it, sure it would fall—and the next moment it had disappeared. Curious, he followed, clinging to the precipice above the green pool and the rushing water. When he came to the place where he'd last seen the sheep, he saw there was a crack in the rock and he managed to squeeze inside. There was no sign of the sheep, but he was able to walk along an interior ledge that led to a cave. And there beneath him was the most beautiful rock pool he had ever seen. The water was a glowing magical green. He sat down beside it and just stared. When he finally moved to stand up, he put his hand on an earthenware jar. He opened it, hoping to find Saracen treasure, but what he found was paper with strange markings on it. For a while he stood, perplexed and disappointed. But as he continued to look, he knew that he had found some kind of treasure after all, even if he did not understand what it was. He emerged from the fissure in the rock face knowing that something extraordinary had happened.

"After that, he often returned to the secret rock pool. The earthenware jar with its treasure was always still there. And each time he opened out the paper, and stared at the signs on it, he began to understand them a little more, as if a mist was clearing. As if he had once known what the answer was, but it had been lost."

By now Dom and I were standing on the stones overlooking the spring. A few other visitors had moved off, and others were lower, out of sight. The illusion was that we were alone there.

"A treasure map?" suggested Dom.

"Poems, which he learns to read."

Rush and gurgle of the water. The high, sheer crags on three sides enclosing us. I sensed I might be losing him, that he might get bored if I continued at this pace, so I pushed on.

"The rest of the story gets really farcical—quite odd, really. It turns out the poems are long-lost ones by Petrarch, in the old Provençal language, and the rich elderly widow is Laura de Noves, who didn't actually die young of the plague in Avignon as she was supposed to have done but managed to pass another victim's corpse off as her own and run away with Petrarch after all. They had five wonderful years together. He wrote beautiful sonnets to their love. Only then they had a child. And Petrarch found this got in the way of the great love affair that he was so keen on writing about, making his great reputation, so he demanded that she give the boy up . . . Can you see where this is going?"

"Not the wild shepherd?"

"Exactly. Paradou. He and the widow turn out, in the best tradition, to be mother and son. They have a great explanation session."

"And then it's happily ever after."

"Oh, no. Not at all. It dawns on the son that Laura didn't hate Petrarch—who subsequently left her anyway to return to Italy, by the way—but that she actually sympathized with him and forgave him for his actions because they allowed him to keep on writing, creating his Great Art. He can't understand his mother's forgiveness, and so he kills her. The son clubs her to death—and returns to the wild."

Dom was silent.

"Bet you didn't see that one coming."

"No . . ."

"They're strange, these stories. You think they're fairy tales, and then they suddenly take on this rather modern cruel twist. I mean," I prattled on, "someone you love just turns around and says, Sorry, I've changed my mind. I hate you now and I'm going to club you to death . . ."

The idea of beautiful Provençal songs I had never heard resounded in my head. I wondered whether I had stumbled on a possible translation project in these tales I had never seen in English. Water swashed over rock. I did not realize for some minutes that I was alone.

"Dom?"

No response. I called again.

Quickly, I started down the path back to the village. Around every corner, I was sure I'd see him but did not.

I was out of breath by the time I doubled back from the paper mill and found him. He was leaning against a tree, back turned to the path.

"There you are!"

He said nothing.

"You just left!"

Silence.

"What's up? Sorry if I was— I didn't realize you'd gone . . ."

"No, you wouldn't have."

"I'm sorry, I was only . . . thinking."

He looked at me then, and his face seemed distorted. Not angry, exactly, though there was some anger in it, but anguished.

"What? What did I do?"

"You looked just like she used to," he said. "You even talk like she used to. I couldn't stand it. I kept thinking, this is all a mistake."

Don't say that, I pleaded silently.

For a few minutes, the sun stabbed through the mottled sky, then all was somber. His pupils shrank to pinpricks in the sudden brightness, and he screwed up his eyes before turning away.

"Why did you split up with Rachel?"

Dom hesitated. I put my arm on his and waited.

But the silence between us stretched until it was unbearable.

The river babbled past. Its rush over rocks and pebbles filled the still air between us, and a bird gave voice to the shrill cry of hurt I had stifled.

Slowly, we began to walk back to where we had left the car.

# 9

I was caught, of course, when I least expected to be.

A few days later, Pierre ordered me up to the blind. I was to collect what I had previously hidden under the stone and take it to the house, where I was to slide it under his bed, right under, so that it touched the wall. It was this detail I was wondering about, why it had to touch the wall, rather than what the mission entailed, when Papa's voice made me start so hard I felt I had lifted off the ground.

"What have you got there?" He came up behind me quite silently while I was digging in the hollow beneath the stone. He must have stalked me like a deer, and I was cornered.

Not waiting for any explanation, Papa reached out and took the sack in his big hands. He pulled it open, and, to my startled bewilderment, he slid out a clumsy black iron implement. It must have been a very old-fashioned one, even then, but it was a gun.

I gasped almost as loudly as he did.

"What. Is. This."

It shook in his hand. Papa's forehead was tight and red, and seemed about to explode. A vein stood out over one eyebrow.

"I— I—"

I was lost for words.

"Where. Did. You. Get. This."

There was no choice. I had to tell him.

**There was** a very small stone store on the olive terrace, with the narrowest of slits for a door. It had once been bricked up for reasons that no one knew, and this is where Papa, in ominous, enraged silence, led Pierre and me and pushed us inside.

It was cold, damp, and dark. Then the only shaft of light was blocked as our father dragged a tabletop against the gap. There were noises outside, like the clunking sound stones make when they hit each other. The noise continued, resonating against the wood, tolling out our father's fury. I wanted to scream. To beg him to stop and to let us out. Somehow I stopped myself, knowing I would make things worse if I did. All I allowed myself was a shivering whimpering that brought some nasty kicks to the shins from Pierre's boot.

Still Papa said nothing. Not even: "I will teach you a lesson you won't forget." Just the heavy sound of the rocks striking the other side of the barricade, the sound seeming to rise up.

"What's happening?" I whispered.

Pierre made a scuffing noise on the dirt floor. "We're being bricked in," he said, as nonchalantly as you please.

I started to cry. We were imprisoned in the cold and dark, with no food or water, and I hadn't even done anything wrong. Then I thought of something that made me shiver so hard it was as if I had been picked up and shaken. This . . . dark space, the size of it . . . It reminded me of the family crypts in the village cemetery. Great boxes of marble with ornate stone and brass carved locks, and names of people with the dates they were born and died.

"Will we die?"

"Of course we will," said Pierre. "Sooner or later."

I hated him then. It was all his fault and he couldn't even apologize when we were under sentence of death for our crime, a crime I had no idea I was committing. Wrapping my arms around myself, I huddled in a ball and rocked. Eyes open or eyes closed, all was black.

After a while, the thuds outside stopped.

Across the dark dungeon, my fellow captive was both invisible and soundless. The walls might have been a touch away or as far as the next hills. I floated in terrifying nothingness.

"Pierre?"

No answer.

Was I dead already?

I pinched my wrist and it hurt.

Then a kind of scraping started. Was that an animal?

"What's that?"

The scrapes became longer and more defined.

"I'm digging," said Pierre.

I knew I could rely on him! "Will we be able to escape?"

"I'm not digging a tunnel."

"Oh."

More scraping.

"What are you doing, then?"

"I'm looking for the treasure of course. This is exactly the kind of place it would be hidden, and it will serve them right when I find it and don't tell them, but just run away with my fortune."

That was typical of Pierre. He didn't even sound worried. Once again, my best chance was to take my cue from him, much though I disliked his arrogant behavior. I curled up on my side, and decided that if I allowed myself to relax enough I might sleep, and blot out the fear.

By the time Papa came to let us out, night had fallen. I was very hungry but we were sent to bed without food, just a glass of water. All night I lay awake, shivering.

**Pierre never** did tell us exactly how he had acquired the Prussian revolver. He admitted a few details to me, which may or may not have been true. Arielle contributed the bulk of the facts and a few embellishments from an overheard conversation between her father and mine.

It seems that the gun came from a dealer at the market who had a quiet sideline in "historical artifacts," specializing in weaponry. Naturally, no questions were asked of the purchasers, who may or may not have had a firearms license, or indeed a genuine interest in antiques. It seems the deal was struck as a swap for some innocuous-seeming mechanical device, which was, in fact, the inner workings of some larger, even more dangerous weapon—and, even worse in our father's eyes, this device had been stolen from the stall where Pierre had been working. The dealer had assumed that Pierre was the errand boy.

What he intended to use the gun for remained a mystery. Pierre himself just shrugged. It would have been useful, he said. He was not yet thirteen years old.

But that wasn't the end of the episode. Far worse was to come.

# 10

It was a creeping unease, at first, which I ignored. Then tightness across my shoulders. All of a sudden, I had the strongest sense that someone was behind me in the kitchen. I looked around. Of course, no one was there.

Dom had gone out to the CD shop in town, where he'd put in an order for some rare recordings of Rachmaninoff playing his own piano preludes. In a feeble attempt at disguising my blue mood that morning, I was preparing a pleasant lunch, hoping to serve it on the table in the south-facing courtyard if the midday sun was warm enough.

I had made an artichoke-and-tapenade quiche, and Dom's favorite crushed potatoes with black olives and olive oil—which I intended to decorate with a sprig of olive branch.

Next I was trying to follow a magazine recipe for *charlotte aux trois abricots*—a moist cake made with three kinds of apricot: fresh; stewed with lavender; and a whole pot of apricot jam. Like so many French recipes, it seemed to assume that time was no object, that cooking was the point of life rather than a quick dash into the kitchen to sustain it. But that was fine. I was happy enough at this table, in this room where the sun streamed through tall windows, and at that point time was irrelevant (apart from precise cooking instructions, of course; there was a certain bossiness in this magazine cook's tone that insisted concentration was required).

And it smelled wonderful already, an olfactory elegy to life in the French countryside. The fantasy life that had seemed within reach but which was even now slipping from my grasp.

**In my** dream state, I must have been unconsciously dwelling on what was happening between me and Dom, and whether it had anything to do with the place we had chosen with such impetuous optimism.

Then, there it was again. The sense that I was being watched, that someone else was there. My fragile mood of tranquility had fractured. I was tense in an instant.

Looking around more wildly now, I could make myself see shadowy groups of previous occupants; oil lamps glowing; spirits lurking in the dark corners of the room; the laughter and misfortunes; children in thick nightshirts; candles that suddenly extinguished themselves, the swish and skitter of mice in the wood and plaster ceiling, the reading of the scriptures with their resonant comfort and hope. Then the sun flared angel-bright, a stark, searching eye. It raked the cuts and crevices of the table and revealed my phantoms for what they were: my own fears.

I stepped out of the back door to clear my head. I leaned against the wall, telling myself to stop being foolish. And then I saw it again. The same figure floating on the path as before. Blue-gray, ethereal.

Transfixed, heart knocking ever harder, I moved slowly and silently down the steps, keeping it in my sights. I left the courtyard and crept into the garden.

It was still there. Then it moved toward me. It was a woman on the path, wearing a kind of loose cloak, and this time she did not dematerialize. She was coming closer.

**In the** daylight, she was older than late thirties, where I'd placed her at a guess in the Durands' hall. The wide mouth had lost the plum gloss. But the well-cut auburn hair was unmistakable.

"I'm sorry, I didn't mean to startle you!"

"It's a public path." I was embarrassed to realize that I was trembling.

"My name's Sabine."

"We met already," I said. "At the Durands'—that wonderful lunch."

"I was wondering if you would remember."

Was she being sarcastic? Possibly she was. The slightly hooded eyes, carefully made up, were watchful and lively.

"It's good to see you again." Keep it calm, keep it light.

"How do you like it here?"

"It's . . ." I gestured around, feeling the tremor in my hand, hoping it didn't show. ". . . it's lovely— fabulous, what can I say? We feel very lucky to be here." But even as I said it, I could not help but think of the damp bubbling the plaster walls, the mossy green streak down the bathroom wall. Shut- ters banged in the wind, a wind that might blow itself into a weeklong mistral at any moment. The sun had gone in.

She nodded, as if that was as it should be, and then made a move to walk off.

Before I realized what I was saying, I was asking her if she'd like to come inside for a drink—a coffee, a tea? Anything to detain her a while longer so that my brain could catch up with my instincts and allow me to turn this to my advantage.

Accepting graciously, she followed me into the courtyard and up the steps to the kitchen.

"Do you live in the village?"

"Just outside, on the road to Céreste."

"All year round?"

It wasn't as stupid a question as it might sound. Many of the local professionals worked in Marseille, or Avignon, or even Lyon, commuting back at weekends. Sabine had the distinct air of a professional woman.

"Half-and-half these days."

What do you do? In the wrong tone, at the wrong time, it can be such a rude question. I hoped she might answer it of her own accord and spare me the difficulty. But she was looking around at the kitchen as if satisfying her own curiosities.

She picked up a chipped porcelain jar, decorated with a picture of serpents sipping from a bowl, inscribed in loopy blue letters: HERBES DES MAGICIENS.

"Left in the house for you to find?" she asked, as if she knew.

I nodded. "We've found all kinds of things here. We call them gifts from the house."

I poured two cups of coffee, and we sat at the long pine table by the window. Through the tall window facing the courtyard, I could see walnuts being shaken from the tree, plopping down into the tufty grass.

There was an awkward pause.

"So much history, so many families must have lived here over the centuries," I said brightly, dismissing any idea of barging straight in with what I really wanted to ask her.

"That's true."

She was watching me carefully. She knew. I felt it as clearly as if she had put her hand on my shoulder and asked to hear my confession. She knew and she was waiting.

"I found a *borie* up in the woods a few days ago," I went on doggedly. I'd found out about these primitive houses made of a round pile of stones. They were all over Provence, probably built by shepherds for shelter. "How long has that been there? I wonder."

"A very long time. Maybe even before this house."

She was looking around again, as if familiarizing herself with some changes. That was disconcerting.

"And this is old enough. It's not in a very good state."

"Do you intend to do much work to it?"

"Quite a bit. The staircase is in a terrible condition—it feels unsafe. And there are great cracks running down the walls where the house was enlarged at one time. There's a buttress, but it seems to have failed."

"That's what they used to do, in houses like this one—when they needed more space, they just built on a new section. They grew along with everything else. What you must not do is do too much."

"I know. We mustn't spoil it."

Sabine seemed to think better of a comment.

"Don't worry," I said. "There won't be any Plexiglas walls or industrial-steel stairs."

"Inside the houses here, parts are left rough. No one cares, especially not the Parisians and other wealthy northerners who come to play at being rustics for a few weeks in the sun."

I'd seen them that summer, arriving in great, gleaming, black four-wheel-drive vehicles that scattered pedestrians in Gordes. Patronizing the crowded, overpriced restaurants for those who are more interested in being seen than being fed. Celebrity- and politician-spotting, then scouring *Paris Match* and *Point de Vue* to see if they were right.

"That's only in the summer, though."

"Generally only for August, the Parisians." She dismissed them with a wave of the hand. "The other nationalities come all through the summer. The locals complain about the crowds in the supermarkets, but you can see all that and still like being here."

"Well, I can't comment . . . being a foreigner myself."

She smiled. "It wouldn't be the same without any of you. I work as a house agent, among other things."

**It turned** out that the other things included running a local glossy magazine and holding a stake in an up-market service company, the kind of place that could organize a chef and a dinner party for twenty with a few days' notice, or find and supply a special kind of chair, or oyster, or work of art to order. She agreed with me that it was almost impossible to find good lighting, lamps that did the job but were not in dreadful taste—I'd decided that the gloomy corners of the house, lit so brightly by sunlight during the warmer months, needed urgent illumination. As winter drew in, the old place was full of dark corners and hidden dangers. She told me where I could find the kind of lighting shop I'd been looking for, and suggested that if we went together she would be able to swing me a discount.

Neither of us mentioned Dom.

When Dom returned for lunch, I didn't mention her, either.

# 11

I was sent on an errand up in the village for Maman the next day. She was still tight-lipped with me, though she had left it to Papa to unleash the stern words I'd known were coming. As I ran into the courtyard, having delivered her message, Pierre was leaning against the fig tree with his hands behind his back.

"You told," he said.

"You know that I didn't."

"I know that you did, Bénédicte. You weren't being careful, like I told you. Either you let Papa see you, or maybe you just told him what you were doing."

"But I didn't!"

"And now you are going to see there are consequences."

"What do you mean?" I was tired of his menacing, tired from the ordeal in the dark store.

Pierre brought around one arm, and I saw what he had been concealing. It was the little black kitten I was allowed to adopt when it had appeared in a thunderstorm, mewling pitifully, a few weeks previously. She was a puny, shy little creature who gladly took food from us but otherwise kept to herself. But as her strength returned, she had started to play, chasing a walnut around the stone terrace outside the kitchen, then flopping over and pedaling at it with her back feet.

The black kitten dangled dangerously. Pierre's thumb and index finger were a noose around her neck.

"No! Don't! Let her go!" I cried, launching myself at him, not caring what he could do to me.

But he raised his arm out of my reach. The cat swung from the gallows of his hand. Maybe I was already too late and he had already strangled it before he saw me. I agonized over whether I saw it move or protest before he made the vicious move.

The light changed and freckled the courtyard. His sneer was hardened by shadows.

Then he smashed the helpless body down. It lay limply on the earth as I could only stare, horrified, tears spilling in a sudden flood.

He took a knife from his belt and looked at me. He bent over and, with one swift, sudden movement, ripped the animal open so that her guts spilled the length of her poor body, matting the soft black fur with quivering scarlet.

I ran. In the orchard, against a plum tree, I threw up until my back hurt.

When I cried, Maman used to hug me and say there were guardian angels looking after us all, watching over this farm; that nothing bad would ever happen to us here.

"Where are they, then?" I asked.

"If you look really hard, and listen, too, then you'll know," she said.

So I strained for a sign, for a sound, but never found the proof.

The same sounds rise now: the goat bells from the fields below, the cicadas and birds. The wind in the plane trees still whispers the old stories. Then it changes to give an impression of a lively stream, or a vehicle coming up the lane. The trees imitate the sounds of life, absorbing and replaying them, according to the type of wind that stirs their boughs.

Bowed down, I went upstairs to find solace in my books. I did not have many, but for my birthday

Maman and Papa had given me a lovely copy of Corio's *Provençal Tales*. It was a medium-size fabric-covered book with a thick dust jacket painted to look like embossed leather. It was the best present I had ever had, full of the stories repeated over hundreds of years by the shepherds as they made their way with the sheep across plains and valleys with the seasons. Stories in which time had no meaning, and life stayed the same; in which good and evil were interchangeable at the flick of a mud-caked cloak, and human nature remained as dark as a cave with no way out.

But when I put my hand under my bed for it, the book was gone.

Though I searched and searched, I never found it. I had no proof but I knew who had taken it, and that there would never be a confession to this crime.

# 12

D om was bunkered in his music room the next day. I opened the door carefully. He was at the piano, his back to me, and gave no response when I told him I was going down to Apt to do some shopping. The music followed me as I backed out and walked across the courtyard and out to the garage.

Uninspired, I bought some bread, cheese, and eggs at the supermarket on the main Avignon road, threw the bag in the trunk, and looked around for Sabine. As I walked back to the entrance, a brown arm emerged from a zippy silver car, and waved me over. As arranged, I got in.

The lighting shop was slightly off the beaten track, about halfway to Avignon. She was right, though. It was exactly what I wanted. Half an hour later, I had placed an order and we were back in her car.

"Now," she said, starting the engine. "I can take you straight back to Leclerc, or we could go somewhere more interesting. What are you doing for lunch?"

"I . . . well, nothing."

She took me to a restaurant in Roussillon.

**The village** is perched on red ochre cliffs that surge like flames out of the valley floor and stand like an island surrounded by pines and dark green cedars. It was one of the features of the sweeping view from the terrace at Les Genévriers, but so far, Dom and I had only been there once for a summer dinner that hardly counted as a proper exploration.

Its narrow streets were notoriously thronged in high summer but now we parked easily in the square. The sandy stucco of the buildings glowed in every shade of orange, red, and pink, from faded watermelon to tangerine.

Up a pedestrian alleyway, past shops selling local wines and olive oil, scented candles, soaps, and sheaves of dried lavender, Sabine pushed open the door of the restaurant.

She was greeted as a valued customer, and it was only moments before we were installed at a corner table by the front window; wine, water, and bread in front of us.

We talked a little about our surroundings, seemingly for politeness's sake, before she asked whether I did anything in particular with my time.

When I told her, after briefly mentioning translation, of my literary ambitions, she seemed genuinely interested. What had I in mind? What kind of book? Whose work did I enjoy reading?

Given that we then struck a rich seam of similar tastes—Pagnol and Magnan among them—it didn't seem strange to be telling her about the ideas I had been mulling over, in which themes were rooted in a spirit of place. Maybe, I admitted, I might even collect some stories myself and translate those.

"You've found the right place to make a start at Les Genévriers," she said, slightly misunderstanding me. "Plenty of stories there. You should research them."

That wasn't quite what I'd meant, but she was keen to offer suggestions, so I listened.

"Marthe Lincel. She would be worth researching. She lived at the farm. The little blind girl who grew up to become a famous perfume creator in the 1950s?"

I hadn't heard of her. "Sounds interesting, though. I might see what I can find out."

"You should definitely look her up. Marthe Lincel."

"I will."

**The conversation** continued pleasantly through two courses of food. Then, when the waiter had cleared our plates and I was wondering how to broach the subject myself, she said, "What happened to Rachel?"

I started. It was not just the shock of Sabine's directness, but the way she spoke the name: Ra-ssh-el, so that the softness at its heart admitted to secrets and warnings. When I did not reply, fighting to recover my composure, not wanting to admit the extent of my ignorance, Sabine rested her chin on her hand and pressed on. "I brought her here once," she said lightly, though on a slightly false note.

"It was a press trip I organized. The journalists stayed in one of our best houses. I took them out to restaurants and one evening the catering company showed what a wonderful dinner they could provide. During the days I drove them around to see parts of the area I thought would make interesting copy. It took place over three or four days. She sent me the piece she wrote afterward, with a sweet letter."

I was thinking quickly.

"I'd love to see a copy," I said.

She was watching me again, in that careful way. As if gauging my reaction to every nuance. In talking to Sabine, each new step had to be placed precisely.

"I'm sure I have it somewhere," she said.

"That would be great."

"It was because of that trip she came back. It gave her an idea. She wanted to do some more research, write an investigative piece."

"So she got in touch with you then."

"It was short notice, but I managed to get her a six-week rental at a good rate. I know a lot of people around here."

"The Mauger house."

Sabine made a quick gesture of acknowledgment by opening her palms.

"And she brought her husband," I said.

"Yes, she did."

"But then—?" I stopped myself going on before I had my thoughts in order. But then, how on earth could he have pretended he'd never seen Sabine before? He must have known that denying it would look strange when they were each well aware of who the other was. It was her job, for God's sake, to take note of the people she was putting in her clients' houses.

But Sabine seemed to read my mind. "I only saw him once. Mostly she was there on her own. As far as I can remember he only joined her for a day or so."

"When was this?" Trying to make it sound casual.

She made a little grimace. "Two, three years ago? A few months after the press trip."

I felt it again, the way she seemed to be evaluating my reactions. "It seems a strange place to rent—just for one person, I mean."

"She was— Well, she was doing me a favor by taking it. She wanted to be in this area; the owner wanted someone there while he was absent. We came to an arrangement that suited everyone."

"*Une bonne affaire,*" I said. A nice deal.

There was a long pause while I considered the possibilities. On balance, the chance of finding out more about Rachel seemed to outweigh the embarrassment of admitting that I knew nothing about her and was avid to know more. What that said about the state of my relationship with Dom was a powerful brake, but it still didn't stop me.

"So—did Rachel find what she wanted, did she write her investigative piece?"

"Yes, she certainly did her research. But as for writing about what she found, I don't know. I don't think so somehow."

"Oh? Why's that?"

"She said she would keep in touch, and for a while she did. There were other avenues to explore, questions she knew that I could help her answer. I helped her a lot."

The searching look again, the quiet attentiveness to my smallest reaction. I stayed as still and as steady as I could.

"But, then—nothing."

Involuntarily, I shivered. Steady.

"But . . . if you were helping her like this—it sounds like you'd become friends. You must have had ways of contacting her."

"I did. There was a mobile phone number—that stopped working. I called the newspaper that published her article, but no one there had heard from her for a while."

"A home address?"

"No reply to my letter. Nothing."

Her words fell like a cold shadow.

Outside, it had started to rain. The patchwork trunks of the plane trees were quickly darkening. I noticed how rusty the metal of the window frame by our table was, like the rind of mature cheese.

"What was Rachel like?"

There was no point in pretending that I either knew more than I did, or was uninterested. In any case, it seemed that Sabine knew very well from the start of this game that she held all the good cards.

She thought awhile. "She was intense, driven—she wanted to understand, maybe even to make a difference. But she had a side of her that was a party girl; she could be frivolous, humorous, and confident. Sometimes people didn't know what to make of her. She was daring and determined, serious one second, flippant the next. That could be unsettling. I could see that others found her difficult. But she was a good journalist. And very attractive—obviously."

I had always assumed that she was. "Which newspaper did she write for?"

Sabine closed her eyes, apparently trying to recall. "It began with 'T' . . ."

"*Times, Telegraph? Travel*-something?"

"*Telegraph*, perhaps."

Her name now.

I took a flyer. "Rachel . . . ? What was her surname, again? She didn't use her married name, did she?"

"Summers."

Trying to nod as if I had always known that, and she had simply reminded me, I asked, "What was it she was working on?"

I was aware that I was bombarding her with questions, and knew, too, how much I was revealing in the process about myself and Dom. I should have backed off then, but I couldn't leave it.

"I could show you if you like. Or rather, I can show you what she saw, what gave her the idea before she began to work. It was not what the story became. That was something quite different from how it started out."

How could I not have been intrigued?

# 13

It was bad enough when Pierre's ghost appeared, so silent and unsettling. He was still lurking around as his younger self, insolent of expression, in the kitchen and my bedroom in the morning. So far, he had done nothing to harm me, but I knew Pierre. It could only be a matter of time.

In the interim, while the precise reason for his reappearance remained unclear, like a cloud hanging over the mountains, a nebulous, dark threat, I had found a way to block him out: I'd close my eyes and pretend everything was normal, and once or twice, when I opened them again, he would have slunk off, or vanished, vaporized, whatever it is spirits do when they have no active mischief to detain them.

But then one afternoon, when Pierre had stayed away for a week or so, and I had stopped tensing at the slightest change of light or shadow on the wall, the haunting started again.

**This time,** it was Marthe. And that's when I knew I was in real trouble. She wasn't a child, you see. She was a woman of means, standing straight and powerful, seeming far bigger than me, although in life we were a similar size. If anything, I was a finger's-width taller. Not then, with me sitting down and her standing, so still.

"What do you want?" I cried out. My outburst was entirely involuntary, and of course I did not expect an answer. Pierre had never answered a single question, even with a gesture.

Marthe did not move. She was a cold statue with hollowed features. If ever a person could represent stillness, she was doing so. Standing barely two meters from where I sat.

Wrenched from my doze by the hearth, I was frozen to my seat. The wind made the catalpa pods click outside the window. A loose shutter banged. Inside the room, the silence began to hum.

Marthe did not react. She remained the embodiment of stillness. For long seconds, I stared, hardly breathing.

Still no movement. Then—and I swear this happened just as I tell you—her eyes began to glow until they blazed red. Her sad, pretty, blind eyes that so rarely seemed to be sightless turned on mine and burned red like coals. Then the skin around them grew a crust of dried blood.

She did not speak, her mouth did not move, but I swear it was her voice I heard inside my own head.

"You thought you'd got away with it, didn't you?" she said.

# 14

It was only a matter of time before I went into the Internet café, the modern equivalent of the magic eye on the world. It felt disloyal, secretive, and wrong. But I rationalized that it was for the greater good, for my peace of mind. I would find out what I wanted to know and that would be the end of it. Wrong again, of course, but how could I have known that as I pulled up in Apt, locked the car, and walked along the embankment to the café?

Inside, it was full of young North African men. It had the air of being run by and for them, but the man behind the counter was not unfriendly when I asked to sign in.

**I typed** her name into the usual search engine. My heart skipped a beat as the screen promised several thousand entries relating to her name. Unable to stop myself, I clicked on "Images" to see if a photograph came up. None of the faces or scenes that filled the screen seemed right. Either they were too young or too old, or clearly belonged to a Rachel Summers in a soccer uniform.

I went back to the original search page and scrolled down rapidly, impatient to get the measure of what was on offer. Among the entries listing the Rachel Summers on team sport lists and schoolgirl social networking sites, a scientist featured prominently, and a musician and an environmentalist. At last, I found a couple of articles from five, six years ago, one from the *Daily Telegraph* and one from the *Traveller.* Then a short piece from a women's magazine. She must have worked freelance, maybe with regular assignments from some of them. But I was only guessing.

As I searched quickly, wondering whether I might get lucky and find a picture of her included with one of the pieces, I had the first sense of unease, as if my subconscious had spotted it first, while my conscious self, doggedly jotting down dates of the more recent articles as they came up, was still struggling to catch up. There was nothing more recent than two years earlier. An interview with Francis Tully in Provence, from the summer of 2008, was the last in the line.

I was so absorbed that it took me longer than it should have to register the argument that had started at the counter. When I looked up, an elderly man in traditional Muslim robes was pointing at me, while the man who had taken my money was clearly asking him to calm down. After a few minutes, during which I did my best to concentrate on the screen, the younger man approached me apologetically.

"I am truly sorry, Madame, but I have to ask you to leave."

"But— I haven't . . ."

It seemed that the elder customer objected to my presence as a young woman alone, and especially one wearing a skirt that did not cover her knees.

"I am very sorry." I thought I detected sympathy in his manner, and a plea not to make a fuss. There was nothing to do but to leave gracefully and hope I might return another time.

"Could you just print this out for me, please?" I asked, indicating the Francis Tully article on the screen as I gathered my bag and papers with a show of uncomprehending dignity. "Then I'll leave."

**In hindsight,** that day marked the start of it: the sense of a separation from Dom. It had crept up on me that we were no longer quite so bound up in each other; that in trying so hard to remain self-reliant and avoid seeming needy and jealous of his past, I had locked a vital part of myself away. Now the realization was like a plunge into icy water.

The idyllic summer was well and truly over.

# 15

*Daily Telegraph Magazine* (London), Saturday, June 14, 2008

## THE CONSTANT GARDENER:
## AN AFTERNOON WITH FRANCIS TULLY
### *By Rachel Summers*

*"Not as many women as Picasso, not as much wine as Durrell, not as angry as Beckett: I could have been so much worse . . ."* Francis Tully upends the bottle of local rosé and pushes a chipped, smeared glass towards me, never pausing for breath.

In the garden that the iconoclastic writer and surrealist has created in the South of France, fragments of stone statues and pediments are placed to amuse: a severed hand here, a skein of petrified ivy linking a group of pine trees, a rococo pineapple in a bed of agapanthus lilies.

Joining us at the stone table under a vine canopy is the headless torso of an archer. He aims his arrow at Tully's head, an ancient version of a gun to the head, although whether this would be to keep him talking or to make him stop is not clear. In any case, stopping him in full flow is not an option.

"Photography and the naïve art are pure ferocity of emotion, as near to the truth as the truth is in people's reactions to it, and in provoking that reaction . . . austerity is the only truth . . . the context must be supplied by the mind. . . . Surrealism is to do with a kind of hoax, a piece of theatre, carrying through a fantasy in a very European way . . ."

And on he goes, a ferment of ideas and associations.

In a green arbour to the side of the house, the ground is scattered with smashed statuary, stone limbs missing bodies like a macabre graveyard. "A work in progress," he says dismissively. He is still working, still serious about his art.

Yet when the eagerly anticipated retrospective of his life's work opens at Tate Modern next week, Francis Tully will not be there. He has no intention of returning to London—ever. His antipathy to his native country remains as strong as it was when he left almost forty years ago.

What I want to ask him about is his arrival here at this house, on this land in the lee of the rocky Alpilles hills, in the spring of 1974, when he put down his stake and claimed his sensuous kingdom; the train journey as he described it in The Rotten Heart: the southern country running past the window where his reflection was a shadow, passing over the fields and the dark trees, the outline of a face without details, waiting to become the man he wanted to be.

The painterly descriptions of stumbling into this wonderful enclosed world "south of the jagged roof of the Dentelles de Montmirail, rock lace natted by the mistral" have enchanted generations and never gone out of print. From the higher windows of his great stone bastide are views over vineyards, "from whence will pour the rich blue-red wines imbibed by the Avignon Popes with their flaccid purple lips, wines that for centuries have fortified the men at their ploughs, uniting all in plum-deep fraternity."

From a distance these villages seem abandoned. Only the geraniums in pots outside windows and doors attest to inhabitation. Far removed from the

Mediterranean world, it is enclosed upon itself, desolate and stony to the casual glance, perhaps, but full of richness for a man like Francis Tully.

As he confessed in The Rotten Heart: "In France, I had all the freedom and ambiguity of the expatriate, the voluntary exile. No borders, checks, or controls. This is what the artist needs: to invent his own country, in which to remake himself."

And the new world in which he remade himself brought friendship and a cornucopia of characters he would immortalise in print: an ex-juggler from the Circus of Dreams; a toothless shepherd; a six-foot-tall Dutch woman whose husband was a banker in Zurich; the brocanteur who collected and recycled junk from the farmhouses and churches and châteaux to the increasing tide of foreigners; the herbalist who grew all his own ingredients, pounding and distilling them into potent cures; and a great cast of fellow drinkers—farmers, beekeepers, winemakers, builders, bakers, engineers, and fellow artists—in the Bar des Alpilles.

I want to ask him how many of these people were still here, still arguing at the tables under the trees while sipping pastis. Was it even a real world, or just one that suited him to portray? But he waves away my questions about the book. "Unimportant!"

*Just like appearances, it seems. He wears a blue jumper full of holes that is visibly unravelling as he stretches out his arm to make a point, as he does often. His shoes are scuffed and the left one is secured to the flapping sole by gaffer tape.*

*When I persist, he fetches another bottle, pulls the cork and says in measured tones:* "Some people prefer lies to the truth. The ambiguities and evasions they live by are what they use to protect themselves. An attempt to know these people is like peeling the layers of an onion. An apt analogy, too, because tears will fall, if you try to love them."

*Erudite and distant, his tone now, with its cut-glass English accent. How much was he talking about himself? I asked.*

*He evades the question.* "But then you can't tie everything into knots and conspiracies. Surely what matters is the great Now, the cadences of the protean, ringing blue of this sky, this moment! This stone! This wine! This annoying wasp! This sudden waft of cistus scent!"

*Does he still see the country in the same way? I wondered. Or has it changed and mellowed with his own long years living here?*

"It's stranger. The more you know, the more you see. Because you are seeing with the addition of another dimension that cannot be seen: time and experience, and all the stories heard and read that are now superimposed. *That's part of the land. It is what makes it.*

"Have you been to Cassis? Look at the paintings done there by Duncan Grant and Vanessa Bell. Read Woolf. See the place where they lived, then look again. Without roots like that, a book, a painting, an installation . . . it's all fraudulent."

He had just returned from a painting trip of his own there, he said. "With a lovely young model. I call her Magie—and she is magic. The best I've had for years. Fearless, you know? I'd like to do more with her. But you should go to Cassis. You'd like it. In fact, come with me!"

When it is time for me to go, we exit through the garden where he wants to show me a metal gazebo he has made for trailing roses. He exhorts me again to go to Cassis and presents me with a granite pineapple and a severed hand.

# 16

A cold wind whipped my hair across my face as I stood by the wall in the garden.

A granite pineapple and a severed hand.

I had assumed Dom had bought them at the reclamation yard. Rachel's words played and replayed in my head. Could they possibly be different ones, bought by Dom, not by coincidence (that would be impossible) but after remembering the ones given to Rachel?

I dismissed that idea in seconds. Surely it would require a great deal of luck to find such specific and odd ephemera.

And yet—what did it matter if she had left them with her ex-husband? Perhaps she had given them to him, knowing how much he would like them. There was nothing sinister in that.

————

"**Why don't** you come and sit here?" asked Dom when I went inside. "You keep scurrying away like a little mouse, always disappearing off to new corners where I can't find you."

He had lit a fire, only semi-effectively, in the sitting room off the kitchen and had pulled a couple of chairs and a low table closer to the hearth. Normally, this room was so bare and chilly we tended to keep to the natural warmth of the kitchen.

I shook off my coat and said I'd bring us some coffee.

"It's made. What have you been up to?" he asked.

"Oh, just . . . nothing much. Looking around the garden."

"Well, come and warm up here."

So we sat together, sipping coffee in near silence. The fire popped and emitted small belches of smoke. After a while I fetched my book. Dom went off to bring in more logs.

Despite the spitting flames, the room was still cold. Flakes of plaster floated down from between the narrow lath beams of the ceiling. More fell on the pages I was reading. After a while, it seemed like snow coming through the roof. I shifted my chair and suddenly wondered why Dom was taking so long.

A long, creaking sound made me jump. A sound like a door forced from the position it had been stuck in for years. Was it Dom somewhere else in the house? I craned my head and listened. Nothing, only the fire. Then another, louder creak. I thought of sailing ships in tempests, and shivered. Another larger lump of plaster came down.

I was almost on my feet when the room erupted. A roaring sound, followed by a huge crash as I was suddenly pulled with some force into the kitchen doorway. The noise of falling masonry and wood shattering on the stone floor was earsplitting. Then a scream, which had come from me. At the moment it happened, I had no idea what had jerked me out of danger.

Then my face was against Dom's chest, and he was swearing and shaking as hard as I was. Only feet away, the ceiling had collapsed onto the chair where I had been sitting. A cloud of gray dust hung over the heap of rubble. Above was an ominous black space. We were both choking.

"Oh my God," Dom said, over and over again. "Did you not realize?"

"I heard some creaking noises, but I didn't think—"

"If I hadn't got back when I did—"

"Don't . . ."

We clung to each other, hearts pounding. I concentrated on breathing, willing the panic to recede. If anything, Dom was trembling more violently than I was.

Upstairs, in an unused room, I stashed the printout of the Francis Tully interview in a box containing files and papers of my own. Even as I did it, I felt guilty. Though that did not stop me thinking obsessively about what I'd read.

Rachel had written herself prominently into the interview. She was there on the page as a character alongside the subject in a way that—ordinarily, at least—only seasoned journalists were. Did that say anything about her, or was that simply the required form of this particular piece?

It was pretty clear that the interview with Tully had been a tricky one, and yet it seemed that they had ended by warming to each other. She came across as patient and resourceful, confident in the manner in which she bearded the lion in his den. He had enjoyed her company enough to give her the stone hand and the pineapple.

Francis Tully must still be living at his house in the Alpilles. Who knew, perhaps—just perhaps—I would go up to his village and hope to find him in the café. I could tell him I remembered reading a newspaper feature, and ask about the woman journalist who had written it. What if they really had got on well after the sticky start, and they had kept in touch?

Then I stopped myself. This was pure fantasy, clutching at straws. Don't tie everything into knots and conspiracies, he had said to her, and I, too, would do well to heed the warning. There didn't have to be a common thread; for all that I was doing my best to spin one out of nothing.

As it transpired, I never had the chance to test my nerve, because when I did go back down to the Internet café in Apt, waiting until the friendly man at the counter had no other customers before being admitted to make a rapid search for references to Francis Tully, I found myself reading obituaries. The old man had fallen down dead in his beloved garden some six months earlier.

**It was** around then, at the time the ceiling collapsed and I found out more about Rachel, that Dom started retreating more into himself during the days, leaving me to my own devices.

He began taking long, solitary walks whatever the weather. He would set off in the car, while I stayed behind, reading and cooking and thinking. When he returned, he was full of stories and small observations, though, and wanted to share them. I rationalized that this was all for the good, that it never seemed we were living together too closely, that it was a way of ensuring boredom would not set in.

If ever I did start to worry, I persuaded myself that this was normal in such a relationship, given that we spent so many hours in close proximity. There were plenty of times when he was attentive and concerned that I was happy; it was my oversensitivity and lack of confidence that made me misread the situation. I was so in love with him that the thought of our life together slipping through my fingers was unbearable.

And we always came together at night. He would put winter's wild offerings from the garden in a vase by my side of the bed: sprigs of evergreen rosemary and pine, translucent dried circles of honesty. He always asked me if I needed anything, and bought me an electric heater for the bare, cell-like room on the ground floor where I liked to sit reading.

One book in particular I kept returning to at that time: *Rebecca* by Daphne du Maurier. It has none of the intellectual cachet of *Madame Bovary*, or *Anna Karenina*, or *Crime and Punishment*, but for me, its modesty is the point. The story has an emotional pull and a truth all its own. Dom's wife was called Rachel, another of Daphne's heroines; was it that coincidence that drew me to *Rebecca* rather than any other novel about a woman haunted?

# Part III

# Part III

# 1

Winters at Les Genévriers were often harsh, for all the luminous skies.

When the snows came, they were heavy. In the severest winters, the path up to the village and the school was impassable for weeks on end and the violet ink in the wells set into the wooden desks would freeze solid.

Then, more than ever, the farm was a community apart, with a sense of isolation even from a village only ten minutes' walk up the hill.

The start of the hard months was marked for us by a change in our footwear. At the end of September, we swapped the rope-soled shoes we wore in summer for winter socks and leather boots. The wind began to bring cold air from the mountains, and carried chilly spots of rain.

There are only three days in the year when one or the other of the Provençal winds does not rake across this land. But the old ways are going—are long gone, in many cases—and soon the millers and shepherds, and farmers and fishermen whose lives depended on reading the winds will have died out, too.

At Les Genévriers, the winds sent word from the north and northwest that September was turning to October, and it was time to taste the *vin de noix*. It was a rite of early autumn, like the preserving of fruit and vegetables in bottles and earthenware jars in summer.

The green walnuts were gathered in June, and distilled with red wine, eau-de-vie, sugar, and oranges. In many ways, this was our most vital crop, as it was our famed walnut liqueur that brought the neighboring families to the farm to buy, some with their own bottles to fill from the barrels for a few sous less.

Papa would go down to the cellar beneath the barn. In this room was the still; then, along a short passageway, was the vaulted, gravel-lined wine cave under the courtyard. From the first barrel, he would draw a glass of sweet tawny wine.

Marthe could smell essences in the *vin de noix* that no one else could.

**Marthe, swirling** the glass of walnut wine and sniffing. The first time she said, to universal fascination,

"I can make out warm caramel, that's the top note. But then, the liqueur stays on the tongue and gives the honey of the tobacco plant, and overripe plums, and heliotrope and cocoa."

Then, as no one broke the silence, she added, "If I really concentrate, there's a hint of the scent of split figs cooked with honey, you know, at the moment they turn jammy under the heat. Only then, at the end, the mellow bitterness of the nut."

Bitterness? Top note? What were top notes? I could see I wasn't the only one wondering.

"Hmmn," said Papa, deciding to play the game. "But what does it taste of? Does it taste good?"

"It tastes all right, perhaps a little too sweet and sticky."

She couldn't have seen the expression of hurt and disappointment on his face, but she went on in the nick of time, "But the aroma! It's so very special, so absolutely right, the scent of these special nuts grown in this place. Just as it should be, quite wonderful."

"Aah, that's true," he said, swilling it around under his nose before taking another great slurp. "A magnificent wine."

"May I be honest, Papa? To be truly magnificent, it should have some bite, some sharp contrast. Perhaps an herbal note that would anchor it, make it a little less fluffy."

"Fluffy?"

"Flabby, fat with too much sweetness."

That made him bellow. "Fluffy? Flabby? Bite? What kind of insolence are they teaching you at this school of yours? Be gone with you and your fancy ideas!" But it was a false bellow that could not conceal his joy at an unexpected source of pride in addition to the wine. He waved us away and settled down with the bottle and a rich satisfaction.

**By that** stage, Marthe was at a special school in Manosque: a school for the blind. I'd finally become aware that she couldn't see very well when I had started at the village school, which at that point she still attended. Every morning at half-past seven we walked up through the woods and she would take my arm, although I was younger than her.

Sometimes a cloud sat on the top of the mountain range like icing on a cake and I would point it out, but, though I realize this only in retrospect, she was always happier noticing the smells and the changes in the springiness of the mud and stone path and the flap of birds' wings above.

This can only have been our routine for a term or two (though, in my mind, it went on for years and years), because Marthe was sent to the special school for the blind when she was ten or eleven.

Strangely, I don't recall being shocked by the discovery of her condition, despite the fact that I had not known of it before. She had not complained. She was a calm, gentle girl, who was happy to sit and study nature in close-up, and we had all accepted this without asking why this should be. If anyone was shocked, it was Pierre, and that was neither for long nor with any sense of remorse. Though, naturally, we did not learn of his involvement until quite some time later.

Even now, I am not sure exactly how or when our parents found out the extent of her loss of sight, how long they had been aware there was a problem. The first I knew of it was when they told us calmly, one evening at supper, that Marthe would be going away.

I was surprised, obviously, but young enough to accept the news without question, as I did so many other new experiences. Later on, I did ask her once or twice whether the onset had been sudden and frightening, but she fudged the answer. Perhaps she thought I was curious for all the wrong reasons and my asking was just prurient. So I was left none the wiser. All I had were my impressions, which may or may not have provided an accurate picture of what really happened. And when the time comes that you really want to find out the truth, there is no one left to ask.

**2**

One morning, the air changed. A light dusting of frost iced the garden. The topiary stood stark-white and petrified. Winter was upon us. Under mercury clouds, the bare bones of nature were being picked clean by bitter winds.

Outside, the atmosphere thickened. Snow was threatening. Static electricity crackled when our fingers touched. We walked through the transformed woods, down to the ruined chapel.

Light changes the scenery. The same place, a different season: the difference is brightness. When the late-afternoon light was low but bright, the tussocks of grass on the fields were backlit into a strange moon surface as we walked. But later, returning to the house with the sun at our backs, we moved into our own shadow, like going forward into the past, back into the fabric of our self-imposed solitude.

The next morning, flurrying and fluttering at the windows, the snow was mesmerizing. Flakes were fat clumps now, the ground so cold that the white was building up into a fleece, sticking to the leaves of the ivy. Wind whipping it in all directions, pulling the gaze from one zigzag fall to another, distorting the perspective.

Outside, the stone pineapple was losing definition, and the hand had accepted a palmful of whiteness. I had said nothing to Dom about their provenance. The stone cornucopia acquired a powdering of sugar: plump, dredged grapes; peaches topped with alien cream. White cushions formed on the wooden benches and chairs, set for conversations that would not take place until the spring.

Snow took hold of the skeletal structures of the garden, coating the seed heads and stalks. Soon the alliums and globe artichoke were extravagantly plumed in winter's coat. Life slowed into a strange calm as disarray and decay were covered over, more thickly smothered hour by hour.

I set up one of the summer garden chairs in the stark room I'd appropriated as a study. It looked out on the courtyard with the blanketed olive tree and the fig, but I put my back to the window to catch the light, writing now as well as reading, with a traveling rug over my knees and the electric fire ticking away.

There was a faint smell of lavender from the dried-out bunch that I'd stuffed in a glass carafe during the summer. At one point, I thought I heard some music from Dom's piano, but it was only a brief, experimental run of notes and ended almost as soon as it had begun.

Finally, my ideas were beginning to crystallize. Everywhere I turned, there were the raw materials of narrative: stories passed on by everyone we met; snippets of information that seemed to resonate. And my own observations: the old keys that didn't fit any lock; the empty wells; the hunters who trespassed in our wood; the discovery of more rooms in the house, secrets that were there all along, only needing to be unlocked; the blind girl who created perfumes.

It was going to be an experiment, but I decided to try writing my own book about the sensuous dimensions of the countryside surrounding us, drawing on the old Provençal tales and setting the story of Marthe Lincel at its heart.

But however much I immersed myself in the past and our enclave, it was hard not to be aware of what was happening in the here and now. Dom spent more and more time in his music room, away from me.

Neither did he seem to have much contact with his family or friends. Nor did I, for that matter. We had received a total of six personal letters, all for me, since we'd been at Les Genévriers. It wasn't healthy being so isolated.

"Do you want to invite your parents down here for Christmas?" I suggested. "Surely they'd love to see the place."

"I can't think of anything worse. Not at Christmas."

"Why do you say it like that?"

"Too many masses, confessions. Too much guilt. I've never been as good a Catholic as I was brought up to be."

"Ah."

"What about you?"

"Well, my mother might like to be asked, though she'd make her excuses," I said. "She likes going to my brother's—being with the grandchildren."

"Just the two of us, then."

Did he say it too quickly?

"Just the two of us," I agreed.

**3**

Marthe did well at Manosque, learning Braille in addition to all the normal lessons. Then, one day, her class was taken on a field trip that changed the course of her life.

The school was tentatively (and perceptively) forming an association with a small local perfume factory. From the second she walked into the blending room, Marthe told me, she knew she was in the place where she was meant to be. Several of the girls showed an aptitude for the work, but it was Marthe who was the most enthusiastic, the one who asked if she could come back soon.

She knew straightaway that she had found her métier. That evening, she sent us a letter, dictated to one of the teachers, which said: "Smell these together.

I think it's beautiful. All best wishes to you all from Marthe." The envelope contained a white rose petal and a twist of dried orange peel.

We were mystified at first, but when we did take her message between our fingers and smelled how the delicate petal and the deep, sharp pungency of the peel did mingle in a delightful way, we began to understand what she was saying. It would have helped to know about the visit to the perfume factory, but that was explained in subsequent letters, when she was less excited.

She made me think, though. How do you describe a scent? The scent of lavender, for example? Apparently, our sense of smell is ten thousand times more powerful than our sense of taste. But that's still not enough for most of us to pin down the scent of lavender in words. Sweet, pungent, woody, spicy, musky, astringent; none of these alone is capable of evoking the unique smell we all know so well. Ask anyone about lavender, and the chances are they won't be able to give you a description of its aroma. But more often than not, they can give you some visual reference. Lavender is color, waving fields of purple, rich blues, and faded mauve. It is the essence of blue and of the warm winds of summer, opulent against the yellow of the cornfield, mysteriously shadowed under the olives that are sometimes planted as its companion.

Even I see lavender like this, in my head. It glows as a memory that grows more vibrant with the passing years. But perhaps the memory is of pictures in books I once saw, or the pictures that other people make for me in words. I'm not sure. All I meant to say was that it was fitting that post from Marthe contained more scents than words.

You could open an envelope from Manosque and find it contained no words at all, just a handful of lavender with a ribbon of dried grapefruit skin, or a sprinkling of vanilla seeds. When we went to see her on a Sunday—though it was not every week, by any means, maybe only twice a term—she would talk about scents in ways we could barely comprehend.

Her favorite flower was the heliotrope. It was all about the sun, she explained once when she came back to us for the long summer holidays. The name means "to turn with the sun." On the southwest-facing bank by the barn and the wine cellar, we'd lie on our stomachs by the clumps of these tiny purple flowers massed in tightly packed clouds as they turned their petals to the light, and to the east at night in readiness for sunrise; I staring deep into the white holes at the center of the flower; Marthe lost in new worlds.

"It smells of cherry and almond and chocolate and vanilla. How can so many aromas be produced in the glands of one tiny flower?" she wondered, rubbing a fleshy, deep-veined leaf between her fingers. "What is the proportion of one to the other? If we could work that out, how much we could learn from it."

She was fascinated by those heady little blooms, and she did learn. She came to understand that scent and tell others in a way that was uniquely hers, but that was all to come.

As her sight deteriorated, her sense of smell became even more acute, until you felt she could read the world through her nose and her instincts. Later, she also seemed to know when I was uncomfortable, and when I was holding back on her, or about to tell her what she had no wish to hear.

But it was good to see that she had found a true calling, and that she was regaining her lost confidence.

**4**

"D on't look now," said Dom.
We were unpacking the car after a trip to the Saturday market. He'd been in an expansive mood, buying sublime venison and a walnut tart for supper, and more wine, chef's knives, and a king-size roasting tin, which gave me quiet hope that we might entertain guests at some stage. His ebullience vanished abruptly.

"Coming our way now," he said. "Down our path."

Sabine was dressed in jeans and boots, so it was hardly incongruous when she stopped in front of our garage and said, "Lovely day for a walk, isn't it! How are you?"

During an exchange of awkward pleasantries, Dom continued to pull shopping bags from the trunk of the car, head lowered. There was no doubt in my mind that he was avoiding Sabine.

"Call me," she said airily, when it was obvious there would be no easy chatter and invitation to come inside. She turned to go, the merest flicker of amusement playing in her eyes, then a wave over her shoulder.

"What was she doing here?"

"Just dropped by on her walk, as she said. You were a bit rude, weren't you?"

"She was trespassing."

"Only in the way everyone else does." I was thinking of the hunters. "Besides . . . I quite like her." I didn't want to be too disingenuous.

Silence.

"I don't like the way she looks at us."

"Dom . . ."

"So what does she want?"

"She lives on the other side of the village. I've run into her before along here. We got talking."

"Why would she be interested?"

"Just curiosity, don't you think? The house, who's finally bought it, what will we do to it. The usual."

I could so easily have mentioned Rachel then, and it would all have been out in the open. Why didn't I? There wasn't anything to hide, except for my desire to know about his life with her, and jealousy of what she must have meant to him.

It was at times like these that I wanted to go away and weep for all that we'd lost already, the innocence and ease of conversation between us, and the trust.

**5**

What I haven't told you yet is that Marthe was beautiful. Her skin was creamy and her chestnut hair was thick and wavy, and fell effortlessly into flattering styles. And her eyes! Those blind brown eyes were deep and intelligent, and the shape of almonds. I know that's a cliché, but in her case it was absolutely true; the cliché might have been coined to describe her. If you looked at her face, there was no hint she was blind, no way of telling as there was, straightaway, with some of the other girls at her school. She had a gentle manner, she was always popular, and she was so eager to learn.

No wonder she got her chance at the perfume factory. As soon as she left the school for the blind at eighteen, she was taken on to be trained as a scent-maker.

We were all delighted for her; and in that way, though not of her choosing in the first place, simply her determination to find some positive outcome from the terrible hand she had been dealt, she was the first of the line to leave Les Genévriers and find work in one of the new industries that were drawing the young to the towns.

Some years ago, I wrote to Marthe again about selling off the farm, but there was no reply. It turned out that the gentle soul had a heart of iron, after all. And as Les Genévriers can never be sold without her consent, I remain here.

# 6

More snow fell, then melted into ridges of mud and water.

"We should go skiing. What do you think?" said Dom.

Skiing has never held a particular lure for me, but I knew he loved it. Suddenly, it seemed like an excellent plan. I was ready to leave the claustrophobic atmosphere of our hillside, the sense of loneliness underscored by the feeling that we were never the only spirits here. I suspect he was, too.

We had a long, enjoyable discussion about which of the small resorts only a couple of hours up the *autoroute* we should try, then he returned from the travel agent in Apt the next day and announced that we were going to Switzerland. He had booked a hotel in Davos. A few days later, we were on Thomas Mann's magic mountain, with its menacing sanatorium above the long, ugly town.

Under clear skies, the relatively shallow runs down the Parsenn were wide, glossy sheets of pure white. Frost sparkled on the packed snow and rocks, and hard exercise in the fresh mountain air pumped optimism back into our bloodstreams. In the great, sweeping bowls, the controlled hum and intermittent clickings as chairlifts were pulled smoothly over their rollers sent a message of strength and power.

Dom was an effortlessly elegant skier, relaxed as he carved wide arcs down the drops. We had some good days.

On the bad days, snowflakes were chips of flying ice on our tight and reddened faces. The whiteout was disorienting. Sweat dried cold on my back. The gray-brown rocks of the sheer outcrops, where the snow could not grip, emerged too late for comfort, for good judgment. For me, on those days, fear of an accident hung like a premonition.

Dom skied ever faster and harder as I struggled to keep up.

**It was** a radiant day, silver-bright and warm in the sun, when he stopped half a run ahead of me on a steep, red piste on the Gotschnagrat. When I drew level, he was bending over, facing straight down the mountain. I made some joking comment about it all being too much for him before I realized something was wrong.

"What is it? Are you sick?"

He shook his head.

Closer up, I saw tears streaming down his face. "What is it?" I asked, but gently this time.

Again, no answer.

Automatically, I thought, Was it me, was I the problem? The sun like a laser. Stinging glare from the slope.

"It was a mistake to come here. We shouldn't have come," he said eventually, his cheeks chalky in the pure, harsh light.

I reached up to his face and wiped away a new trickle without understanding that he was unraveling from the inside out. How could I have done?

The snowfields rippled out below us. Salt tears and the afterimage of the searchlight sun blurred my own vision.

Dom just stood there, silently, while I was powerless to help.

It was Thomas de Quincey who wrote that it was never possible to forget, only for a thousand accidents to serve as a veil between our present consciousness and "the secret inscriptions on the mind." That's a beautiful phrase, and one that we all recognize even if we could not have distilled it so perfectly into words.

We cut our week short and returned to Provence. He didn't explain then, and later tried to shrug off the whole incident. He was quiet but didn't seem unhappy with me. In fact, he was more loving than ever.

# 7

The summer I was fifteen, I went up to the mountains of Valensole for the lavender harvest. It was Marthe's idea, she who persuaded our parents to let me go to see for myself how the ridged uplands had been transformed into purple carpets where the scent was born.

Well, not only to see for myself: to see for her.

"I want you to look really hard, just like we used to, look right into the heart of the flowers and the spiny leaves and the earth and describe it to me. Use all your senses to make the pictures come alive for me. Would you do that, Bénédicte, would you? I need to know, to put the pictures in my head, so that I'm not missing any single aspect as I try out my ideas. I don't want to be just a blender of scents who follows set recipes,

I want to follow my own instincts. I want to see it all, the whole process, and you're the only one who will understand, who can do it in a way I can see and who won't think I am mad!"

My immediate reaction was delight. I was so grateful to her, for handing me this chance to experience some independence, to find out for myself what had so enthralled us all from her descriptions; and, not least, I was grateful to be asked to perform this service for her, to show her in such a practical way how much I loved and admired her.

Neither was there any objection from our parents. I would be working outside the farm for the first time and earning a little money. There could be no argument raised against that.

The night before I went, as we said good night, she pressed a little notebook and pencil into my hand.

"Remember, you are my eyes now," she said.

The lavender road winds eastward from our farmstead, up through the hills of northern Provence. I was conscious that I was following in her footsteps, that this was the road that Marthe took when she was younger than me, and that she had found new prospects for her life at the end of it, when all might have been so dark.

The prevalent view at the time was that lavender was work for the young, and the women, too. After the Great War, there was an effort made to increase lavender production as a way of halting the exodus of young people from the villages. Then, in 1920, the hybrid lavandin was made by crossing pure lavender with hardy spike lavender, which was tough as well as aromatic, and the ideal crop had been discovered. Little by little, the old, pure lavender was replaced by the new wonderplants, and by the summer I arrived, it was becoming more and more established.

And it was wartime again, 1941. The men who could were fighting, underground, any way they could. Even Pierre, like all the others his age, was waiting to be called up, though in the unoccupied south, our so-called Armistice Army was playing a waiting game. It was said our boys were hiding arms in the hills, for the uprising against the Nazis when it came.

More women than men were in the fields, which may have had a bearing on our parents allowing me to go. I remember being happy at the prospect, not thinking of it as war work. I wanted to see for myself the violet waves on the hillsides, the crops planted on slopes—never on flat land, because that's where it will attract the frost—but on slopes, where the cold air cannot settle. I was proud to be earning some extra money for the family as well as fulfilling my promise to Marthe. It was a heady feeling, that first taste of independence and responsibility, and it was with a sense of excited wonder that I reported to the lavender farm, a letter of recommendation from my sister and her teacher at the school for the blind tucked into my leather pouch.

At a stone hut, which must once have been a shepherd's *borie*, I was directed to a field about a kilometer away. I arrived to find a field of hunched backs, the blue rows reverting to dusty green behind the women curled over like commas, cloth bags slung across their bodies.

A man in a white shirt and open waistcoat, the only upright figure in the panorama, beckoned to me. When I drew closer, the sun caught a gold tooth at the front of his mouth as he spoke, and I stared, having never seen such an ornamentation.

I was given a bag, a small sickle, and a starting place. Although he asked my name and nodded, he did not introduce himself. For several days afterward, until I got to know some of the other girls and exchange information, he would remain simply the man in the waistcoat.

"Watch out for the bees, and the vipers," he said.

"Vipers?"

"They hide under the flowers."

I put on my apron and pulled my cotton scarf up over my head. My eyes were already hurting from the relentless sun.

Nervously, I began. It was tiring work but I was keen to prove myself. The bag grew heavier and bumped against my legs. The scent was heavenly, all around in heavy fumes, so intense that after a while it seemed to pulse.

The other women ranged in age from girls of about thirteen to grandmothers. We were spaced too far apart for any conversation. We bent and cut and pulled, making sheaves as we went, tying the bunches with twine as they became unwieldy, then transferring these to our canvas bags. All was quiet save for the drone of fat bees and other insects, and the scrape of the sickle as it tore the stalks. Now and then, a mouse would cause a rustle.

When each bag was full, we took it to the end of the row, where the flowers were all laid out in the sun to dry for a few hours before distillation.

Eventually, a cart like a hayrick wobbled over to the growing piles of flowers. It was pulled by a noble horse so calm that it seemed drugged. Perhaps it was, by the mysterious olfactory properties of the flowers. It was a discovery, how much horses and donkeys, even sheep and goats, enjoy grazing on lavender. Not many years later, they would start to use tractors with iron wheels to pull the heavily laden ricks, but that summer, with petrol so scarce, the power was still provided the old-fashioned way.

Men with pitchforks were throwing the stalks and flowers up like hay. Another stood on top of the shaggy load, shouting. Then, when it seemed not another petal could possibly cling on, and the mauve tassels were dripping in every direction, the order was given to sway off to the corner where the alembic had been pulled in by a donkey.

It was a strange and primitive contraption, this double-boiler copper still. In appearance, it was like a potbellied stove with a substantial round column for a chimney. I watched (we had taken a break for a drink of cool water) as water was poured into the belly of the machine and it was set to boil over a fire. Meanwhile, the lavender blossoms were beaten from the stems and packed into the chimney above for the scent to be extracted by steam.

"How long does it take?" I was thinking, of course, of the notes I would make for Marthe, determined to remember all the details. I picked up one of the broken stems and examined the spiky end where a few minuscule petals clung feebly.

"About thirty minutes from the time the water boils," said the man in the waistcoat.

It was a straight answer, but I realized from the tone of his voice that I might have gone too far, been too familiar perhaps. Did no one else want to understand how it all worked? Feeling I had overstepped the mark, I kept my head down and my work rate up for the rest of the day.

When the whistle finally went for the end of our shift, my back was so stiff I could barely stand up straight. Slowly, we filed to the entrance of the field, past the boss. He seemed to stare intently at me as I passed, so I dropped my eyes and hurried on. It was a walk of a couple of kilometers back to the farmhouse.

**We seasonal** workers were lodged in a group of primitive wooden huts. Meals were all outdoor affairs, taken at a long wooden table outside the dormitory hut. The food was rationed and meager. I was more interested in making friends with the others, to keep life pleasant, and the others must have shared this aim, for generally there was quite a party atmosphere, especially in the evenings.

Our beds were narrow thin mattresses on planks with sacking for sheets. Luckily, we had no need of these, as the nights were so warm, and sleep was only possible in the stuffy dormitory if you laid yourself out uncovered on top of the mattress and stayed as still as you could. Sometimes, when there seemed no breath of air to spare, we dragged the mattresses outside and slipped into sleep under the bright stars.

As a group, we were mainly girls and young women. The older women apparently came from the nearby villages in the morning and went back each evening.

It was all pretty friendly. Being one of the youngest, I wasn't of much interest to the ones who were over twenty and wanted to talk about hairstyles and their romances with men, but I found easy company with a couple of others more my own age, Aurélie and Mariette. Aurélie was the tallest girl I had ever seen, taller even than Papa, and with long, thin shins like a giraffe I had seen in a book; her back often hurt her, perhaps because she had farther to bend. Mariette was the daughter of a cheesemaker at Banon. She would always share sharp white patties made of goat's milk, wrapped in dry brown leaves, which she brought from her family's farm. Her generosity didn't make her popular, she was too awkward for that, but I liked her. I sensed we shared a similar lack of ease away from our own family land, though neither of us ever admitted it, being committed to claiming success in striking out on our own for the first time.

Among the field workers were Spanish and Portuguese, men and women, regulars at harvesttime, and paid by the task. They were polite to us, extremely voluble among themselves, and kept slightly apart. What they were doing there during the war, I don't know. Perhaps the authorities didn't, either, but they were obviously known and trusted by the farmers, so perhaps they had simply stayed after other harvests and been assimilated into the land, just like us.

They slept in a tent at the side of the fields and cooked for themselves on a camping stove. What they thought about sleeping so close to vipers slithering around the flowers, I never got the chance to ask.

# 8

I thought they were icicles, at first. But as I drew closer, I saw they were fringes of glass shards hanging in the olive tree in the courtyard: the remains of the little jars I had wired to the branches in the summer to hold tea lights, their bellies blown away when rainwater they had collected had frozen and the ice expanded.

As I unwound the wires and picked more sharp slivers off the ground, it seemed a long time since Dom and I had sat outside each balmy evening.

When you first meet someone and they tell you stories about themselves, you generally have no reason to doubt these are true. You take them on faith.

Here's the rub: Dom never told me anything that wasn't true. In any case, at this point, I thought I was the one who had reluctantly begun to keep uncomfortable truths to myself. I wanted so badly for the reality to match up to the dream. Right at the start, I had promised myself I would be bold. Before, I had been so shy and scared of a serious relationship—so scared of life, sometimes—but I trusted him with my hopes and expectations. Now I was experiencing the painful realization that real trust only comes with real knowledge of someone else. The truth was, beneath all the excitement and romantic backdrops, we were two people who really didn't know each other very well at all.

When Dom was not immersed in his music, he was reading science books, books rooted in complex physics, about string theory, time, and the universe. It didn't occur to me to question his motives, to wonder if his interests were an avoidance strategy. Perhaps another woman might have, but I did not. I understood all too well about having a vibrant, satisfying inner life that complemented the outer one. It was a place of refuge, too. When I was reading and writing, I was in that exhilarating place where the life of the imagination is more real than the tiles and soil and rock under my feet.

If we shared that, I reasoned, surely it was a mark of our compatibility. If he didn't seem to want to see other people, well, to be frank, neither did I—not all the time, anyway. I was reveling in the freedom to think and research and experiment.

So I put my faith in the hundreds of everyday details that showed we loved each other, not the great, showy speeches and excesses that had marked the beginning of our story, but the subtle gestures and kindnesses: the smiling eyes and plans, the soft, silent kisses as we passed, the pieces of music composed in my name, the rolling conversation and exchanged understanding over cups of tea, and wine, and the food we cooked together, his endless generosities, the way he touched me.

**There was** balance in the relationship when we were both occupied with our own interests, so I followed up Sabine's suggestion and visited the public library in Apt to research Marthe Lincel. The idea of blindness and scent was a compelling one.

"I finally went blind when I was thirteen years old, and it was the loss of my sight that took me to places I might never have seen."

These are the first words of Marthe Lincel's own memoir of her life as a perfume creator, published in Paris in the early 1960s.

"In the village, they said our family was cursed, and that my blindness was this generation's manifestation of it. I never thought that. We were caught in a cruel vise between past and future, ground by the wheels of progress, no different from any other family, perhaps with a little less luck than some."

She, or rather her ghostwriter, describes the journey she made at eleven years old: from the farmstead in the Luberon valley to the lavender road that winds eastward up through the hills to Manosque. It would lead her to Paris, where by the 1950s, at the age of thirty, she would have a shop in the Place Vendôme and fame in her chosen career.

"Would that be considered a curse?" she asks.

To the east of Manosque is the Valensole plateau, nursery of the lavender industry. *Vallis* and *solis*—the Latin for "valley" and "sun." It was here Marthe Lincel learned the craft that would make her the highest-regarded perfumer of her generation. Her talent for blending scents was so prodigious that each one was a story, a sensuous journey that developed on the skin for up to ten hours.

Photographs show a self-contained young woman with dark hair, fine-boned and attractive. From the photographs, perhaps carefully composed, her blindness is impossible to discern. There are no photographs of her after the age of forty.

Her family, the Lincels, lived at Les Genévriers for as long as anyone could remember. The years were marked by vintages of walnut wine and olive oil, each one a variation of the *terroir*, the land that produced it, a reflection of its soil and gradient, height and angle to the sun, that year's temperature fluctuations and winter rainfall. In vaulted stone caverns under the main house and courtyard, where barrels creaked and cobwebs laced the ranks of bottles, their labels were the only written history.

When Marthe created her signature scent, Lavande de Nuit, like the winemakers and the olive farmers she bottled the past. Then she walked away.

She left Paris at the height of her success and disappeared without a trace.

# 9

Work in the lavender fields was hard but not unbearable. I was well used to bending and cutting and picking, and the man in the waistcoat was a fair master. He did not tolerate idleness but made sure we had iced water to slake the terrible thirsts that seized our throats after a few hours in the dry, perfumed dust under a fierce sun. His name was Auguste, I learned, and he was the son of the farmer who had brought most of the new lavandin to this plateau. He had negotiated a lucrative contract with the scent distillery.

So, all in all, despite the physical aches, I was not at all unhappy. The change of scene, the new vistas, new mountains and lines of the horizon were all an adventure, one that helped to blot out the terrible stories we heard of executions and Nazi atrocities from Paris and the rest of the Occupied Zone in the north.

**Sometimes, when** work was done, I took myself off for slow ambles in the lanes around the fields. My eye was drawn to a corner where a neighboring field of sunflowers had tossed up golden heads in sumptuous contrast to the palette of blues. The bands of yellow ochre sang with stinging clarity between ropes of indigo on the tilting fields.

In other areas, where lavender rose upon lavender in a hundred shades of mauve, twilight brought a deep, unreal violet to the plateau. One evening in late July, I watched, transfixed, as the undulations merged into a mysterious landscape where no boundaries were definable between flower and sky, between falling shadow and the darkening blue. For an hour or more, perspective ceased to exist.

I stared into the secret openings and whorls of flowers, then up into the vast new views, making sketches to help myself focus on the detail, always trying to find the right words to describe them. I was beginning to understand now what my sister had been saying, with the envelopes containing petals.

Then, just as I hurried away in what was left of the light, a black shadow lengthened under a solitary olive tree in the middle of the field and detached itself. It set a course in my direction. Unsure what to do, and feeling that to stand still might be taken for an admission of guilt in the course of some misdemeanor, I put my head down and continued on the path.

It was not until the man's footsteps crunched hard by my own that I looked around, although I did not stop. It was Auguste.

"You're a quiet one," he said, coming straight to the point.

This came as a shock, for I had been making a great effort to be sociable, and indeed had spoken to more strangers in the past weeks than I had in the whole year previous.

"Where have you been this time, all by yourself?"

"Just . . . walking," I said.

He nodded. He had a grave manner.

"This . . . this place with so many purple fields . . . I've never seen anything like it." I was stumbling on, with my mouth as well as my feet. "It's so beautiful."

He asked me where I came from, and told me he had heard of it. He might have been being polite.

"I had you down as a clever one, who thought she could wangle a beater's job at the still by seeming to express an interest," he said.

It's true that with a table set up for the job, separating the flowers from the stalks meant less backbreaking bending, but then again, it was only fair that the older, frailer women had that privilege.

"No, I wasn't."

Another grave nod.

"There was a reason but it wasn't that."

And I told him about Marthe as we walked, side by side, through the cicadas' deafening evensong, back to the farm. All around, a scented veil blurred the rows of lavender and the coming night.

# 10

I did call Sabine.

She asked me what I'd been doing, and seemed so delighted I'd taken up her suggestion, so warm and friendly, that I immediately accepted her invitation for a day out. I told Dom, and he made no comment.

A few days later, she drove by to pick me up and we set off east on the road to Digne and Sisteron. When she'd told me our destination, it seemed it simply couldn't have worked out better: Manosque, the town where Marthe Lincel had learned her craft.

A route sign indicated that we were heading into the Alps of Haute-Provence. The road swooped in and out of plane tree avenues. By early summer, they would form green tunnels under a high canopy of leaves, a reminder of the old rural France.

"They are gradually being uprooted due to the dangers they are said to present," said Sabine. At the wheel, she was assured and purposeful. "Too many accidents caused by wide modern trucks; drivers plowing head-on into the thick trunks; drunks at the wheel veering off course and crashing into a wall of wood, hard as iron. They say the flickering light between them triggers headaches and even epileptic fits." She exhaled an expression of exasperated disbelief.

I agreed that the dappled arches over bright country roads were a symbol of an older, slower time.

"Two-hundred-year-old trees they are destroying! If you hit a tree, it is the tree's fault?" she demanded, smoothly passing the car ahead of us.

She was interesting, charming, and helpful. Part of me thought that I could come to relish her friendship, if indeed that was what was on offer; and part of me was wary. Given how eager she was to discuss Rachel, she was using me for information every bit as much as I was using her. As things stood, the balance between us was just about even.

From a distance, this time of year, the lavender fields were dull brown corduroy. But in the background, the Montagne de Lure floated above forests, and behind that, the peaks to the north stood vast and wide, still capped with snow.

The sunny day was cold as steel. Pink and orange tiled roofs were outcrops of illusory warmth under the blue vault of the sky. Half-forgotten hamlets in rolling hills, the last shudders from the formation of the Alps. I had been reading Giono, immersing myself in his otherworldly stories of harsh existence on these uplands, the vastness of the lonely country and the subtlety of the barely perceptible difference between success and failure.

A little way out of town, the Musset perfume factory was a modern plant, short on romance, too. A few token oleanders and tubs of lavender softened the entrance and the parking lot. "A very long time since the days of Mme. Lincel of Les Genévriers," said Sabine.

"But look," I said. A map in relief pointed the way to a library of scents in the grounds, and a closer look revealed that tags on the plants were in Braille.

"You know, a lot of people assumed she came back to the village when she left Paris," said Sabine, as if she hadn't heard. "But if she did, she didn't stay long. She cut herself off, just like that. No one knows where she went."

We took the tour, but I felt curiously disengaged.

Sabine was right. If we had been hoping to find the spirit of Marthe Lincel, it had long since evaporated, along with the scents she had conjured and captured in glass.

**We drove** back to the outskirts of Manosque, past billboards advertising the local supermarket, roadside fruit stalls, garages, and building-supplies stores. Sabine parked with skill in a space I would have sworn was too small, and we walked through a medieval arch and tower into the center of the teardrop-shaped town. The narrow streets of its heart were restricted to pedestrians, and there was a bustle about it just before the shops closed at twelve thirty.

Sabine suggested lunch, but neither of us felt much like eating. Instead we wandered past weathered stone doorways and out into a sunlit square lined by the familiar flat buildings of the south, ochre-plastered and shuttered, which rose above the tree line. Here and there were tall palms, and umbrellas were appearing over café tables. Many of the shops and restaurants were Moroccan. Pungent *tagine* spices overpowered more delicate scents. A horsemeat butcher had closed down; flyers on its grimy window announced a meeting of the Jeunes Communistes. African women offered to braid our hair, and in dark doorsteps, their men sat wearing mismatched clothes of clashing patterns, watching mutely as we passed.

In another square, secondhand books were piled on tables, the dealers watching from inside their shops. On a stone bench outside a chapel, in a sheltered corner, we sat and let the sun's rays warm our faces for the first time that day. I closed my eyes and felt the red pulse of the heat.

Sabine caught me off guard. "So tell me what really happened to Rachel," she said.

"What?"

"Rachel. I really would like to know."

Even to my own ears, my voice sounded unnaturally high and grating. "But I have no idea!"

Sabine didn't respond but fixed me with an unsettling, penetrating stare. It reminded me of our first lunch.

"I wish I did know," I said. I could feel a deep flush spreading up my neck.

"They were happy together," said Sabine. The fierce way it came out was nothing less than an accusation.

"She was long gone when I met Dom. Nothing to do with me, I can assure you."

Another long appraisal, which I sat through with discomfort. "You see, when I last saw her, she and Dom were talking of coming to live here, of slowing down a bit. She was going to do some work with me. And she had just had it confirmed that she was pregnant. She—they—couldn't have been happier about that."

I had to look away then.

Sabine spared me having to respond by going on: "So what happened after that?"

I thought of Dom on the ski slopes, his head in his hands. The way he withdrew from me at Les Genévriers. The sad, sad melodies that floated up from his music room. All the months I had known that something wasn't right. I'd thought that it was my fault, but I was wrong.

"Are they divorced now?" asked Sabine.

It was a very direct question. A good one, too.

"Yes," I said dully.

At least I had always assumed they were divorced. When I'd asked him right at the start, he told me he wasn't married, but that he had been. He didn't say he was separated, there were no tussles with the ex-wife, no communication that I knew of, so I took that to mean that they were already divorced. Now—well, suddenly I wasn't so sure.

"You said . . . did she have the baby?"

"That I don't know."

The fact that I obviously didn't know either whether they had had a baby together hung unspoken in the air between us.

Surely, surely Dom would have told me if they'd had a child.

"There's no child," I said, to myself as much as her. Then, more certainly, "Dom doesn't have a child. If he did, he would see it, be a father even if he and Rachel were no longer together."

Sabine's expression was impassive.

"And sometimes . . . the happiness or otherwise of other people's relationships is difficult to ascertain, even when they seem happy enough on the surface."

"Perhaps," said Sabine.

A pause, before she asked, a little slyly, "Are you happy with him?"

"Of course I am," I said.

What I should have said was, "Why do you ask?"

After that, we didn't linger in Manosque. We walked briskly through slightly down-at-the-heels streets back to where the car was parked. I didn't even look out, as I'd intended, for the plaque on the wall marking the house where the town's most famous son, Jean Giono, was born. By then, all I wanted was to be alone with my thoughts.

**Sabine dropped** me off on the road above Les Genévriers, and I walked down, feeling guilty and evasive. I let myself in by the kitchen door, trying to compose my expression to greet Dom. But subterfuge was unnecessary. He wheeled around from the sink where he was scrubbing his forearms.

"Dom, your face!"

I was taken aback by the sight of him. His cheekbones were badly scratched, as were his arms and hands. The water in the sink was tinged red.

"It's nothing."

"What on earth—? There's blood everywhere!"

"I was walking—caught my foot and fell."

"Walking where?"

"Does it matter?"

I stared.

"Over by Castellet. Too many rocks and thornbushes."

"Let me help you," I said, coming closer.

He pulled away from me, splashing bloodied water. "I told you. It's nothing. Don't make a fuss."

"But Dom—!"

"Just go away, and leave me to it!"

I ran upstairs. A door slammed behind me, accidentally, but I was glad. Shaking, I slumped down on my side of our bed. A nasty surge of suspicion took hold: was he telling me the truth? His response had been clear: back off or risk the consequences of one of his abrupt mood swings.

Minutes passed with no sound from below. Then the quiet was shattered by a loud blast of Oasis from the CD player. Did that mean his temper was worse, or that the outburst was over? Already I was reminding myself that I knew the way he walked: fast, carelessly sure of himself, hardly looking where he was if his mind was elsewhere. I could picture just how it had happened. I was making a drama out of nothing. I was the one who was on edge and feeling guilty about spending time with Sabine, asking questions behind his back.

It was no good. I still couldn't shake the feeling that something wasn't right, that there was more to it than that. You can't put fears away until you know they are unfounded, and this persistent anxiety was a mark of how my trust in him—and in myself, for that matter—had been eroded. I wanted so much for him to be the person I believed he was, but now I doubted my own judgment. What if Dom . . .

I stopped myself. This was ridiculous! I was being silly and childishly dependent, constructing a melodrama from my anxiety that Dom was drifting away from me. A few deep breaths, and I went back downstairs determined to act as if nothing had happened.

# 11

The next day in the fields, during our break for water, I asked the others how they would describe the blues we could all see. It was a case of trying out the words to convey to Marthe the startling beauty all around.

"Blue like the stripe in the rainbow," said Aurélie.

"No, more purple," said Mariette.

"Not that dark."

"A mauve, then. Don't forget the green and grays underneath, and the chalky pink and brown stones in the soil between the lines."

"A color that hesitates between blue and purple," Auguste cut in. He did not usually join in our conversations. I found I liked his phrase very much.

We pulled our aprons straight and adjusted whatever arrangements we had made to keep our hair off our hot faces. A dragonfly swooped on its hunt for other insects, leading the way back to the rows we had been working.

As I was turning to go, Auguste pulled me aside. "Come and beat the flowers," he said.

"Me?"

"You."

"Certainly," I said, pleased at the prospect.

"This way, then."

As I went to follow, I hesitated. "Perhaps . . . it should be Aurélie . . . she was in pain last night."

But Auguste did not even pause. "Don't think that it isn't tough work," he said, striding out.

The water in the still was bubbling merrily. At the table, one of the much-older women, known to us simply, namelessly, as Madame, was thrashing the head of a sheath against a box to break off and collect the flowers. Then, with one deft sifting motion, she showered the ground with any remaining remnants of stalk and leaf, and an even more intense cloud of lavender scent exploded into the warm air.

"You tip what's left here." Auguste pointed to a line of boxes where the flower heads lay packed like grain. "Make sure you are thorough and careful. We want the best yield possible."

Next to the alembic was a copper cylinder, fed by a pipe that looped up from the top of the still in a swan's-neck shape and then down into this smaller mechanism for the next part of this mysterious process.

"This is the cooling chamber," explained Auguste. "Once the steam has risen through the lavender flowers it is pushed up through the pipe that comes out of the top, and then down through the cylinder here."

"How does it cool?"

"Cold water. The cylinder is full of cold water and the coils spiral round and round inside. At the end of the process—here"—he touched a neat, narrow spout—"the liquid contains the essence of the flower, its oil and scent."

The other woman had stopped work, with an odd look at him and then at me.

"You never told me that," she said.

"You don't have a blind sister," replied Auguste. It was a brusque explanation that left her none the wiser, judging from her face.

As soon as we were alone, he asked me if I would like to go out with him one evening.

We went the very next day. Flames licked the belly of the alembic still as we left the fields. Burning wood and resin released gusts of molten sugar and toffee.

It was the first time I had been into the town of Manosque at night. I was excited. As we approached on foot, we were dwarfed by the height of the stone buildings that rose steadily on the mound where the town had grown in ancient times. The center was mazelike, the plaster of the tall tenements elaborately veined with long creases, here and there chalked or scratched with stones with V for victory. Half-curious, half-unsure whether I should be there at all, I let Auguste lead me farther into its heart.

The traveling cinema was set up in a tree-lined square. Wooden chairs stood in rows in front of a number of tables placed on their sides and covered with a couple of white bedsheets nailed tightly across.

"That's where the show will be projected, from a machine at the end of the aisle," said Auguste.

He bought me some lemonade and steered me to a seat near the back. "You don't want to be too close. It's bad for your eyes."

Soon, night was a black tent over the proceedings. The audience took their seats, and those who were unlucky sat on the rim of the stone fountain, or brought up the municipal benches, or begged chairs from the surrounding houses. Candle lanterns and oil lamps were lit, and the reek of paraffin mingled with the sweat of farmworkers, homemade potions of rosewater, the ubiquitous sweet violet warmed on the skin of women and girls, cigarettes on the men, and garlic from all.

Excited chatter and shouting all around. Soldiers in French uniform, watching us uneasily. On my tongue, the sharpness of lemonade.

The movie began. It was *Angèle*, based on a Giono story but made jollier by Pagnol, who seemed to make all the movies I ever saw as a young person. The actor Fernandel was soon pulling his long, elastic face with its horsey teeth into expressions of disbelief and mock-horror, and the audience rocked with laughter.

The plot involved the young daughter of a farmer, who runs away from home to follow a handsome young ne'er-do-well. I leaned between the heads of the people in front of me, and tried to concentrate. It wasn't easy.

There was the pressure on my left leg from Auguste's hand to contend with, at first. Then, as I leaned forward to get a better view, there was his arm snaking around my waist, and the nearness of his damp armpit. Then he was stroking my arm, and whispering into my ear. When he tried to kiss me, I pushed him away. That wasn't what I had agreed to. I enjoyed talking to him, that was all.

One section of the screen started to pull away from its pins so that the actors now billowed and deflated as they played out the terrible warning of what happened to Angèle when she succumbed to the advances of an opportunistic young buck.

Afterward, we walked back to the farm a long arm's-width apart and in silence.

**In the** lilac satin of early mist over the fields the next morning, he looked tired and hardly glanced in my direction. He gave some other girl a turn at the still after that, but I wasn't too bothered, as I'd gotten what I needed by then.

# 12

At one of the regular *brocante* markets one week-end, Dom stopped at a collection of old scientific instruments set out on a mat on the ground: micro-scopes, mechanical measuring devices, barometers, medical implements, and music boxes. Picking up an unfamiliar-looking item, he examined it closely. It was made of black metal, rather battered, the size and shape of a round cake pan in an upright spindle.

"What is it?"

"An instrument of optical illusion," he said, set-ting it to spin, which it did with a wobble. "I've always wanted to find one of these. It's a zoetrope."

He pulled off the lid and showed me. It was just pos-sible to see the faint script on it: LES IMAGES VIVANTES. Then he held it up. "See these narrow slits in the drum.

You have to look through one of them at the images on the opposite wall inside."

When it was spun, the images appeared to move, on the same principle as the simple moving cartoons produced by flipping pages of a notebook: a portly policeman chasing a child thief, and another of a ballerina.

"It's mid-Victorian, I should think—1870s or 80s. It really was the beginning of moving pictures, the step before finding how to project the images. As stories go, they weren't long—just a simple action, really."

"And a bit repetitive."

He smiled. "Now we just have to find the picture strips to put in it."

Putting the lid back on, he took it over to the stall-holder and began to haggle.

He returned triumphant, the zoetrope carefully cradled under one arm. He tucked the other around my waist and we went off, happily discussing where we might be lucky and find some more pictures to go inside. This was a good day. Anything might happen.

**He placed** the zoetrope on a table in the upstairs sitting room next to the shelves that held all our books. I looked up zoetrope in a dictionary (it was the same in English and French): from the Greek zoe ("to live") and *tropo* ("to turn"). The wheel of life, in other words.

To the accompaniment of Satie's piano pieces on the CD player—the *Gnossiennes* and the *Gymnopédies*, the *Pièces Froides*, softly overblown and melancholic— he began reading a book called *Eyes, Lies and Illusions*, then left it open, facedown next to the zoetrope. When he left the room, I picked it up; I wanted to know what was in his mind. The book was full of the art of deception and how it triumphed; tricks of the light and the inner eye.

We never did find any more picture strips to fit the zoetrope, though, for my part, I can't say that I tried very hard.

**That afternoon,** as I left him in the kitchen and went upstairs to the library room, a light switched itself on. One moment, I was on the twilit stairs, carrying a notebook in one hand and a cup of tea in the other, and the next, the room ahead of me was flooded with brightness.

I stopped and listened. No sound.

Moving to the threshold of the room, I saw that it was not an electric bulb but a burst of western sun hitting the bull's-eye window that had filled the space with a searing, concentrated light. Just as though the light had switched itself on.

On the table, the dull, blackened metal of the zoetrope caught a gleam.

I tried opening a book I'd bought, on the history of the lavender industry, hoping to gain some insight into the background to Marthe Lincel's work, but my thoughts were elsewhere. The rows of books seemed to mock my efforts, my vanity in even attempting. The notes about the perfume distillery hastily scribbled on paper after I got back from Manosque seemed slight and irrelevant. I wanted to write but could not find a way of proceeding that did not draw on the personal.

Anything but the story of the husband who makes a mystery of his first wife. Nor the composer who will not play the music his first wife loved. The wife who disappeared. The Bluebeard legend: the man who tells his new wife she may have the keys to his castle, she may open every door except one; the door she does indeed open to find the floor awash with blood and the bodies of his former wives hung from meat-hooks around the walls.

Unsettled, I turned to the pictures in a book of old Provençal photographs. My head began to hurt as I tried to concentrate on the grainy images, to see through them to re-create the surroundings of a girl who once grew up here, among the biting insects and hungry wasps, darting brown lizards, the grass drying to straw while still growing on the hillside. The complex visual patterns of field and hill overlaid with mosaics of uneven tiles, stones, brickwork, all expressed in black and white, light and shade.

It was no good. The pictures I wanted to see were of Rachel. Rachel and Dom.

One afternoon, when he was out, I had a thorough look through the house, in out-of-the-way drawers and cabinets, in all the places where boxes were stored, searching for an album, or an envelope, even—anything that contained a link to Dom's past, but there was nothing.

From my weakness, the doubts that kept returning to my state of not knowing, Rachel was like a ghost materializing. And with her strange presence came that scent, romantic and cruelly mocking, that drifted lightly from room to room, though the courtyard flowers had all died back. There seemed no possible source other than my own overwrought imagination.

**One night,** the lights flickered, then died. An outage. It was the first of many that winter, as it turned out, for which we became prepared.

The first time, there was no flashlight ready by the side of the bed, or on the table in the library where I had been sitting. Slowly, I edged down the staircase, feeling with my feet for the bends in the steps, and with my hands for the unstable balustrade. I called again, but Dom did not answer.

Down in the kitchen, a feeble light came through the glass of the back door, and I groped my way toward it. All was silent. Then came a noise like hail on the unshuttered window. Hail, or the ringing splatter of stones being thrown.

I stopped and listened, feeling my heart beating faster.

Nothing more.

"Dom?"

No answer. Gingerly, I opened the door. A half-moon was enough to make the outside brighter than the inside, enough to find my way to the garage where I knew there was a flashlight.

On the path to the garage, I stopped. There was someone in the garden.

I called out, but there was no answer, so I changed direction for a few paces and went toward it. I seemed to be in the person's line of sight, but they had stopped moving. Then I stopped, shaking my head at myself. It was the statue of the Greek boy on the lawn. In the half-light, he seemed less solid; his lichen-stained skirt flicked up around his thighs as if caught by a playful gust of air; his petrified gesture of anguish was all too real.

Get a grip.

I made for the garage ahead. My feet were soundless on the grass.

But, again, there was a movement at the periphery of my vision. A light, this time. A glimmer of light that was moving slowly up the path, swinging slightly as if held by a night watchman. It came from the direction of the wild orchard, a patch of yellow brightness, like the glow from a hurricane lamp.

As I waited, shivering, it seemed to wait, too, suspended in the black air. Too low for a star, too near to be light from the hamlet on the facing hills across the valley.

Then the light dimmed.

By the time I had opened the car door, found the flashlight, and locked up again, the land was almost totally dark. A cloud covering the moon, perhaps. I waited expectantly for footsteps to come up the path, but none came.

I switched on the flashlight and was astonished to see that, by my watch, it was past midnight. I headed back to the house, still calling for Dom. I found him on the sofa in the music room, fast asleep.

**In the** next morning's milky daylight, a tarnished, old-fashioned lantern sat in the middle of the track. It was the one with the curlicue top we had found with a mountain of rubbish in the corner of the courtyard when we had cleared all the overgrown bushes. We'd kept it and used it in the summer.

Someone must have taken it. It had been deliberately placed on the path, it must have been. Had Dom done it? Could the light I thought I had seen be connected with this battered old thing?

I picked it up and brought it back. The candle had burned down completely. There wouldn't have been much left anyway, there never was when we blew it out at the end of a long summer's night.

When I asked him, Dom knew nothing about it. He seemed to think I might have dreamed the whole thing.

# 13

When the harvest was in, I took a job at the factory, helping to make the soaps and weak perfumes and potions.

Beyond the use of lavender in perfumery, there was hardly an ailment that the plant would not cure, it seemed. Of course, I knew that Maman made lavender infusions for nervous emergencies, and that Old Marcel rubbed it on his dog's paws if they became cut and infected. But it was news to me that it was also considered to have properties capable of healing everything from asthma to fever, fainting to stomach disorders, headaches to rheumatisms. That, and its widespread use as a cheap antiseptic in hospitals, was the reason the fields were still in production.

The factory at the foot of Manosque made a particularly potent brew that would stop an epidemic of influenza in its tracks, according to Mme. Musset, the wife of the owner. She was also the potions manager. That was her official title, and it suited her, this small, bony woman with a prominent nose; there was a touch of one of those elderly women in fairy tales about her, both good witch and bad witch. Certainly she turned out to be Marthe's fairy godmother.

Due to her fondness for Marthe, and her desire to nurture my sister's talent in every way possible, Madame was very kind to me. She gave me a personal demonstration of how the influenza cure was made. A liter of water was boiled, to which was added a whole fifty grams of flowers, left to infuse for several hours. When required, it was to be reheated, and the sufferer made to drink it all. They would sweat profusely, and have to run for the privy, but it was deemed to have an impressive effect on the system.

"They say Napoleon got through sixty bottles of lavender essence a month," said Mme. Musset happily. "He even drank it before rising from his campaign bed and appearing on the battlefield! I must say I have my suspicions about the level of preserving alcohol in that consumption, though."

More conventionally, the Musset factory followed a traditional recipe for lavender aperitif by marinating lavender flowers in white wine. After a week, we filtered it and added sugar and honey, then it was bottled.

I found it a strange taste. "It needs to be served very cold," explained Madame. "For myself I prefer the emerald." She made an unnerving sip-sip noise through teeth yellow as pumpkin seeds.

The emerald liqueur hardly involved lavender at all, just a few flowers, as the marinade was predominantly herbal: angelica, sage, rosemary, bay, rue, absinthe, and thyme. It also called for a liter of ninety-degree-proof alcohol, which gave it a stronger kick, and, once sweetened, was quite delicious, though advisable only in extremely small doses.

Madame showed me how to make a powder to perfume the house by taking lavender flowers, thyme flowers, and mint leaves, and letting them dry, then adding several cloves and pulverizing them before leaving out in open bowls.

After the war, all these products, decanted into pretty bottles and jars, were sold from stalls at all the markets of Provence, along with biscuits studded with dried lavender buds, and rose-petal meringues. When I was there, that would have been an unspeakable indulgence.

Every evening, I would return to the room nearby where Marthe lodged (and I was sleeping on a camp bed), and relate to her the minute details of everything I'd seen.

**14**

I tried to imagine what it would be like to see the world only in scent and sound and touch. To understand without ever being able to see the way the hills swelled up to the sky in sea-green waves, or the contrast of the time shadow on the crumbling sundial, or the geometric patchwork of the aromatic fields. To smell the pungent herds of goats blocking the narrow lanes, and the yellow banks of wild broom at the edges but not experience the myriad colors, or the cloud patterns sweeping over the empty flatness of undulating fields. To be able to combine scents but not to know the exact hue of the eau de cologne in the glass bottles.

"Have you found a project?" Dom asked one evening as I sat scribbling.

252 · DEBORAH LAWRENSON

"Not so much a translation project as trying out an idea, but I think I could be onto something."

"What's that?"

"I've been following up a story I was told about a girl who was born here at Les Genévriers in the 1920s. It's fascinating, quite a mystery. Her name was Marthe Lincel. She began to go blind when she was only five years old, but she developed a prodigious sense of smell."

He was silent.

"That's how it all began, with the flowers and the patches of lavender right here. By the time she went to the perfume factory for the first time, she could already distinguish between the different types of lavender and sometimes even the slopes where they were grown, what angle they were to the sun. She became a renowned *parfumeuse*, a creator of scents—in Manosque. I've been there already, but I want to go again—will you come with me?"

Disconcertingly, the question was met by an expression of bewilderment that quickly turned to blankness.

"If you're not interested I'll go on my own. It's not a problem."

No response.

"Dom?"

"Why are you doing this?" he asked, barely controlling the anger in his voice.

"What?"

"You heard. Why did you choose this?"

"Well, I—" I was about to say that Sabine had told me, to admit that I had gone to Manosque with her, but Dom had closed his eyes as if he was steeling himself for the worst. He was rigid with tension.

"Dom, it's only a— There's nothing to react like this about—"

He opened his mouth, then clearly changed his mind.

"What?" I persisted.

"Oh . . . forget it. You know what, I really don't want to know."

"Dom, what is it? What did I say?"

He turned and went out of the room. Hours later, when I had heard nothing, not a note of music, not even a movement throughout the rest of the house, I poured two glasses of red wine and followed. I found him at his piano, head in his hands, elbows on the keys. The solidity of his despair stopped me in my tracks.

On the threshold of the room, I quietly turned back.

# 15

Marthe and I went home together at Toussaint, the first of November.

While the men were out hunting, and Maman and I plucked and butchered and stewed whatever game they had shot or caught in snares, Marthe sat by the hearth and listened. She had so many questions, wanted to know so much.

I did my best to find the words to reanimate the pictures imprinted in my memory, struggling to stitch bright patches of summer over the fallen leaves and the sound of cold against the windows.

Even the scents—especially the scents—were fleeting, hard to pin them down in words. The way the resinous fire beneath the alembic still candied the soft summer nights. The warm human odor as the audience squeezed together in front of the cloth cinema screen in the town square. The smell of a man pulling you toward the mysterious underside of his chin in darkness lit by flickering black-and-white pictures, I kept to myself.

I was not Marthe, with her extraordinary concentration and attention to detail, but through her, I was becoming ever more alert to the sensuous power of smell. They say that the loss of one of the senses makes the others more acute. I'd go further: it makes the senses of the people around them grow more intense, too. Not only was I smelling in the way she taught me, but I was seeing, really seeing, details on her behalf that I might never have noticed otherwise.

Like an atmosphere, like a taste, it is felt and experienced, and then it is gone. You can't record it like music or conversation or a picture. You have to smell it again, and remember.

**Marthe's masterwork,** the perfume that made her name, was based on heliotrope and lavender.

I often wondered, later, whether the perfume she created was the tangible form of her memories of the farm, an idealized version of her childhood, or perhaps even a hymn of praise and thanks for what we once had. The times we'd immersed ourselves in the flowers on the bank by the barn where the walnut wine was made, and watched, or seemed to watch, the purple blooms turning to the hours of the day.

When I smelled that perfume, I was drawn back helplessly into a sunlit world of Maman's flaky almond biscuits with their hint of bitter apricot kernel, earth like cocoa powder clinging to our bare legs, light, warm winds sifting sugared scents from the kitchen where the orange mirabelles were being bottled; and on, far beyond the aromatic, to the distant sound of the goat bells, and the whispering of the trees, the butterflies on meadow flowers and the scrubby spikiness of the land underfoot as we chased them, the taste of dried cherries sucked from their pits and of the honeyed nut wine; the soft, guttered candles waiting on the table in the courtyard where we dined at night, cool at last, a floury embrace before bedtime: all the fragrances in one, of the four months of the year when we all lived outside in the immense wide-open valley, a season of warmth and enchantment, safe from all horrors, or so we thought.

# 16

I gave it until around seven o'clock. Then, aware that I should not leave him to his private mood too long, I ran noisily down the steps into the courtyard and into the music room to ask if he wanted a drink and what he'd like for supper.

Dom was not there.

Setting off into the garden, I called his name. There was no response, but I assumed that meant that he was up in the woods, or wandering in the orchard.

I turned back toward the main house. The sky above was a tumbled bed of dark clouds; lights blazed on the top floor. I went back inside and called his name as I climbed the stairs to the bathroom. But he was not there, nor in the library.

Still unconcerned, I opened a good bottle of wine to let it breathe, studied the contents of the fridge, and began to cook, expecting him to push the back door open at any moment.

An hour later, it was completely dark. He wouldn't still have been wandering the land. Not knowing what else to do, I called his cell. It went straight to voicemail. I tried again, once in the house and once down in the music room, but there was no corresponding ringtone in either place.

He was not there. Neither was his phone. And neither, when I ran to the garage with my heart beating wildly, was the car. How could that be? I had not heard it go. I was sure I hadn't.

I spun around, perplexed. My flesh puckered into goose bumps as I wondered who had switched on the lights in the upper rooms.

**The hands** on the clock slowly ground out the night hours. Familiar night noises, the ticking of tiles as the temperature changed and small animals scurried took on a new menace. Every sound was a threat.

Where was he? Had something happened to him—an accident? Why had he gone out without saying a word? I sat in the kitchen, then went upstairs and lay awake asking the same questions over and over until they gave way to others I had long avoided: What was I doing here? How well did I really know him?

Then, at about two o'clock, I thought I heard the sound of a car. I rushed up to the open window, heard nothing more, and so went out onto the terrace.

A faint light flared.

"Dom?"

Silence.

I leaned over the terrace wall. Vines scratched my bare legs as I pushed myself as far out as I dared. The light was there all right: it was quite a way down the path. I squinted, trying to make it out. Was it moving? Could it be Dom holding a flashlight? Then I started to tremble.

It was moving closer. It seemed to be—it was—the glow of a lantern. The same pattern, the same yellow dance of a guttering flame inside the metalwork frame as it moved up the path. Who was holding it? I blinked, wondering if this could be some kind of a dream.

I couldn't make out anything else, but the lamp was still there. I watched it until the light vanished, just as before. Now I was spooked.

All was dark again. I went back into the bedroom, still shivering. Minutes later, I thought I saw him, or someone, behind me reflected in the mirror over the dressing table. The shudder down my back was like a convulsion. It seemed to push me with a cold, cold hand.

I shut my eyes. When I summoned the courage to look again, there was nothing. It must have been a trick of the light.

"Dom?" I called out again, heart hammering.

No answer.

**In the** empty bed, with no comforting arms, no warm breath, the night was an expanse of space, an absence.

A faint breeze puffed through the window, bringing a delicate vaporization of the mysterious scent whose source I had still not located.

Had I relied on him too much, and fallen into the trap of thinking that my happiness depended on him? In my determination to convince myself otherwise, had I failed to understand what was really going on, that the relationship had reached the point where it could not be saved? That he was even now in the arms of some other woman, grown tired of me and my inexperience, my failure to give him what he was searching for?

It was impossible not to feel the hollowness of loss. For the first time in a long while, I had to admit it. I was lonely; I missed my family and friends.

I thought back to previous relationships, one in particular. How, when love had soured in a morass of lies and betrayals, I'd stayed for too long, believing nothing he said. No more of that, I'd promised myself. No more suspicions; no more questions and examining the answers for deceitful chinks; no more loss of trust and stomach-churning paranoia in the long reaches of the night. And now what was I doing but repeating the same pattern?

Perhaps this time, though, it was a different story. It was, as everywhere around us, a matter of perception. Like the zoetrope, each picture slightly alters the previous image to create the illusion of movement. But that's a hopeless analogy, because it's the same movement repeated endlessly, or until the spinning motion stops. Each act has an effect, a ripple that cascades into another.

# 17

The perfume was called Lavande de Nuit. Years after I helped make the potions in order to be able to describe every detail of the factory to Marthe, it was her blend of flowers and herbs that changed the fortunes of everyone concerned.

While the war dragged on, the frustrations of the Vichy years, when our so-called leaders and army never did turn against the oppressors as expected, the rise of the Resistance and through to the painful liberation of the country by the Allies, the Mussets and their employees kept their heads down. It was a solid provincial business, of use to all sides, and it continued to manufacture basic lines in antiseptic lavender water and soap. While others became heroes and traitors, Marthe, blind and considered no use to anyone, was quietly experimenting with scent combinations, not using expensive ingredients like ambergris or violet-leaf absolute, but those close to hand, from plants that grew freely all around, the familiar scents of her home.

When the war was over, she had a catalogue of creations made from practically nothing. For the next five years, the Musset factory put them into production and saw profits grow beyond all estimations.

It's no exaggeration to say that it was these years that transformed the lavender fields and steam factory distillery between Manosque and Valensole into the far more prestigious Parfumeur-Distillateur Musset, and Marthe Lincel into a creator of perfumes.

No longer were their products sold from market stalls, but in shops in Aix and Avignon and Marseille; then—the crowning glory—from the Musset *parfumerie* in the Place Vendôme in Paris, which opened in 1950 to herald the new decade.

**Occasionally, Marthe** would send me magazine and newspaper clippings. The photographs showed a slim, elegant woman with a beguiling expression. Often she would be posed in front of a counter full of scent bottles and their fashionable striped boxes, or sitting, wearing the latest look, in a chic sitting room. The photographer would never get too close; it was barely possible to discern in those pictures that the pretty, laughing eyes were empty.

Even more occasionally, the same envelopes would contain a leaf or pod or sliver of wood that allowed me to smell what she was working with, for old times' sake.

Over the years, I asked her for money now and then, toward the upkeep of the farm, and she was always generous. At first, she would send what she could from Paris, then more, as she became more successful. She had a good head for business, and without her ideas and help, the place would have gone under long before it did.

Of course, I never did leave or fulfill my ambition to train as a teacher. It was not to be. But I did complete my education, on my own, for my love of books never diminished. I loved Balzac and Zola, who could move me to tears, so I knew the harsh truth about society and thwarted dreams, and the resilience of the human spirit. I always made a point of reading modern authors, too, especially those who described the lives of young women in Paris.

If anyone had ever said to me there would come a day when Marthe and I would have nothing to say to each other, that she would become too grand for me, that she would forget all that we had ever been to each other, I would have cried out that they were wrong.

Marthe and I were part of each other. I shared my sight; she taught me to see with my other senses.

# 18

I still could not sleep.

The scent was growing stronger. I got up and ran around the room, stood at the open window and tried to identify, once and for all, where it was coming from. But it seemed to have no source. It surrounded me now. The more I concentrated on it, the more suffocating it became.

And just as before, for no reason, it made me think: Rachel.

In the absence of hard facts, the mind locks—taking pictures one after the other, putting them together, hoping to transform them into a coherent story.

Intense, driven, clever: that was what Sabine called her. But also humorous and confident. Frivolous, even. A girl who liked a party, but was equally a daring and determined woman. She sounded like someone it would be interesting to know. No. Not to know. To be.

She was clearly much more of an extrovert than I am, much more assured in social situations. Rachel was already a published writer, of course, while I was still only dreaming of that. But the writing and the thoughts behind it, the fascination with stories: we shared that. The way she phrased and described was uncannily close to the way I would have done.

Dom had loved her enough to marry her. What had happened to the happily ever after?

And what about money: Did Rachel take a chunk of Dom's wealth away with her? His generosity was unarguable. I had had to fight to be allowed to contribute to the running of the house; he would have paid for everything without a word of protest if I had let him. For my own pride, I was not about to let that happen. I did ask him once, right at the beginning, when we discussed living together, how he stood financially, and was vaguely shocked by how much he had. Not then or afterward did he ever complain, not a word, about handing over sizeable alimony payments; nothing like that had ever been mentioned.

No, Dom never told me anything that wasn't true. But it may have been the kind of truths that lawyers deal in. There are degrees of honesty. How much detail is the right amount? There is omission, and holding back and misleading statements. But there are confidences to honor, too. There are white lies that spare someone the hurt of too harsh a truth. And there is simple restraint: always thinking before you speak, and a precision in one's choice of vocabulary that can conceal a multitude of ambiguities.

This was what I was thinking, my mind clogged with suppositions and imaginary dead ends, as the scent grew still stronger. I was angry with Dom for disappearing without a word, hurt and nervous, too, at being on my own in this situation. I was aware that my breathing was fast and shallow, that I needed air.

I went back out onto the bedroom terrace. A three-quarter moon hung over the hamlet, dropping puddles of gray light over its domestic landmarks. Enough light to see that I was no longer alone.

Relief flooded through me, pushing aside anger. "Dom!" I called down at his shadow.

He did not reply. My anger reignited and I shouted again.

Still no response; no movement, either. Then—did a cloud move and the moonlight gleam brighter?—I saw that the figure was not Dom.

It was a woman standing below on the path. She was completely still in the dark, looking out to the hills, her back to me. I couldn't think what she was doing there, or who she was. Or why she was out in the middle of the night and chose to stop just there.

My first thought was to call down and demand an explanation, but though I opened my mouth, just as in dreams, nothing came out. As though my subconscious took over to pull me back from the brink, I stopped.

Whoever she was, she was an unlikely intruder. Hardly more than a silhouette, she simply stood there, small and fragile and utterly calm. Perhaps the barest ripple disturbed the fabric of her skirt, and brushed her hair back from her face, the face I still could not see.

Uncertain, I held back.

The world stilled. The temperature plummeted. Night noises faded, leaving absolute silence.

I lunged back into the room to find the flashlight. How stupid was I, to do nothing? I switched on the beam as I fumbled with the other hand for my phone. Then I edged back to my vantage place. I shone the light straight down at her.

She was gone. There was nothing there.

My body knew it before my mind. In the minutes that followed, as I pressed my back into the stones of the wall, heart pounding, a thought came into my head. It arrived with all the slippery discomfort of a recovered memory: on some primal level, I knew who she was. I had felt her presence, and now, fleetingly, I had seen her. She was one of the women of the house, one of the spirits.

I closed my eyes, feeling my skin tighten all over. There she was again, already stamped on my memory. It was the very ordinariness of the vision that was so chilling. As if nothing in the world could be relied on not to shift shape, as if this was the visceral knowledge we learn to suppress: that childhood terrors are all too real.

It was only then, as I sat trembling on the bed, fighting waves of panic and fury at Dom, that the scent gradually ebbed away.

## 19

It was a terrible spring that followed the winter Marthe went to Paris to make her fortune.

As late as March, the frosts lay like foam on the cherry, plum, and pear blossom, killing most of the fruit before it had even formed. There were very few branches that managed any yield that year. It rained so hard that the springwater overflowed the spring over several weeks and washed away the sloping field of lucerne below. The damp penetrated the sheepfold and the animals sickened. Too many lambs died. Our hopes of a good return at the market dwindled and died.

Our summer passed in a desperate race to compensate. We planted and gathered as many vegetables as the soil could throw up, and rushed to preserve as much as possible for another hard winter. No rot-blown plum or pepper was too soft or small or pocked to have the bad parts excised before being added to the pile for bottling. Our thumbs bled as the juices ran and the small fruits slipped under the knife. We sowed and nurtured pumpkin and squash. The hunting season began. The guns brought back thrush and blackbirds; now and then, a partridge.

The first low clouds of autumn came in like wisps of smoke across the mountains. The walnuts we had left to eat were dropping, quickly blackening, eaten inside out by earwigs. We harvested what we could, then the ladder came out and we snapped the crop from the trees, hustling to get them into the barn before more rain came. We worked as fast as we could, to the music of the changing winds, our hands stained yellow by releasing the nutshells from their pods.

After heavy rain, the wild tangle of green grapes and wisteria outside the windows dripped like a shower. The scent of fig mingled with wood smoke and warm, wet earth, and, for years after, was synonymous with despair.

**In the** midst of all this, Pierre left.

There were arguments in raised voices, and slammed doors, but Pierre was determined. He dressed his abandonment as an opportunity to take the best of all worlds, that he would return with money and still be able to work here when he could, but no one was fooled.

Then Old Marcel died, leaving two distraught dogs that howled all day and night for ten days.

Papa became dejected. Whatever suggestions Maman put forward were swept aside as worthless. We had never seen him like this, nor heard our parents arguing with such ferocity when they thought that we had gone to sleep.

Then, one evening, Arielle's father, Gaston Poidevin, came and told our parents that his family, too, would be leaving Les Genévriers. He had been researching the opportunities in the new industries for some time, he said, and it was with great regret that he had decided to reestablish his family at Cavaillon, down in the plain on the road to Marseille. "Treachery" was the word Papa used, rejecting his old friend and tenant's reasoned arguments.

"You realize you are making, at a stroke, our lives here twice as hard?"

I do not remember the response. There was nothing Poidevin could have said. If Papa hadn't been able to persuade his own son to stay, how could he succeed with anyone else?

Maman was as close to Marie Poidevin as I was to Arielle, and we cried for the loss of our friends, though without letting Papa see us. Tearfully, Arielle and I vowed everlasting friendship, no matter where we came to rest in the future.

For a few weeks after that, Papa tried hard to pull his spirits up. We had our backs to the wall, he admitted, but we would never be defeated, it was not in our bones to give in. We had our land, and, with hard toil, we would make it pay. We gave a cheer at that, and hugged one another. The arguments with Maman ceased, at least within our earshot.

As the months crept into winter, though, it became clear there was an artificial aspect to our spirited pride. Our father, exhausted and ashamed, took to the walnut liqueur.

Christmas was a muted affair. For the first time, neither Marthe nor Pierre returned. For the last time, we ate the traditional Thirteen Desserts with the Poidevin family, and Arielle and I placed the clay *santons*, the little saints, around the holy crèche in the hall. I added a new one, a lavender girl, to our battered collection of figures: the shepherd, the miller, the carpenter, the tambourine player, the dancer, the baker, the woman with a bundle of sticks.

A few evenings later, none too steady, Papa had been cleaning his hunting rifle. He could have put his cloths away, but instead he decided to go rummaging in one of the many shelves of the basement under the house.

He returned with the Prussian revolver that Pierre had once stolen. None of us knew he had kept it. But, somewhere, he had. Maman said that he decided to use the remaining oil on the cloth to give it a polish.

We told everyone it was a freak accident. Maybe it was. But maybe it wasn't. We all had different reasons for suspecting it was what he had wanted to do when he went and fetched that dangerous old gun from its hideaway—a gun that hadn't seen the light of day for years—a few days after that cold, strained Christmas when both Pierre and Marthe stayed away.

I was outside when I heard the shot. There was a glorious sunset in a red-and-violet mackerel sky, and I was watching intently as, for a few minutes, the distinct clouds were rimmed with scarlet light. A moment later, the light shimmered in shock and went black as the report rang out, so close by. All thought fractured in the second or so needed for surprise to turn to panic. Suddenly, all luminosity was extinguished, leaving a heavy, blue-black glower reaching up over the valley to the house.

# 20

The next morning, I was shaky from lack of sleep, still chasing logical explanations for the events of the night before.

It was one of those searing, blue days when everything seems painfully sharp. I was sitting on the steps down from the kitchen with a mug of strong coffee, feeling unearthly, as though I was suspended in liquid, when I heard the car pull up. A few minutes later, Dom came into the courtyard. He looked awful, as if he had not slept, either.

Holding back all the questions and accusations, wanting and not wanting him to know how scared I had been, desperately relieved he was back, yet furious he had left me, I stared at him dumbly.

He stopped at the bottom of the steps. "I'm sorry," he said. "I'm so sorry."

"Where the hell have you been?" I spat out the words.

Coming up toward me, he seemed older and more battered than I had ever seen him, with that air of vulnerability that confused me. His stained shirt hung slackly outside his jeans.

"Where? Just driving . . . then too many beers in the pub in Apt."

"And?"

"And nothing. A room in the hotel in the back square. Drunk, but not quite drunk enough to risk being stopped by the police and losing my license." He put his hands gently on my shoulders. I shrugged them off. Up close, every line on his face was vividly etched.

Even if he hadn't wanted to risk driving—and over that short distance, on deserted roads, most Frenchmen would have—I couldn't understand why he hadn't called a taxi to get himself home.

"I'm not sure I believe you."

"It's true. Stupid, but true."

"What was so bad, Dom?" So bad that you had to stay away.

"You'll think it's idiotic—"

"Tell me."

He looked away, up toward the roof. "It's . . . what you were writing about. The blind girl, Marthe."

"I know that, but—"

He shook his head wearily. "It's what she was doing. Rachel. Exactly what she was writing. Now do you understand?"

**That same** day, Fernand gave me a photograph of the Valensole lavender pickers in the 1930s. I'd asked him about the old times up there, and we'd had a lengthy conversation about times gone by. I was touched that he'd gone to the trouble, though, clearly, this was no longer a subject I would be able to write about.

The two men in the group picture took the dominant positions: one in the center of the front row, the other leaning on a pitchfork on the left flank. The women ranged in age from teenagers to grandmothers. Their checked dresses were utilitarian, most crossing over the chest and tied at the back. They wore aprons, too, and cotton scarves, which they knotted over their shoulders. In their arms, they cradled sheaves of lavender, like trophies. Faces dark, and eyes squinting against the sun. Hair was short, in the fashion of the time, and pulled back in clips. I was bemused to see how stylish these women were until I realized that, for many, this was their adventure, their time to leave home for new sights and experiences, even if they were only twenty kilometers away.

I looked deep into this photograph for a long time, knowing that I ought to abandon the work I'd done, but unwilling to do so.

**I wish** I could say that I hadn't known about Rachel and what she was working on, but I think, on some level, that I must have. At the time, I thought that morning was the tipping point in my relationship with Dom. If only it had been. If only we had both had the courage to speak then. As it was, I didn't even tell him about the figure I thought I saw on the path. He would have called my fears excessive, and perhaps he would have been right. I'd had a panic attack; that was what it was.

A few days later, the newspapers again were full of stories about another girl who had gone missing near Castellet and about the discovery of her battered body. It took all my reserves of sense and sound judgment to strike through that flooding paranoia, the unwelcome pictures that flashed through my mind. Dom's night away. The woman on the path. The last photo of the girl alive. The last known sighting of her in the area where Dom said he'd been walking. The deep scratches that had scored his face and arms.

Then I stopped myself. I was letting my jitteriness get the better of me. How could I have thought that, even for a moment?

# 21

The first I knew that Marthe had come back, that she had not left forever, it was a signal so subtle that I hardly realized that was what it was.

I had stirred early in my bed. I was warm and comfortable in my nest and I could smell lavender. The scent was quite distinct and pleasant. It was a while before I thought to wonder where it was coming from. Was it from the chest of drawers where I had placed a small cotton bag in with my nightwear? The drawer was closed, and the scent was too strong. I supposed the cleaning fluid I'd used on the tiled floor might have contained lavender, but, in that case, why hadn't I smelled it before I went to bed? Some of my perfume bottles stood on the mantelpiece about two meters away, but I had never been able to smell their contents from this distance before, and, in any case, there was no pure lavender among them.

All I knew was that the scent was coming up the hillside and in through the open window. It was delicious, full of childhood memories and flowers. I luxuriated in it for a few heady moments before dismissing the thought as impossible. The scent was too strong, too immediate, to be coming in from outside. I could not understand it at all.

Later, when I went up to the room again and there was no perfume but that of cool, clean air, I decided that I must have had the remains of some scent on my wrists and neck, which had somehow been warmed and activated in the coziness of the bed. But I wasn't convinced.

Somehow I knew, deep in the fibers of my being, what it signified.

Yes, I yearned for Marthe to return but not like this.

I confess: I did not like it.

Even before she appeared in front of me, I knew she was there. Can a house retain scents of the past? Are they such potent spells? Or can the mind trick the body into believing it is actually smelling a concoction that exists entirely in the memory?

Or, if we are to talk about haunting: Is it the house or the resident that is haunted?

Whatever the answers that might be given by medical scientists or philosophers, I know what I smelled. Marthe's presence. Day by day, piece by piece, all the components came together—the first, flirty trail of fruitiness, the vanilla and cocoa, the cherry and almond and hawthorn and wood smoke—until I could hardly breathe for her perfume.

# 22

Then it was spring again, almost a year since I had first seen Les Genévriers.

Under diamond-bright sun, brown expanses prickly with last year's dusty thyme and lavender were being overwritten by meadow flowers. Tight blue grape hyacinths sprang up in the lawns. Daffodils, primroses, and violets pushed aside drifts of crisp brown oak leaves, and white blossom burst out of the plum and cherry trees.

For weeks at a time, all was good. Better than good. It was as though the season of renewal and rebirth had reinvigorated Dom's mood, and I responded with almost manic relief. We talked and laughed and drew closer again. I shut away any uneasy thoughts, blaming my own psychological shortcomings, my tendency to worry unnecessarily. Dom and I were spoons in a drawer, complementary personalities in perfect balance: we had rediscovered our sweet spot together. We spent days outside, feeling our winter bodies lighten. Dom hacked at the ivy strangling the deciduous trees, I cleared beds for planting, and we made a joint attempt to build a low wall from rubble we found in the wood.

Desire would spark mid-afternoon. We might draw out a deliciously languorous display of restraint until disappearing formally behind the closed shutters of the bedroom. Or I might surprise him in the shade of the garden.

We felt quite restricted (and had to become more inventive) when the masons arrived back to "butter" between the stones of the outside walls of the main house: *beurrer* is the term they use to describe the filling and smoothing of the gaps with lime mortar. I liked that.

The swimming pool contractor came to take soil samples and detailed measurements. A tangible sense of purpose reemerged. The sounds of physical work were oddly soothing. I no longer started at sudden noises. Dismissing any lingering suspicions as so many misunderstandings, cold thorns of the winter months, and too much melodramatic literature, I began to recover my sense of self.

**The sound** of shooting in the woods stopped, and M. Durand sowed lucerne for his sheep in the fields below our land, as he had done the previous year. It made me nostalgic for the sound of their bells, and for the perfect summer we had spent, even if it had been illusory.

It reminded me of the barrier of branches that had been dragged across the *chemin.* How it had concerned us until we saw it was only part of the process of providing a temporary enclosure for the sheep. (I would do well to remember that more often, I told myself. There was almost always a simple explanation.)

M. Durand was keen to tell me about the sheep, and the old ways: how the shepherds used to travel the traditional grazing routes by night, and talked and drank, ate and rested by day. "At night, they carried hurricane lamps. The hooves made a skittering noise on concrete roads, the whole herd running, dogs barking, bells going crazy. It was a hard, hard life. You can understand why hardly anyone does it now."

"But some do?"

"These days the shepherds drive their vans and the sheep are transported in trucks. You can't do it the old way anymore. Too much traffic. Shepherds use off-road motorbikes to get from pasture to pasture. They get supplies dropped by helicopter. But the best parts are still there: the sound of pure springwater falling. On the high plateaus, the grass is eaten so smooth it could be the lawn of a grand château."

**But even** so, despite the influx of new people and the day's activities, the odd incidents continued: other signs of life that I could not read, sources of energy I could not trace, signals I was unable to decipher. All around, there was perpetual movement even when the men had packed up and left for the day: the rustling songs of the trees; the light flickering on the walls; the smells that rode up the stairwells on dust motes and collected in corners.

One evening, I went into the upstairs sitting room and found the radio playing softly, the radio that neither Dom nor I had switched on. Another time, the zoetrope seemed to be spinning of its own accord, though when I went over to look closer, it was quite still. In the hall, I found a picture on the floor in a mosaic of glass shards. A rattling sound, like stones thrown at the window, woke us up one night. There were more power outages.

One afternoon, as I was idly looking down over the lower terraces at the stone walls, my eyes fastened on a wooden beam in the wall attached to the first stone arch. Moments passed before it occurred to me that what I was seeing was a lintel, and that there had once been a door underneath it. It was there, very faintly, in outline. Another room, possibly, blocked up with stones.

I made a mental note to ask the architect if he might try opening it up and investigating the possibility of using it for some kind of studio.

# 23

It transpired, many years after the event, that Marthe blamed the family for her total blindness. I was honestly shocked by that.

It was true that, after she was pushed by Pierre and fell so hard from the window, and I had run with him from the scene of the crime, there had been a great row. But had that really worsened her affliction? According to her, now, after all the intervening years, it had. This was a different story than the accepted version. It was certainly not in the book that was written about her.

After she ceased to reply to my letters, I took that book down from its pride of place on the shelf and moved it to the table by my bed. I went through it word by word, looking for clues. I have it on my lap now.

I searched so hard one night that my eyes hurt. The lamplight went cloudy, as if the bulb was glowing from inside a shell, leaving the room nacreous as an early morning when mist still covers the sun.

Why had she never told us this before?

**If I** had not heard it, face-to-face, from someone she trusted and who knew her well, I would never have believed it. But there it was. Marthe had had a change of heart. We were all to blame: Pierre had been too rough, always out of control; Maman had been too uncaring, hadn't taken her seriously enough; I had held my tongue, when I might have told the whole truth, out of fear of provoking Pierre into taking his usual reprisals out on me; Papa simply didn't want to know when things went wrong, he had enough on his plate running the place.

Our father's version of events was that the window from which she fell and banged her head was not a high one—if it had been the bedroom window three floors up, it would have been an impressive fall (assuming she hadn't been killed by the courtyard cobbles), but this was only the ground-floor window, where she'd been sitting on the sill inside. Children were bred to help, not to create more problems. He was a countryman through and through, unsentimental to the bone. Characteristics she shared with him, as it turned out.

**So now,** I found myself shouting at her silent, accusatory spirit: "Is that what you want? But it wasn't me! I had nothing to do with it! You know what Pierre was like!"

But did she? Did any of them, really? Sometimes it seemed I was the only one who could see it.

# 24

The *terrassier* arrived for the swimming pool excavation. He and his men were soon in consultation with the contractor, and more men arrived on site. Earth, stone, roots, and rubble began to move. Metal claws gouged into the walls of the old pool.

With this added impetus, Dom and I walked around the garden, marking where new walls and landscaping would enhance the setting of the pool. Then, while he played the piano for a few hours, I sat in the warm shelter of the courtyard with my books and notebook and let my thoughts float in counterpoint to the music.

Carefully, I mentioned nothing more about my writing, and he did not ask. While I read in the evenings, Dom developed a new interest. He acquired a telescope. Night after night, he trawled the sky, convinced he was spotting stars few had the chance to see through the orange scrim of city streetlights. Sometimes I joined him, but more often than not, I was happy with my books.

Soon we would be sitting under the bright, burning dome of the summer stars again, the Milky Way pouring a silver arch right over our heads. A long, hot summer when everything would be perfect, from the new swimming pool to the buttered walls and the garden where we would sit with friends, sharing our good fortune.

Life seldom works out as expected.

**As noise** and activity levels rose, I spent the afternoon combing through the various building permits, construction quotes, and contracts. Primarily, this was because Dom's French was not as good as mine, but also because I had realized by then that he did not relish administrative detail. Left to himself, he would have taken the architect and the builders at their word and never so much as glanced at the fine print. It didn't seem to square with his experience in business, but I put that out of my mind to concentrate on the job at hand. One of us had to do it.

Determined that every cent should be accounted for and every clause honored, I checked, cross-referenced, and made a file for the sheaves of loose papers.

---

**Mounds of** gravel to drain and stabilize the soil were delivered the next morning. Among hillocks of mud and rubble, groups of men stood in earnest conversation. Engines fired, and stones clattered in the excavator cradle.

Dom was in the music room. I was digging in one of the orchard terraces.

When the rattling and whining over by the pool site ceased for a moment, I took a break from the plum suckers I was trying to uproot, the shoots as strong as wires, stinging even through gloves. Shoulders loosened in the sunshine, I stood up and drew in the relative silence with pleasure and purpose. A break from the noise at last.

It was such a beautiful morning.

As the quiet stretched into a longer calm, I went over to the excavators, intending to offer coffees and trying to remember which fruit juices I had in the fridge.

The men were staring into the hole, arguing respectfully among themselves.

"What is it?" I asked.

Bones, they said.

**They had** been brought up when the concrete floor of the old pool was lifted. It wasn't that surprising, in a spot where a farm had stood for centuries; they would be animal bones, I said. The place where a loyal farm dog had been buried, I suggested. Or a favorite horse.

No, they said, these were human bones.

As time came juddering to a sudden stop, it was the small details I noticed: the shard of green printed pottery pointing up from the recently moved soil; the mud caked on a man's boot; the black rime on another worker's fingernails; knobbles of rubble; the broken piece of brick; the individual blades of grass.

Piano notes ascended, Dom too intent on his own sounds to register that others had been silenced.

# Part IV

Part IV

# 1

Old bones, I repeated.

Almost certainly, said M. Chapelle, the *terrassier*. Human bones.

Old, but perhaps not all that old, others ventured to suggest, offering their countrymen's wisdom, their instinct for nature and the soil, the seasonal ranges of temperature and probable rate of decomposition.

They were discussing what to do next, as if I weren't present. Should they leave the discovery there, or investigate further?

"I think you should leave everything exactly as it is," I said.

"The police will have to be informed," said M. Chapelle.

"Of course."

"It is just a formality, Madame. Probably it's nothing."

**By the** time I had gone to get Dom, and the two of us had hurried back, several of the men were on their cell phones, and the rest were engaged in urgent debate. Already the theory was gaining currency that, far from nothing, they might have found a link to the missing girl students. It seemed to me a wild assumption, born of the frenzy in the newspapers, though, naturally, my own instincts had immediately taken flight in that direction before I forced myself to think logically.

"Surely it can't be . . ." I began.

"We don't know what it is yet," said Dom, attempting to assert his authority as the owner of the property. He admitted afterward he suspected it was a builders' ruse to spin out the job and claim daily rates of pay for the apparently unforeseen delay.

One of the men, one of the older ones, stocky, with bandy legs, ignored the shouts and advice of his colleagues and jumped back down into the pit. He picked up a spade and started scraping away at the soil near the muddy exposed ridges that were the cause of all the drama. Soon curiosity overcame all our reservations.

"Anything more?"

"What can you see?"

The scraping stopped.

**Dom swore.** "This is the last thing we need," he said.

"I know."

We were standing within sight of the scene but away from the men, as we all waited for the police and whatever story was about to unfold. I felt a bit shaky and I think Dom did, too. As I relate this now, it seems an absurdly selfish exchange, but that is what we said. We were both shocked, of course, but also resentful that our idyll had been corrupted in such a chilling way. That here, in our paradise, was death, and suffering—the stuff of horror stories. That our privacy was about to be invaded; our hamlet, perhaps even our life here, was about to become public property. It was an honest expression of that, nothing more or less.

In the pit, the exposed outline of a skull grinned atop a mouthful of earth.

**An hour** later, the police were with us, and the work site was cordoned by iron stakes and fluttering plastic tape.

"I am Lieutenant Marc Severan of the judicial police."

The officer in charge was a tall, solid man in his forties, with wide, slightly pockmarked cheeks and a disconcerting way of looking beyond our shoulders as he spoke. "I have to tell you, as a matter of courtesy, that there will be extensive searches of the house and grounds in addition to the immediate site of the investigation into what has been found."

Even as he was informing us, a team of men and women in white forensic jumpsuits descended on the pool site.

"We will, of course, need to talk to you," added Lieutenant Severan.

"We don't know anything more than anyone else here!" said Dom.

The investigator did not reply immediately, letting Dom's words and his harassed tone die away, becoming more ridiculous as Severan made a face that suggested suspects do not always tell the truth.

"That is precisely what we are here to find out, monsieur," he said.

As the uniformed gendarmerie and detectives from the judicial police invaded, and the curious, alerted by the marked cars and unnecessary sirens, began to arrive from the village and beyond, we sat with M. Chapelle and his men and two gendarmes in the courtyard. Conversation was stilted. Dom stared into space. I tried to read. One by one, we were called into the kitchen to speak to Lieutenant Severan.

I knew we had nothing to fear from speaking, from putting what little we knew into words, but I was fearful. Fearful that, somehow, we—Dom and I—would be misunderstood.

Dom was summoned after M. Chapelle. I worried, even as he went up the steps, that his reasonable but imperfect ability to express himself in another language might leave his words open to misinterpretation and further difficulties. Naturally, I had suggested to Severan that Dom and I be questioned together to enable me to translate.

"I will see everyone individually," he replied firmly.

After about twenty minutes, Dom emerged pale but composed. He nodded to me but there was no opportunity to say anything. It was my turn.

**2**

When Papa used to say, "I know where the treasure is," it was never in a way that gave us any intimation he would tell us. Perhaps, as young children, we felt it fell into the category of mysteries that adulthood would eventually reveal, such as why the men spent so much time sitting at tables in the bar at the corner of the market square, and why our parents' bedroom door was locked on a Sunday afternoon.

As I grew up, I came to realize that there was no treasure. What he meant was that the treasure was the magic of the place, the rare atmosphere of calm and the wind sighing in the tall trees that only grew because of the underground river. Or the treasure might have been the underground river that flooded out of the spring in winter and made a stream down the alley between the main farmhouse and the row of cottages, ensuring that we always had water.

It was because of the treasure, in this form, that we knew we could not give up. We were so blessed, it was inconceivable that we could not make a living here, when so many others down the centuries had managed to, had considered themselves rich, even.

So we struggled on with the help of the remaining tenant family, Maman and I. We continued in the old ways, trapping and foraging to supplement what we grew, and bartering with other families in the commune: gathering wild salads—usually dandelion and sorrel, wild asparagus in season—and mushrooms, and, led by Old Marcel's dog, truffles from a very special place only ever known to two people at a time.

**The next** ghost to appear was not a person but an object. It had never occurred to me before that ghosts could be inanimate, but perhaps that was just prejudice, or lack of understanding. There was another difference, too. It was the first to come to me in darkness.

I have always struggled to cope with the dark, ever since I was a child, but somehow it didn't occur to me to worry about apparitions at night. When I heard the gate clanging in the wind, iron banging on iron, I went out, unthinking and unafraid of anything but the blackness, to secure it before retiring to bed.

Out beyond the courtyard, on my way to the gate, I paused. The familiar landmarks were picked out in pinpricks of light as usual: the lonely settlement of Castellet across the valley was a string of diamonds, and the constellations winked from the high vaults above. I took a moment to breathe in the scent of slightly damp pines. All was quiet.

And then, I saw it. Low on the ground, riding a rut of the path, a flame flickered through the sparse hedge of firs. I felt the old start of the heart. How could this be? All logic denied the probability that this was real, but there it was. I drew closer, stared, blinked. There it was: the candlelit lantern.

Our signal. In the happiest year of my life, the lantern on the path was the sign that my fiancé, André, was waiting for me. André. I had not thought of him for so many years, and there it was, our sign, about twenty meters beyond the gate, as large as life.

Convinced I was mistaken, or that it was a memory I saw—so clear in my head that it seemed to be real, just like the pictures of the Valensole lavender fields I had trained myself to retain for Marthe—I moved slowly toward the light.

It was cold, and I was shivering. It had been dark for hours. The nights were falling earlier now, and chilling as soon as the sun dropped over the western ridges.

The candle bloomed inside the lantern. I was astounded. It was the very same lantern he once used, with its familiar iron frame and pretty curlicues. The same one in the same place. I had not seen it since the last signal he set. I reached out a hand, wanting to touch. My fingers were almost on the loop on the lid, by which it could be carried, almost touching it, when—

The lantern flew away down the dark path.

I watched as it rose into the air and hung for a moment in the night, floating in the boundless black. Then, in a blur of amber, it shot away from me.

What is uncanny is how, once the mind has accepted the existence of a terror, of fear, it is able to cope. The important thing to say is that, by this stage, I did not think there was anything unusual about a ghostly appearance. Possibly I was less frightened by this one, as I had not been harmed physically by the shades of my brother and sister, and felt that there could be no malice in a simple lantern.

It came to rest soundlessly, this small, metal ghost, another ten meters or so ahead, on a rut in the track.

I shut my eyes and counted to ten. Opened my eyes. The lantern still burned brightly ahead. A sudden squall of wind rifled through the black trees and filled the dark with the sounds of a waterfall. The candle flame did not flicker.

# 3

I t was less an interrogation than a dance of extravagant politeness.

"First I must ask you, is this a holiday house or do you live here all year round?"

He must have asked Dom the same question. I stuck to the facts without making assumptions about any future plans. "We have owned the house for approximately one year," I said. "We first saw it in May last year and the final contract of sale was signed at the beginning of July. Since then we have lived here continuously except for one short break in Switzerland."

Severan made notes, and we exchanged a few comments about the attractions of the area in terms that might almost have been social. How did we choose to buy here? Dom already knew the region, I said. Had we had many visitors? Not really. Which guests had come to stay? None. We had had no visitors staying with us, not French nor any other nationality? Not even in the summer when so many visitors come to the Luberon? No.

"That is strange, is it not?"

"Not really," I said. But it was an effort to keep my voice steady. Did I really believe that?

"A couple like you, you buy a beautiful and expensive property and you don't have family and friends to visit, to show it off, to relax with them in the sun?"

Why? Why exactly hadn't we invited even a few friends? I wasn't sure I could give an answer to that.

"You hesitate," said Severan.

"There are several reasons," I said, striving to remain calm, outwardly at least. "As you can see, there's a great deal of work to be done on the house. It isn't yet renovated the way we would like. The upper floors are barely habitable, with only one small bathroom for the whole house. It simply isn't ready for visitors." That was enough, surely. It was a good answer.

"Several reasons, you said."

Already I felt cornered, not as sharp as I thought I was.

"None as clear-cut as that. We— We've wanted to spend as much time together, alone together, as possible. Our families have their own busy lives. We've both had busy lives up until now . . ."

Severan supplied a cold, polite smile. "Do you work?"

"Not at the moment."

"A career break?"

"A change of direction."

"And your husband?"

"The same."

He asked me what we both did, before we had this wonderful opportunity to take time off, and I watched his pen as it carefully inscribed a version of what I told him. He needed to ascertain exactly how we had managed to finance this new life. Not many local people would be able to afford it, he said, to take on all the work. I made no comment.

Severan shifted in his seat. "Have you ever seen any person acting suspiciously on the public path that goes through the property?"

"Not that I can think of, no."

"Any unusual activity? Anything you were not happy about?"

"No."

"Anything odd at night? A vehicle maybe?"

"It's very quiet. The only vehicles that come past are farm tractors, and those only rarely."

"There's no fence around the garden."

"There will be. We have to install the new swimming pool first. The builders' trucks need access. When the pool's in, we can fence the garden."

He tapped his pen on the notepad.

I wondered whether to remind him that the bones were found under the old pool, that they must have been there for decades. If he was asking whether anyone could have come into the garden, the answer would be yes, but they couldn't have buried the bones under concrete.

"No sign of earth being disturbed—apart from the pool works, of course?"

"No. Nothing."

"So . . . no disturbances, night or day, that could tell us anything about this . . . matter?"

"No . . . nothing I can recall."

**Too late** an image flared in my mind: the battered old lantern with the stub of candle left burning. The puddle of light on the path. But by then I had been dismissed and was on my way out. I could have turned back and mentioned it. But I didn't.

Neither did I say anything about the figure on the path, or the ethereal trails of scent. How could I, when part of me did not believe I had actually seen the woman, in any real sense? I had half-convinced myself I had been dreaming, had dreamed the whole episode of smelling the perfume and getting up in the night and seeing that still, silent form.

It was afterward that it grew in importance, along with a slithering worm of self-doubt. Severan had asked about Dom and called him my husband; I should have corrected him, but it didn't seem relevant. Then there was the issue of our near solitude. I had not realized, until in the hours following that interview I allowed myself to face the truth, that I might have failed to answer too many simple questions, both Severan's and my own.

# 4

I was waiting for the visitor who would frighten me the most.

Surely it was only a matter of time. The pockets of fragrance, the lantern, the guests who arrived uninvited, the stream of ghosts crossing the divide after Pierre first broke through . . .

Who were they? After a while, when I had had long enough to think as rationally as I could, I became convinced that they were nothing more or less than the stirring of my conscience.

And so, in dread, I waited for her.

I listened to the sounds that could reassure me, temporarily, of normality. The leaves rustling down the alleyway, scraping the pebbled concrete with their imitations of light footsteps.

The *loirs* scampering between the terra-cotta tiles of the roofs, and balancing in the electricity wires like a high-wire circus act. We never succeeded in getting rid of them, you see, not since the time when André worked for us. These funny, rodentlike creatures—a kind of gray squirrel with larger eyes and ears—are becoming braver, promenading along the beams of the little terrace roof outside the kitchen.

Roof tiles crashed off in high winds. More creaking presaged the fall of more disintegrating ceilings. I was alert for the pattering of crumbling plaster, followed by the crash of falling masonry. When I dared to go up to check, ambushes awaited, startling reflections in windows blacked out by shutters, glimpses of shadows, odd people at odd angles.

Doors slammed in the wind, forever slipping their catches but impossible to lock, because keys no longer turned and steel would not dock in holes that have shifted out of alignment with the weight of the house.

I, too, could feel myself shifting.

**5**

A soil specialist was called in. The bones were pho-tographed in situ, and then gradually uncovered. The earth was being brushed, grain by grain, from the remains until they were exposed and raw. Not only the bones but the soil itself would be analyzed.

It was a clear spring day, new leaves translucent. On such a day, when the land was washed clean of winter, it seemed a desecration: the macabre evidence in the pit and the surrender of normality to dispassionate, vaguely hostile professionals. We were numb.

Outside the fluttering police tapes around the hamlet, rumors were spreading fast. Naturally, con-nections were being made to the missing girl students. Word was that these were the remains of the first to go missing, a nineteen-year-old from Goult, who had failed to arrive home after a party more than two years previously. All unconfirmed, of course. But everyone knew it must be so. Speculative headlines screamed from the front page of *La Provence*. The fate of those girls was so well established in the public consciousness that while a spokesman for the gendarmerie tried to play down the certainty with bland statements, no one seemed willing to believe the police could not advance the obvious theory with all this new evidence.

"Where exactly were they found?" "How old were these bones, then?" "What happens now?" the locals asked us.

We all wanted to know.

After a while, we stayed inside and tried to ignore the coming and going as the forensic scientists dug and scraped and came to their meticulous conclusions. An archaeologist was introduced to us, but Lieutenant Severan remained implacable. His big presence seemed to be a permanent feature of those next few days, during which he stared deep into the garden and across to the mountains and answered no questions. "We have recovered some items from the scene, which are being examined," was all he would allow us.

On the morning of the third day, I sat on the steps, waiting for him to appear in the courtyard.

When he approached, I asked, "Is it all right for me to put some things through the washing machine?" I indicated the full laundry basket at my side. It was a challenge of sorts. Were we suspects or not?

He waited for a few seconds, perhaps for me to say something else, then reached in, groping among the sheets and pillowcases and T-shirts that made up the load. It was an uncomfortably invasive and confrontational action.

"Go ahead." Brusque, but smiling, as he removed his hand from the basket. As if he was waiting, that "go ahead" meant something more.

I responded cautiously. "Are you able to tell me yet what you've found?"

"In addition to the remains . . . . tissue fragments and scraps of fabric."

"Clothing?"

"Seems so."

"But it can't be what they're saying, can it? The student . . . in the papers . . ."

"Everything must be examined before we draw any conclusions."

His manner was still watchful, evaluating, superficially polite but stiff.

I was about to point out the obvious, that the bones had been found under the pool floor. They must have been there for years.

"Why didn't you tell me someone else was staying here?" asked Severan.

"There isn't anyone."

"Then who was the woman who was here this morning?"

"What woman?"

"She was leaning over the forensic tape having a good look at the site where the bones were found. This morning about eight o'clock."

"I've no idea. She must have wandered down from the village."

Severan waved his hand dismissively. "It's all sealed off. I have men at both ends of the track to keep the public away. She can't have got in, or out for that matter. So she must be staying here."

I shook my head. I didn't like the notion of strangers arriving to gawk, but had to accept that they would. "Didn't you ask her?"

"I saw her as I was parking in front of the *bergerie*. When I got out of the car and went over she was gone."

A sudden brief vision fell like a shadow across my mind's eye. "What did she look like?"

"Not very tall, slim, dark-haired, gray-blue dress . . ." Severan patted his pockets, perhaps for his cigarettes, never taking his gaze from mine.

Involuntarily, I shivered as I said, "I think I may have seen her before. I don't know who she is."

Severan was watching me carefully but said nothing.

"I wish you had asked her name," I said.

He might have been about to press me on that, when the electronic jingle of my cell sounded. Left to myself, I would have ignored the arrival of the text. With Severan studying me intently, that was not possible. Moving away, I opened the message.

It was from Sabine. *Call me urgently.*

I did not want to. Not after she had set me up by suggesting I research Marthe Lincel. I was sure now that she had done so deliberately. She had used me to rile Dom, and I found that deeply unpleasant. Perhaps I had misjudged the depth of Sabine's friendship with Rachel, and this was all some sisterly demonstration of loyalty. I hadn't seen her since our day out in Manosque, and although I'd thought I might run into her in the village—at the post office, in the café, perhaps—where I could tell her what I thought of her, our paths hadn't crossed.

I snapped the phone shut.

Severan was staring high into the catalpa tree, at nascent leaves lemon-lime against the sky. "It really is a splendid spot," he said, almost companionably.

"Yes, it is."

"My aunt and uncle had a place—"

There was another electronic interruption. Again, our separate pretenses.

Sabine was insistent.

*Meet me now in the Café Aptois,* the text commanded.

"Ah, technology," said Severan pleasantly. "Whoever sent it can tell when someone has read their first message. You can't ignore it now. Who is it from?"

# 6

The body lies silent in its earthen vault. No marble and stone in the public cemetery for this one, no carved tribute, nor dates that testified to a full life well lived.

For me, she was there in the wind that sent cool rivers running through the trees and carried the warmed scents of summer. And then, she was there in the angry mistral that cleansed and neutered all scent, in the winds that snatched tiles from the roof like malevolent hands, tore up delicate petals, and wrenched the top branches from the oaks and planes. Some people claim to be able to see the mistral, literally see it as an evil force, tormenting humans and destroying their work and spirits.

On the worst days, I hear it howl and recognize it as retribution.

I did so very wrong. What use now would be confession?

There will be no forgiveness. The ghosts tell me that.

**Little by** little, I took on most of the day-to-day responsibility for the farm as the last of the tenant families reluctantly handed in their keys and moved down the valley to work for the expanding candied-fruit factory with its new machinery and higher wages.

With every departure, there was less help, and less money.

No money to pay for repairs. There never was, but what this place did once have was manpower. One or other of the men would devise some means of solving the problem, or a team would form, my father directing operations. Arielle's father, Gaston, and Albert Marchesi were always there to pitch in, Gaston tall and mournful, Albert with his quick, efficient trot. At the very worst, help would have been summoned from the village, and the work paid for in kind, or in walnut wine and mutton.

I was twenty-seven. Maman was frailer than she should have been for a woman not all that far into her fifties, but she was ground down by grief as well as the grim physical work of subsistence. Naturally, we tried to get replacements, but no one was interested. We asked around, even going so far as to leave notices in the shops in Apt, but had no luck.

The tide was flowing the other way. Young people were moving to the towns, to work in the new factories and earn steady wages. The villages were emptying. Even those who were happy with the old ways in the country were setting out farther afield to look for work. The life of the hillsides had always been harsh, but it was becoming ever bleaker.

Without family—without sons—it was hard. Pierre had no intention of returning, that was clear. The last time we had seen him was at Papa's funeral, and that was our first reunion in more than a year. He told us he was earning good money making agricultural machinery, though he was vague, I thought, about where exactly the factory was.

"Looking at onions" is a Provençal phrase, which means keeping an eye on the neighbors to see that standards are upheld. We worked so hard to ensure that our onions were better than ever, but we couldn't do everything on our own.

When André appeared on the path to Les Genévriers, he was the answer to our prayers. He was a jobbing mason, he told us. "And carpentry, too. Any jobs you need doing I can turn my hand to, even roof tiling. I don't mind getting up on a roof; I have a good head for heights."

The hardest part was disguising our desperation so that he would not charge us double.

"We might let you have a look at the barn roof, as you're here now," said Maman with a dignity that was only slightly stiff.

He was quite young, about my age, I guessed, as we took him around to the other side of the courtyard. The hole in the barn roof was the size of a manhole. Tiles had slipped and been loosened further by the squirrel-like pests we never quite managed to control.

"*Loir,*" he said.

"That's right," said Maman. "They may look sweet but with their incessant games hiding nuts, and building nests up in all the roofs between the rafters and the tiles . . ."

"It's an infestation," said the young man. "They'll dismantle the place if you give them half a chance. There are a few tricks I know with them, but first we need to make the roof watertight again. If you show me where I can fetch a ladder, I'll get up there and have a proper look."

His clothes were the dustiest we had ever seen, so there was no point in wondering if he would change into any kind of work overall. He shucked off his jacket and set to.

As he climbed up, I saw that his shoe leather was holed and patched with bark. Sometimes he took his shoes off, he told us later, tied the laces together, and slung them over his shoulder in order to save the leather on the soles.

"I could do that in a day," he said, after what appeared to be a serious inspection. He named a price that seemed reasonable, so we agreed on the spot, and that was the first job he did for us, beginning at first light the very next day.

# 7

"Rachel left this with me," said Sabine. She passed a flash drive across the table. "I don't read English so well. I'm not sure exactly what the files contain but I need to know. She gave it to me before she left and said it was important. She was acting a bit strange, told me to keep it safe, she'd be back when she could to pick up where she'd left off. So I did what she asked. But then she never came back for it, never asked me to send it on to her."

"She was acting strangely in what way?"

"She seemed . . . evasive, angry maybe. She went in a hurry—looking terrible I might add, as if she hadn't been sleeping."

"Didn't you ask, if you were worried about her?"

"She said she was pregnant, and that unfortunately it wasn't agreeing with her."

"And you thought that was strange?"

"I didn't think anything much about it," said Sabine, as if wanting to close down that line of conversation and attend to her own agenda. "Only that I have been trying to contact her for a long time, but I can never reach her. Then I saw her husband with you at the Durands' house."

Her husband.

I picked up the flash drive and turned it over. "You want me to look at what she was researching? To translate it for you?" I asked. I hadn't yet made it clear how I felt about her using Rachel to unsettle Dom and me, how angry I had been to be drawn into her game.

"I think it needs to be done."

"But, now . . . with everything else that's going on? I'm sorry but I really think—" I was dumbfounded by her insensitivity.

"No," said Sabine. "It might be to do with what's been found and why the police are at your house. You're not letting yourself understand what I'm telling you."

A pause.

"Dominic knows," said Sabine. "And I'm doing my best to help you."

It was the way she said it, the curious emphasis that made it clear she intended more meaning than was explicit. That was the crossing of the line, the tacit acknowledgment that we both knew something was wrong.

**I inserted** the flash drive into my laptop and downloaded the files.

Most were dated October 2008. That squared with what Sabine told me, that Rachel gave it to her for safekeeping at the end of that month. As I worked my way through the list, one title sprang out: LUMIÈRES—MISSING GIRL.

I clicked it open with trembling hands.

*It's 8 A.M. The dust and gravel village square at Lumières howls and seems exposed now the bus has left.*

*On the autoroute north from Marseille the overhead warning signs were flashing, ever more bossily:* AVERTISSEMENT: VENT VIOLENT. WARNING: STRONG WIND.

*"Soyez prudent," warns the woman in the bakery where I buy myself breakfast. Outside trees are bending and loose leaves ride on air down the sloping street. The wind is getting higher.*

*I have every intention of being careful, not only when I am out in the mistral, but when I'm asking* the questions I have come to ask in the places I have come to find.

For this is where the girl set off, the last time she went home.

Her face is on the poster in the bakery window. Another is on a plane tree where the bus pulled in, though how long it will be before some powerful gust pulls it free is anyone's guess. It is already tattered.

Missing for more than a month now.

Lumières is not even a proper village. It is a kind of anteroom to the much larger Goult just up the hill.

The girl's name is Marine Gavet. She is a student, nineteen years old. This is her family home, where she grew up with an engineer father and a mother who is a part-time secretary. In the picture on the posters she is smiling and pretty, but sensible and serious-looking as well. Her face has become familiar throughout this northwestern corner of Provence, gazing out from posters tacked up in cafés and shops and on lampposts, trees, bus stops.

She had been visiting a boyfriend, though she had reportedly ended the relationship the day before her disappearance. It had ended badly. So badly that the young man, Christophe LeBrun, became the prime suspect despite his protestations of innocence and fury at the waste of police time when they could have been finding her.

The last confirmed sighting of Marine Gavet was at the bus stop in the square, boarding the bus for Apt, about sixteen kilometers east along the N100, the main route between Avignon and Forcalquier. Christophe had last seen her at 11.30 P.M. the previous night when she walked out of a party in Bonnieux. Other guests saw and heard the argument, and gave statements to the effect that he remained at the party, drinking steadily for a further two hours.

She was due back at university for the start of her second year ten days ago. She was popular and hardworking. Not the sort of girl to take off without telling her family and friends.

Hope is still strong, of course, that she will not be found dead, as so many are in such circumstances. What is the best outcome when this happens? Before it happens to you, it's tempting to think that perhaps it is better not to know, and to go on in the hope she is alive and happy in the new life that has overwritten the one she was supposed to live. But according to the family, what they are seeking, every day, is certainty and closure.

*Not far from Lumières, on the road to Avignon, is the castle at Lacoste that once belonged to the Marquis de Sade. Already notorious when the Marquis arrived to claim it, it was the scene of the rape, torture, and murder of three hundred members of the heretical sect of the Vaudois. From his prison cell in later years, the Marquis made it the setting for the literary flowering of his own notoriety in Jus-tine and* One Hundred and Twenty Days of Sodom. *These days, it is owned by the veteran designer Pierre Cardin and is the centerpiece of a summer music festival.*

*That does not mean that a dark underbelly no longer exists in this glorious countryside. Of course it does, no less than in other places of beauty.*

*In Avignon, high summer has gone, and with it the troupes of festival players, the gilded steam-driven fairground ride and the bunting flags, the music and indulgence in the warm evening air. Soon the plane trees lining the boulevards will point gnarled witches' fingers up into the blackness above the city.*

*Homeless North Africans are already huddled in dark doorways, shivering like the litter that stirs in the wind, features flattened by sodium lighting from the windows of Galeries Lafayette. The shop* dummies, too, are harbingers of winter, blank-faced in their jackets trimmed with fake fur.

Marine had a week to go before she was meant to be traveling to Avignon, with a ticket booked to Lyon, heading back to university. That should have been her route.

Instead she was seen—for the last time by a witness who was prepared to come forward and give a statement—climbing into a bus bound east, not west.

According to the police, the last person officially to see her was Mme. Christiane Rascas, the baker's wife who has just sold me my croissant and warned me about the wind.

"Soyez vraiment prudente," she tells me again when I tell her I intend to walk up to Goult. "Be really careful."

I'm not sure whether it is just the wind she means.

# 8

He had traveled from Sault to Coustellet, and then
on down the valley, calling at all the hill villages
until he reached us. He had walked and taken rides on
farm carts all around the area, and once he had delivered a secondhand bicycle from Roussillon to Saint-
Saturnin at the request of the buyer, which proved
useful for everyone, as he had work waiting at the other
end. Now, if only he could get word out somehow that
he was reliable and available for transport deliveries,
that would suit him very well as an itinerant worker, he
said wistfully.

He was a nice-looking boy—young man, rather. An
air of innocence and idealism made him seem younger
than he was. That was what drew us to him. Dark hair;
eyes that glistened like black olives in oil and held our

gaze reassuringly as we spoke; arms muscled like tree branches, testament to the drive with which he worked; a gentle manner. We couldn't have dreamed up such a paragon.

When he had finished patching the roof, taking some trouble to match the old tiles from the stacks in the undercroft, he insisted on holding the ladder while I climbed up over the edge to check his work. "There are some who would do a botched job thinking that two women would never know," he said.

The work was done well, I was relieved to report to Maman. "The tiles he's replaced are on firmly—I prodded them hard with a stick—and you can't even tell where the hole used to be!"

André smiled. "What else can I do for you? If you let me stay here tonight, there'll be no charge for the first job tomorrow."

He joined us at the kitchen table for a chickpea stew and a little cheese, and ate with relish what we could offer. I had the feeling he hadn't eaten much except for what he had foraged from the hedges and orchards for many days. In return for supper, he stacked a good pile of logs in the wood store.

That night he slept in the old Poidevin cottage. We made him up a bed in the room where Arielle and I used to share secrets.

For the next few weeks, we developed a routine. When he had finished one job, André always asked what his next would be. "We can't pay you much, but we can offer you a little food and wine, and somewhere to sleep," Maman would say.

"I accept your terms," he'd reply.

It was unsaid, but we knew he was very grateful.

There was nobility about him. To me, as I came to know him, André was like one of those universal figures of Provençal folklore: the shepherd, the farmer and his hired hands, the priest, the mayor, the knife-grinder, the miller, the troubadour, the baker. He was hewn from the long history of the struggle to survive in isolated homesteads, across the barren hills and plateaus, in the perched upland villages.

Marine Gavet was the first girl to go missing. Why had Rachel chosen to write about her? I would have to go down to Apt and check at the Internet café, but I was sure that at the time Rachel was writing this, none of the other girls had yet disappeared.

I stared blankly at my laptop screen. This was Rachel's second article about a person who was absent, missing. First, there was the interview with Francis Tully, in which he justified his nonappearance at his own prestigious retrospective exhibition; the visual tricks he played with in his work. Or was I straining to find connections where none existed?

The other files on the flash drive were all titled LINCEL. I only looked briefly to check, but they concerned Marthe Lincel, her work as a perfumer and her blindness.

Marine Gavet. Francis Tully. Marthe Lincel. There was no connection, unless I thought of Rachel herself, who seemed to have vanished into the ether. Disappearance in the abstract. Different kinds of disappearance. Various kinds of silence.

Rachel herself. Was this a theme; was it coincidence—or a prefiguring of her own situation?

I had no idea.

**I would** have liked to relay all this to Dom, to show him her research, but how could I? Doing so would have meant admitting I had been fretting about Rachel and talking about her with Sabine. Even though the atmosphere seemed calm on the surface these days, he could still be distant and quick to anger. The waiting while the police completed their work was unbearable. We both felt it. But Dom seemed determined we should suffer it separately.

It was that distance between us that unsettled me. No matter how I tried to tell myself I was overreacting, I could not shake off the sense that Dom had not been completely honest with me.

When I did go into the music room with two mugs of coffee, he gave me an odd look before he spoke.

"Was that you, earlier?"

"Me what?"

"Singing."

"No."

A pause.

"What kind of singing?"

"Just . . . nothing. Forget it."

It might have been the trees, I suggested. Perhaps it was.

But he had already cut me off, waved me away, and I was adrift from him again. I went outside and listened closely, but heard nothing.

**That afternoon,** Severan announced that forensic analysis of the bones confirmed they were the remains of a woman aged around fifty.

"And you still cannot tell me who she was, the woman I saw hanging around the site?" he asked.

I could not.

It was hard to tell whether he believed me.

# 10

One evening, as I sat sewing, a thin strain of flute music drifted into my consciousness. Haunting, melancholic notes on the air, floating up from the lower terraces like the accompaniment to some forest god of the ancient world. The musician was André.

That night, it began; as the notes insinuated themselves into my senses, so did my thoughts of him. I began to be more and more aware of his handsome face, his strong arms. Innocent as I was, I felt scorched by the warmth of his flesh in the merest brush of our fingers as I handed him a glass of water, or a cup of hot chicory, or passed him a plate.

I realized after a while that I always knew where he was on the land, no matter whether that was in the woods above, bringing down stones for a wall in our brute of a tin wheelbarrow, or filling the cracks in the plaster that appeared like old enemies at the end of each dry season.

In the absence of Pierre, it was not long before Maman began to treat André as an adopted son. She gave him her lovely smiles and washed his shirts and trousers, and patched them, taking great care to match the fabric, even asking our neighbors if they had scraps that were more appropriate than ours.

He took a shower in the alley, which made me feel strange, just thinking of him without his clothes.

**In the** dull glow of the oil lamps on the dinner table outside, I watched surreptitiously as the shadows contoured his smooth skin, the way he drank his wine, held his fork, the movements of his mouth. The textures and tastes of the food on our plates, the flicker of a candle in a jar to catch the insects, the rustle of the vine above, the splash of water poured into a thick glass and transformed into amber as it caught the light: all seemed larger, fuller, more worthy of attention than before.

One evening, he caught me looking, and smiled.

The next, he caught my hand as Maman turned away with the dishes and I noticed his shirt was torn, from a thorn perhaps. I must have been unable to look into his eyes, too shy.

His hand was large and warm, and overwhelmed mine. I could hardly believe that what I felt, the pressure on my palm and fingers, was really happening.

"You have a tear in your shirt."

The words were out before I knew it. They hung, stupidly, over us, over his warm touch.

But he laughed lightly, easily. "Would you mend it for me?"

So, not much later, after Maman had turned in for an early night, I collected a needle and thread. Back at the table, I drew the oil lamp closer, so I would be able to see my stitches, and André slipped his shirt off.

"No one can see us," he said.

Tracing the line of my face with his fingers, he drew me toward him. We paused, exchanging warm breath. I knew what he wanted, and I was scared. But this time, I wanted it, too.

From the first touch of his lips on mine, the warmth and softness of him, I was changed. For the first time in my life, I loved the darkness. I embraced the black, as we kissed, and I lost myself in the smell and the taste and the feel of him.

# 11

Outside the kitchen door was an odd clicking noise, irregular. At first, I dismissed it as one of the strange little rodents in the roof, but the sound was insistent. After a while, I got up and went out. At my feet was a sweet-faced black kitten chasing a walnut.

"Where do you come from?"

The kitten paused, looking into space, then flopped over onto its side and pushed the nut around with its back feet.

When it was still there an hour later, I put down a saucer of milk, but it didn't drink any.

Beyond the courtyard, the pool site still swarmed. Despite the announcement, there seemed no letup in the frenzied activity down there, with cars arriving regularly. Some brought journalists, who barged their way into the main house to ask their questions. I let Dom tell them, in his most terrible French, that we couldn't help them, that they should ask the police.

We just wanted this to be over. For the builders to fill all the holes in the walls and give the place a renewed solidity, to finish the pool. We wanted to plant our garden and light our candles and play our music and be left alone.

**People did** disappear.

That was what was absorbing me, as we waited. Dom retreated more and more often into his own thoughts as well as his music. Perhaps the problem for both of us was that our dreamy preoccupations had left us badly prepared for the real world.

People did stop working, or rather, they stopped what they were doing before, for all sorts of reasons. Why, hadn't I done exactly that myself? People left failed marriages every day. Had Rachel simply met someone else, and Dom's pride was still too wounded to admit it? How I wished it might be that simple.

Rachel's piece on the flash drive about Marine Gavet seemed unfinished. I came back to that notion again and again. Had it ever appeared in finished form in a newspaper, and if so, when?

I needed to know.

It occurred to me that the library in Apt might have Internet access. I was about to go looking for Severan, to let him know I was driving into town, when his heavy footsteps sounded on the stairs. He stood in the open doorway, filling the space, head nearly touching the lintel.

"Where is M. Ross?"

"Dom . . . he's in the music room, I think."

"I just looked there."

"I'll go and find him."

"Stay here. Don't you go anywhere." It was a command.

He went off again, shouting for one of his officers.

I sat down, feeling sick to my stomach. I should have left sooner. Not for the first time, I cursed our isolation.

Dom was sullen as he preceded Severan into the kitchen, giving me only the quickest of glances.

Severan waited until we were both standing in front of him. "We have now found the remains of a second body. It was a few meters away from the first. I can tell you it is the body of another woman."

# 12

It was an old-fashioned lantern, with a frame of wrought iron that held four glass panes, and a lovely curlicue on the top, and another that held the catch to open it to light the candle. The kind of lantern that had been used for a hundred years, perhaps by a night watchman dangling it by its loop on a hook at the end of a pole.

André was still lodging in the old Poidevin cottage, and said he found it in a cellar there. Wherever it came from, the lantern became our signal: I want you. I'm waiting for you. You are not alone in the dark.

Of course, a secret code was hardly necessary. Maman must have known what was going on; most likely, she was actively encouraging us. But it was the romantic gesture that we found so appealing. He would

take it from a stony shelf behind the lilac in the courtyard, and place it, lighted, on the path. Then, playing
the game, I would slip in through the dark alleyway
when the coast was clear.

**Battling the** winds and rains of winter, and the
chronic decay all around us, André soon became our
mainstay. Without him, we would have gone under
far earlier. Every other weekend, he went back to his
village to check on his parents and to see his brothers
and sister and their children. It was a great big family,
by all accounts. After he'd gone at first light on Saturday, cycling off on Pierre's old bicycle, I felt empty, as
if part of me was missing.

As summer came, he began to miss a few of those
fortnightly visits. On the Saturday evening, we might
take the horse and cart into the next village and treat
ourselves to dinner at an inexpensive restaurant. Sun-
days would be for walking in the woods and on the plateau, taking wine and food, eating in the great wide
silence, then finding a shady hiding place in which to
sleep, stuck together.

When he asked me to be his wife, it was a moment
of pure happiness. I accepted him in the sure knowledge we would have a wonderful life together. I didn't
receive a ring; he gave me a much more original symbol

of our love and commitment. He began to build his gift to me, in stone, painstakingly bringing the rocks down from the woodland where some listing walls had collapsed.

I said earlier that André seemed to me like a figure from the traditional tales of Provence. Perhaps he was more like a character from Jean Giono's books, those almost mythic men who give his stories such a universal appeal. The messages were simple: have faith that the gods of nature will prevail, faith in hard labor on the land, and celebrate the determination of the peasant and the artisan to redeem the harshness and transform it into beauty and a symbol of that endurance.

It was André who built the two Romanesque arches in the gardens. He called them, in all seriousness, his monuments to our love. Complete follies, and the most wonderful presents I had ever been given.

We still lit the lantern, though the message had changed subtly. It had come to mean, I love you.

As he worked, and the arches slowly took shape, I dreamed of a simple but gloriously happy wedding in the village's small church, saw the flowering rosemary strewn on flagstones as I walked up the aisle to him. The beignets and pancakes made with white flour for our special day. The long table set under the vine-and-fig canopy in the courtyard for the feast. The friends and neighbors from the village arriving with ribbons streaming from their carts.

**My fiancé's** other present was less of a success. One evening, he arrived with a great unwieldy object, over which he had thrown some sacking.

"What on earth is it?" I asked, noting that it seemed to have some kind of independent movement as he held it out. The muscles in his arm were straining.

"Open it."

I pulled back the sacking. Two black, beady eyes met mine through the bars of a cage. Instinctively, I pulled back. "A parrot?"

"A parakeet."

It had been given to him by an elderly lady in the next village after he passed through on his way back from town and saw her fall from a loose stone she had been using as a doorstep. It was so typical of him that he mended it for her and took no payment other than a basket of apricots. She insisted he also take the bird in a cage.

The birdcage, a large, ornate cylinder affair made of thick wires, was placed in the corner of the sitting room. From a riot of bright green and yellow and red feathers spouted a vicious, hooked beak. When it launched into a stream of loud expressions of indignation, you could see a devilish blue-gray tongue, which neither Maman nor I could bear to look at.

In short, the bird was a brute, and it soon became obvious why the old woman could stand no more of its squawking. We put it outside by the wood store in the courtyard, and both sides declared an uneasy truce.

But the whole episode did make us laugh.

"If Pierre were here, he'd sell it at the market," said Maman ruefully. "We might get a few sous for it."

It wasn't a bad idea, and André said he would give it a try himself. He came back with it in the afternoon.

# 13

The second body was that of a younger woman.

This time, the remains were exhumed not from the pool area itself but from the raised bed that formed part of the ornamental stone crescent at its head. Weedy clumps of fast-growing herbs had been pulled away by the police team, and they had found her there.

We couldn't believe it. How was it the police search team had found exactly what it seemed they had been denied with the first discovery? What made them keep searching? Had they been looking for further evidence linked to the first when they found the second body, or had they always believed they would find another? I begged Severan to tell us what was happening. His mood was grim exaltation, with a dash of vindication perhaps.

Then he arrested Dom.

"We now have the remains of two bodies on this property," he said curtly when we both protested loudly. "What do you expect us to do?"

They took Dom to police headquarters in Cavaillon for questioning. Severan would tell me nothing more.

**Where lies** the line between books and life, fact and fiction? Of seeing and being seen? It was only now, when events were unfolding, that I recognized, from books rather than experience, that I truly appreciated the boundaries between reality and art. Before, I would read to understand, to think: yes, that person has a dilemma, those were the options available, and—for better or worse—that was the solution she or he chose. I have always argued for the fundamental honesty of fiction. But now I could see more sharply where the honesty lies. Possibly not in the stripping bare of the soul or on the crest of high drama, but in the small details and observations.

Dom hunched over the silent piano, his elbows on the keys. The wave of frozen discord. The great dark space of his absences. His face visibly closing.

**The next** morning, following a sleepless night, strong winds were brawling over the garden. Flowers and shrubs billowed and feinted, flattening themselves under the blows.

In the kitchen, sunlight filtered through the movement in the leaves of the courtyard trees, rendering the white plaster walls inside diaphanous and transitory, like fluttering muslin. A bright, Christmassy scent of freshly peeled oranges was all around. I couldn't think where it came from, as we had only apples in the fruit bowl.

Feeling disoriented, and still in my nightdress, I let myself into the music room, looking not for Dom but some other resolution. Apart from the books of piano pieces—his favorite Schumann, Rachmaninoff, and Chopin—and loose pages of scribbles on staves, there was nothing. I supposed that if I had known more about music then I might have been able to read something into his choices and his own markings, but it was not a language I instinctively understood.

It seemed to me then that I knew as little about Dom as I did on the first day we met, and that any knowledge I had gained in the interim had made him more mysterious to me, rather than less.

Craving a sense of normality, I showered and dressed, then walked up to the village to buy milk and bread.

I trudged up the woodland path and emerged on the road up to the village. The first person I saw, her car parked at the side of the road just by its junction on the last bend, talking rapidly into her mobile, was Sabine.

She waved, rolled down her window, and then stepped out.

There was no escape. She was eager for every last detail. It goes without saying that she already knew what the police had found, and had a firm grasp of all the latest wildfire theories. She knew better than we did what was likely to happen next.

It occurred to me then: was it Sabine who had tipped off the police about Dom? What did she suspect, Sabine who seemed to know more about all of us than was comfortable, and who enjoyed the power it gave her?

**Outside the** café in the village, where we sat for a morning coffee, the sky was a few shades too bright, the clatter from inside a touch too loud.

Sabine considered what I'd just told her. "Why didn't you say something before?" she asked.

Nervously, I twisted the bracelets on my wrist. As I went through some of the incidents that had spooked me—the light flickering on the walls, the sound of stones against the window, the eerie evanescence of scent, the power outages—I felt more stupid. None of these could possibly be anything but random and un-related. It was a relief to be able to tell someone, though

I had to be careful. Not too much information; just enough to prompt her to tell me more than I told her.

Mercifully, she did not seem to know about Dom's arrest. And, above all, I had to deflect her from that.

My gaze rested on the fountain in the square where we sat: black-green with lichen and moss, the water spewing from the mouth of a gargoyle so flattened and worn by age it looked like the head of a tortoise, water as cool and dark as the Styx.

"I thought it was nothing, just . . . crazy incidents, that I was . . . overreacting."

"But you are clearly upset."

"Yes."

"Quite a lot of odd things, all happening in a chain together."

It was a question of relationships, perhaps, between the infinite numbers of unconscious perceptions we make based on our own experience. It is a sum of impressions, in other words. Tricks of the light, yes. But of the inward eye, too.

"I was more scared of making too much of it," I admitted.

"Some of them could easily be accidents, coincidences—the picture smashing, for instance. That happens. The glue on the backing tape dries up and gives out after so many years."

"I know."

"And power outages happen. They happen a lot here sometimes."

"Of course."

"But then the stones at the window . . . those are deliberate actions," said Sabine. "So then you must ask who would be doing these actions deliberately."

"Kids . . . bored kids, having a laugh."

"It's possible. What does Dom say?"

Careful now. "He doesn't."

"But you've told him."

"I don't mention it anymore."

"There is another explanation, if you want to call it that," said Sabine quietly.

It was unsettling how serious she looked. I dropped my eyes and let them wander beyond our table to where the uneven, cobbled road led away up the hill.

"Do you believe in ghosts?"

"No!" I thought she was joking, and laughed, but her composure suggested otherwise.

"No—not at all," I repeated. "Why, what makes you say that?"

"I shouldn't have. Forget it."

# 14

There was a boy in the village I had always been friendly with. He was in my class at school. Henri claimed he was in love with me, but I never had those feelings for him. His jaw was too heavy, and his bottom lip seemed to swing pendulously. It grew worse as he aged, which was a shame. He worked on his family's farm on the other side of the hill; they kept a large herd of goats and made cheeses, good, strong cheeses, and the smell of that always seemed to linger around him and leave savory trails in his wake. He was a musician, too, and played in the band at the fetes in the small villages in this eastern end of the valley. Unloosing his accordion to squeeze out torrents of notes, Henri was the star of the show with his fine renditions of popular songs as well as the complex, swooping rhythms of the traditional dances.

When I danced with André in our village, Henri never took his eyes off us. I was uncomfortable and flattered all at once. But then, at the end of the set, when the band was taking a break, swigging rough rosé, he leaped down and caught me by the arm.

"Sorry, so sorry," he said to me. "But I have to do this."

Before I could ask what he meant, he had swung for André. Blood dripped from André's nose and formed rosettes on his white shirt.

"What are you doing? What's going on?"

By now, other people were gathering to enjoy the spectacle.

"Ask him. Get him to tell you."

"I don't know what you're talking about."

There was a tone in his voice that didn't ring true. "André?" I asked. "What is he talking about?"

"I have no idea."

"Roussillon. Ask him how much fun he had at the Roussillon fete last week. Go on, ask him."

"Oh, for goodness sake, come on Béné, let's go."

"No, André, wait." I couldn't conceive that my old friend would be behaving like this for no good reason. "Last weekend you went back to see your family, didn't you? You weren't even in Roussillon."

"No, of course not." He rubbed his palm across his bloodied face.

"Yes you were. You were with a pretty woman and two small children who called you Papa."

"What?"

"I was playing with the band. Their accordion player was sick and I was the substitute. I recognized you and watched you all night from the stage. You barely left your family's side. You kissed your wife a few strides away from where I was having a drink and promised your work would be finished and you would be back for your fifth wedding anniversary next month."

I turned to my fiancé, incredulous. "Is this right?"

It was obvious from his sudden sheepishness that it was, but I persisted. "I ask you again. Is this true?"

"I never wanted to hurt you."

"So it is true!" I felt my bones melt, as if I might fall down on the spot. Other people had stopped speaking nearby, the better to take in the drama. "Then why? Why ask me to marry you? Why lead me on when you already had a wife and children back home?"

He sighed and shook his head. "Because . . . because . . . I care for you so much, Bénédicte. I could not help it, and . . . no, don't turn away, listen to me! There's a long story. I was pushed to marry her. Our families always wanted it, not me. Why do you think

I spent so long away? Because I wanted to escape. Because I found you, and I thought there might be a way for us, if we could only find it!"

It was a pretty speech. I even found I believed some of it, probably because I wanted to so badly.

André reached out to touch me.

I drew back sharply, all too aware that we had an audience. "What are you doing? Go! Please go now! Don't make it any worse!"

By then, some of the other men had started jeering, telling him to get out of the village. Henri put a protective arm around my shoulders.

André had no choice. He turned and walked away.

I was hollow. I felt as if my insides had disappeared and I was just a shell. The ax had fallen so swiftly, entirely without warning.

André left that night. I have no idea where he went; he just walked off into the blackness.

For weeks, I was inconsolable, unable to sleep or eat. I dragged myself through a dank imitation of life, in which every action seemed to require too much effort. I barely spoke, even to Maman. I retraced the paths we'd walked, and cried until it felt like there was not a drop of moisture left in me.

Then, late one night, long after I would have gone to bed if there had been any point in doing so, I saw it—

the light on the path, in our secret place. I shuddered, sure I was imagining it. But as I approached, I heard my name being called in a whisper.

I jumped. "Who's there?"

It sounded like him. It couldn't be him.

Again, my name. Then he stepped out from the shadows by the *bergerie.*

André had returned.

I would have leaped into his arms. More than anything, I wanted to, yet I held myself in check.

"What do you want?" I asked in a small, flat voice.

"A chance to explain."

"Please don't lie to me again."

"I won't lie. And I never lied when I told you I loved you and I wanted to marry you, that you were the most lovely girl I had ever held in my arms."

"And you never wanted to hurt me," I said mockingly.

He protested, of course. But there was nothing he could say that could alter the situation. He was married. It was impossible.

For the second time, I sent him away.

The next morning, I found the birdcage was open, and the parakeet gone. I remember feeling glad about that, considering it an act of mercy. As André well knew, I never liked the bird, and I didn't want it there to remind me how badly I'd been deceived.

So, that was how I once had a fiancé. Or, rather, to be more accurate, how I once had a lover, since there were fundamental reasons why André was never my fiancé, not really. In the space of a few cruel minutes, out under the lights of the village square, with everyone watching, he stopped being my André, and became someone else's husband and father of two small children.

It was such an abrupt end to my dreams; and such a long time before I came to terms with it. So many different facets of the story held me back. He must have loved me—he couldn't have faked that, the way he held me with such tenderness. It must have been an impossible situation. A genuine love story that had begun when we had least expected it. He was not a terrible person. Then again, perhaps he was just an adventurer with a glib line in explanations.

I found it hard to trust people after that.

Funny enough, we kept the cage after the fiend flew away. I suppose we must have thought we could sell it if a dealer from one of the traveling secondhand markets ever called. It was an interesting-looking object, and strong, too. Someone might have been able to make use of it. But that was another opportunity that passed us by. As far as I know, it's still there, by the wood store, rusting and empty.

Everyone and everything is gone, except me. Maybe if I could find the courage to step out beyond my bars . . . But, you see, I never had a reason to go.

And now they are all coming back. Perhaps it wasn't a light on the path, after all. Perhaps it was the spirit of that parakeet trying to materialize. Now that would worry me.

# 15

Taking a deep breath, I asked Sabine, "I suppose you still haven't managed to track Rachel down, since we last spoke? I felt a bit uncomfortable with the idea of translating her notes, as if I was taking something of hers without her permission."

The inference couldn't have been louder and clearer.

This was the real reason, of course, that I'd agreed to sit down and drink coffee with Sabine when all I really wanted was to be on my own with my hurt and confusion. And however wary I was of Sabine and suspicious of her motives, she was the only key I had to understanding. Rachel was the link. Knowledge was power, and what I needed was some more of it.

Sabine studied her cup before she replied. "No. Still no sign of Rachel."

As usual, she would talk about Rachel, though.

"Rachel was a curious person."

Did Sabine mean that Rachel was a little odd, or that she often showed curiosity? I couldn't help but be drawn in.

"There was a story that Rachel told me once, about herself," said Sabine. "I suppose I remember it because it's a tale that appeals to me."

"What was it?"

Sabine settled herself more comfortably. "Rachel liked talking to strangers, which was how this incident began. She was on a train journey, and a conversation started between her and a couple sitting opposite. They were very charming, only a few years older than she was.

"They all got on extremely well, and when the time came for her to change trains, it turned out they were making the same stop. It was lunchtime, and she had a couple of hours to kill before making her connection, so when they asked her if she would care to join them for a meal at a local café in the square, she accepted their invitation with real pleasure.

"The train pulled in. It was a small town, but more akin to a large village in atmosphere. They walked from the station to the prettiest square, shaded with plane trees, which cast dappled light over the shops and houses. It was a *place* such as one always hopes to find.

The scent of newly baked bread from the *boulangerie*. Busy and friendly but not too crowded. They sat outside, where they were served delicious food and wine, all the time still enjoying a wonderful conversation, a real meeting of the minds.

"The couple even walked Rachel back to the station and waited with her until she was safely on the right train."

Sabine paused. I was beginning to wonder what the point was.

"A few days later, Rachel was flipping through a newspaper when she saw a picture of the young couple. She was sure it was them, and the first names matched up. They had died in a plane crash, an accident in a small private aircraft, the same day as she had met them, but, oddly, the crash happened on a flight between two airfields hundreds of kilometers away from where they had eaten lunch."

"It might have been possible, depending on timing. Or she was simply mistaken—it wasn't the same couple," I said.

Sabine nodded. "Of course. But now here's the thing. For years after, Rachel carried the image in her mind of the perfect lunch in the perfect square, knowing she would have to return one day to see if it was as lovely as she remembered. The only thing she could not remember, and could not work out using even the most detailed maps, was the name of the town. And when at last there came the chance to take the same trains south, she decided to break the journey in the same town in the same way. But a connection was no longer possible. The trains ran direct to her destination. So she decided to drive.

"She approached the area where the train must have stopped, but none of the names of the towns and villages along the railway line was the right one. She drove all along the route, dipping in and out of the places that could possibly have been reached on foot from the station, but none of them opened out into that perfect square."

"She never found it again?"

Sabine shook her head. "Never."

"When did all this happen—just before you met her?"

"No, several years before. But it's a poignant story, no?"

I wasn't sure what to think. It reminded me of something. It might have been one of those apocryphal tales of la France profonde, like the strangers who find the perfect restaurant and eat the most wonderful pâté they have ever tasted, then disappear, only to be minced by the chef, added to the other ingredients in the ambrosial recipe, and offered to the next customers.

Was Rachel's a true story? I didn't think so. It had too many shades of romance. And I found it hard to believe that a seasoned journalist like her would forget the name of the town if it had made such an impression.

It was nicely open-ended, too. There was no spine-chilling detail about the couple being ten years younger at the lunch than they were in the newspaper, and it being ten years since the trains had ceased to connect at the town's station. It was simply about the power of the imagination, and the way it can affect memory.

"It's a good story," I said.

A clatter from the café kitchen seemed to make Sabine refocus. "What does Dom say about her?"

It was the way she said it. Knowing. Waiting for me to catch on.

"Nothing. We don't talk about her," I said automatically.

"He used to get angry with her."

"You saw that?"

"Rachel told me."

A pause.

Sabine went on, forcefully, locking the beam of her eyes with mine: "He's never admitted, though he pretends not to know, that she might be still here in Provence after all? But that she might be dead?"

It was a terrible thing to think, let alone to say out loud.

"What exactly are you saying, Sabine?" I said slowly.

# 16

Without André, it was hard to keep up with the chores. Neglect, of the land, of the buildings, of myself, crept in for far too long until you could hardly think it was the same place that once had so many people living here—four, even five families with children, and all the animals, too.

Animals drinking springwater at the trough under the fountain, the stone bowl giving the scene a decadent air, had been a symbol for so long of the farm's unique blessing, and now the trough filled with dead leaves whirring down from the plane trees.

I should have—could have—married. A good, strong husband could have taken charge, but after André, strange as it may seem, I never met a man

I loved in that way. Henri (he of the accordion and the unfortunate lower lip) asked me, naturally, and I even seriously considered accepting, but in the end, I turned him down. I liked him too much, you see, to shortchange him like that. It would always have been a compromise of feeling. Besides which, I'm not sure I could have gone through with . . . the physical aspect, not with him, not after knowing what it could be with André. So that was that.

Marthe once said I was shooting the messenger, but she was wrong.

**Marthe wanted** me to go to Paris, and I did—for a visit. What she had in mind was for me to live with her there, and gradually make my own way in the metropolis, taking advantage of all the introductions my sister would have been able to give me in scent firms and shops, but I always felt uncomfortable in a great city, and longed to be back on the hillside with the valley spread out before me.

Besides, I had to get back to Les Genévriers. I wasn't feeling well and needed to be home.

**I have** heard it said that a happy childhood is a curse, because what follows can never measure up. All I can say is, those people must want too much; they can't accept that life is a series of struggles and that happiness can be found in overcoming them, drawing strength from the reserves laid down in the good years.

Back at the farm, I tried to soothe my ills by lying in a bath infused with lavender essence. I put my faith in its healing properties, in a fog of forgotten prescriptions of the nuns who grew it as a medicine, and sent the buds to be strewn on the stone floors of palaces and monasteries to mask foul odors and fight disease; the good witches' herb, believed to repel evil spirits from entering the house.

As I lay soaking, I summoned the scents of the past. The spicy blue junipers and the lemon thyme on the hot, dry slopes below. The winter heliotrope, also known as sweet-scented coltsfoot, which grows in hedges and at roadsides, by streams and even on wasteland. There is nothing rare or precious about it. It is treated as a weed, an invasive nuisance, but it always reminded me of Marthe and our childhood, and spurred me on as I tried to block out the pain and the growing certainty that I knew what was wrong.

**So it** was that not long after I returned from Paris, I went to see Mme. Musset in Manosque.

Marthe had spoken fondly of her, and then given me a selection of perfume samples, which I offered to take to her old mentor. I suppose I could have sent them in a parcel, but I chose to take them myself on the bus and the train. I had realized by then, you see.

I needed help, and Mme. Musset was the one person I knew who could supply it.

# 17

When I got back, Dom was there.

He was sitting at the kitchen table, head in his hands. I was so choked by angry questions that I could only stare at him, trying to pretend I wasn't frightened by what might happen next.

"Sorry."

He sounded defeated. I turned away instinctively from whatever it was he was sorry about. I didn't want to hear any more lies of omission. It was obvious that he had been hiding a great deal from me, but I couldn't decide whether hearing it was worse than not.

"They let you go, then."

He scarcely managed to raise his eyes, let alone meet mine.

"Are you going to tell me what happened?"

At that, he blanched. I had never seen the color physically drain from a person's face before.

"Happened?"

"With the police, at Cavaillon?"

"I don't . . ."

"Let me guess. You don't want to talk about it."

He closed his eyes tightly.

"Why did they take you in, Dom? On what grounds?"

A shake of the head and a mumble I didn't catch.

I had no idea what to say next. My head was bursting with frustration and anger. I wanted to rush at him and lash out, pound the truth out of him, but of course I did not.

"What is wrong with you?" I shouted at last.

Slumped at the table, he seemed to shrink.

"Why do you not want to tell me anything? Whatever it is I would help you but you push me away all the time! I'm not stupid, I'm not insensitive, but I need to know! Otherwise . . . otherwise what am I to think! Please, Dom . . ."

My words seemed to ring, too thin and high, all around us in the silence.

Then he broke. His head went farther down and his shoulders rose. A horrible sound came from his chest. I stood there, waiting, still furiously running through possibilities in my mind, waiting for him to tell me something—anything. It was a few minutes before I realized he was sobbing.

Even then, I couldn't bring myself to comfort him. I continued to stand over him, as his shoulders heaved, and the strangled noises from his mouth made me feel hard and brittle and confused.

Sabine's parting shot still reverberated. How could she suggest Rachel was still in Provence, maybe even here on this property? That made no sense. But then Dom's arrest made no sense to me.

"They released me without charge," he said.

His voice was so quiet I had to lean in close to hear him. Through the window, the hills were misted, each a darker tone; the effect was that of a Victorian silhouette panorama in a box, so flat was the light. A thunderstorm would break soon.

"So . . . why arrest you in the first place? Just because you are the owner of the property? They had no other reason than that, no?"

"I suppose."

"What did they want to know that you hadn't already told Severan here?"

"They just kept asking the same questions."

"Did they ask about Castellet?"

He looked at me as if he hadn't heard right. "What?"

"They didn't mention . . . Castellet?"

"What's that got to do with anything?"

I reined myself in. "And could you tell them any-thing more—about the bones?" I asked, with a small measure of relief.

"How could I? Of course not."

"It's just that . . ."

"How could you ask that?"

"How?" I shouted. "Because you won't tell me any-thing! How do I know you're not guilty?"

"Guilty . . . ?" His face was still drained. Tiredness and tension were etched into every line.

"Guilty, Dom." I knew I was twisting the knife, but I had no intention of stopping now, not after all the evasions and uncertainties. "Guilty of something, I'm sure of that. You've been secretive. There's more locked away than you will ever admit, but you get so angry if I ask . . ."

He was waiting, making me come out and say it. Terrified as I was of the answers he might give, I blazed on. My eyes stung with the effort of hold-ing back the tears. "You say it's not true, but I can see you're not happy! And when I look back to see whether it's me, what I've done wrong, I keep coming back to the same point. Me wanting to know about . . . Rachel."

The light outside was now a deadly ocher.

Dom's hand trembled. His posture, his expression, his voice: all were deadened. "Why does everything come down to Rachel with you? What has this to do with her?"

I swallowed. "If I ask you some questions, now, would you answer them?"

He stared somewhere beyond my head, and nodded, imperceptibly.

"Did you and Rachel have a child together?"

"No."

"Do you still love her?"

It was as if I had hit him in the face. "You've asked me that before."

"Because . . ." I went on shakily, "Because I'm trying to understand you, and—and you make it so hard. Because I'm beginning to wonder if I know you at all, and what I'm doing here."

There, it was said.

"Are you telling me you want to leave? Please don't . . ."

"No . . . I am not saying that."

It seemed he hadn't heard me. "Because, you know, I don't think it would look good . . . Not right now, the police . . ."

"I won't—"

"I need you, Eve. You have no idea how much. Promise me you will stay with me, even if it's only until all this is over. After that . . ."

"So answer me. Did you leave her, or . . ."

The silence seemed to stretch forever.

"She died," said Dom at last.

I knew it. All around us was a sense of fruitlessness, of utter weariness. It was a while before I could even say it. "Why didn't you tell me before?"

# 18

Maman died in her sleep.

She was too young to go, but she looked far older than her years, by the end. The doctor couldn't find a reason, any heart attack or stroke. One day she was there, and the next she wasn't. An awful time, I don't want to say more.

As for Pierre, he returned briefly to lay our mother to rest after Marthe and I put a notice in the newspaper. I had no idea where he was. I had no means of contacting him, and neither did I have any particular wish to. Like so many of the young men, he went away to the town sure that he knew everything about modern life.

Meanwhile, I stayed, occasionally feeling betrayed, usually just lonely.

Poverty is stunting. Even the threat of it bears down on the human spirit. For centuries, people had known what it was to be poor: it meant that there was no choice but to go on scratching what they could from the soil, and gathering what grew wild. Now there was a choice. The wheels of industry were moving, drawing people down from the old life—the old imprisonment—in the hills. Many did not realize they were exchanging one kind of poverty for another.

In the past, there was never any poverty of purpose, of love, of faith, of companionship, of family support in the villages and farmsteads. For all the back-breaking work and the unpredictability of due reward, there was richness for the senses all around. Independence, neighborliness, and mutual understanding.

**When Marthe** suggested selling the farm, I said no. Under no circumstances would I be willing to sell, which was a display of bravado, partly an unwillingness to admit failure, and mostly stubbornness. I did not say that to her.

Anyway, my position was irrelevant. The truth was, without being in touch with Pierre, we were stuck. We could not sell without his consent, consent between the three siblings clear for all to see at the notary's office.

And who in their right mind would want to buy a failed farm? If we, who had lived there for generations, could not make it pay anymore, what hope for anyone else? Besides, the *paysan*—the country person—is custodian of the land, and it must be worked; that was what Papa always said. I struggled on.

As the years passed, the world's turning brought with it the hope of a solution, of sorts. This region had always attracted summer visitors, and now, with the success of the great move to the big, industrialized centers, the workers were returning, hoping to renew themselves with a week or two under the southern sun.

By the 1960s, more and more people had money to spend on travel. All they wanted was sunshine and scenery for a few weeks. A few forward-thinking families had begun to offer rooms to rent at reasonable rates, and found themselves doing well. Many letters passed between us, and in the end, using Marthe's money, we decided to repaint and repair the cottages to take in paying guests.

Thanks to Marthe's prestige in Paris, among the growing number of her happy clients were plenty who were charmed by the suggestion of staying at her childhood home. They came and stayed, and spread the word. After a few years, we were able to afford to employ a young couple to help. Soon we were opening at Easter and receiving guests until mid-October, when the sun's sorcery was finally dampened by rains and the approach of winter. They were good years.

The couple, Jean and Nadine, stayed for five summers. They were hard workers and we got along well. The more acclaim Marthe's perfume shop received, the greater was the demand for our cottages. The visitors would ask all about my sister and I was content to tell them tales of our life here as a family, though carefully omitting any mention of the precise circumstances of Papa's death.

Over time, visitors began to include wealthy foreigners—northern Europeans, who rarely saw the sun, and Americans, who roamed our country and others in their big, bright clothes.

It was after the stay of one friendly, boisterous family from California, in 1972, and on their suggestion, that Marthe and I decided to invest some of our profits in a swimming pool.

If we hadn't had our magnificent source of springwater, we wouldn't have entertained the idea. But it all seemed to make sense at the time. It was to be a very basic affair, using local men to dig out the hole and line it with concrete, but it would be an added attraction, commensurate with the cachet of Marthe Lincel's name, and it would certainly give us another advantage over other local holiday properties. To be honest, the pool was never really very good. It would go green in the heat of August, and it always leaked, in a slow, dispiriting seep. But that was later. I am getting ahead of myself.

# 19

I spun the zoetrope.

Through the slits, the pictures blurred together inside the wheel to give the illusion of movement. A miniature dancer kicked one dainty leg and then the other. Over and over again, for as many times as I cared to spin the device. The story would never change. The only way it could alter was in the mind, in the understanding of it from a basis of newly acquired knowledge.

Rachel was dead.

"How?" I'd asked. "When?"

Dom had his head in his hands. "Please don't do this . . ."

"But I need to know! For God's sake, why can't you understand that?"

A silence, which I was not going to break.

"It was nearly two years ago. She had cancer. She was ill, and she died. I should have told you that before, and I made a mistake, okay? I'm sorry. It was hard to talk about, you know?" He finally looked up, but couldn't hold my eyes.

"But—"

"No, I really don't want to talk about how I feel, then or now. It won't help. Believe me, I know, it will not help. Please." Please leave it, he meant, don't make me think about it anymore, I don't want to talk about this, nothing has changed.

What could I say? It was trite to tell him I understood he was still grieving, that maybe he hadn't allowed himself to grieve properly, so I had to drop it.

And so, incredibly, on the surface, nothing did change between us. For a few more weeks, anyway. I kept up my side of the charade, my emotions in turmoil, locked into inaction. Because something had happened—was happening—that made me need him, quietly, more than ever. It was dreadful timing, and I wasn't absolutely sure, but all the signs were there.

**As we** maintained our composure, Dom at his piano, I with my books, what we both sensed, I think, was the desperation behind our efforts, the drive to understand. I did not know how music could change and charge the emotions, where it came from. It was too wide and deep and haunting for me, a person who needs to pin down and unravel emotions in words.

We were both afraid, in our different ways.

At night, he held me tightly and whispered, "I promise you, absolutely promise you, that we will get through this. I know it all seems as if it's all going wrong, and it's horrible, but it will be all right, I promise. Nothing changes how I feel about you. If it's possible, I love you more now than in the beginning."

I wanted so badly to believe him, to trust in him—more desperately than ever. To be reassured that I had not lost all reason when I fell for him.

**Memories form** in counterbalance with forgetting. You can look at a photograph, years later, of a place that is vivid in your memory, and find that it looks nothing like the pictures filed in your brain. Only a few specific details will tally exactly, making the rest a strange reminder of what has been forgotten. Do photographs and memories complement each other, or do photographs inevitably prove more dominant, ultimately taking the place of the true memory?

Sight offers such a powerful and immediate understanding that an image always seems more persuasive, a proof of what was once seen. We believe the evidence of our eyes. When we hear, think, touch, smell, there is always the suspicion that we might be on the wrong track, we might be mistaken.

And the interconnections we make between pictures can produce a dangerously subjective narrative. If I had succeeded in finding a photograph of Rachel stowed in a drawer, would I really have seen her, or what my own assumptions supplied?

I would have seen her beauty for myself, and one of the reasons he loved her. My mind would have grasped on to the way he had tried to love someone else in her place and had clearly failed. In these scenes, I would never be the woman Rachel was, only a pale imitation. No matter how hard I tried to be a better partner, I was only a partner, not a wife.

Yet, whatever Sabine said, Rachel did not have his child.

Rereading Rachel's articles, I was struck again by her resourcefulness. The way she wrote, too. It was obvious she liked stringing along a story. There may not even have been much of a story—no proper ending—but that didn't matter. It was a world in miniature and it spoke of human nature. Sometimes I think that's really all you need in a book, though it's rare to find it in a newspaper article. I admired her.

I could understand why Dom would want to marry her.

She seemed to care, too, about the outcome, about the people she met. And it seemed they warmed to her; otherwise, how could they have opened up as they did?

Perhaps this was the key to my own peace of mind. I needed to recognize that here was someone with strength of character and purpose. She was her own person and she had died. Dom had come to terms with that, and now I had to, as well.

Toward the end of the Francis Tully piece, I came to the part about Magie, his young model. I call her Magie, he'd said. That implied it wasn't her real name, or even the one by which most people knew her. Perhaps we are all different people, depending on whom we are with.

## 20

It was after the work on the pool had begun, under the chill blue skies of spring, when the rains had ceased, that the first intimations of a downturn in our run of good fortune crept in. As I have said already, in a big old place like this, objects always appeared and disappeared. But when items of more value began to move, it was something different.

First, it was my silver hairbrush, bequeathed to me by Mémé Clémentine. I searched and searched, all the while knowing that I would never have put it anywhere but in its usual place on my dressing table. I was upset because it was so precious to me, a symbol of all I remembered about her. The idea that it had been stolen was horrible, yet what other conclusion could I draw?

Then a small picture went from one of the downstairs rooms that were normally left shuttered. By the time the gilt clock in the hall disappeared, I was beside myself, forced to suspect the pool contractor and his men as the only possible perpetrators, and all the while wondering how they thought they would get away with such dishonor among neighbors. Unpleasant scenes chased through my head. It was reminiscent of Pierre's old tricks.

So I shouldn't have been that shocked to find, quite soon afterward, that he had returned, bold as brass, with no explanation or apology for his prolonged absence.

**The day** I went to the secondhand furniture store to find some bedside tables with the right degree of age and patina on them, I returned to find an unknown car held together by corrosion and postal tape, and Pierre in the courtyard, looking around at the trees as if perturbed by how much they had grown since he had last seen them. "They say places seem smaller when you come back after a long time," he said. "But I'd forgotten how big this house is. And what the hell are you doing in the garden?"

His face had changed. The eyes that used to glint with mischief had grown dull, the skin around them puffed and baggy. He had lost his athletic body, but then what grown man stays the same as he was as a youth? He was now just over fifty, but even so, the transformation since I had last seen him was radical. What was most painful to see was the sneer now permanently embedded in the lines and flesh of his face. He made no observation about my own personal changes beyond a swift, appraising stare.

He walked around the place without saying another word, which immediately put me on my guard. I had no idea what he wanted.

I made up a bed in his old room, and he ate most of the supper I prepared. Conversation faltered, the atmosphere became strained and belligerent when he admitted he was after money.

"We need to sell this place," he said.

I told him how Marthe had once suggested selling and how we had decided to develop it instead. "That was a wise move," I said emphatically. "We've built up a good little business here."

"Let's see how she thinks now, then. Get her here."

It was hard to eat when my crossness with him was nearly choking me, but my childhood ability to suppress my emotions in his company still worked, it seemed. He retired early, after drinking a bottle of good wine from the cellar.

I sent a telegram to Marthe from the post office the next morning, knowing there would be no peace until I did. "Pierre has returned. Wants serious discussion. Please come soonest."

**Despite the** urgency implicit in my message, it was nearly a week before Marthe was able to travel. She had commitments in Paris, and then the added complication of arranging a visit to Manosque on some kind of business, which she could explain in due course. We had to be content with that.

The days with Pierre did not improve. He continued to march around with private purpose and sullen expression. He made a few disparaging remarks about the food I served, complained about his raffia mattress, drank wine, and refused point-blank to enlighten me about his current circumstances. At a guess, they were not happy ones.

I was relieved when he took himself off to town, saying he would wait there, where there was life and good company, until Marthe turned up. I was to leave a message at the bar on the corner of the square, the Lou Pastis, when she arrived.

The silver candlesticks and Maman's mirror disappeared at the same time. I didn't care for the objects themselves, but it was the principle of the matter, and what it said about Pierre's attitude toward the family, that hurt.

**On Thursday,** Marthe finally arrived, accompanied by a young girl, the two of them escorted by a polite young man in a smart suit. The girl was about sixteen, and very shy. Marthe introduced her as Annette, who was to be her new apprentice, and told us proudly that she came highly recommended by the school at Manosque. The warmth in her voice was clearly intended to reassure the girl, and indeed, Annette smiled and seemed to relax a little.

"Come in, come in!" I tried to emulate my sister's tone.

Annette patted her hand along the top of her valise before she found the handle.

"Do you need to take my arm?" I offered.

"No, thank you."

Confounding my expectations, she then seemed to have no trouble finding the start of the steps leading up to the kitchen.

"She's not completely blind. She's partially sighted," said Marthe, as if reading my mind.

I set out some cake to welcome them, and put the coffee on the stove. My fingers were trembling. This small show of domestic harmony could not protect any of us.

Barely had I shown Annette to the bathroom to wash her hands after the journey and returned to pour the coffee, when Pierre crossed his arms and stated his case.

"The farm must be sold as soon as possible," he announced. "I have instructed a land agent."

He hadn't even waited to ask Marthe her news.

"Why?" she asked reasonably, though with a harder edge to her voice.

"I need the money."

Marthe's shoulders stiffened visibly.

"This is my inheritance as much as yours," he went on. "I want my share."

He had a point, of course he did. "You'll get your share," I said, emboldened by Marthe's presence. "We're not trying to deny you your share, it's just that—well, this is all a bit too sudden. You go away for years and years, while we find a way to keep everything afloat, quite successfully at the moment, as it happens . . . and now out of the blue you come back making demands. We will sit down and discuss this calmly and rationally. Later."

Pierre picked out a sharp knife from the drawer and began to clean his filthy fingernails. "We need to get on with it," he said.

"Yes, thank you, Bénédicte, I will take some coffee," said Marthe pointedly. "And the cake smells delicious—lemon with a hint of ginger, am I right?"

The young man from Manosque took his leave soon after, and, luckily for us all, dinner was not a long, drawn-out affair. Annette, tired and overwhelmed, had respectfully requested an early withdrawal to the bedroom I had hastily made up for her.

The argument downstairs could begin.

**Marthe was** even more resolute than me. The years in Paris in business had left her well able to stand her ground and put forward her opinions emphatically yet with an impressive detachment. Inwardly, I was cheering as she said quietly but firmly: "Your demands are completely unreasonable." His attitude, too, though she did not need to say it.

"Without our consent you cannot sell, so the instruction of a land agent is a waste of his time and yours. You want the money that would be raised by selling. You left the family and the farm long ago, so we can assume no great attachment to the property. This is a question of money. The money does not have to be raised by the sale of this place. If it's money you need, then we can go to the notary and come to some formal arrangement whereby, perhaps not in full but partially, we can buy you out."

"Why do you need so much money right now, anyway?" I wanted to know.

Pierre tossed me a glance of sheer contempt.

"Yes, it would be nice to know what has prompted all this," said Marthe. "What kind of trouble are you in?"

"I'm sure you would like to know, but it's really none of your business."

"But this is our business!" I cried, meaning the farm. "And it's a good business now. We're doing well! Why not let us continue with it?"

"While your own flesh and blood starves . . ."

He did not look as if he was starving, and I was quick to point this out. "Anyway, it's you who doesn't care about the family! We did think of selling a few years back, when things were really hard here, but we couldn't. And why not?" Expediently, I glossed over my objections at the time; the point was what was important. "I'll tell you why not, because you were nowhere to be found. Couldn't even let us have an address, could you?"

Pierre waved that away, an irrelevance. "I want what is due to me, and for it to be divided now. Why should I let you keep the property only to see that you are twice as rich from it in ten years? That would be unfair."

"But that's the way it works, Pierre," said Marthe. She looked so tired as she took him firmly but kindly through the principles of ownership. "If you want your share out now, you get the current price. If you stay in, maybe with some of your share released in advance, it will be calculated as a percentage of the current price, but you will still have a stake in the property, the same as we do."

What she could not see was that she was not speaking to a rational person. Pierre, hunched inside his dusty coat, picked his teeth with the point of the knife and waved away her reasoning with a hand that trembled.

"You just don't want me to have what's mine. But I'm here to tell you that you will do what I say. Bitches!"

"But it's working. It's a good business," I said.

"Gah! This is just a little toy for you now, this place. You don't farm. How can it be a business?"

"A good business," reiterated Marthe. "Which could be worth a great deal more in years to come."

"A blank no, then, is it?"

It was, we said.

"That's it, then."

"Not exactly," I said. "Where are Mémé Clémentine's hairbrush, and the candlesticks from the dining room, and Maman's old mirror, and the clock?"

Pierre exhaled heavily to demonstrate his irritation, then threw the knife into the wooden table with such force that it stood quivering on its tip.

# 21

Lieutenant Severan began, in the indifferent voice he used when delivering more bad news, "We are calling in a specialist, a blood-spatter analyst."

"Blood?"

"Where have you found blood?"

He ignored us.

"This analyst is stupendous. He can see the story in the patterns on the floor and walls like the rest of us can read a map."

All the time, he was studying our reactions.

Something was going to happen.

"We would like to seal off the house, and search it thoroughly using all the most up-to-date techniques."

"Have you found something else?" asked Dom.

If they had, he wouldn't tell us.

"You can leave. Go wherever you want. You must report to a police station in person every day, wherever you decide to stay."

"When you say, 'You can leave,' you are really saying that we are now required to leave our property and turn it over to the police investigation," I asserted.

"That is correct."

"And this is because you have found blood, what, here in the house?"

"Yes."

"Where?"

But Severan would not tell us that, either.

**No matter** how unpleasant others can be, the pain we are capable of inflicting on ourselves is far sharper. When Dom asked, in deadened tones, if there was anywhere in particular I would like to go, I said: "Cassis."

I suppose I wanted to gauge his response.

"Why there?" he asked.

It was what I'd expected him to say, but what I had not anticipated was the way he said it—as if he were resigned, defeated even.

"A couple of reasons," I said.

He didn't ask what they were.

"If you wish," he said.

"I've always wanted to go to Cassis," I said, justifying myself even though he had asked for no justification.

# 22

What happened next, I would give anything to change.

Pierre let out a terrible, growling sound. Then he ran out of the room, shouting incoherently.

We listened, horrified, as fury carried him through the house, pulling pictures and hangings from the walls, smashing china and glass. Neither of us said a word. For a few moments, we were too stunned to react. The sounds of his destruction were getting louder and more crazed. Oh, how I wished there were other families still living in the cottages, whom we could have called for help and known it would have come in the reassuring bulk of Gaston Poidevin or Serge Barberoux.

"Annette," whispered Marthe.

"I'll . . . Don't worry . . . I'll . . ." Not knowing what else to do, I charged upstairs to the girl's room, whispered something I hoped was reassuring, then quickly locked the door on the outside and pocketed the key.

Down in the kitchen, Pierre reappeared in the doorway with another bottle from the cellar. "So," he said. "You still think you know best?"

We didn't answer.

"All this is mine too! Do you hear? Mine too!" He pulled out a drawer, throwing knives and forks and other implements to the floor as he scrabbled for a corkscrew with one hand and held the bottle in the other. When he couldn't find it, he let out another cry and smashed the neck of the bottle against the top of the table. Red wine dripped obscenely, splattering the floor, as he decanted what was left into a large water glass and drank deeply.

He turned then and walked out. We heard his heavy tread on the stairs, and for that duration, I think, we both felt a flood of relief that he was taking himself to bed to sleep it off.

Marthe's face was pale, her voice shaky. "How long has he been like this?"

I realized then that I should have explained the situation better to Marthe. I had thought I was using my discretion in front of Annette. I assumed that Marthe would grasp straightaway the state of affairs with Pierre by the smell of drink and dirt on him, that she did not need to see his reddened, dark-rimmed eyes above their baggy pouches, the lack of pride in his dress and long, unkempt hair. Perhaps that was just another shame I wished to hide from her.

I had to remind myself that Marthe would never have to make adjustments for all the years she had been away, would never see the disappointing present reality of her childhood home; in her mind, it would be exactly as it had always been. I thought of all the times, too, when our parents had turned their own blind eyes to Pierre's darker nature, his cruelty and arrogance, his reckless disregard for any of us. Was it possible that Marthe really had no idea, that she was shocked by what she was hearing? In trying to protect her, what damage had I done?

**Blows exploded** on a closed wooden door. The only door that wouldn't have yielded was the one I had locked upstairs.

We rushed up, Marthe holding on to my skirt.

"Stop this now, Pierre. Leave the girl alone. This is nothing to do with her." Marthe's voice rang out clearly, but even she was beginning to lose her nerve.

By that time, I was desperately trying to pull him away, to stop the battering. From inside the room came the sound of sobbing.

Maybe I should have run to fetch help from the village, but there was no time. I should have picked up the jagged bottle and hit his back with it hard enough to inflict an injury that would have made him stop. There was no time.

The door gave.

With a roar, he sprang inside. Annette was huddled in the corner, curled up on the bed, petrified by the noise and commotion. What must she have thought she had been brought into?

She screamed as he grabbed her.

"You want to help her, a stranger, more than you'll help me!"

"That's not true, Pierre."

Instinctively, the girl bit the arm that coiled around her waist.

"This girl has sharp teeth," said Pierre. "That can be dangerous."

He pulled her off the bed and dragged her roughly past us, despite the fists and scratches we were both trying to land on his arms. But it was as if he were possessed.

We followed them downstairs, then out into the dark courtyard, and the garden beyond. The girl was not so much screaming as yelping, as if he had his hand over her mouth.

"Stop this! Stop this now!" cried Marthe, behind me, clinging to my arm. "What are you doing?"

Two by two, we were stumbling farther into the garden. There was no moon to illuminate the scene. When Marthe and I fell, I had almost as little idea as she did of where exactly we were. By the time we were on our feet again, I could no longer make out any movement ahead.

"Pierre!" I shouted.

"Annette!" called Marthe.

When I felt my leg hit against stone, I realized we were at the low wall near the great hole the contractor had dug for the swimming pool.

"Wait here," I said to Marthe. "You can sit on this wall. Let me go after them."

My eyes were getting more used to the pitch-black. Sure I could make them out ahead, I pushed on, not daring to think what Pierre had in mind for the poor girl.

Suddenly my feet went out from under me. I was grabbed from behind, and my arms were twisted up behind my back. Wind rushed in the trees, or perhaps it was the blood in my head, pounding like angry waves, which seemed to pull me down. As I fell, my head hit rock.

I lay semiconscious and helpless as Annette's screams cut through the night. There was no doubt what our brute of a brother was doing, and I was powerless to help her.

# 23

"W e are leaving," I told Sabine. She had wandered down the track again on one of her well-timed walks now that Severan had unblocked the way.

"Bloody stalker," muttered Dom, as he turned back to the house to avoid her.

"Can you leave?" asked Sabine.

"Lieutenant Severan isn't stopping us. This really had nothing to do with us, we just happen to be the fools who blundered into it."

"Where are you going?"

I debated whether to tell her, and decided against it.

"South," I said, and gestured vaguely.

**I sometimes** wonder how much of our life is rooted in the imagination, in the stories we tell ourselves and others in order to make sense of what has happened along the way. Unable to accept the unvarnished truth of our situations, we have to make them more palatable to ourselves as well as to others. I always say, for instance, that my father is American and my mother half-French. How much does that cover up? The clash of cultures and personalities that left me feeling like its physical embodiment, something tossed up from the storm. I never talk about the nights they screamed and shouted downstairs while I lay wide-eyed with horror in the room above. The insults that were hurled. The empty bottles of wine and brandy, far too many of those. The books in which I took refuge, under the covers, hands over my ears.

We all tell stories about ourselves, some repeated so often that we can honestly believe them to be the truth. Stories are our self-protective coating. Everyone has them, not only the people who have survived terrible families, though clearly they will have a larger canon than most.

And what narrative had I invented for my life with Dom? There were plenty, I now realized. Nothing important at first, but that's the thing with stories—like lies, they start small. You play around to see what feels comfortable.

**Sabine still** wanted to talk about Les Genévriers, to know exactly what was going on, but I resisted. Was I really so lacking in confidence and overwhelmed by my new life that I had allowed her to undermine me? Had she deliberately and intentionally punished me for having the temerity to take Rachel's place?

Of course not. I could not claim that she had. It was all in my own head. Sabine had been using me for information, as much as I was using her.

For whatever reason, I didn't tell her then what I knew, that Rachel had died.

**"Be careful,"** she said, as we made our farewells.

I would, I thought. I would be careful not to dwell on what she meant by that. And neither would I think too much about her reference to some drama at Les Genévriers she wrongly assumed I knew all about, or the implication that not only did I not understand the complexities of Provence life, I did not even understand the man I was with.

"I mean it. Be careful." She hesitated, then came out with it. "Rachel once told me her husband would kill her."

# 24

I came around, disconcertingly, in blackness.
Long after the sounds of dawn told me it was
morning, it was still dark. Under my trembling fingers
was a bump on my head that throbbed, my throat was
parched, and my eyes were stuck shut.

I spat on my fingers and rubbed crusted blood from
my eyes, blinking painfully as sight returned. From
the way the sun hung over the orchard, I guessed it
was about nine o'clock. Slowly, I got up from the grass
where I had spent the night and made my way to the
house.

Pierre was snoring at the kitchen table. His head
was slumped on a muddied cushion and his hands hung
down. I stared at him dumbly, utterly defeated. Under
my observation, he stirred.

His pallor was shocking. His clothes were ripped and dirty, as if he had been sleeping outside for days. This was someone I did not know at all, corrupt, but by what I did not know, either.

I rushed past him, unable to think what I could possibly say that would convey my rage and disgust. All was quiet at the house. I put my face under the tap, and drank deeply.

"Marthe!" I shouted. "Annette!"

I shouted again when there was no reply.

Their rooms were empty. I rushed downstairs, head hurting worse than ever, flinging open doors and hurling myself down into the stores of the undercroft. Back into the courtyard.

They were in the small barn, huddled together.

"Stay there, I'll go to get help," I whispered. They both seemed asleep, though Marthe nodded, as if she heard me.

As I backed away, Annette stirred. "We have to go!" she whimpered. "I don't want to stay here!"

"Don't worry. I'm going to get someone who will help." I felt her desperation, heard again in my head her cries the previous night.

I hurried back into the house for my coat and purse. But as I came down from my room, Pierre was awake in an instant.

"Where do you think you're going?"

"It's market day. We need food."

Pierre grimaced. "I don't think so."

"Annette's not well. We need the doctor for her."

"No."

"We're responsible for her! If she's hurt . . ."

"I said no. She's fine."

"Please, Pierre!" I was begging and I knew you should never beg Pierre. It made everything worse, it always did.

"No doctor. Do you want to get into trouble?"

"What do you mean?"

"This is all your fault."

"Mine?"

He stood, hitched up his trousers in a loutish gesture. Then he seemed to have a change of heart. "Okay. You go and get food. But you come back with anything more than food and . . ." He picked a knife off the table and ran his thumb down the blade.

Heart pounding in my throat, I turned and went. I took the path up through the woods, wanting to be as quick as possible. But it was a disastrous decision. My head throbbed. I felt giddy, then fell and blacked out. I came to—how long I'd been out for I don't know—and all but crawled up to the village.

By the time I made it and knocked on old Mme. Viret's door, I was gabbling nonsense. She took me in and made me a tisane. I was begging her to call someone strong to take me back and deal with Pierre, or I thought that was what I was saying. I said Marthe's name, and Pierre's, but Mme. Viret tried to put me to bed. When I wouldn't lie still and quiet, she went to call the doctor. I should have defied Pierre and let the doctor take charge of us all, but my brain wouldn't work properly. I took my chance and fled back down the hill, tripping and falling and worried about leaving Marthe so long. Hours must have passed since I'd left.

**I stumbled** up the steps to the kitchen.

Pierre was standing, smoking, at the open door. "You took your time," he said. "Where's the food?"

"Marthe and Annette . . ."

"They're gone."

"What do you mean, gone? Marthe wouldn't have gone without saying good-bye. Don't be stupid."

A shrug. "Looks like she just did."

"I don't believe you. She would have asked where I was."

"I told her you'd gone out. You felt like a saunter round town."

"But that's—! And what, she just went without waiting for me?"

"As a matter of fact, she went after I reminded her that she was the first of us, years ago, to suggest selling."

How I wished I'd never told him.

"And told her that if she only had eyes to see," went on Pierre, "she'd know you were taking her for a ride. That if she could see the way this place is falling apart, she'd know the business was in trouble, and you'd be hitting her up for more and more money to keep it going."

"But that's a lie—all right, the buildings are shabby but the tourists find that's part of the charm. The business is fine!"

"So she now knows the facts, and agrees with me. One-third of this place each, as soon as it can be sold."

"No!"

"Anyway, I fixed what food I could find for them both, and our sister couldn't wait to get away from here. In the end I drove her and the girl down to the station and put them on the train."

"That can't be . . . She would never just have gone without waiting for me, without speaking to me about this!"

He flicked the butt of his cigarette onto the floor and ground it with his heel. "Maybe she doesn't think as much of you as you think." Such a cruel remark, thrown out without a care. "You've always wanted too much from her. She said quite frankly she was glad I'd told her and she agreed with me, it was time to sell up here. You have been a drain on us for long enough."

"I don't believe you."

He was heartless. What had made him like that, the same flesh as us?

"Tell me now what she said. And where she is—so that I can go and hear it from her! Let her tell me that herself!"

But he just turned his back.

"Tell me!"

His shoulders hunched as he wrenched himself around. "She's gone back to Paris. You want me to tell you what she said before she went? All right, then, I will. She hates us both, and blames us, all the family, for what we have all become. And finally . . . finally, she's come out and said it. But now it's out, it's the end. Of the family. Of the farm. Of everything."

He paused, breathing heavily. "Are you satisfied now?"

I sank down on a chair.

Within the hour, Pierre had packed and left, too. And you know what? He was right. It was all my fault. I shouldn't have left the house. I shouldn't have left her with him for five minutes, let alone for hours. I should have known from hard experience that it never worked to confront Pierre head-on, nor to give him time alone with Marthe to persuade her around to his way of thinking. To put pressure on her, more like, with his usual threats and intimidations. I couldn't blame her for leaving as soon as she could. But I could blame myself for subjecting her to his bullying lies.

# Part V

# 1

We found Mme. Jozan's hotel on the coast quite by chance. A wrong turn off the *autoroute* from Marseille meant we approached Cassis from an unexpected direction, with the great red rock of Cap Canaille across the bay in front of us, and a syrupy, blue-black sea to our right. We were on the road that runs past the Hôtel Marie, whitewashed survivor of a bygone age that clings to the rocks above the sea. It looked like a blank wall from its landside approach, anonymous except for a small sign on a gatepost. Neither of us suggested staying at one of the town's big, flashy hotels; we were in agreement from the start that we weren't here for all the usual summer pleasures.

The Hôtel Marie was perfect. The rooms were white and spacious, the other guests quiet and discreet.

Pleasant nods were the currency of communication, as if we were all in on a secret no one wanted to spoil. At first, it felt one step from going into hiding. As arranged, we told no one we were here, except the police.

It was already July when we arrived, and the town was filling with vacationers and their sailing boats, excited families and lissome girls in miniskirts. In high summer, this fishing port, bustling since Gallo-Roman times, is the epitome of what people imagine a small town on the French Riviera to be: its timeless crescent of sandy pastel buildings along the waterfront, drawn shutters above the awnings, bars and restaurants beneath, boats lined up in the marina, a short stroll from the beaches.

Dominating the eastern side of the bay, a medieval château-fort sprawls across the towering rock of Cap Canaille, which surrounds the town like a huge protective arm. As the sun sets over the sweetly curving harbor, the castle catches flame from the west, and burns blood-gold for up to an hour each evening. We would drink an aperitif there, once we had been mesmerized into action by the deepening red of the rocks below our balcony.

The air warm on our shoulders, we dined in restaurants overlooking the sea, and drank crisp white wines from the vertiginous vineyards a mile inland: cautious sips for me, ever larger amounts for Dom. In any other circumstances, it might have been a treat. As it was, we hardly spoke.

I would look up from stiff, overelaborate menus on which I could find nothing I wanted to eat, to find Dom staring at me. It was always a look of such intensity, but the distillation of exactly which emotion eluded me: a mixture of pity and noncomprehension, as though he could hardly remember who I was or what I was doing so close by.

At night, though we shared a bed as usual, each was careful not to touch the other. Trapped in the clammy heat, we lay awake for hours, wordless and hardly daring to breathe. Between the white walls and polished stone floors, the air was stagnant. A ceiling fan slogged above us to no effect, as mosquitoes whined and dived. We lay on a single cotton sheet, finding no comfort even though Mme. Jozan had exchanged the neck-cricking bolster roll for more pillows.

Then, when sleep did come, and the first unsettling dreams began, I was back at Les Genévriers, hearing Dom scream; as his cries grew louder, I ran through the upper floors but could not find him, until I realized he had climbed through a window onto the roof, which gleamed with ice. He was hanging on to the edge by a hand, desperate for me to help him. I woke with a start, as I knew I could not leave him to drop, but equally there was nothing I would be able to do to pull him back. It was a three-story drop down to the stone of the courtyard. So I climbed out, knowing he would pull me down with him, that it was the end for both of us.

I lay there, heart hammering. What was I trying to tell myself? Rachel was dead. My thoughts swung agonizingly between the logical and the paranoid. For all that I wondered about Sabine's motives in planting suspicion in my mind, did I fear she was right? That Dom was a man who was capable of killing his wife?

In the morning, we were dazed and flattened. I felt nauseous. Nothing seemed real except my fear that I was wrong to have trusted him, that any lingering faith was irrational, an aberration born of need. I worked up the nerve to call someone, a friend back in London I could talk to, but I stopped myself at the last minute. What could she do but tell me to leave? It was too long a story, too long kept to myself; my brain was too muddled with fact and supposition, embarrassment, humiliation, and pride, to tell it.

# 2

He was clever, Pierre, always had been. There was always the possibility he had made it all up. Yet what if he had not? Was it I who had badly misinterpreted Marthe's words, her actions, her whole demeanor that night? How could I have? But as the weeks and months passed, I began to doubt myself.

The swelling on my temple took a long time to go down, and I had begun to suffer excruciating headaches. If I was honest, I could not recall precisely what had happened during Marthe's last visit. Had it really happened as my instincts told me, or had my mind stepped in and overwritten that which I feared to see?

Marthe was so radiantly reasonable, never raising her voice, perhaps all along it was me she had been seeking to persuade, not our brother. But I had a picture in my head of him reaching for Annette in the upstairs room, and the sickening roar of him in his cups, the darkness.

My mind was stewed in uncertainty.

It was so strange how Marthe went without a word. I supposed I must have distressed her greatly by leaving the house that morning without explaining properly, and for that I was truly sorry. I wrote to her in Paris to reiterate what I thought she had heard me say, that I was going to seek help to get Pierre away from us, reassuring her that the business was solid, but had no reply.

**3**

Our first morning in Cassis, we rose early after a fitful night, while there was still a vestige of coolness in the air. Dom was as keen as I was to walk, so we took the path, then the road, down to the harbor at Cassis.

There I bought a guidebook to the Calanques, the deep and narrow inlets, like small-scale fjords, that suck the turquoise sea into wind-scarred cliffs of dense white limestone along the coast between Cassis and Marseille. Where the land holds firm at the end of these sharp, steep incisions, harbors and beaches are formed on an intimate scale. For centuries, millennia even, they have provided shelter to sailors in tempests and rolling sea storms.

Crisscrossing these high cliffs are miles upon miles of signposted walking paths. Some of the suggested walks are timed at four hours, some six or seven. A head for heights is necessary, as is the ability to scramble over rough terrain of loose rocks in places.

"They've discovered more underwater caves recently, some with prehistoric paintings. There's wonderful diving around there. The water is so clear. Just look at the creeks," I babbled nervously, holding up a page of photographs in the guidebook.

I let him think I had wanted to see the Calanques for quite a while. Well, that was true: I had, but only since reading Rachel's interview.

"Cassis stone was used for the base of the Statue of Liberty, for parts of the Suez Canal, and the seafront at Alexandria. It has great durability and was used to build lighthouses at Cassis and Marseille," I read from the book.

We descended a cobbled street and walked around the harbor. Shadows of palm trees brushed giant blue feathers across the facades of the sea-facing buildings.

"Did Rachel ever follow Francis Tully's advice and go to Cassis?" I asked directly.

I knew what I was doing; I wanted him to react. I wanted to be sure, one way or the other.

I waited for the outburst, but there wasn't one. "What are you talking about?" he asked lightly.

Staring into his eyes, I was looking for annoyance or duplicity, but there was none that I could detect. He paused, and lightly touched my cheek. "We can make the best of this, you know, Eve. It doesn't have to be doom and gloom. No one would have chosen this, but what's happened has happened and we have to live with it. Let's just . . . try to get back to where we were, what we were . . ."

Did he really believe that was possible? It sounded like he was trying to persuade himself, as much as me, that it was. But there was nothing to be gained by arguing, so we walked back at an oddly jaunty pace, holding hands and swinging arms.

**It was** as if Dom had suddenly decided that this was a clean slate, we were going to recover what we had lost, and we had to leave all the arguments and disagreements and misunderstandings behind us at Les Genévriers. If only it were that easy. With each step, I was tamping down unwelcome emotions: fear of what I might discover; the terrible disappointment that our new life had been so ephemeral; fury at my own gullibility, my lack of confidence and judgment.

All I knew for certain was that Dom was guilty, of something, and I had to know what that was. He was right, though. However we played it, we couldn't go on as before.

# 4

Two months after Marthe's ill-fated visit, when she still had not answered any of my letters, the telegram came from Paris. "Why Les G not yet sold. I will not return. M."

That was the early summer of 1973; the year Picasso died in Mougins and the whole of France was vibrant with reproductions of his paintings. But for me, all brightness faded when I read that telegram. I wrote again, apologizing for whatever I had done, and begging her to explain. Still no word came back.

Bewildered, I traveled by train to Paris to find she had packed up the apartment she had rented for ten years and left no forwarding address. At the perfume shop in the Place Vendôme, I was told that Marthe had taken indefinite leave and was currently on a long sea voyage. She had charged our brother, Pierre, with collecting her effects, and he had cleared her office a month or so previously.

It was at the shop that I fainted. When I came to, a well-dressed, exquisitely made-up woman appeared. She said she was Marthe's administrative assistant and good friend. I can't remember her name. She was not Annette. We talked for a while and she was kind enough at first. It was thanks to her that I had the second shock of the day.

She did not seem to think it strange that Marthe had not been in touch with me. Indeed, she blamed me for the suddenness of Marthe's departure.

"But what did I do?" I cried.

"You wanted too much from her."

"No . . . no, I—" I shrank into myself, feeling insubstantial on the firm daybed where I lay. Was that true?

It could have been. Perhaps we always want too much from family, and those we love. I had assumed until then that that was the point of it all, why I stayed with Maman, why I went to pick lavender at Valensole, why I never really hated Pierre when I was younger.

Worse, this woman, Marthe's friend, corroborated what I had been hoping were just more terrible lies from Pierre. That Marthe blamed us for her blindness, and me for continually holding her back with demands from the place she had always wanted to leave. I was, indeed, the one who had misunderstood.

I left as soon as I had the strength. "Tell Marthe, when she comes back, that I'm sorry," I said. "What else can I say? I had no idea. I'm so sorry. Please, please will she call me."

**Marthe never** did.

One thing, though. I would not agree to the sale of Les Genévriers until I had the words from Marthe's own mouth, and I kept to that principle. Nothing would move me on that. Oh, I let Pierre think he had won, and the land agent came scurrying around with his measuring instruments, but I would never have signed any of the documents that would appear on the notary's table if a buyer was found.

In any case, as the farm slid into disrepair and I did nothing to stop the process, no one did want to buy.

# 5

We made one false start to the Calanques.

"An extremely photogenic day hike with no real difficulty," advised the book on the Morgiou and Sormiou walk. It promised views across the azure sea to the fort of Bormiou, smugglers' paths and a hidden valley lit up with wildflowers.

Mme. Jozan provided us with a picnic in old-fashioned waxed paper and a canvas bag, and we set off soon after breakfast at seven thirty. The air was cool, so we decided to walk to the fishing village of Morgiou instead of taking the car. Perhaps if we had done that, we wouldn't have been hot and thirsty by the time we got there, and even better, we would have arrived early enough to take the trail to the creeks. But I misread the guide, and we left not realizing that the stated twenty-minute journey referred to one made by car rather than on foot.

The walking trails were open only between six and eleven in the morning during high summer, because of fire risks. The brush and tinder-dry trees on the hills catch light at the slightest spark from a cigarette or piece of foil, explained a warden. We could cover part of the way, but we had to be back at the start by eleven. It was already nearly ten. There were no exceptions. The fires were an ever-present danger in the south, starting so quickly in the brittle scrub, some the fault of a careless smoker, others the unaccountable malice of arsonists. He left us in no doubt of what he thought about the mental capacities of those people.

We found a bench and consulted the map. There really wasn't much point in going ahead with so little time.

"It doesn't matter, does it?" said Dom.

"No."

**The sun** beat down. Being out in its hot glare felt like an end in and of itself. I tried to relax into the feeling. Dom looked as I felt, with both his elbows up on the back of the bench, sweat on his brow. We made a start on the picnic. He stroked my arm and smiled, and all at once I was back at Yvoire the first day I met him.

First impressions are valid, no matter how vigorously we dismantle them as we come to know more. We all construct stories from visual clues, making snap judgments that draw on our own past experience. Sometimes we react against instinctive judgments, because we can't rationalize them. But all the time we are picking up thousands of cues, both rapid and subtle, and using them to form a fuller picture of a person or place.

Those first few seconds can shape the entire outcome. But now I thought of the glitter in his eyes at that lamp-lit table in the café, and wondered. What if it had an entirely different meaning than the one I gave it?

My phone bleeped.

As Dom looked at me, I opened the text, fervently hoping it would not be Sabine.

It was, of course. "Are you OK?" it said.

"What does she mean by that?" asked Dom, looking over my shoulder.

I shrugged, hoping to make it clear I knew little more than he did.

But as we began a slow ramble back to Cassis, I had started to worry again. Sabine's reminder was all it had taken to crumple my wafer-thin confidence. Perhaps nothing about our presence here was as simple as it seemed; maybe the police were counting on Dom to lead them to some answers.

There was a time, of course, when I could have left, gone back to London alone; but that was long past. The police, my reluctance to release a dream that had disintegrated in my grip, my pride: none of these motives was holding me as strongly as the growing conviction that I really was pregnant and would have to tell him soon.

**Lunch by** the marina at Cassis consisted of a shared plate of crayfish and a large carafe of wine: half a glass for me and the rest for Dom. The alcohol and the sun-baked day combined to evaporate Dom's easy mood, leaving him edgy. I suggested going back to the hotel for a well-earned siesta, but he was having none of it. He was soon arguing, ever louder, that we had come for a vacation and that was what we were going to have. So we took a boat to the nearest inlets.

I felt detached as our fat, tourist-laden craft churned toward Port-Miou and back into the Calanques, past warty outcrops that stood up from the dark amethyst of the open sea. The stubbled white-gray cliffs were topped with wide pines like open parasols. And then, ahead, there were glimpses of the famed emerald and peacock-blue waters of the first *calanque* as they reached into the land.

Alternately drowsy, dehydrated, and sick from the motion of the boat, I was not enjoying the experience. Or perhaps it wasn't seasickness.

We chugged farther into the creek. The scent of pines mingled with coastal brine. Holm oaks stood proud on blasted brown strands of grass. White pebbles and shingle created bathing places, and people were having fun diving from rocks. Neat white sailboats skipped like butterflies across the glittering water.

"Each inlet has its own character, elemental, teeming with microscopic life, bizarre shapes, and special atmosphere," intoned a disembodied voice from a loudspeaker, which made me jump.

More boats bobbed at moorings in this long, narrow space, and my queasiness increased as ours made a tight turn. We were not stopping; this was only a short trip.

Out to sea again, the wind picked up. We headed toward the Calanque of Port-Pin. Shuffled slabs of white rocks, Aleppo pines, the clearest of green waters. On the rocks, according to the commentary I was trying to block out, rosemary and thyme, cistus everywhere on the scree slopes, and yellow thistles; eagles, falcons, and rare owls. A grotto where the sea rushed at the rock, making sea-music. The sound could be heard a hundred meters away when the wind was up, as waves were sucked in and pushed out through an air duct somewhere.

"What's he saying?" asked Dom. "What's a *trou-souffleur?*"

I steadied myself. "A blowhole."

"Where?"

"Over there, I suppose, where everyone's looking."

"Are you all right?"

"Not sure."

He put his arm around me, and I wished desperately that I could just take that for what it was instead of feeling on guard.

I closed my eyes and breathed deeply. Better to keep my eyes open and on the water. Ahead was a great, looming rise of rock, the Calanque d'En-Vau, the highest and most spectacular inlet. This one was stripped bare, naked and vulnerable. Exposed yet bearing up to the elements.

But we were only taking a glimpse before heading back, for which I gave silent thanks.

Back on dry land, I told him I needed some aspirin from the pharmacy in Cassis. He waited outside while I bought the test kit that later confirmed what I already knew. Even then, I did not tell him.

# 6

It must have been about a year and a half later that a man came to the farm with bad news. He was carrying Pierre's clothes and a few sorry possessions in a cardboard box tied with string.

Pierre had died in an industrial accident in Cavaillon. It involved some kind of machinery in a fruit-packing factory. The man spared me the details, and I'm sure he was right to do so. All I could feel was a dull loss and relief that Maman and Papa had been spared the news and the circumstances of his passing.

"What about the funeral?" I asked.

"All taken care of."

"When is it?"

"It's been. This is just to inform you."

"I don't understand! Why wasn't I told before?"

The man had the decency at least to look ashamed. "We didn't know where you were. As you can see we've only just been able to find you. The factory paid, as was only right and proper, but the boss couldn't hang around forever."

I didn't know what to say, what to feel.

The boy I had known was not the man I had last seen.

"Marthe, our sister. Have you informed her?"

"No, I'll leave that up to you."

So I wrote again, but never had a word back.

**I mourned** the whole damn lot of them then. Mémé Clémentine. Papa, Maman. The Pierre who once was, and, perhaps most of all, Marthe.

It's no exaggeration to say it took years for me to feel right again. No, that's not true. I have never really felt right since.

But I wouldn't give up. I wrote again and again to Paris, until the letters came back in a thick bundle, marked "Return to Sender."

**I have** had so many years to think about Marthe's departure from Les Genévriers, and the misunderstanding we must have had. How many times have I reproached myself? It was a terrible misjudgment on my part not to make Pierre's instability clear before she arrived. I should have thought to write a warning letter or telephone her, but I didn't. As it was, she walked unprepared into the storm. Then I left her too long to Pierre and his foul lies.

In my mind, I revisited the Musset boutique in Paris, looking for clues I had been too distressed at the time to pick up. It had occurred to me, too late, that what the assistant there had told me about Marthe—about her blaming us for all her difficulties, in particular her blindness, which she had never done before—might have been a repetition of some conversation with Pierre while he was there to collect her belongings. Not necessarily true, in other words.

But whatever the reason, it made no difference. Marthe had cut me adrift.

Our estrangement caused me physical pain. I ached with bewilderment that after all the years we had been so close, it was over, all over, in a single evening. She could not forgive me for my stupidity, and I could not forgive myself.

I have not thought of myself in the same way since, though I have never stopped looking for her. Looking for her in the sense of hoping I might know where she is, but in the sense, too, of the way she once asked me to look at the world.

There is always a part of her still inside me when I see the apricot trees flame red to yellow in November, like ranks of burning torches in the orchards, or the ruby vines dying back against a contrast of silver-green olives, or the lavender pruned into shivering ice-blue rows for the winter. I store these sights away, for her.

# 7

It was Dom's idea to walk to the forbidding stacks of the Calanque d'En-Vau.

We researched it properly this time, taking plenty of water, food, and sunblock.

"Seasick pills?" he joked.

I forced a small smile.

The path to the spiny cliffs was beautiful. Here and there were silver shivers of olive trees. Each level of the rise was marked by green scrub, and where it flattened into an exposed spot, geriatric trees bowed over, bent by the legendary winter winds, mop-tops of stinging green against the blue all around.

The trail was fairly easy going, just patches where the pebbles rolled under our feet like ball bearings, or slices of exposed rock that had been polished by the passage of other hikers. Mostly, we walked in silence.

At one point, he drew close and disconcerted me with a soft kiss. I hesitated, wanting to say something but not knowing what; wanting to be here, with him, in any other circumstances; wanting to be able to tell him about the baby and knowing I couldn't, not until I knew what Dom was, once and for all.

So we continued in silence. We were both breathing heavily when we reached the top, but there, laid out before us, was a panorama of such loveliness that it took what was left of our breath away. It seemed as if bands of mountains had reared up from the darkest blue sea, one behind the other, dancing whalebacks of land before a misted horizon.

The *calanque* was below us, such a long way down. I shivered involuntarily. On one vertical drop, human climbers scrambled like lizards, searching out holds in the scarred rock faces of the cliffs. Turquoise water shifted far below, sprinkled with silver flakes.

Adrenaline fizzed in my veins, provoking that surge of self-doubt you get sometimes on the edge of some high place, that you might—just might—throw yourself off, powerless to stop it from happening. My feet stood firm, but I did what I knew I shouldn't. I let loose the first of my pent-up questions.

"Dom, did you always know what Rachel was writing about?"

He wheeled around. "What?"

"You knew she was writing about Marthe Lincel. Did you know about Francis Tully, and the first girl who disappeared?"

His look was incredulous, as if I had slapped him. "Eve . . ."

"I want to know, Dom. I want to know everything. Now."

"What?" he said again, but helplessly resigned this time.

"Francis Tully, the artist. Rachel interviewed him. The piece she wrote was in the *Telegraph*."

Dom shook his head. "Did she? I don't remember . . ."

"He told her to go to Cassis."

He waited, nonplussed by this outburst he clearly hadn't seen coming. "I still don't understand where this is leading."

"So humor me. Did Rachel ever talk about Francis Tully?"

He sighed deeply. "I suppose . . . probably. Why do you want to know?"

"I have so many questions . . . but let's start with this. It was Tully who gave her the stone pineapple and the hand, wasn't it? The pieces you let me believe you had bought along with the rest of the stone for the garden."

"Is that what this is about?" He was looking at me as if I was crazy. "Does it matter that they once belonged to Rachel?"

"Oh, no. That's just the start. Hardly important at all, except that told me you did lie to me, after all, even if they were lies of omission."

The sun was so bright it darkened his face. "Okay. I knew that she was interested in the missing girl. I knew about that. She was always curious. Of course it seems suspicious now. But it's just one of those horrible coincidences, nothing more."

"So tell me how Rachel died. How she really died."

Dom put his hand under his sunglasses and pinched the bridge of his nose. A seagull squealed and seconds ticked by.

"What happened to Rachel, Dom? Because you see, I need to know. I can't go on not knowing. You telling me I can't ask. That it's too painful for you to talk about. But that means I can't help you! And I want to, so much. It may not seem important to you, but to me, it's grown into something that's . . . that is spoiling everything. It's even . . ." I gave a laugh that sounded off-key. "It's making me go slightly crazy . . . thinking I see and hear stuff that isn't really there, in the house, in the grounds. And then with what actually has happened back at Les Genévriers . . ."

I expected bluster. I expected anything but this: as I was talking, he started to shake. I fought the instinct to reach out and hold him. He was two feet away from me, shaking. And I watched him, carefully, yet helpless as ever.

Then he turned his face to mine, a flinty set to his mouth. He started closing in on me, very slowly, like he did in the dark, the first time we kissed. Only this time it wasn't excitement and desire I felt. It was pure fear.

He moved toward me. I backed away from the edge.

Then I was fastened to the spot, his grip so tight I could feel the bruises forming on my arms under his grip. But I couldn't stop myself. I had always been reckless with him, hadn't I?

"So tell me the truth, Dom. I can't bear it any longer. Tell me now exactly what happened to Rachel and why it is you feel so guilty!"

Perhaps I was crazy. God knows it had felt like it at times. I had come so far, had seen my dreams turn to ashes, when all I had wanted was to love him and empathize, and make him whole again.

His thumbs gouged my flesh as he pulled me across the scrubby ground. The sea seemed to rush up toward us.

"This has nothing to do with you but you wouldn't leave it be, would you? You are determined to know, and all I have been trying to do is protect you!"

"Protect me how?"

"From knowing what kind of person I am."

"What do you mean, Dom? For God's sake . . ."

Far below, the sea heaved under its tight, sequined skin.

"What do you mean?" I goaded him. "That you might throw me over the edge? You would throw me over the edge and say it was an accident! Was that what you did to her?"

"Stop it! Just stop this!" He spun me around, and the sea and the sky spun, too. Then Dom was shaking me. Or was I trembling? "Stop this! Listen to yourself, you're hysterical!" he shouted. It was, I realized, the first time he'd ever shouted at me in anger.

"So tell me . . . the police are right to be investigating you, aren't they? In fact, they're probably still investigating you."

But the thoughts behind the words I was flinging were becoming muddled. What did he mean by saying he wanted to protect me? Why had they

allowed him to leave the area? Why wasn't he in cus-
tody—?

Gulping down air, I realized my face was wet. I was
crying. "Are you out on bail?"

"No. I told you. There are no charges against me."

I concentrated on lowering my voice, trying to
regain reason and composure. "But this is all to do with
Rachel, isn't it?"

A secret can rot the soul. Unspoken, it seeps into the
subconscious, it penetrates the body, the character of
a person, until at last it takes over all reason and reasoning—until nothing is left but the secret that cannot
be told and that must be kept tight inside at all costs.
This is devastation, the inner waste.

I thought I could see all this in his expression, the
horror and the ease with which evil can be covered
over, and the knowledge that this can only ever be temporary, just as the soil gives up the history hidden in its
grains.

It was the end of everything. No more pretense. I
had no idea what either of us was going to do next.

Far too close by, the cliff dropped sheer away into a
glistening blue oblivion.

# 8

When my bundle of unopened letters was returned to me from Paris, I went to see Mme. Musset in Manosque. I was desperate to know: had she heard from Marthe?

A tear trickled down one wrinkled cheek as the old lady told me Marthe had broken off relations with her, too. Mme. Musset blamed me, of course. She had only done what she did out of loyalty to Marthe. And now look where it had led!

Vehemently, I protested. It was twenty years ago, all that! Why should it suddenly make a difference now?

I told Madame, if only I could have done things differently, I would have done! But I had no option back then. I did the best I could at the time, the only course of action that made sense. I have been paying the price ever since. And anyway, I just didn't believe that an event so long ago and so nearly forgotten could have any bearing on Marthe's present estrangement. How could it, when it was so long past and had never made any difference before?

But for Marthe's old mentor, who had felt for my sister all the pride of a mother and had been brooding on the facts for many months, there was no other plausible explanation.

**Perhaps I** should never have told Marthe what Mme. Musset did for me. That should have remained forever between the two of us.

But the urge to confide in Marthe was too strong, at a time when I was not getting better. Each day was a struggle. It didn't seem I would ever get over it, and she did ask. Marthe asked why I was so cold and thin under her hands, and this was many months after the dreadful event. So I told her, with a gush of warm relief, and Marthe was kind and concerned. I never felt she reproached me, not then, or any time afterward.

Which was why I found it so hard to believe it was the reason Marthe had broken off all contact with Mme. Musset, when the two of them had always been so fond of each other. It seemed odd that it never affected their relationship until around the same time as

Marthe cut me out of her life. But I was certain of this: one way or another, I was to blame.

**And now,** now in old age, when I was sure there could be no more to pay, the spirits were proving me wrong. And others were arriving. All unknown, these others . . .

I was supposed to be safe there, in the house I had known all my life. Never before had I felt frightened here, for all I have suffered. And now . . . Was I losing my mind? To help calm myself, I made soup the old-fashioned way, with stock made of chicken bones and whatever beans, vegetables, and herbs I could gather. Soup is good. It softens the bread from the bakery that the girl brings every other day; by the second evening, it is too hard and crusty for me to swallow without soaking it first.

Sabine is a good girl. Sent by her grandmother, of course. She is very like her, and of course that brings back the past in yet another way.

My nights were disturbed by then. I was no longer alone and no longer sure of myself, sure of my own spaces, of my place in the world. The spirits were slipping in like water and air, and my defenses were failing.

Pierre was a persistent presence, although still re-markably trouble-free, always silent and very often still. He made no attempt to scare me by leaping out or by playing other unsettling games, for which I was grateful. Red-eyed Marthe did not come back, thank God.

But others were coming now, strangers. Strangers to me, that is. Perhaps they were not strangers to the house.

# 9

D om held me against him, roughly. My heels were off the ground.

It was just as they say. At such moments, there is an element of dreadful clarity. All that I was and had been was compressed. All meaning was compounded into this one act of straining to understand what had happened to us, what Dom would say next.

The French have exactly the right phrase for the perfect word or expression, which we lack in English: *le mot juste.* I work within the parameters of other people's words, faithfully reproducing what they are trying to say, not how I would have phrased it more felicitously. It is a balancing act, an attempt at understanding their intentions, alive to nuance, shades of irony, occasionally showing compassion for their mistakes. Yet all that was easier than understanding real, live people.

Slowly, shakily, he released me. He seemed to read my thoughts: he kept it simple. In a small, broken voice, he said, "You're right. I am guilty. I killed her."

I held my breath, hardly moving as he whispered, over and over, his face pressed into my neck, "I'm so sorry, I'm so sorry."

**On pitted,** wind-polished rocks high in the air, he began to tell me.

**Dom and Rachel** were married for five years, together for eight. They met in London, where they were both working, he with his geo-tech company, she as a journalist. They were both in their early thirties.

Rachel was everything Sabine told me she was: attractive and vivacious, hardworking and determined. But the longer Dom lived with her, the more he realized that there was another facet to her. She would delight in telling him of her many professional triumphs, and he was happy for her, but she would rage at the slightest downturn in her good fortune. Anyone who stood in her way or crossed her would be subjected to vindictive character assassination. Often this was extremely funny, and her renditions of events that led her to take revenge would make her the center of attention at the pub or party where she was surrounded by admiring acquaintances. She had a wide circle of friends, who forgave her faults for the amusement and glamour she brought with her.

But as Dom discovered, little by little, there was another side to these performances. Rachel would lie, easily and often. She would lie about minor incidents, and big issues such as whether she was faithful to him. It was hard to deal with, ever more so as her habitual infidelity became more daring. These episodes were not affairs but one-night stands with strangers, from which the marriage always seemed to recover. She managed each time to persuade Dom that they meant nothing. Perhaps they both used them to inject some extra thrill into their relationship. When they were together, she was exciting; part of him enjoyed the drama of uncertainty, being kept on the edge.

Yet they argued a great deal. Any confrontation could make her extremely difficult and unpleasant for days to come, and was often followed by more lies. What was real in Rachel's universe and what was invented? She set herself up as a journalist, a seeker after truth, yet she continuously spun tales that had only the thinnest thread of reality in them. And she was worryingly persuasive. Other people believed her stories, and she came alive in that belief.

Eventually, he went alone to a psychotherapist specializing in marital problems, who confirmed he was suffering from severe stress and suggested that while no diagnosis was possible without seeing a patient, Dom himself might benefit from doing some research into narcissistic personality disorder. Even then, as Dom reluctantly followed this advice and recognized in the papers he pulled off the Internet not his own but his wife's familiar patterns and traits, he wondered: Was Rachel really as bad as this? Could it be a question of enough love? If he had shown her the love she craved, the acceptance of who she was without embellishment, could he have brought her back into normality?

But then again, was it the psychological issue that was responsible for the serial infidelities, the broken promises and schemes, the arguments—or was that simply her true nature?

The difficulty was that Rachel was so plausible, and so slippery. She might have paid lip service to the idea that she needed help, but she had no intention of accepting any. Why should she, when she had no problem? Plenty of other people accepted her as she was—indeed, were full of the admiration she craved.

Take Sabine. Sabine clearly believed Rachel was an admirable person and that she always told the truth. I remembered the story Sabine related, in all seriousness, of how Rachel supposedly met the interesting couple on a train. The way she had lunch with them in a town that did not seem to exist afterward, the apparent connection to the couple whose death was reported in the papers. I had not known what to think about that until now. At last it made some kind of sense.

**When Dom** told Rachel he was leaving her, he half-anticipated disaster. He knew what the effect would be, but by then all he wanted was to extricate himself. But to his amazement, she took it well. She offered to be the one to move out, and he was more than generous to her, agreeing to pay the rent on her new apartment and allowing her to take what she wanted from their house in North London.

He and Rachel had been separated for six weeks when he arrived home to find her waiting for him, having let herself in and started on his vodka. He had not thought to change the locks, so amicable had been the split.

"I've changed my mind," she said.

And, by the way, she was pregnant.

Stunned, he tried to explain to her that they would still be better off apart. That he would support the child. That nothing could be gained from trying again. The marriage was over.

She pleaded. She could and would change. What had happened in the past was all just that—the past. She played on his guilt, the reaction of his family if he were to abandon her.

In the teeth of Dom's resistance, she moved back in. He knew it was a mistake.

**Dom withdrew** into himself. He swam for hours every day to avoid going home.

In the year leading up to the sale of his company, he volunteered for the lion's share of the traveling. He traveled a great deal, across Europe and to the Far East. The more she tried to stop him from going, the longer he stayed away. In London, his friends placed their spare rooms at his disposal.

He ignored her. By that stage, it was clear there was no baby. Even when she had admitted to Dom she was not pregnant, she still told other people that she was. When he refused to react, the lies became more and more hurtful, more outrageous. She told friends and family that he had alcohol and drug addictions, that he gambled recklessly, that he was turned on by seedy clubs and underage girls. Then he was questioned by the police after she claimed he had broken down and confessed to her that he was the man who attacked and raped a woman in a horrific case that had been widely reported in the newspapers. Luckily, he was able to establish beyond a doubt that he was out of the country at the time.

Then she claimed she was seriously unwell. He knew that; by then, he was certain that she was mentally unbalanced. If she would only accept professional help, all might not be lost. But Rachel laughed at the suggestion. She was sick, she said, physically, terminally sick.

He didn't believe her, of course, certain it was yet another one of her attention-seeking stunts. Their arguments escalated. She played on his ingrained sense of loyalty, the power of the marriage vows, and his conscience. Effectively, he had left her anyway, even if he had not formally made the break.

She begged him to come back; he had to, she needed him desperately. He ignored her ridiculous pleas and extended his visit to Hong Kong and Japan. But, against all odds, all the stories and fabrications, this time she was telling the truth.

By the time he did return, it was almost too late.

# 10

I t wouldn't be long now, I could feel it.
More and more of the others, the strangers, were coming. For nearly a week, I lived in trepidation, worrying about who would turn up next. By now, they were being announced by neon flashes. Light would flare on the ceiling and the walls when wind brushed the leaves back and forth outside. Even with the shutters half-closed, I found this an uncomfortable sensation, like a quick, silent explosion. Flashes followed: white rushes of rapid movement with streaks of green and yellow and red. I was reminded of the bird André gave me, or rather, more accurately, that the old lady gave to him; there's quite a difference.

Then I'd see another of them arrive. And so many were children. Not just Pierre, but a whole raggle-taggle gang of them, none of them familiar. Staring at me, waiting for me to say something.

**Then, on** the sixth or seventh day, it was the turn of the kitchen wall to behave oddly. The kitchen is painted white, has always been white, but suddenly, when I opened my eyes after a mid-afternoon doze in the chair by the hearth, the walls were covered in a profusion of flowers, garish, scarlet poppies wide as dinner plates, with creeping stems like bindweed.

As I watched in amazement, the flowers seemed to open and close, and tendrils grew in sweeping curls. The wall was alive with color and movement. There was no sound but the beating of my heart. Within moments, red blooms were pulsing in time to my chest. I looked up in horror at the ceiling, and saw the inexplicable display had begun to take hold there, too, the tendrils would soon have the lamp in their grasp.

I ran. Fumbling at the door catch, my vision blurring with fear, I tilted down the stone steps into the courtyard and made for the open ground. But the disturbance had followed me.

The land was rotating. Round and round it went, all around me. Alternating blackness and light that made the world flicker like the first moving pictures.

I was off-balance, standing in the middle of a fair-ground ride. But these were live horses, and a full-size black steam engine pulling train carriages by, at speed, on the dusty path to the fields. I raised my eyes to the sky, and a great eagle hovering overhead transformed into a carnival clown.

It will soon be over, I remember thinking. I closed my eyes.

# 11

I n London, even then still unsure whether he was being played for a fool, Dom drove her to the private hospital for another scan and a second opinion.

A large part of him held back from her. Yet he was there with her in the consultant's room when the news was broken. This was no lie. When Rachel first turned to Dom, she wanted him to tell her that everything would be all right. They were going to fight this, he told her, and she would pull through. So that's what he did. That's what anyone would have done.

Then she got angry with him. "It's not you who's got this, who's going to have to do the winning. It's me, that's the bottom line."

She was wrong, though. It was happening to both of them, for better or for worse, in sickness and in health.

She was coming to terms with her mortality, but so was he.

Outside the hospital, the world seemed cruelly normal. For once, Rachel was scared. "I'm so sorry," she said. "For putting you through this. For everything I've done."

And he did believe her.

Yet, as the months went by, they had to accept that the cancer was spreading, that she was not going to get better, no matter how hard she fought.

In their bedroom, she would turn her face to the wall. She was having hideous dreams, she said. Her voice was barely recognizable. Gone were the confrontations and provocations. The only comfort Dom could give was to agree to two requests.

**The first** was that he would support her in her wish to refuse more chemotherapy and live as normally as possible while she still could. She wanted to go to Provence and to work. Dom protested that he could only spare a couple of long weekends and a few days here and there away from his business; it was just at this time that the negotiations for the sale of the company were getting complicated. Why choose to go there, why not stay in London?

She was determined.

"One last good story," she said. "Maybe more than one, who knows?"

It energized her, she told Dom, to have goals. She wanted to get away, to go somewhere she could immerse herself in other stories and forget her own. He began to think that maybe she really had miraculously turned a corner, that she could get better if he supported her. Deep in his subconscious, he knew it could never be that simple, but there she was, in front of him: she glowed, she was the woman he had first met. And she wanted to be somewhere she knew he would want to be, too.

Rachel's will prevailed: she rented the Mauger house for six weeks. Dom visited her there as often as he could, and was heartened by what he saw. She looked healthy enough, though she battled terrible exhaustion. He had no reason to doubt the veracity of the stories she told him of her experiences here. Perhaps there was no need to invent them, they were rich enough. She was researching Marthe Lincel, and began making her own inquiries about the girl who went missing from Goult.

The rental agent dropped around a couple of times to check that all was well. Rachel had made a friend for life, it seemed, by agreeing to investigate Marthe Lincel's story. That was the way Rachel operated: she won people over by giving more than they could ever have expected. The agent seemed pleasant enough but she hardly registered with Dom, so intent was he on keeping an eye on Rachel. It was a short but peaceful interlude, during which he scrutinized her behavior and agonized over making the right decision when the time came to fulfill his second promise.

**Rachel was** the one who found the clinic, made the appointment, booked the travel tickets and the hotel in Geneva. They went to see it, took in the impersonal, cream-painted walls and beige carpets, and she deftly interviewed the soft-spoken, middle-aged Swiss couple in charge.

They did not see anyone else there, which was a relief. She was asking questions, as she always did. The man seemed suspicious at one point, as if he could tell she was a journalist and suspected her motives. She was very quiet after they left.

"If I have to, I will," was all she said. "I want to die on my terms."

Dom, still profoundly disturbed by her decision, said nothing.

**They found** a small apartment to rent nearby. During the following weeks, they sought a third and then a fourth opinion. The doctors' brutal confirmations were the same.

They were running out of time.

As the pain increased, Rachel scripted her final lie: her family was to be told that she died at the flat they were renting near the hospital where she was being treated, that the end was sudden, that no one had suspected she would go so soon. It was what she wanted. What difference could one more lie make? For once, it was a lie intended to spare others from hurt.

Even when they returned to the clinic for the last time, they saw no one except for the quiet, middle-aged couple and a nurse who provided the morphine that would make her as comfortable as she could be. The room was functional, completely sealed off from the outside world. Dom dreaded what would happen there, not daring to think ahead. But Rachel smiled, and squeezed his hand.

Was she as numb as he was? Doubts churned ceaselessly. Of everything that she had put him through, this was the worst. Was he truly trying to do the best for her, what she wanted? Or was he acting for himself? Could they have tried any harder for a cure? No. Would he do what she asked, when she called time?

They were shown how to operate the morphine line, then left alone.

I will not write down exactly what Dom did. It was enough. He did what she had demanded of him. It was brutal and ugly, as she raved and cursed and needled him. It was not a good death. Nothing could have been further from the peace she craved. Then, when the unbearable worst of it was almost over, came the words that made the difference.

"I've changed my mind," she said.

Such an innocuous phrase. A brief string of ordinary words. Words she had used before.

He heard the familiar mockery in her voice. Saw, behind her half-closed eyes, the lizard watching, waiting for him to react in those seconds of poisoned calm. Had all this been a setup? Would she go that far, could she be that twisted? Even now, with the last of her strength, was she tormenting him, or could she not stop herself from leaving him with one more terrible uncertainty?

Dom did not stop. He heard her speak and his body reacted instinctively, viscerally, to her voice and he could not stop. He kept right on with what they'd started, with what she'd claimed she wanted. What the practical and compassionate Swiss couple had heard her say she wanted. What her signature on the consent forms indicated. And part of him wanted to do it, was fired by so much anger that he had never wanted to do anything more. Sensing a trap, furious with himself for walking into it, needing it all to be over—he crossed the line only he knew was there.

Suicide? Or murder?

Afterward, when the staff at the clinic had moved in, discreetly and swiftly, Dom was left agonized and isolated. In the weeks following Rachel's death, he was physically ill, shaking and nauseous, as if his own body had turned on him in punishment when no one else would. When his guilt almost broke him after silent months on his own, he confided in his sister, a doctor, and found himself a pariah in his own family, more alone than he had ever thought possible. And when he had looked to his churchgoing parents for support, he found none. Only a tacit understanding that he was no longer the son they had brought up to know right from wrong. If forgiveness was possible, it would be a long time coming.

# 12

For two days after that, I stayed in bed.

There were two possibilities. Either I was in the presence of evil, and the farm was possessed; or I was losing my mind and these hallucinations were the proof. But how could the house I had known all my life be haunted like this when it had never been before?

Hour upon hour, these thoughts chased each other through my head, while in my room I watched a procession of angels with halos, halos without angels, silver mists, and golden blurs, dimming, shafts of clarity, and brilliant flashes of light.

The doctor came on the third day. I have never been so relieved to see anyone in my life.

**They must** have drugged me at the hospital.

When I saw the doctor, he told me I had been asleep for two days and nights.

"Have I gone mad?" I asked, all fight gone.

"No, not at all."

"Am I possessed?"

"No . . ."

"What has been happening to me, then?"

It was bad news, he said softly. He reached out and took my hand that was lying on the cover. I'd had enough of that, I replied feebly.

"I am sorry to have to tell you that you are losing your sight, Mme. Lincel."

I closed my eyes and pushed my head back on the pillows. I felt more pressure on my hand as he squeezed it to show he cared.

"But all the visitors!"

"There is an explanation."

"But they were there, completely real . . . people I knew!"

"The brain has an extraordinary capacity to evoke sensations and visions . . . a heightened reality . . ."

"But I am not crazy . . ."

"No, not crazy at all."

"But how?"

"We don't know everything, of course, but there is a medical condition—an optical syndrome—

that might explain what you have experienced. We will need to conduct some tests, with your consent, before we can say with certainty this is the explanation."

Wearily, I agreed.

# 13

There will always be those who believe that what
Dom did deserves the harshest punishment.
Deaths in euthanasia clinics have led to murder charges;
often there is a trial, followed by acquittal and useless
expressions of regret that the matter was ever brought
to court.

It is against the law, as well as the natural order, even
if committed out of compassion. But Dom knew that
he had crossed the boundary at the very end.

"I'm not the person you thought I was," he said.

That was only true up to a point, as he well knew.
Until then, he had revealed what he chose to reveal
about himself, nothing more. Reading between the
lines, I found not necessarily a different man but a far
more complicated one.

"Perhaps I saw the person you always were, until then," I said carefully.

He closed his eyes, and it was written all over his face, his shoulders, his chest, that a weight had lifted. In my hands, his were trembling.

"And, the police know . . ." I went on. I saw it now. "Severan knows. When they arrested you, they must have known."

"They checked with the clinic, made me sweat. Made me tell them over and over again until it sounded false, like a story I had made up and was failing to tell exactly as before. All night they kept on, question after question."

"You told them the whole truth?"

He made a noise in the back of his throat. "Very nearly."

"Does that mean yes or no?"

I waited, hardly able to breathe.

"No."

I started to shake harder. I think it was relief. "They let you go."

"The whole situation . . . it's a very gray area, but so long as no one wants to make a show trial of it like they do in the U.K. . . ." He hesitated. "In the end, where is the line if the prosecutors want to draw it? It will be all right. I think the police are more interested in their own case and the pressure to get that solved."

But there was also the incident with the police back in London, thanks to Rachel's spitefulness, when he had been questioned about the rape. That was on record, too.

"So . . ." I was still having difficulty coming to terms with what he had told me. "All this . . . whole dreadful story, all the worry, but you didn't think to tell me?"

"No."

"You don't think that maybe—?"

"It's a terrible thing, to have killed someone. I thought, if you knew . . ."

"What, I would leave you?"

He didn't answer.

But I was thinking of the weight on his conscience, the effort of living alone with that knowledge. In this instance, knowing that part of him wanted her gone, wanted her to die—that he killed her knowing she had changed her mind. And I wondered, from what he had told me about her, whether Rachel said what she did to leave him with one terrible, lasting wound.

When I met Dom that day, a hundred years ago, on the shores of Lake Geneva, he had been back to clear out the flat and hand over the keys before the lease expired. The skiing trip with friends was true enough, but he had always intended to do this, had steeled himself to do what he hadn't been able to face before.

Almost a year had passed.

He was in Yvoire because she had wanted to go there. It was a final farewell to the girl he had once loved very much, before all the lies and unhappiness.

"Then I met you and it was the first time I had allowed myself to think about moving on. There had been nothing—no one—until then to make me remember that the future could still be good."

"Perhaps it was too soon."

"I tried to let you go."

I thought of the afternoon in Hyde Park, when he seemed to be telling me it was over, that he was moving to France. The occasional meetings in London followed by distressing silences that preceded the real beginning of our relationship, which I had airbrushed out of my version of our whirlwind romance. And now I understood the subtext, his dignity and quiet grief. How it began to eat away at his spirit, and then mine. His fear when the remains were found beneath the old swimming pool, the police investigations. His certainty of what would follow when they discovered his wife had died under suspicious circumstances. The way events spiraled to implicate him, just as he had dreaded.

Dom would look in the mirror and hate what he saw. The sadness and guilt spreading like an invisible yet fatal disease. He was already serving a life sentence. While I feared I was haunted by the house, he was being haunted by Rachel. As was I, though in a different way. In thinking it was the spirits of those who had once lived here, I was too literal-minded; it was the spirits we had brought with us.

# 14

The daylight is still playing tricks on me. What should be bright and clear is smeared with mother-of-pearl. It clots and breaks up my vision so that what I see is becoming more and more like van Gogh's spirals and waves. He came south in search of color, and then went mad. I am still not convinced that I am not suffering the same fate.

Since the doctor gave me his grim diagnosis, I examine what I can see with minute attention, fear barely contained beneath the surface.

Being blind is not like closing your eyelids; that merely reduces the light entering the eye from the pupil. What is blackness and what is nothingness? Did Marthe see darkness continually or did she experience reaction to light? Did her memory of light make the empty void into a darkness she could relate to? The blackness into a remnant of vision?

**There's something** else.

If all this was in my mind, there can only be one cause.

Who were those unknown children who came to see me, you may ask?

# 15

Dom and I stayed on in Cassis. From time to time, we thought about progressing along the coast in the direction of Nice, but in the end, we felt comfortable in Mme. Jozan's white hotel. Weeks went by and still we stayed away from Les Genévriers.

Through the heat and sleepless nights, we rode out the summer. Dom was like a victim of shell shock, as if, with his confession to me and the dismantling of his emotional defenses, he was only now allowing himself to react to the police investigation and the grisly discoveries at the house. It would take months for him to come to terms with what had happened.

I stood back and allowed him to be, listening when he wanted me to listen, reassuring when he seemed to be asking for reassurance, turning to him at night when he felt for my body, wondering if he would discover the secret I still kept. When would be the right time to tell him? It seemed too demanding of the future, to risk telling him before he had come to terms with the past. Perhaps telling him would give me fewer options than not telling. I was thinking of my own independence.

As the summer faded, we found an approximation of peace. The walking helped, sometimes with Dom, more often not. Between the tumbling slopes and steep, pine-bristled ravines, the sea was a constant companion. Its dazzle lifted the letters off the pages of my walking guide until I could see precisely how each black mark was stamped on the soft paper.

At night, I dreamed of the crumbling hamlet on the hill. I sensed it always was a place of secrets. It was, in my old understanding, like a sentence hung in midair: abrupt, unresolved. Surely there should have been another page, but that was all I had, the ghosts and intimations of a half-told story.

Perhaps the house in the dreams (that was and was not itself) had come to stand for our relationship. I was afraid it might.

**One day,** I bought a local newspaper at a kiosk and took it down to the harbor to read while I drank coffee. Three pages in, my heart lurched as I read the words "missing students" and the name "Marine Gavet," "also known as Magie." A grainy black-and-white photograph in the paper showed her laughing, caught on a security camera at a bank where she had recently opened an account. Her parents had arrived from Goult. Anyone who saw her should call the Cassis police.

Magie. What Francis Tully called his young model. I debated whether to call the police myself, with my feeble contribution, my hunch that she arrived in Cassis with Tully and posed for him. Perhaps she stayed on; perhaps she had caught a glimpse of another life and decided to grab it. Perhaps speculation was pointless.

I was still undecided when the call came from Severan that evening. The rocks burned below our balcony and the sea shuddered, and we were summoned to return.

# 16

I killed her, you see.
The unknown children who came to haunt me:
I did know them. Not in appearance, but in essence. I
knew where they had come from.

When I returned from visiting Marthe in Paris in
the months after André had left, I did not know where
to turn. As realization of my situation crept up on me,
I had to act quickly.

The only person I could think of was Mme. Musset,
she who had taught Marthe and me so much. I said
earlier that she was the one who helped me. The truth
is, I went to Manosque and I begged for that help. She
did not give it willingly.

I was carrying André's baby.

What was I supposed to do? I had no hope of him,
no longer even raged at him, felt only sadness and

contempt. I could not have the baby, alone and unmarried. I would not allow my kind friend Henri to settle for a farce of a marriage.

So I went to Mme. Musset, who made up a tincture: parsley and angelica and pennyroyal that smelled of spearmint. I had to drink it diluted with warm water every hour, and also to take the juice of as many oranges as I could afford, to ingest high doses of vitamin C. She wasn't happy to do it; she made some comment about me making a habit of leading men on, which made me wonder whether she was thinking of Auguste, the field supervisor, all those years before. But she did it, for Marthe. Because she thought Marthe had advised me to come to her, she gave me what I wanted.

**First, I** had to deal with Maman.

It was only fair she should take a holiday, I insisted. After all, I had been to Paris and left her to cope. I told her Marthe had sent the fare and paid for the hotel on the coast, which was partly true. Marthe had given me some money, and we had both decided that Maman needed a break.

The day I waved her off on the bus, I took the first sip of the tincture. My cramps began on the third day after that.

I prepared a pile of clean towels, boiled water and bottled it, and waited. I was on my own, the most scared I had ever been. For hours, I thought nothing would happen, that the pain was all I had provoked. Then I started to bleed.

I must have been further along than I thought. After the spasms of pain and the blood, came the tiny form of a baby. Not an unidentifiable entity but a shocking, stillborn baby, formed more fully than I ever thought possible. A girl.

Desolation, pure and complete.

**The next** day, I lit the lantern, our lantern, for the last time, using the biggest candle I could find to keep the light alive for as long as possible. It flared into a fat crocus. Then I placed it on the ground in the old storeroom next to the arch her father had built. The crocus glow warmed the black space as I dug.

When the grave was deep enough, I anointed the baby with Marthe's perfume, made the shape of the cross, then buried her in her own vault. It was the best I could do. When the light went out, she would sleep held safe inside the ribs of its crude wooden beams.

A prayer, and then I bricked it up, stone by stone. Next to the arch that stood for love, it was all my own work. The masonry I learned from silently watching my lover when he thought I was busy elsewhere.

So, the baby was laid to rest among her ancestral stones, though she would never open her eyes in the morning to the great curtain of blue mountain that hangs beyond the bottom of the path, or feel the soft breeze coming off the sea of hills, or taste the wild plums and the cherries dried on the tree, or smell the lavender and thyme and rosemary. But neither would she be hungry in winter, and feel the sting of ice through the holes in her boots, work hard and love with good intent only to lose it all, or know how it is to be desperate and alone.

I once thought it was better she did not know sorrow. I realize now that I can never atone for what I did. I carry her still, knowing that the greatest betrayal was mine, of her. I will never forgive myself.

And I will never leave her.

# 17

In Apt, the seasonal crowds were thinning at last, tempers calming in the supermarkets where the locals had been making their frustration and displeasure known since the second week of July, at the lack of parking spaces and the lines at the checkouts. The tourist surge had been weathered, the money taken.

We shopped quickly, and then headed up to Les Genévriers.

In our absence, paradise had overreached itself. The courtyard was dense with chaotic inflorescence. The fruit was splitting on the fig tree; giant hornets gave full song to their thirst. The earth was warm where summer sun had burned away the grass.

Beyond the courtyard, the statues stood reproachful—lonely spirits stuck in this all too earthly world.

Work on the swimming pool looked like any other building site where work had stopped. It was a mess of abandoned digging and plastic wire guides and stones. Hardy grass and wildflowers had sprung up on the piles and banks of exposed soil.

The grapes were almost ripe, the prettiest mauve and purple baubles under the vine's dry, rustling leaves. Greengages, too, pulpy and darkened on the grass beneath the tree, crusting with a lichen of mold, were being devoured by insects, birds, and small animals. Too high on the tree to pick, too many to eat; the joy of plenty turned to decadence.

**The key** stuck as we tried to open the shutters to the back door, as if the lock had rusted since we left, and we had to walk around to another door to the main house and find our way in from the alleyway between the two main buildings.

Inside, the house was dark and silent and cool. As we passed through each room, we threw open the shutters to the light and felt the stones breathe and familiar shafts of brightness sweep the floors and walls. Pockets of scent stirred the senses: here, old soot and cloves combined in imitation of church incense; there, lavender and citrus.

The wooden monk in the hall had lost his sheen. Our secondhand furniture simply looked used up and shabby. In the music room, spiders scuttled across a floor speckled with dead insects. On the mantelpiece, an untidy slew of leaflets for all the summer concerts we had missed.

By four o'clock in the afternoon, the light receded. In the west, it was gray-yellow over the valley, and by five, a thunderstorm had started. Forks of lightning pitched through the blackened skies. It was warm, too, the warmth building to suffocation point. In the fountain trough, the water was an ominous, toxic green, fronds of algae waving mistily from its floor, clouding like the sky. In the air, an odd, almost ginlike tang.

Dom and I stood together on the covered terrace and watched as white explosions flashed on a hillside below us.

"Look down there," he said.

Lightning had struck an electric cable, and fire was sparking its way along the wire, from pole to pole.

Then the rain came down, beating emphatically on every surface, cascading off the roof tiles like a sheet fountain.

That evening, when the sky was clear and red, we set a table on the covered terrace, as we had done so many times that first summer, and lit candles. With tangible relief that we had a neutral subject, we discussed the state of the house and what needed attention. Evening breezes took the flames in hand and ripped them down the tall dinner candles in twenty minutes, leaving stalactites of wax in mysterious shapes to drip onto the table and the plate of cheese. But by ten o'clock, another wind had pounced. It picked up the tablecloth and yanked it roughly aside, like a failed trick. A glass tipped over, then the empty wine bottle, and we went inside.

**The next** morning, Severan and his assistant arrived promptly at nine. Sitting astride a kitchen chair, Lieutenant Severan accepted a cup of coffee, as did the woman officer he introduced as Adjutant Grégoire. She was about my age, with hazel eyes that locked onto whatever had her attention. After she finished with us, the oven and the work surfaces came under scrutiny.

"Are you baking?" she asked.

I shook my head.

The adjutant breathed in deeply. "Smells like almond biscuits . . . lovely."

"It's . . . this kitchen, I think."

Severan sniffed but made no comment. Tapping a sheaf of papers on the table for our attention, he got down to business. "We have collated the results of our forensic tests. The first remains to be found were those of a women in her late forties to early fifties. The second set of bones belonged to a young girl between sixteen and twenty. According to our soil specialists, they had both been interred at the same time. The bodies and the blood are too old to be linked to the cases of the missing girls. Both have been in the ground for several decades."

"Do you know who they are—were?" asked Dom.

I am sure I saw a glance pass between them, a compassionate kind of look that may have held an element of unspoken apology. At least, I like to think so.

"We have a theory, but as yet no actual proof."

We waited as he took a sip of black coffee.

"We have reason to think that the remains of the older female are those of a woman whose family lived here for generations. Her name was Marthe Lincel."

"Marthe Lincel!" I couldn't help it—I gasped.

"You know who she was?"

"Yes . . ."

"No relatives survive, so it is impossible to make any kind of DNA comparison, but what we know of her age and size, last known whereabouts, approximate dates of her last activity, and the length of time her body has been in the ground, all support the theory."

I was racking my brain trying to remember what I had read about her. It all seemed a long time ago, in another life. "There was a ghostwritten memoir of sorts, that covered her life up to the age of forty or so. Wasn't it assumed that she retired after that . . . ?"

"That's the story the Musset boutique puts out," said Adjutant Grégoire. "Perhaps it suits their dreamy wholesome image of Provence. Perhaps that's what they were told and they never thought to question it."

"She must have been a loss for them, though," I said.

"That's true . . ."

"Is it possible to tell how they died?" asked Dom.

"The same method in each case," said Severan. "By a blow to the back of the head with a heavy object. Both skulls were subjected to a brutal assault."

There was a pause, in which we all seemed to contemplate the possible realities of that.

"How—" I just couldn't leave it. "How did you come to the conclusion it was Marthe Lincel?"

Severan rubbed his hand over the stubble on his face. "We talked to many people in the village. Her name came up several times. She lived here, after all. The other is as yet unknown."

"Is that it, then?" Dom wanted to know.

"We will continue making inquiries, but I have to say this will not be a priority."

"A woman called Sabine Boutin and her mother seem to know more than anyone about the Lincel family," interjected Adjutant Grégoire.

I had the impression it was she who had been tasked with most of the Lincel line of inquiry, and was proud of a job done well.

"The Boutins were old family friends of the Lincels," she went on. "They have been trying to discover what happened to Marthe Lincel for many years, and have been extremely helpful. If you want any more information, perhaps you could get in touch with them in the first instance."

"Perhaps I will," I said, looking at Dom.

"And naturally if anything else comes to light—in the house or grounds—you will get in touch," said Severan, standing to go.

"What about the bloodstains?" asked Dom suddenly. "You said you found bloodstains here that could be read like a map."

"Old, too."

"Where, though?"

Severan winced, and pointed to a patch of tiled floor not a meter from his boots.

It was the stain I had been scrubbing to no avail since we arrived.

# 18

While I was still at the hospital, a distinguished gentleman came to examine my eyes and talk to me. He was Professor Georges Feduzzi of the University of Avignon. It was he who suggested I make these recordings.

He told me, in his warm, clever voice, that it would be a great service to his scientific researches, to the understanding of blindness, and of Charles Bonnet syndrome in particular. When I agreed, he took my hand and squeezed it softly.

It may seem strange, but I actually felt proud.

As you have heard, the stories tumble out of me. Perhaps I could have written it myself, once, with great effort of will. But, for once, I admitted I needed help. I can no longer see the words on the page.

As I have made these recordings, I have become less afraid. As I accustom myself to the idea of blindness, of what will happen to me, of the loss of my reading, I find I miss the prospect of Marthe appearing. With every day, I feel her within me, like the house is around me. You cannot be here, among these stone walls and rocks and paths and gnarled, wind-twisted trees, without being aware of the passage of time and the spirits of the past. I'd felt so alone with only the cloudiness and the scents, first of lavender, then of heliotrope and milky almond woodiness; the scents of Christmas and baking; on warm, stormy nights, the sharp hints of gin from the junipers that grow wild on the scrubby slopes below.

Understanding is all. The visitors come more and more rarely. That is consistent with the syndrome, too. There is a period of intense activity within the brain, and then it subsides. The doctors predicted that, and they have been proved right. The family and all the forgotten strangers only appear regularly in my dreams now. If one of them does come home during the day, I try not to worry. Instead, I make mental notes of what I think I see, and I speak them into these tapes.

And I am happy, in a way, because I know that at last I am fulfilling my ambition. I am passing on learning. My account will be studied and used by doctors and students at the university. I have become a teacher.

# 19

We steeled ourselves and called Sabine, invited her for a drink that evening.

At six, I set a scented burner on the fireplace, and a light cinnamon trail rose, overlaying the random bursts of diverse scents that had come and gone since our return.

Sabine arrived, intent and eager for information and bringing light footprints of figgy mud over the threshold.

Dom poured some wine, and together we told her the truth about Rachel. The truth that Rachel had been sick and the truth that she had died in a clinic in Switzerland. Not quite the whole truth, but as much of it as necessary.

Sabine shook her head slowly from side to side, seeming to restrain herself from saying what she really thought. "I knew it . . . I knew that something had happened to her . . ."

She threw me a beady glance, as if she thought I was holding back or dissembling. Well, I had been holding back, but only about how little I knew of Dom's wife, and how uneasy that had begun to make me, and because I felt disloyal to Dom.

I looked over at him now, willing him to dispel her lingering suspicions.

"I should have said, before now. I'm sorry," he said.

There was a charged pause.

Silently, I urged him on.

"She didn't know either—not at first," he said, meaning me. He put his hand over mine. He began with a stutter, then continued. "This has been a difficult time for me. Perhaps I shouldn't have come back here. But can you begin to understand why I did not want to talk about my wife's death?"

Sabine put her head on one side. "Of course. Of course I can . . . but—"

"And Rachel . . . she wasn't well, she used to say things she didn't mean," I said. I looked steadily at Sabine, trying to communicate what, in particular, Rachel had not meant.

Neither of us was going to say it.

"I'm sorry if I appeared to mislead you," I said. "I overreacted and . . ."

"It wasn't her fault," said Dom firmly.

From the way she raised the side of her mouth, it seemed that Sabine was about to air some other discrepancy, but she let it go.

"Lieutenant Severan and Adjutant Grégoire were here this morning," I said, changing the subject to one I knew would interest her. "I gather there's a new theory as to the identity of at least one of the bodies here."

**Sabine was** keen to tell us her own stories. More wine was poured, and she explained how her family and Marthe Lincel's had been intertwined for generations.

"My grandmother Arielle was a childhood friend of Bénédicte Lincel, the younger sister. Her family, the Poidevins, were tenant farmers here at Les Genévriers. Well, as you probably know, the farm gradually failed, the tenants all left, the son of the family left, Marthe was in Paris with her perfumes. Then there was only one old lady living here. That was Bénédicte.

"She was on the point of ruin. She was advised to sell off some land, but selling the farm was the only way forward for her. Much land had already been sold, or let to another farmer for his goats."

I thought of the fields below, owned now by the village's most prosperous farming family, a clan destined for success from the moment the third son was born, and then, almost excessively, blessed by the births of the fourth and fifth. The view from the back of the cottages is now another neighbor's wheat field, and his vigorous golden crops roll right up to our chins, or so it feels. All that came with the hamlet were the scrubby woods, the garden, and the steep orchard terraces.

"Bénédicte needed Marthe's help, and urgently. But the sisters had gone their separate ways, or rather, many years before, Marthe had cut Bénédicte out of her life after some argument. So we tried to contact her on Bénédicte's behalf, and got nowhere. Everywhere we tried ended in a dead end." Sabine laughed drily and took a sip from her glass.

"So," I said, suddenly understanding, "when a talented journalist came looking for local stories, you put her onto Marthe and gave her all the help you could. You even encouraged me to take up where she left off."

Sabine smiled. "We all wanted to know what happened to Marthe. Bénédicte made us promise to find out what happened to her sister, where she was if she was still alive. It was always possible a fresh mind would turn up some fact we hadn't found, see the story from a different viewpoint."

We all seemed to think about that one.

"When the police ran forensic tests on the bodies, and announced the age the woman would have been when she died, and the length of time she had been in the ground, they came around to everyone in the village, asking if anyone had any clues as to who she was. My grandmother, my mother, and I dug out old diaries and with those and what we could piece together from memory . . . It turned out that the woman was the age Marthe Lincel would have been when she was last known to be here, which also fit approximately with the time when Bénédicte last saw her."

"And Bénédicte is dead—the police said there were no relatives," said Dom.

"She died in 2007. She had been living with us for some years by then. She couldn't stay here alone."

"So they can't be sure it is Marthe Lincel."

"No. It's all circumstantial evidence."

"Who was the other girl, the young one?" I asked.

"No one knows, poor soul."

A noise against the window made us all jump. It was a hornet, so big it clunked its head against the glass trying to reach the light inside.

"What do you do about these?" asked Dom.

"Find the nest," said Sabine.

"The police found bloodstains here in the kitchen," I told her. "They thought they were relatively recent, but it turns out they must have been here for decades. If they'd only asked I would have told them."

"Dark stains on the floor tiles—and then some like droplets?"

We nodded.

"I tried to scrub them," I said. "I never had any idea they were . . ."

"It's not a happy story," said Sabine. "You may not want to know."

Of course we did.

"Bénédicte and Marthe . . . their father shot himself. It was the first act in the family's downfall."

**We showed** her to the door and she was gracious. She might even become a friend, I felt, at some stage, if we decided to stay.

I remembered, just as she was leaving, standing in the open doorway. Raindrops threaded through basil and lemon verbena in the pots at the top of the steps, making an infusion of pungent leaves.

"If you would still like me to, I will translate the research Rachel left with you on the flash drive for safekeeping," I said. "If that's okay with Dom."

# 20

I n the end, it was Rachel who led us to the answers.
This was among the files on her flash drive.

**Marthe Lincel's** most famous scent was a runaway success in the early 1950s, Rachel wrote.

Lavande de Nuit starts as a winter-white scent, and turns into summer on the skin. The first burst of powdery sweet heliotrope and white iris develops a sharper note of wild cherry, drying down to a milky almond base with a signature flourish of the unexpected, in this case, a bracing dash of hawthorn. After a few hours of warmth, it pulsates with wild herbs and lavender in sunlight. A faint mist of caramelized hazelnut and vanilla emerges, and finally a deep, smoky lavender. It is one of those scents that seem alive on the skin, subtly incubating, insinuating its personality, and leaving an enchanting trail.

It is still made today, in bespoke quantities, by the Musset boutique, now part of the huge BXH luxury-brand empire. The original elegant frosted glass flacon has been replaced, and the composition using modern commercial ingredients is heavier on the vanilla notes, which were such a joy when they unfurled more slowly, like the telling of a secret. But it is still a wonderful perfume, one of the greats, even if it is only available these days as part of a library of classics maintained by a small but highly regarded Parisian house.

The perfume was born, like Mme. Lincel, in Provence, in the hamlet where she was born and where she lived until she went away to Manosque. It still stands: Les Genévriers (The Junipers) is a hillside farm overlooking the great blue ridge of the Luberon chain to the south, and the wide sweep of the valley to the west.

Old buildings can weave their own magic, and this one has a powerful presence: for all its failing structure, left to rot for years now, the unsafe walls and skewed lintels, it has a monumental quality. It must have been like Cold Comfort Farm in winter.

This part of Provence is a country of contrasts, the searing heat and the bone-biting cold; the golden days of heat and the violent storms; sweetness of the soft perfumes that pulse in the sun and the treacherous changes of mood. The wind is the pacemaker of the day's rhythms, from the summer zephyrs that sustain the spirit to the savage howling of the mistral.

These days, Les Genévriers lies abandoned. Spectacular views roll out from all four compass points: views that Marthe would not have seen since she was a very young child. It seems encased in another era, one with a tragic air. Once you know Marthe's story, and that of her family, it's hard not to feel that the tightly shuttered windows echo her sightless eyes and the way those who were left turned their backs on the world.

For the biggest mystery is Marthe herself. What became of her? How did her story end? Where did she go when she left her boutique in Paris for the last time in 1973? No one knows.

**According to** the local administrators at the *mairie* in the village at the top of the hill, the property had been put up for sale many years previously but so convoluted is the inheritance division among family members—a regular complication of French property—that the legal tangle had defeated several sales. Now the last of the family to live there was dead.

Others claimed the property was haunted, that this was the reason it had lain not only unsold but uninhabited for so long. When I mentioned the name of Marthe Lincel, the woman in the grocery store nodded enthusiastically, and said, "Of course!" as did a small gaggle of customers waiting at the post office. But it transpired that it was the family name they knew, as everyone in the village knew the names of all the prominent families linked to the land, and not specifically of her renown as a perfumer.

Sabine Boutin, a local businesswoman, walked around the hamlet with me and did her best to put Marthe Lincel in the context of her family home.

"If you speak to anyone in the village, they will tell you that they remember the place from their childhood. This was the place where they could be given little jobs, like collecting walnuts or picking fruit in the orchard, helping with the drying or bottling of the tomatoes. Later, when it went to rack and ruin, their children came to explore and to play. It was considered a dare to steal into the vaulted cellar through the open wood store and defy the ghosts to play games and tricks around the pillars. It was considered the local equivalent of a forgotten castle in a fairy tale. After Marthe's sister died, there was no one there, only spirits and mischief."

I assumed the stories of hauntings started then.

"No," said Sabine. "That was a much sadder story."

**Marthe Lincel** was, by all accounts, an excellent student at the school for the blind in Manosque. After the inevitable difficulties of settling in away from home, she made friends and was remembered by all as kind, determined, and perceptive.

Then came the dark days of the Second World War.

Marthe's younger brother, Pierre, was twenty-two when the war in France ended. He had joined the army but spent most of the previous two years marching around a parade ground in Marseille, having convinced the medical examiners that some problem with his sinuses would prevent him from being much use in combat.

Then, when it was over, like so many other young men, he could see no future in subsistence farming. Marthe's memoir gives a picture of a cocky lad with plenty of different girlfriends, all giggly things wearing cheap scents and the sweet aroma of honey soap. He headed for a fruit-preserving factory at first, then worked at one of the new agricultural machinery plants. The family rarely heard from him. Much later, word reached the village that he had been killed in an industrial accident.

But there was an earlier tragedy.

Marthe left for Paris, her fortunes rising. But at the farm, it was another bad year. The weather veered from severe frosts to torrential rains through the early and late summer, which took the crops in the fields. One by one, the tenants were leaving. Without them, the work was doubly tough and demoralizing.

Then Cédric Lincel was killed by a shot from an old revolver he was cleaning.

**Only the** younger sister, Bénédicte, clung on with their mother.

Bénédicte was pretty and clever, they said, and had several local suitors but she never married, even after their mother died and she was free to live her own life. Instead, Bénédicte became a recluse. Those who visited the hamlet began to come away with unsettling stories: the family was cursed, and the tragedy foretold; spirits danced in the darkness and shared the rooms with the living; strangers materialized out of nothing; a mysterious and dreadful stench was emanating from the courtyard of the big house; lanterns flickered and died for no reason. An atmosphere of fear grew and took hold.

As Bénédicte aged, alone, the farm falling into ruin around her, the village children dared each other to venture there by night. Odd occurrences continued to be reported, but they were never convincingly anything more than rumor fueled by idiotic pranks.

One day, arriving at the farm with provisions, Arielle's granddaughter Sabine found Bénédicte trembling and unable to speak coherently. Not until the doctor was summoned was she able to tell them of the horrors she had witnessed.

# 21

The key to Bénédicte's experience was in the other files on the flash drive: notes marked with precise library catalog numbers from the research archives of the department of ophthalmology at the University of Avignon. They led to an extraordinary collection of tape recordings made by Bénédicte herself in 1996, when she was seventy years old.

Terrifying though Bénédicte's ordeal had been, it was never a haunting. There was an earthbound, though equally distressing, explanation.

Visual hallucinations such as these are known as Charles Bonnet syndrome, and it is almost certain that Bénédicte was suffering from this mysterious condition. Phantasmagoria, or visions, were a manifestation of a certain kind of progressive sight loss.

Charles Bonnet, a natural philosopher from Switzerland, was the first man of science to attempt to understand the visions from which his own grandfather was suffering, including a distressing parade of people, vehicles, and horses that were not actually there. In the eighteenth century, Bonnet developed the theory that these, along with moving landscapes, geometric patterns, and disembodied faces, were actually a symptom of macular degeneration.

Strangely enough, he discovered, even people with healthy sight could potentially experience these hallucinations if they were blindfolded for long enough. They seemed to be caused by lack of visual stimulation rather than madness, by the brain trying to make up for fewer impulses from the nerve cells in a damaged retina. When the brain does not receive as many pictures as it expects, it tries to compensate by drawing on the areas it has always used to process faces, surroundings, patterns, and colors.

But normally, the condition was an indication of age-related macular degeneration, one of the most common causes of blindness. And, unnervingly, visions most often occurred when the subject was in a state of drowsiness or relaxation, which would explain why Bénédicte was most often affected as she sat by the hearth to rest.

Was there a genetic predisposition in the sisters that was responsible for them both losing their sight? It seems likely. Like her sister, Bénédicte was to put her blindness to admirable use. She collaborated over several years with the eminent ophthalmologist Professor Georges Feduzzi at the university in Avignon to produce a scientific paper on the disease, its purpose not only to present research on a little-known condition, but also to reassure its terrified sufferers.

# 22

That transcripts of the tape recordings made by Bénédicte Lincel were released is a tribute to Rachel, her persistence and genuine ability that she had no need to exaggerate for effect. All Sabine knew was that Bénédicte had been treated by a professor at Avignon University and that the bulk of the Lincel estate was bequeathed to the ophthalmology department there when Bénédicte died. Rachel did the detective work and had the intuition and persuasive skills needed to gain access to the archives.

I'm not certain how well she was able to translate the files. Well enough, I think, with the basics of the story already understood from Sabine. But, for whatever reason (her illness, most likely), she hadn't managed to unravel the story in its entirety by the time she left the flash drive with Sabine; and though Sabine would have been able to read the files, the mixture of English and archive reference numbers meant nothing to her.

In the many hours of recordings, among the vivid first-person accounts of the onset of her blindness, her confusion and terrors, is her account of the last time she saw her sister and Marthe's young apprentice, Annette.

**There was** never any proof that Marthe Lincel lived beyond her early fifties. The Musset boutique allowed their loyal clients to believe that Marthe had retired to her native Provence. Perhaps the Mussets, sadly and slyly misinformed by Pierre, genuinely believed that was the case. A quiet death would have been in the natural order.

Here, after my reading the transcripts of the tapes and much discussion with Sabine, her mother, and eighty-four-year-old grandmother Arielle, is what we believe happened to Marthe and Annette.

When the last meeting took place between the three siblings, the garden beyond the courtyard was being dug up in preparation for the installation of the pool. The hazards would have been difficult for anyone to negotiate, but for Marthe, trying to navigate from memory, it would have been impossible. Nothing was the same as when Marthe knew the ground so intimately. Walls would have crumbled when she reached up to steady herself. Piles of soil would have given way.

We know she held on to Bénédicte as they stumbled out after Pierre's drunken raging, but after he attacked Annette and struck Bénédicte unconscious, Marthe and Annette would have had no bearings.

We can't know what exactly happened to them that night. It seems no fatal harm came to them, because Bénédicte found them huddled together in the courtyard barn the next morning. Possibly they were injured. But they were gone when she eventually returned, concussed and panicking, from the village.

Whether one or both of them fell by accident into the excavation, or whether Pierre cold-bloodedly set about bludgeoning them with his fatal blows once he had led them over to their grave, no one will ever know. What can be said with certainty is that Bénédicte's account of that night and the following day strongly implicates him.

Bénédicte found it hard to believe that Marthe would leave without speaking to her. There was no previous indication that the sisters were about to be estranged. The next day, Pierre had hours in which to commit murder and bury the bodies.

To the world, Marthe left Provence, and then Paris. Pierre played the helpful brother to collect Marthe's possessions from the boutique and her apartment, and explained that she had gone away, perhaps even that she was not well. He left a few more drops of poison for Bénédicte, in case she ever came looking, and no doubt found some way of putting an end to any other suspicions. Annette had no parents, which was one of the reasons the kindly Marthe was keen to support her. The teachers at the school for the blind saw her off to Paris with the famous Marthe Lincel. When they never heard from her again, they must have presumed she either never succeeded in her chosen career, or that she simply stopped work to marry and raise a family as so many young girls did.

Why didn't Pierre kill Bénédicte, too? Perhaps he was so drunk he was barely aware of what he was doing until it was too late. Perhaps with Bénédicte dead, too, he would have been too obviously a suspect when he came to take over the farm. Did he have reason to sense that the net was closing in on him and fake his own death for Bénédicte's benefit? No one will ever know.

# 23

As for my own unsettling experiences here, there are some I can explain, and some I cannot.

I am fairly sure that it was Sabine who set the lantern on the path. She has never admitted it, but a few months ago, Dom and I were invited to her family house. It was a sultry night and we all sat outside under a vine canopy. On a stone wall was the lantern. I hadn't seen it since before we left for Cassis. It was in such a prominent position, and the curlicue of a handle was so pretty and distinctive that I am certain it was the same one. I chose to interpret it as a message, an unspoken apology and reassurance that it would not appear at Les Genévriers again.

Or was that all my imagination, a creation of my craving for security? Who knows?

What Sabine did admit was that she had been shocked and disappointed when the house was sold and the proceeds donated, according to Bénédicte's wishes, to further ophthalmological research at the university. For a decade previously, apparently, the property was the subject of a will that would have bequeathed it to Arielle and her family, in recognition of all the support they had given. Sabine had planned to renovate the farm and run it as a modern version of the holiday rental business that Bénédicte and Marthe had started. When she found out that it would not be coming to her, as she had always believed, she worked hard to raise the money to buy it anyway. But that took years, and she was ultimately outbid by Dom.

So was it spite? Did she think that we might not stay if we felt uncomfortable, that we might sell up quickly? I may ask her one day, but not yet.

As for the rest of the odd manifestations, I have no easy explanation. I know what I saw on the moonlit path below the terrace; there was no mistaking the outline of a small female figure, and she was not Sabine. If I go out there on a warm night, even now my instincts are to look steadily up into the constellations. Then, half-afraid of what I might see on the path, I quickly glance below. I have not seen her again.

Inside the house, especially in the kitchen, I still sense that we are not alone. When I stand cooking at the island, with my back to the hearth, I often turn to check behind me. A feeling, no more, no less. It makes the atmosphere no less radiant; in fact, it may even be its origin.

There has been only one unnerving incident in the kitchen. I had left some books on the table. One of these was the old children's book I found hidden in the hayloft, the Provençal tales. I was standing by the kettle, waiting for it to boil, when I heard a crackle behind me. I turned to see the book open like a fan and its pages flip over. Now, the back door was ajar, so it was just possible that a stray wind could send a few breaths across an open book and riffle the pages. But the book had not been open. I know with absolute certainty it had been closed, because a minute before I got up to make tea, I had it in my hands. I ran my palm over the pretty design of the cover and felt the pleasure any child would have had to possess such a volume. Then I placed it carefully back on the table.

I watched as the pages turned, not too fast, not too regularly, as if a fastidious and learned current of air were flipping through them. Then it stopped. The pages stood up in an arc but with no more animation. All was still. The merest hint of smoky church incense hung in the air like a blessing.

An incident as meaningful as the imagination wants to make it. Perhaps it was a matter of physics. Perhaps it was a sudden draft from the chimney. Perhaps I fell asleep and dreamed for a minute. Or perhaps it really was the spirit of Bénédicte leaping up from her place by the hearth to seize the book I now know she lost all those years ago. Just because Bénédicte's ghost visitors were not what she feared, does not mean that all can be explained away

Throughout the autumn, the police have worked doggedly on the cases of the girl students. At one time, I even wondered if Pierre Lincel might have had a hand in them, but it seems that he, too, died, a decade or so out of reach of Severan's men. They found him in an urn at the crematorium at Orange that no one had come forward to collect. It seems his messenger lied to Bénédicte about his death in a fruit-packing plant when he handed over her brother's supposed last effects. Just one more lie that now surprised no one.

The first girl, Marine, was found alive, well, and protesting in Cassis, shortly after we left. She had, indeed, worked as Francis Tully's model, then joined a squat full of other young people who moved south and neglected to leave explanations.

In November, a jealous ex-boyfriend, a computer technician from Le Thor, was charged with the murder of the girl found close to Oppedette by the truffle hound. The third girl, the one who disappeared near Castellet, was the victim of a hit-and-run driver, who eventually came forward after suffering months of remorse and posttraumatic stress. The fourth had dyed her hair and joined a religious sect.

All of which goes to show how dangerous it is to assume connections where there are none, to link events that have no link, to want tidy storytelling when real life is not like that, to draw too much on the imagination when it is so often misleading.

**So we** stay, Dom and I, as another winter approaches. The hornets are gone, the spicy black figs long finished. Walnuts drop from the trees like fat, brown tears.

We have to sweep up the vine leaves out from the terrace, but the grapes are dark purple and seemingly everlasting. They hang in straggly triangles, oozing floral muscat essence over the table where we can still eat lunch if the sun shines. It can shine any day of the year here, and often does.

Dom calls me, and he uses my real name. I walk over to where he has found some new beauty in the garden and we stand together, his hand proud on the swell of my belly.

A late bud has opened on the white rose I planted by the arch on the grassy terrace below the main house. Its perfume is exquisite: musky honey and spun-sugar and orange blossom, and its petals in bloom have the soft luster of baby skin. It has taken well to this spot, where I've pinned a bough to the lintel of what seems to be a blocked-up store. I think it must be the vault where Bénédicte buried her baby. I hope so. This is for her.

The atmosphere around the house has lifted, and our spirits with it; we live easily again with the past and the histories here, as we add our own to the stones. Our love story is a good one, deeper and stronger by the day.

Even as winter comes, mornings are crisp, and the big, blue sky seems to hang newly washed over the sea of hills.

# Epilogue

A sudden ripple of descending piano notes makes me start.

It comes from the other side of the courtyard.

There it is again! Tinkling like the cascade of a waterfall.

For such a long time, there was no music here. Now there are always soft bursts of piano music. It comes from the visitors, but I don't mind. I have gotten used to them. Hearing this music is delicious. It releases me, makes me feel like a girl again.

She looks very like me, the woman. She is younger than the man—about the age I was when I was in love with André. I think, after all, I am pleased they have stayed. They are kind to each other, and they care for the house, bringing it back to life, mending it stone by stone, tile by tile.

And once more, the house has a child. Such a sweet little cherub, who watches me with endless wonder.

**I say** that the young woman looks very like me, but I mean what I looked like then, not now. I have no idea what I look like now. Pierre took Maman's mirror. I would feel for the wrinkles and deeper crevices on my face, but I can feel very little. Perhaps my fingertips have lost their sensitivity. The pads are hardened. I can pick up hot pans from the range and never feel pain.

Some tasks I can still manage, but many elude me. I have to relax and breathe and draw on all my inner resources. The other night, I managed to strike a flame quite easily, though.

I had been thinking of André, of how, when I was alone and scanning the seascape of the mountains, I told myself: "This is my ship now, and I am sailing on." But then, the waves banked higher and the winds convulsed the sky, and I was clinging on alone in the tempest, the first mate deserted, the cargo lost. Where was he now? Was there a chance he might be within reach at last?

So I lit our lantern and set it on the path.

Then I watched the candlelight dance as it sent the signal: I am waiting for you. You are not alone in the dark.

# Acknowledgments

The hardest words to write are the really heart-felt ones. So it has taken days and days to craft adequate thanks to Stephanie Cabot, my literary agent. Without Stephanie's steadfast belief in me and wise counsel this book simply would not have been written. Throughout every meeting in London—lunches at La Poule au Pot for French atmosphere—and all the transatlantic phone calls, Stephanie was at her brilliant best: calm and pragmatic, sensitive to every nuance in the text, and above all, as fiercely determined as a lioness on my behalf.

Huge thanks also to her colleagues at The Gernert Company in New York, especially Rebecca Gardner, Will Roberts, and Anna Worrall.

It has been a real privilege to work with Jennifer Barth at HarperCollins. I could not have asked for a more empathetic, incisive, and measured editor. Thank you, Jennifer, for taking such infinite care. Jason Sack and Olga Gardner Galvin have also been marvelous.

In London, Araminta Whitley at Lucas Alexander Whitley came in and gave us some more firepower— and a crucial tweak to the manuscript—before closing the deal with Orion. I'd also like to thank Harry Man at LAW.

A great big thank-you to Kate Mills at Orion for being so enthusiastic, warm, and in tune with this book, and for being such a generous editor, and to Susan Lamb and Jon Wood for immediately making me feel it was in the best possible hands.

At home, Robert and Madeleine allowed me, as always, to disappear upstairs to my desk for whole days at a time without ever making me feel I was being self-ish. Joy, Stan, and Helen Lawrenson let me drone on about Provence without too often showing an excess of France-fatigue. My mother, Joy, and Robert were, as ever, the highly valued first critical readers of the draft manuscript.

For encouragement and continuing support in various ways while I was writing, I thank Felicia

Mockett, Josina Kamerling, Louise Piper, Lucy and Jonathon Hills, Tanya Alfillé, and Juliet Gowan. Judy Barrett not only designs lovely websites, but was there at the desk as I made my first tentative posts as a blogger.

Merci to our friends in Provence and those who have been there right from the start of our French adventure: Ann de Boismaison White, William Bris, Julie Beauvais, Fernand Constan, Françoise Vuillet, Olivier Buys, Gérard de la Cruz, and Roger Allard, bighearted plumbing boss who investigated the mysteries of our missing water and electricity while we had to spend a week back in the UK that first summer, leaving the hamlet a daunting, overgrown, and very dry place.

I would like to acknowledge that the idea of writing about a blind perfumer came from the realization that there were strips of Braille on the packaging used by beauty product brand L'Occitane en Provence. In 1997 the company created the foundation Provence dans tous les sens (All the senses of Provence) to introduce visually impaired children to the world of perfume creation. In the novel, Marthe finds her true talent as a perfume "nose" after a visit to the Distillerie Musset in the 1930s. The Distillerie Musset is entirely imaginary but the scenes at the modern plant owe a debt to my visits to L'Occitane's factory shop at Manosque. And, of course, just like Marthe, they create wonderful natural fragrances inspired by the scented landscapes of Provence.

Thanks finally, and very importantly, to Brian Rees for inviting me to his house in Viens all those years ago, and for being so pleased and excited for us now.